The Body
ON THE ROUNDABOUT

The Body ON THE ROUNDABOUT

FAITH ECKERSALL

embla books

First published in the UK in 2025 by

embla books

An imprint of Bonnier Books UK
5th Floor, HYLO, 105 Bunhill Row,
London, EC1Y 8LZ

A CIP catalogue record for this book is available from the British Library.

ISBN: 9781471419928

Also available as an ebook and an audiobook

1

Typeset by IDSUK (Data Connection) Ltd
Printed and bound in Great Britain by Clays Ltd, Elcograf S.p.A.

FSC www.fsc.org MIX Paper | Supporting responsible forestry FSC® C018072

The authorised representative in the EEA is Bonnier Books UK (Ireland) Limited.
Registered office address: Block B, The Crescent Building, Northwood, Santry, Dublin 9, D09 C6X8, Ireland
compliance@bonnierbooks.ie
www.bonnierbooks.co.uk

For Ashley, for everything

Prologue

Page 6, the *Guardian*. 14 January 2021

A journalist who was sentenced to a year in prison, after admitting breaches under the Data Protection Act, has seen his sentence suspended on appeal.

Harold Rupert Hedges, 37, of Fulham, London, had admitted to breaking the law while working as a correspondent for the Daily News *newspaper but went on to appeal the sentence.*

In a statement released after the hearing, Daily News *proprietor, Sir James Knox, described Hedges as 'a disgrace to our industry and our nation' and said there was 'no place for this type of reprehensible behaviour' in his or any other publication.*

Chapter 1

The red petrol light had been flashing since the Bournemouth Spur Road. Now the amber oil light had decided to join it. All his ancient Mini Cooper needed next was the battery light to start up, and his dashboard would resemble the full Blackpool Illuminations.

Harry felt as if he'd been on the A31 forever. Thank God he was nearly there.

He indicated right, started driving north on the A350 and, after several miles, found himself approaching a large roundabout, from which assorted foliage bristled, like a giant green and yellow pirate's beard.

Where was the bloody sign?

Too late he clocked the notice indicating that the centre of Historic Piddlington Minster was the exit he'd just missed. He jammed down his right brogue on the accelerator as he made another attempt to arrive nearly on time at his new place of work.

As he did so, a small, elderly woman on the pavement suddenly brandished what appeared to be a placard on a stick, right in front of the bonnet. Harry yelped and closed his eyes as he swerved away from her.

As he opened them again, he shuddered; the last thing he needed was another brush with the police. The old girl must be off her head.

He immediately juddered to a halt, having managed to place his size-11 foot on the postage-stamp-sized brake pedal – a six-foot-three journalist isn't ever a good idea in a vintage Cooper. Judging by the car-horn symphony behind him, you'd think he'd stopped in the middle of the M25, not this obscure Dorset backwater.

Harry flipped his blonde fringe out of the way and looked round for the placard-waving pensioner, who had mysteriously disappeared. He beamed nervously into his rear-view mirror at the baleful woman driver of the tractor-sized motor which had nearly shunted him.

Looking like a younger and taller version of Hugh Grant used to be such an advantage in life, he thought. Nowadays, he may as well resemble Donald Trump, for all the good it did him.

He fiddled the sulky gearstick into neutral and gently turned the ignition.

Nothing. Unless you counted the flashing lights. Harry began to feel immensely warm under his tweed jacket, which was far too heavy for early September, but the only one he possessed now. The bailiffs had seized all the others when he stopped paying rent on his flat.

'Sorry!' he said, as if every other driver backed up behind him could hear. He tried the starting procedure again. Miraculously, the car sputtered into life. Ramming the gear into first, he successfully exited towards the town centre, trying to ignore the radio which had jolted into life again and was fading in and out of two separate news bulletins, surreally jumbling a story about antiques thefts and the rate of inflation.

According to the guidebook he'd surreptitiously thumbed through at the M3 service station as he fled London – his ancient iPhone had long been out of data – Piddlington Minster could be approached in three ways. He was coming over the stone, humpbacked bridge option, which afforded 'heart-stopping views' of the twin-towered minster: a mellow, medieval building, which looked as if it had been lovingly constructed from artisanal loaves, glowing in the sunshine.

If Jasper Grant, his former school chum and newsroom boss at the *Daily News* was correct – and Harry wouldn't put it past him to have lied about this, too – following the road should allow him to find his new office quite easily, as he spooled through the town's one-way system.

Having overshot the correct route, he found himself in what looked to be the town square, clattering past a knot of youths on bikes, a health food store and a statue of Queen Victoria, who was glaring right at him.

* * *

He was looking for the newspaper's premises. In the old days – twenty years ago, probably – a paper like the *Piddlington Gazette* would have occupied the best part of a beautiful Georgian building, all symmetrical sash windows, like a doll's house. It would have had a Downing Street-type door – complete with a spiderweb fanlight and a hand-painted sign, proudly declaring that this was the office of Your Local Newspaper.

But those days were long gone, melted away with publishing it all for free online, a collapse in advertising and the faint but lingering taint caused by various journalistic scandals.

So, while he knew he was looking for a Georgian building with three steps up to the front and a door in 'Arsenal red', as Jasper had put it, he also knew that this part of the edifice – 'the good bit' – was now occupied by a lifestyle boutique. Jasper had explained that he'd probably have to guide the Cooper through the building's old coaching entrance at the side and into a courtyard, where he'd find the former outbuilding, which now housed the newspaper. 'They used to keep pigs there,' said Jasper. 'Supposed to be haunted. By a two-headed pig, or so it goes.'

Harry had asked him how he knew that and been answered with a chuckle. 'Must have done a story on it, back in the day.'

He'd been so desperate to work again that he'd grabbed the opportunity. *So long as there's a parking space*, Harry prayed. The parking space was crucial, because it would mean he would have to pay out less money.

And that was vital, for the simple reason that he didn't really have any. *What Had Happened* and the resulting court case had seen to that. Paying the barrister had burned through the inheritance left by his mother, Isabella, and he was living on an overdraft the size of Wembley Stadium.

Of course, he could have accepted his father's kind offer to integrate him into the family's luxury wastepaper-basket manufacturing business as a means of paying off his gargantuan bills.

But that would have meant giving up journalism. Frankly, he'd rather cut off his right hand. Which would be far less painful than doing a proper job, he reckoned. Especially in luxury wastepaper baskets.

After extricating himself from St Basil's College Sixth Form, he'd joined a regional weekly, working there two weeks until his interview with the notorious Colombian drug baron, *El Rato*, went global. As someone who enjoyed the happy knack of being in the right place at the right time, and often with exactly the right people, he didn't see the point of telling anyone that he'd only obtained the world exclusive after freeing the notorious criminal –and, it turned out, clandestine claustrophobe – from a locked toilet during an unscheduled layover at São Paulo airport. Harry had promised not to reveal the sobbing gangster's embarrassing secret in exchange for the interview everyone wanted, before segueing seamlessly onto the *Daily News*.

As he braked, gently this time, not wanting to miss the newspaper's entrance, his excitement rose at the thought of actually getting into a newsroom again. It would be the first step in his grand plan to rehabilitate himself and earn a few quid to help pay back his father for his assistance with the legal bills. Newspaper work had provided Harry with a fabulous living and helped fill the hideous void of loneliness and pain he'd fallen into after Isabella's death. His handsome face, velvety brown eyes and ability to make interviewees feel as if he'd spent his entire life waiting to meet them had landed him a string of effortless front-page splashes, not to mention some reasonably successful investigations. From getting Princess Anne to admit she'd sung happy birthday to her horse, to *El Rato*, he'd sailed along. Until that fateful day, when an envelope of what appeared to be conversation transcriptions had arrived on his desk with a scribbled note about 'turning them into stories'.

He'd been busy at the time, working until stupid-o'clock each night, so he'd just added the extra work to his pile and cracked on.

When he'd mentioned it to Violett Travers – his long-term reporter colleague with whom he'd enjoyed a brief liaison – she'd shaken her long, glossy dark hair and sympathised.

'Tell me about it! I've been working on them all day too – should we complain to Jasper, do you think?'

Even now, like a comedy thermometer, he felt the heat of shame travelling up his neck and face. Never having had any formal journalism training, he hadn't realised the transcriptions were of recordings which had been illegally obtained.

Violett had been broken up for him when it all came out: 'My God, Harry, how has this even happened?' But then had come the rumours, the police investigation and the reckoning. Jasper had ordered them to his office and put it brutally simply. 'This is what's known in the trade as a monumental fuck-up,' he raged. The bastard politicos were on the rampage and the organisation needed to look willing. He needed someone to admit to the wrongdoing. 'It's you or her. I'm going out now, so you can sort it out between you.'

In the end the choice was surprising easy. Firstly, because he knew that unlike him and Jasper, the tear-blotched Violett had been raised in the kind of London postcode where gritty police dramas about violent drug gangs were filmed. She hadn't gone to a posh school; she'd started working at the newspaper as a cleaner. He knew and understood how hard she'd had to slave for everything she'd achieved.

And secondly, after arriving back in his office and ordering Violett to get a tissue, Jasper told Harry that if he fessed up to it being his idea and went quietly, it would all blow over and he'd get a caution 'tops' and his job back. So he said yes.

And very soon found himself the poster boy for everything that was wrong with the British press. Thank God his father was so wealthy that he could afford the kind of barrister who specialised in convincing flinty judges that everything that had happened was simply a *frightful* mix-up.

It had been, therefore, a *frightful* shock to find himself sentenced to a year in prison. This had entailed a sizeable chunk of the family fortune being spent on convincing even flintier appeal judges that an eye-watering fine and the public shredding of his character were punishment enough.

* * *

As he swung into the first part of the one-way system, past a row of Georgian and Victorian buildings belonging to solicitors and estate agents, he spotted the Life & Style Store, on the right, with its glossy red door. And there was the passageway at the side. For once in his life, Jasper Grant had told the truth.

As he changed down and manoeuvred the Mini towards the cobbled entrance, Harry grimaced. It had been over two years now, but he still couldn't smother the horror of being marched away from the newsroom, head bowed so he didn't have to see the mortified faces of his colleagues, as the Operation Knacker coppers pretended they were arresting Gordon Gekko in *Wall Street.*

As he drove through the narrow brick archway into a courtyard, he looked up to see a faded wooden sign propped against the flaking, whitewashed wall of the one-storey building at the courtyard's rear: *The Piddlington Gazette.*

After parking the Cooper, he turned off the engine, shoved open the door and stepped out. Straight onto a giant dog turd.

A sickening odour zoomed up his nostrils. Oh, great. Just great. His shoes may have cost £300 but that was a long time ago and they now had a hole in the bottom that he couldn't afford to repair. After much vigorous foot-wiping on a handy clump of dandelions that were sprouting through the neglected cobbles, he knocked on the sad-looking office door, with its three panes of mismatched glass.

Silence.

There was an electric bell attached to the jamb and a security light, but the number of wires sticking out of both made him fear for his personal safety. He tried the push-down handle instead. Surprisingly, it opened.

The room was lit by a lone and flickering fluorescent light, suspended from the apex of the converted stable roof. The remainder of a piece of Christmas tinsel hung from it – an exotic turquoise caterpillar, twisting in the breeze coming from the open door. To Harry's left was a row of wonky metal shelves bulging with files, curling notebooks and ancient, yellowing newspapers. In front of them was a battered metal desk whose surface was mostly taken up by a huge, archaic-looking computer monitor.

Upon that desk there were also a round circle of wood with a metal spike on it, a model of a submarine, a glass etched with an old-fashioned dolphin and emitting what smelled suspiciously like an alcoholic substance, and a crumpled copy of the *Racing Post*. To his right, immediately beside the door, was an imposing brown wooden desk with a green leather surface and a dusty flatscreen.

The desk's top was as lifeless and devoid of personality as the moon itself. As there was no record of any living journalist keeping their workspace this tidy, he assumed that was where his predecessor had sat, before he had, according to Jasper, 'run off into the night'.

To the right of this desk, under the grimy windows, was yet another. It looked like a skip salvage job, but someone had decided to brighten it up by spraying it bubblegum pink and attaching fairy lights and a hand-painted notice to the front, declaring: *Hot Desk!!!!* Its top was encrusted with lidless pens, dishevelled reporter's notebooks, mismatched mugs with unicorn cartoons on them, two half-finished glasses of water, and various ornaments, including a panda, a polar bear, a pig and an inflatable cactus. At the side, a flimsy-looking retro wire-basket tower was so piled up with papers that it tottered like a drunken model on a catwalk.

But it was what lay at the centre of the room that really grabbed his attention. On top of an old duvet, covered with a fleecy Union Jack blanket, was the biggest, floppiest, daftest-looking chocolate Labrador that Harry had ever seen.

'Hello, boy!' he said, in what he hoped was a friendly voice. 'What are you doing here? Where is everyone?'

The dog regarded him with dark, solemn eyes. He bent forward to pat the creature. The dog seemed to like it, so he carried on.

'What's your name, then?'

He reached towards its worn leather collar to read the brass identity disc that dangled underneath. And then retreated with a yelp as the beast clamped its entire set of teeth round his right hand.

'Christ!' he screeched, yanking it away. The dog growled.

A faint set of red speckles on his hand proved it had drawn blood. Now he'd probably need a tetanus injection. He looked round. Across the room there was another office door with two mismatched glass panels in the upper part, and the lower one badly repaired with hardboard. *Must be the kitchen. Or the loo*. He stepped towards it. The dog rose majestically and growled again.

Shrinking to the perimeter wall, he proceeded to creep round until he could pull the door open with his foot, then slunk into a dank room containing mildewing back copies of the newspaper on shelves, a toilet cubicle, and a tiny sink, kettle and unwashed mugs.

Harry ran the cold tap. Nothing. He opened it a little more. The tap began to vibrate. He opened it another turn, and it made an explosive noise before water spurted out, making an appalling and inevitable beeline for his crotch.

Horrified, he stared down. He looked as if he'd developed raging incontinence. Selecting the least crumpled paper towel by the sink, he wrapped it round his injured hand and tried to push the door to the newsroom back open. It wouldn't budge.

He shoved again. The wood couldn't have swelled up in a few minutes. Maybe it had got jammed. Desperately, he pressed his face against the upper reeded glass panel and, looking down, saw an ominous brown blob. The Devil Dog again.

'Get out of the way! Shoo.' More shoving. 'Move. Move!' ordered Harry. It didn't.

For a second, he allowed his memory to drift back to his time at the *Daily News*. A metropolitan paradise where ergonomic seats with memory-foam cushions came as standard, along with beverages supplied by a well-known chain. In a situation almost unknown in British publishing, the kitchen fridge even had its own cleaning lady.

He was jolted out of this daydream by a new sound. As if someone was moving around in the newsroom.

'Hello, Ignatius darling, are you all right? Are you warm enough? Shall I get you some tea?' It sounded like a teenage girl.

Harry gave the door an almighty shove. Unfortunately, the dog had chosen this moment to move, and so he barrelled out of the kitchen-cum-dungeon and halfway across the office, tripping over the dog bed and landing face down on the sticky blue carpet tiles.

'Oooof!'

When he rolled over and looked up, he found himself staring into a pair of hazel eyes. They belonged to a girl. She looked about twenty, with thick hair the colour of salted caramel curling round her face, which was dominated by a pair of over-large, brown-framed glasses.

'You poor thing! Are you OK?'

He opened his mouth to answer, when he twigged that she was actually talking to the dog.

'Hello, my name is Harry Hedges,' he said, standing up and brushing himself down. 'I think I'm right in saying that I'm probably your new editor.'

The girl stared, the glasses emphasising her huge eyes.

'Well, you should be more careful,' she snapped. 'You really scared poor Ignatius.'

Ignatius? 'Is that dog yours, then?'

She smiled. 'Sort of. Isn't he gorgeous?'

'Very,' he lied. 'But he can't stay here.'

'Stay here? He *lives* here.' She then proceeded to explain how, when she'd started a couple of years ago, aged eighteen, as the trainee reporter – 'Not that I've had any proper training; I've had to train myself.' – Ignatius came to live in the office.

'You can't have dogs in offices,' said Harry, more firmly than he felt. 'Health and safety won't allow it.'

'Karl Lagerfeld had a cat. And I bet the Queen had corgis in her offices,' said the girl, as she moved towards the pink desk. He couldn't argue with that. Mainly because he had actually visited Her Late Majesty one time, with his Royal Warrant-holder father, to hand over a new, ceremonial luxury wastepaper basket, and had noted that she did indeed keep corgis in the royal office.

'Look, he can stay for today. Then you'll have to take him home. Sorry, nothing against him but it's health and safety.'

She looked upset.

'Hey,' he said, in an effort to get on the front foot. 'I don't even know your name.'

'It's Hattie.'

'Do you have another name?'

'Watson. Like Dr Watson. Sherlock's mate.'

'Great, I love Sherlock Holmes.'

'So do I. He had a dog in his office too.'

Only sometimes, thought Harry, but something told him that Miss Watson would be a tough nut to crack, especially where that mutt was concerned. And while he had been quite happy cracking tough nuts in his day – from *El Rato* to Princess Anne – he realised he'd never actually managed any staff, just been managed. And not always very well, come to think of it.

Feeling less sure than he hoped he looked, Harry asked Hattie to make the coffee. That was all right, wasn't it? It wasn't exploitation or anything. He was the editor; he could do this.

* * *

Hattie pushed up her glasses and stalked into the kitchen. This bloke didn't look like an editor. Not that she knew many, she would have to acknowledge. He looked like that actor off those old romance films. He was good-looking and extremely posh but, she wondered, should she tell him about that dodgy stain across the front of his trousers?

He'd guessed correctly that the empty desk was his; it was the biggest. It was also furthest from the office's two mean little radiators, which he wouldn't notice until winter, Hattie hoped. As she rattled the office mugs, she tapped at her mobile.

Raymondo, she messaged. *New ed here, hurry up!*

She prayed her colleague would see it before he got stuck into his morning bets. Ray Featherwaite could, like most people these days, place his daily bet online. But he was old-school. And besides, he fancied the woman behind the bookie's counter even though, as Hattie had pointed out on several occasions, 'She's gay, you daftie.'

As she walked back in with an instant coffee for Harry, she noticed him staring at the unoccupied desk.

'Here you are,' she beamed, thumping down the chipped, brown mug.

'Oh.'

'Something wrong, Mr Hedges? Not enough milk?'

'Er, no, it's just that I'd normally have macchiato espresso.' Hattie blinked. They didn't have any espresso, or macchiato, whatever that was. Ray – her absent sub-editor colleague – only drank tea. And the occasional nip of rum. That left Ignatius, who also liked tea: very milky, poured into his china bowl.

'Maybe I'll go out and see if I can get one. See a bit of the place. There must be one decent coffee shop in this town,' Harry declared.

'OK!'

As he stood up, his landline rang.

'Hello?' It sounded like an upper-class elderly woman. At the bottom of a particularly deep well. 'I'd like to speak to the editor.'

'I am the editor,' said Harry, straightening his back and enjoying a tiny thrill of importance.

'Are you sure?'

'Yes, madam, may I help you?'

'Indeed, you may, but I'm not going to talk to you on this thing. I shall expect to see you at 11 a.m. tomorrow. I have a story for you.'

He scrabbled in his desk drawer for a pen and asked if he could take a few details.

The woman snorted. 'Surely you can spot the problem for yourself?'

'Sorry, madam, you may have to enlighten me – I only arrived here about half an hour ago.'

'What kind of timekeeping do you call that?'

He let it pass. 'It's just so I can prepare in advance of our meeting,' he busked. 'I do think it's good to be prepared, don't you?'

'In that case,' she said, 'I can tell you that it will be about an extremely serious matter. Corruption on the town council!'

Harry sagged. Town council corruption. Only about a million people had ever rung their local newspaper to inform them about this. In about three of the cases, it had actually proved to be true.

'Do you have evidence of this alleged corruption?'

'I do indeed. Firstly, the town roundabout is a disgrace. You must have noticed.'

He had, but he wasn't going to admit it, because it would only add to the bonfire of indignation that was blazing merrily down the line. But how was that corrupt? He had a feeling he'd soon find out.

The woman continued. 'It's so bad, I had to conduct my own protest down there this morning. I nearly got run over by some idiot. Anyway, young man, I am vice-chairman of Piddlington in Bloom and I can tell you now, we won't even go through to the second round with a mess like that confronting the judges as they arrive. It's a deathtrap.'

He wanted to point out that messy roundabouts were neither evidence of corruption nor portenders of sudden death but felt he did not have all day, and so asked for the woman's details again.

'Robarts. Mrs Prudence Robarts. Thank you, I will see you tomorrow. Remember, 11 a.m. Good day.'

He looked up to see the eyes of the office upon him.

'Don't worry, Mr Hedges,' said Hattie. 'She's just the town busybody. Always banging on about something. She's obsessed with that roundabout but next month it'll be something else, you'll see.'

He groaned inwardly. He didn't feel like going out now.

'Do you think you could go out and get me a real coffee or something? A proper one, with a lid on it, which actually tastes of coffee?' he asked, simultaneously wrenching at his anorexic wallet, which he'd stuffed into his back pocket. He fished out £5 and pushed it towards her, and she smiled and stepped towards the door, Ignatius padding at her side.

Harry dashed into the kitchen and swiftly tipped his 'coffee' down the sink. He arrived back in the newsroom to be confronted by a round, moustached man, possibly in his seventies, ensconced at what had been the empty desk. This must be the other member of staff mentioned in his brief appointment letter: the chief – and, indeed, only – sub-editor.

''Ow do,' said the man, not standing up. 'You must be . . .'

'Harry Hedges. Your new editor.'

'Ray Featherwaite.' The man coughed and shifted on his axis. 'Well, I don't know about you, Mr Hedges, but there's the most disgusting smell in here – someone should do something about it; it's not right we have to work in these conditions.' And with that, he heaved himself up and walked towards the kitchen.

Harry bent down and sniffed in the direction of his beloved brogues. Something would definitely have to be done about that dog.

Chapter 2

An exhaustive search of the office had revealed absolutely no instruction manual or any indication of how to revive the moribund newspaper website, whose most recent news story had been uploaded over six months ago.

It *had* revealed a washbag and towel belonging to Ray – 'I wondered where that had got to . . .' – a cupboard filled with bright metal tins of 'Premium Senior Dog Food' and what appeared to be luxury dog biscuits. 'Poor Ignatius has got sensitive digestion,' said Hattie. Harry decided to ignore her remark, given that she'd managed to get him some chain-store Americano: 'It's from the machine at the petrol station which, if you ask me, is a major cause of global warming *and* litter.'

The office search had also revealed that while the surface of Harry's desk was devoid of any accoutrement, save the flatscreen, the same could not be said of the drawers, which were crammed with tatty reporter's notebooks, defunct biros, old business cards and several obsolete phones. Worse still, there were also the remains of a packet of pork scratchings which looked as if they'd been collected from the feet of Tutankhamun's mummy. Harry recoiled as he slowly and carefully emptied each drawer into a plastic rubbish sack and deposited it in the kitchen, ready for bin day.

He had insisted on a complete office clean-up and managed to get a resentful Ray and a mutinous Hattie to dust and hoover the dismal space. 'Poor Ignatius is scared of the vacuum cleaner,' said Hattie, which presumably explained why the floor had a carapace of crumbs all over it.

'I don't care if Ignatius is scared,' he said. 'This place is a pigsty.'

'I'm not surprised, lad,' piped up Ray. 'Didn't you know, it used to be a pigsty? They used to slaughter the pigs out there, on those cobbles.' His laugh was brought to an abrupt end by a violent bout of coughing.

The gruesome images did nothing to improve Harry's growing headache, which had started with the flickering fluorescent light above him. It was like a medieval form of torture, as were Ignatius's intermittent farts, which were of Chernobyl-like intensity.

He'd busied himself with knocking out press releases, instructing Hattie to scroll through the local Facebook 'to see what people are talking about' and 'visit her contacts', as well as suggesting she walk the streets and look at the *For Sale* and *Wanted* notices in the local newsagents and post office. 'They are still great places to find stories; people selling off weird things or reporting lost pets,' he told her, remembering his early reporting days.

Probably at the thought of writing lost-pet stories, Hattie brightened up. 'I'm on it!' she said, packing up her pink rucksack with her crumpled notebook and clattering through the door again.

Ray made to move too, back to the betting shop, if Harry had guessed rightly, to collect yesterday's winnings. 'Not you, Ray. I need to understand how the paper's all laid out.'

Ray explained it was done on his time-worn monitor, via an editing package so ancient, it predated the twenty-first century.

'At least until we get to understand that newfangled thing,' said Ray.

The newfangled thing appeared to be the sub-editing software package, which, in any normal newspaper, allowed the subs to place stories on the pages, fit and place headlines, and add images and captions with relative ease. It appeared that the reason Ray couldn't use it was because he hadn't downloaded the software for his computer. And the reason for this was because he hadn't bothered to unpack the new flatscreen – 'There was nowt wrong with the old one.' – which still lingered in its box, next to a broken office chair.

After heaving the old monitor onto the floor and setting up the new screen, Harry rummaged hopefully in the system preferences and was amazed to see a message flash up, indicating that the software was miraculously downloading.

'Still not sure it'll work properly,' said Ray, placing a large, ruler-type object on his desk with a smack.

'Blimey, that should be in a museum,' remarked Harry, just about recognising it as an Em rule, beloved by sub-editors in the early part of the last century as the way to ensure that copy fitted on a page.

'Nowt wrong with the old ways,' muttered Ray.

* * *

It was at 4 p.m. that Harry realised he was supposed to have checked into his accommodation at the local inn by noon, on pain of losing his room. 'We are always very busy,' they'd explained. Given that Hattie had returned with two interesting stories – one about a family who were selling a coffin 'never used' and the other about a child who wanted to give his burgeoning stick-insect collection away – he decided to call it a day.

'Don't worry about locking up, Mr Hedges,' said Hattie. 'You must be so busy. Why don't you get off? Me and Ray are used to sorting everything out.'

Harry glanced round. There was still the faintest whiff of dog poo, the room was stuffy and that evil hound was staring at him as if it knew something he didn't.

'Well, if you're sure?'

'Run along, lad,' said Ray. 'We know what to do.'

'That's great, thanks. But one thing.' Was it his imagination, or did they look worried?

He smiled. 'It's Harry, not Mr Hedges. Please, call me Harry.'

'OK, Harry,' said Hattie. Ray nodded. And, for the first time, he felt like a boss. Even if he wasn't exactly bossing it just yet.

Tiptoeing through the courtyard, Harry unlocked the Mini and folded himself in. There was just enough room to turn the vehicle round before he managed to launch himself back into Piddlington Minster's now rapidly flowing one-way system. But it took two more twirls round the square before he spied the hanging sign for The Ball Inn, at the end of the High Street.

He trundled round to the small rear carpark of the black-and-white beamed building. The fish-tiles and shape of the windows showed that while it may look Tudor, the pub was probably thrown up during the Edwardian era. Anyway, it was cheap, and the website described it as: 'A beautiful market town hostelry with traditional comforts.' Hopefully, he could get a drink to celebrate his return to journalism.

As he opened the car door, he stared carefully at the ground before swinging his legs out, peering at each sole before taking his suitcase from the back seat. Louis Vuitton was probably far too flash for this place, but the suitcase had belonged to his late mother, and his father had never seemed to want to use the thing after the accident.

The rear entrance was in gloomy contrast to the brightness outside and he blinked as he adjusted to the lack of light. The narrow, parqueted corridor led to a larger space nearer the front, with a cubbyhole and a table displaying some leaflets advertising Jurassic Dino World and Piddlington in Miniature – a model village – as well as a dried-flower arrangement that looked as if it had been directly transported from the table at Miss Havisham's wedding breakfast.

'Hello?' Harry felt like an intruder.

'Coming!' fluted a female voice with a strong Dorset accent. There was the sound of very high heels clicking furiously across wood. Emerging from what he surmised must be the bar area came a short, platinum blonde, extremely pretty woman wearing rhinestone jeans and a dazzling white blouse, which strained to cover her ship's figurehead of a chest.

'Who are you now, m'love?' she enquired as she squeezed her incredible frame into the cubbyhole, before flicking furiously through various sheets of paper with scarlet-nailed hands.

'I'm Harry Hedges.' More flicking.

'Laurence Anderson? No, sorry, he never turned up, did he? Nigel Panfield – no, no, there was that awful business with the sheep. Ah, here we are. Mr Harry Hedges of . . . ooh, London!'

She said it as if the idea of someone from the capital staying at The Ball was an excitement or a rarity.

'Could I just trouble you to fill in the form?'

As Harry nodded, she started picking up his suitcase and bag.

'Oh gosh, don't worry, I can manage,' said Harry, whipping out a chewed Biro from his jacket pocket before scribbling away.

'Wouldn't dream of it,' she said and, before he could object, she grabbed the Louis Vuitton and started clattering towards the staircase. Pint-sized she may be, but she was pretty strong.

'Now, it's up here, on the right, down these two steps, on the left and just over the entrance hall,' she instructed as they walked. As she unlocked the bedroom door, Harry was blanketed by a waft of air that appeared to have been trapped there since the 1970s. 'Nice and quiet for you.' She smiled, throwing the suitcase on the bed's mint-green candlewick cover. 'The bathroom's down the hall.'

Hadn't the website said en-suite? 'Excuse me, Miss . . .?'

'Oh, don't bother with all that m'love, everyone calls me Cassandra,' she said, false eyelashes beating like dancers doing the cancan.

Harry wrenched a crumpled printout from his jacket pocket. 'I do apologise, but I ordered a room with an en-suite. Look, it says en-suite, right here.'

Cassandra pored over the sheet, her chest rising and falling. She looped a strand of hair out of her eyes.

'I can tell immediately what's happened. Silly boy! You've mixed us up with the Ball Hotel, haven't you?'

Had he? No wonder it was so cheap. But what about the en-suite?

As if reading his mind, Cassandra started explaining. She had been telling the website man *for ages* to remove the mistake, but it appeared he still had not.

Harry smiled. He wasn't falling for that.

'Look, I'm really sorry if there's been a mix-up but I think I should pop along to the Ball Hotel, Cassandra. I am so sorry for what's happened.'

He made a move towards his suitcase, but Cassandra was too quick, diving across the bed and creating a human barrier.

'Now look, Mr Hedges. I can understand if you think my little inn isn't good enough for someone from London, all la-di-da and all the rest of it. And before you say it, I know we're not the Ritz. But do you really think it's a good idea to be walking out on one of your biggest customers?'

What was she on about? He was tired, he wanted a beer and he wanted a bath. In a tub. Not a shared shower down a long, dark hallway.

'What do you mean?'

Cassandra proceeded to inform him of exactly how much advertising the inn placed in his newspaper every week. 'We advertise the quiz night on Mondays, the Shove Ha'penny Festival every month, the snooker league and the Pie Night. You won't be getting none of that from the Ball Hotel, m'dear. They only do it online. And,' she added, 'we're not full up like they always are – you're our only guest, so plenty of time to give you the treatment you deserve.'

Harry opened his mouth to ask why, if there were no other guests, the inn forced visitors to check in so early but felt too tired to argue. If he really was the only one there – and leaving aside the worrying implications of that thought – at least he'd get all the hot water and it would be a bit like having a private bathroom, hopefully.

'I'll expect really tip-top service, then.'

Instead of looking annoyed, Cassandra beamed. 'I'll see to that, m'love, you just wait!' And she winked, turned on her heels and squeezed out of the door.

He looked round. The room gave him a commanding view down the High Street, which was a pleasing jumble of charity shops, a bookstore, a ladies' outfitters and an antiques emporium, as well as the flashing yellow sign of the ChickinBiteTonite fast-food shop. His head gave a warning throb.

The bed was one of those dour 1950s affairs, like the ones at his old boarding school: dark, varnished, with a slatted headboard and a rattly wood-and-metal frame. The cover looked like so many lines of furry mint-green toothpaste, and the sheet and pillowcase were made of scratchy linen and smelled as if they had come off the Titanic: damp and, even on this early autumn day, cold to the touch. Still, low-grade bed linen was the least of his problems, Harry thought. He forced open the window and was rewarded with a blast of warm air while he inspected the musty old cupboard and chest of drawers. After putting away his shoes and few clothes, he decided to check out the communal bathroom.

Surprisingly, it was spacious and very clean; green-and-white tiles, with a giant rectangular tub and separate shower unit which actually seemed to work. He put in the bath plug and turned on the enormous taps, tipping in the last vestiges of his almond bath oil. There would be no more luxuries like this, unless he could work out a way to get back to London, journalistic civilisation and proper wages.

As he lowered himself into the bath a few minutes later, he breathed in and started to feel his muscles unknotting. Most baths were too short for a man like him but this one allowed him to lean back and, within a few minutes, he could feel his eyelids closing. Perhaps he could walk along to the Ball Hotel for dinner and then come back here to kip. And he'd certainly start organising that office, sort the website and get rid of that dog. With his head full of these soothing thoughts, Harry drifted off.

* * *

He didn't know how long he'd slept but he was awoken by a piercing scream.

'Oh my God!'

It was Cassandra. And she was groping around in his bathwater with her right hand, while clutching his head to her bosom with her left, and uttering a mantra of: 'Oh my God.'

'What's the matter?' he shouted, rapidly trying to cover up all the necessary bits.

'You didn't come down for ages and I didn't hear the water go, so I thought you'd drowned,' she said as, finally, after stabbing those nails far too near his important places, she yanked the plug out. 'You might have caught your death in there in all that cold water.'

Next thing, he was being heaved to his feet and Cassandra was wrapping him in a bath towel.

Pink with embarrassment, he tried to apologise.

'Look, I'm sorry if you've had a shock but really, I was just tired and I fell—'

'And you might have drowned!' she shrieked. 'And then where would we all be?'

'How did you get in?' He knew he'd locked the door.

'I've got a spare key,' she replied, staring at his dripping body.

'It's awfully kind of you but I think I can probably manage from here on.'

Cassandra looked reluctant. 'You might fall over or something. Or faint. Here, let me help you dry yourself.'

The last time anyone had dried Harry, he had been six years old and that person had been his mother. He refused to count the appalling ministrations of Mr Dingle, the sports master at St Basil's, or St Bastard's, as the unfortunate inmates had called it. He had got to the age of thirteen before realising that sports teachers were not required 'by law', as Dingle had insisted, to ensure that their charges were 'warm and thoroughly dry before commencing their next lesson'.

Backing away, Harry assured Cassandra that he wouldn't drown, catch his death, faint or get eaten by a stray lion.

'There's no need to be sarcastic,' she said, peering intently at his semi-naked torso. 'Tells you what, I'll pour you a nice glass of brandy in the bar to warm you up.' It really was the only way of getting rid of her so he agreed, then shuffled along the hallway with as much dignity as he could muster, before locking the bedroom door and wondering if he should wedge a chair under the handle.

Ten minutes later, clad in his favourite jeans and the Paul Smith T-shirt that Violett had once admired on him, Harry contemplated how he might leave the premises without joining Cassandra in the bar for a drink. Mentally, he prepared his escape but realised that the passageway to the High Street led straight past the saloon.

'Harry? Is that you?' Cassandra's voice trailed out of the bar. 'Don't be shy.'

No point in that after what had just happened. Sighing, he obeyed. He wasn't in a mood to argue. As he entered the bar, which was as dark as the hotel entrance, he was delighted to be welcomed with a perfectly pulled pint of Old Piddle: 'Something tells me you're not a brandy man,' she winked. 'At least not before dinner. It's won a lot of awards.'

'Thanks, Cassandra.'

She smiled. 'You look like you could do with it; it's a right proper job you've taken on at that old newspaper.'

He sipped and nodded. Bright and hoppy, Old Piddle wasn't bad at all.

'And we're all hoping in this town that you do better than the last one. A right pig's ear he made of it, if you ask me. Running off like that.'

He remembered the report in the *Press Gazette*: 'Editor quits after month at new job'.

'Kevin Fewtrell,' said Cassandra, expertly reading his mind.

'Did you know him?'

'Mr Fewtrell? Oh yes. He stayed here, just like you. Had the same room, as a matter of fact. Very cagey, though. Always seemed a bit nervous. You know . . .'

He didn't, actually, but Harry rearranged his face into his 'fascinated journo' one, leaning forward and nodding furiously at everything Cassandra said.

'What on earth was he scared of?'

'Hard to know, really. All I do know is that he skedaddled off in the night without even saying goodbye or paying his tab, and he didn't look the sort for that. No forwarding address or anything.'

Harry drank all this in, along with the dregs of the Old Piddle. Jasper hadn't mentioned any of this when he'd called out of the blue and, in a burst of uncharacteristic generosity, tipped him off about the job.

'Did anyone try to find him?'

'Police said that in Britain it wasn't against the law to disappear and that I should sue him in the county court for the bill. As if I've got the time.'

Harry decided to change the subject. 'Have you ever met the newspaper's proprietor?'

'Good lord, no! No one's ever seen him or even knows his name. Have you?'

He hadn't. He'd been appointed by letter from a PO box address after having had to apply by letter, too. Cassandra nodded. 'I mean, there's always rumours – I've heard people say he's one of those Russian oligarchs, or a publishing magnet.'

'Publishing magnate,' corrected Harry. 'Which he would be, if he owns a newspaper.'

Cassandra gave him a look. He was desperate to find out more, but he was also desperate to eat. 'Look, it's been really wonderful to chat but I'm going to pop off for dinner. Perhaps we can resume the conversation later?'

'I can rustle you up something here. Egg and chips?'

'No, that's really kind but I think it's best if I get out and, you know, see the place, show my face around.'

'Right you are, then.'

That was easy.

* * *

The Ball Hotel was along the road and round the corner, in the town square. Bathed, well-watered with Old Piddle and in anticipation of a decent dinner, Harry felt better. Never mind what Fewtrell had done, he wouldn't be making the same mistake. He was going to get back to London by turning round this ailing publication: he would increase advertising, bring the staff into line and become so successful that he'd make the lead story in the *Press Gazette* for all the right reasons. 'Disgraced Hedges rises from the ashes' – something like that, only without the disgraced bit. Hopefully.

It was only after he arrived back at The Ball Inn, after a passable seafood linguine – thank God for overdrafts – that he realised he still had no idea why Fewtrell had run away in the middle of the night.

Still, he thought, *I'm too tired to worry about all that now.* Yawning, he opened the inn's front door and started to trudge up the stairs. He'd use the bathroom now, and then just clamber into bed. After carefully locking the bathroom door, Harry washed his face and brushed his teeth. As he unlocked the door, he peered down the hall. Was that a footstep? He listened. Nothing.

'You're tired, old boy,' he told himself and entered his bedroom. As he looked at the bed, he realised it had been turned down and a chocolate in the shape of a kiss placed on his pillow. Smartly, he locked the door and dived under the covers. Cassandra wasn't hiding there, then.

But as he'd already learned, in Piddlington Minster, you couldn't be too careful.

Chapter 3

It had been a blissfully uneventful night. He hadn't been plagued by the recurring nightmare of his arrest: looking down at his shoes, Violett red-eyed, trying to maintain her composure as he was shuffled by, the deathly silence from his colleagues. Newsrooms only ever go quiet for very serious reasons.

The morning shower was surprisingly hot and powerful and, as he knotted his tie, Harry decided to be the first one in the office and drove off at 8 a.m. sharp. Arriving at the courtyard, he looked carefully about for tell-tale lumps masquerading as cobbles, before jumping from the Mini, which had risen to the occasion by starting first time.

All he needed now was a proper coffee and maybe a croissant or pain au chocolat, and he'd be set for the day.

To his enormous surprise, Hattie and Ray were already ensconced at their desks and chorused, 'Good morning,' as if he were some kind of headteacher. Ignatius, thank God, was nowhere to be seen.

He decided not to mention it, relishing in silence his easy victory, and called an editorial meeting, asking Hattie and Ray to bring their 'coffees and ideas' to his desk. He also decided to ignore their pulled faces.

'Before we get into the day's list, I need to know a bit more about the proprietor. I need to ask him a few things,' he said. 'Hattie, what happened the last time you met him?'

She looked bemused. 'I've never met him. If it is a him. It could be a woman.'

'Who employed you, then?'

'Ray, of course.'

'And who employed you, Ray?'

'Ooh, that was a few years ago . . . My old mate Ron Handley told me there were a job going and I enquired, and they said yes.'

'Who are "they"?'

'I don't know, I had to send the letter to a PO box and one came back telling me when to start. From a secretary, I suppose.'

'So, no one's met our proprietor?'

'I looked them up on Companies House but there was nothing helpful. Our wages arrive in our bank accounts and that's that,' said Hattie.

'Don't you wonder who's paying them?'

They both shook their heads.

Ray spoke up. 'It were always said, and this is going back a bit, that it was owned by a family who all fell out and threatened to close the newspaper. Then it was sold off, very cheap, to a staff collective and then, when they fell out, it belonged to an Englishman, an Irishman and a Scotsman . . .'

Harry put his hand up but Ray continued: 'Who—'

'All went into a bar? Or did they all fall out too?' finished Harry, scratching at his ankle.

'So, you do know, then?' enquired Ray, indignantly.

'I'll have to get hold of him – or her – somehow because I'm planning a few changes around here,' said Harry.

He noticed their glances. 'I don't think it will affect your hours, it's more about how we approach things.'

Hattie looked up. 'Yes, what a good idea, I think there's a lot of stuff that we could do – don't you, Ray?'

Ray nodded vigorously. 'Oh yes, lots and lots,' he said, loudly. 'In fact, I was only going to say . . .'

Their sudden burst of chatter couldn't hide the fact that there was an odd, rhythmic thumping from the direction of Hattie's desk. A horrible smell began to pervade the room.

'Hattie!'

'Yes?'

'Is that dog still here?'

She looked mutinous. 'If you mean Ignatius, then yes, he is. I told you: this is where Ignatius *lives*. It's his home. If he goes, he'll have to be sent to the dogs' home and no one will want him because he's old and . . .'

'Smells disgusting,' finished Harry. He didn't want to be unkind but also felt that, if he wasn't careful, he could spend the rest of his life trying to outwit the creature.

Hattie glared.

In an effort to be conciliatory, he said, 'Look, he's got until the end of this week. If he isn't gone by then I'll . . . I'll, well, I'll . . .' he petered out.

To distract himself, he started firing questions. Who was in charge of the website, who was doing the social media, and what were they putting on the Twitter or X feed, as well as Facebook and TikTok?

Two pairs of eyes stared back. Three if you counted Ignatius, who had heaved himself out from beneath the desk and was now panting near the door.

'We've never updated the website,' said Ray. 'Fewtrell set it all up and then, when he left, no one knew how to get in and change it. It was a right mess; loads of stories you couldn't open up or move and . . .'

'So,' added Hattie, 'that's why there's no social media. Because what would be the point?'

I'm in the Middle Ages, thought Harry. He wanted to ask about Kevin, because he was professionally intrigued by his disappearance, but there were more pressing issues, such as finding some stories to publish.

'Right, what's on the newsdesk diary for today?'

More blank stares.

'Oh, come on, there must be a diary.'

Hattie stretched over to her desk and picked up a large, pink-jacketed book. 'We always try and do the mags' court and, if there's an inquest, I can do that. Ray buys the newspapers every morning and goes through them for stories we can localise. Sometimes people ask us to cover stuff, so I put it in my diary, too.'

Presumably, next to the reminders to buy dog biscuits and fluffy toys from charity shops, thought Harry.

'What about the local police?'

Hattie pulled a face. 'They are sooooo horrible. The sergeant who runs the police station is really old and grumpy and she hardly tells us anything. We stopped going in the end and I just try to pick stuff up off their county Facebook page.'

Harry imagined that Hattie's idea of old and grumpy was probably a thirty-something person who had told her she was too busy to help at some point. 'What about the fire service and the local paramedics?' Were they being regularly contacted in person and online for good-news tips? Apparently, Ray had a lady friend who did the cleaning for the local fire brigade, and she brought in bits and pieces of news. 'You know, like if they are going to have new flower baskets outside the station or something.'

Harry scratched his wrists while he thought of something to say. This was horrendous. The calls, as they used to be known, whether online or in person, were traditionally the backbone of local news gathering, along with the council's drains or AI policy sub-committee working party agendas and the sent-in reports from the Townswomen's Guild and the WI.

As his stomach rumbled, he was reminded that not only had he eaten no breakfast, he'd had no coffee, either.

'Right, I'll do the calls personally today, and on my way, I'm going to get something to eat,' he announced.

As he approached the door, Ignatius wagged his tail. 'He likes going out in the mornings, too,' said Hattie.

'Well, he's not coming with me.'

'He wouldn't want to. He goes off for about half an hour and then comes back and has a sleep. Goodness knows where he goes.'

Too weary to argue, he leaned over and opened the door. Ignatius trotted out, his tail metronoming happily from side to side.

Harry followed. There had to be somewhere that sold proper coffee. As he approached the entrance of the courtyard, he caught a sniff of something glorious: Number Five – French roast, very possibly. Even though Ignatius was now padding purposefully along the pavement in front of him, he decided to go that way too. It was down here somewhere; he could smell it.

As he walked along, he noticed the dog was received with much affection by the townsfolk. 'Hello, boy,' said a man emerging from a key-cutting shop to give him a biscuit. Another stepped out from a pharmacy with what looked like half a ham sandwich, which Ignatius devoured in one gulp.

As a lorry navigated the one-way system, Harry lost sight of the dog. But who cared about that – the coffee smell was intensifying. He quickened his pace, past the betting shop, past a boarded-up fast-food store. The aroma appeared to be coming from an alley, where it hung, like an invisible finger, beckoning in the air.

As he breathed in the wonderful scent, it was joined by another – melting chocolate. The alley was really dark and narrow . . . Surely there couldn't be a shop or a café down here? But the walkway broadened out to a cobbled space, like the courtyard at the *Gazette*. He walked forward. The building at the end had a glass door and he could see inside the Café Bar Parisienne's interior. It was Ignatius, who was being fed little pieces of what looked like glistening croissant by a smiling, middle-aged man.

Harry could stand it no longer and knocked on the glass.

'I'm so sorry, please excuse me, but I smelled the coffee and wondered if, er . . . if you sell it,' he shouted, aware of how pathetic he seemed, like an addict knocking on a dealer's door.

The man shouted back that they did. But not until 11 a.m. 'Until then, we only serve dogs.' He chuckled. 'Me and Ignatius go back a long way, don't we?' Then he patted the Labrador and broke up yet another croissant, which the dog gratefully devoured.

* * *

After a few more seconds of being ignored, Harry decided he may as well go straight to the police station. Maybe someone would take pity on him there.

Like many rural towns, the police station wasn't actually at the police station building; that had become a 'nitespot' called The Old Police Station, which appeared to have closed down. 'Nah, mate,' the road sweeper outside told him. 'You want the old library.'

'Was it always a library?'

'Yes, they just call it that because it was built before the new one. That got turned into a fitness place after the cutbacks, so they moved the new library back in the old one, along with the cop shop.'

As he walked back through the town, Harry noticed how many stores and premises seemed to bear no relation to their original purpose in life: The Olde Bakerye was now Hardaz

Nailz Bar; the former tobacconist's next door – identified by a faded ghost sign above – was now Crafty Crafters; and The Tannery, which appeared to have been an ironmonger's, was a place full of DIY sunbeds with neon-orange people walking in and out of it.

The police station was indeed at the rear of the old library, a pleasant, red-brick Victorian structure with two tubs of multicoloured pansies at the entrance and, inside, a glass kiosk with no one sitting in it. Obeying the instructions to ring the desk bell, he waited. A tall, slim-built officer with close-cut afro hair and a friendly smile emerged from a side door.

'Hi, I'm Harry Hedges, the new editor of the *Piddlington Gazette* and I'm here to see if I can have a chat with the person in charge about sorting out the police calls.'

'Come again?' The officer had a broad Irish accent.

Harry made a second attempt. 'I'm sorry if there's been a breakdown in communication in the past between our two organisations, but that's the reason I've come in person.'

'Right.'

'So, er, would you be able to go over it all with me, please?'

'We'll have to see, won't we, Mr Hedges?' said the officer who, according to his badge, was PC P. Collins.

'OK, PC Collins, thanks, it's the kind of thing that's normally done by a junior reporter but—'

The policeman cut him off with a hand wave. 'Are you sayin' our station isn't good enough for the editor of the local paper? Is that what you're sayin'?'

'Gosh no, I mean . . .'

PC Collins's face cracked from ear to ear. 'I'm joking you. I'm named after the finest Irishman ever to have walked God's earth and it's nice to see some interest from the paper at last. I'll get the iPad.'

Feeling as if he'd scored a major victory, Harry sat down. PC Collins returned with a red-covered iPad and, in a further encouraging gesture, unlocked the glass screen and swung it open, so Harry could hear better.

'It will all eventually go on the county Facebook feed, but you can have this now,' said PC Collins, running his elegant finger down the screen. 'Right . . . it says here that overnight, a giant great sinkhole appeared in Piddlington High Street.'

Harry scribbled furiously. How had they missed this?

'Where, exactly? Anyone hurt? Any reports of car accidents? Is it cordoned off?' Perhaps Hattie could start a live blog – sink-holes were click-central; the reading public loved them.

PC Collins sounded grave. 'All I'm prepared to say is that police are looking into it!'

Harry looked up. The officer was shaking with mirth.

'Police are looking into it. Ha! Do you get it? It's a hole and—'

'Yes, very good,' muttered Harry. The oldest one in the police-men's book, wheeled out for all new reporters everywhere. And he'd fallen for it.

PC Collins went on to describe a few outhouse burglaries, the arrest of a man caught urinating in the town water trough – 'Disgusting!' – and appeared to be searching other windows for more snippets.

'We've had reports coming in about the theft of toilet seats at the police station in Lower Gusset.'

'Lower Gusset? Where's that?'

'Near the village of Far Corfe, as far as I can remember. Anyway, what you need to know is that, as of this moment, police have nothing to go on. Go on! Get it? Police have nothing to go on!' And he started laughing again.

It didn't happen very often, but Harry's temper snapped. 'I suppose you think this is hilarious, don't you? As if I didn't have enough to deal with in this stupid town where even . . .'

He must have raised his voice, because a uniformed woman stepped into the room from a side door. Short, with polished titian hair pulled into a tight, hard, neck bun and with the tiniest trace of makeup, she frowned at them both.

'PC Collins?'

'Sorry, Sarge, just having a bit of banter with the local press.' He slipped deftly from behind the desk into another room, leaving Harry to face the senior officer.

'That idiot has been wasting my time for the past half an hour,' he complained.

'Are you calling my officer an idiot?'

'Yes. Well, no, but . . .'

The woman pursed her lips. She was actually very attractive; instinctively, Harry stole a look at her ring finger. It was empty.

'Just so you know, I am the sergeant here and we don't have the facilities to deal with prima donnas who seem to think they can just turn up and waste police time.'

Her eyes, which were actually a pale, luminous green, glittered. He calmed down; no point in upsetting her, but he could now understand Hattie's reaction to her brusqueness.

'I'm sorry, this has got everything off to a bad start,' he said. 'I'm Harry Hedges, the new editor of the *Piddlington Gazette*.'

'We all know who *you* are,' she said, mouth twisting.

Harry decided to ignore the barb. 'And you are?'

'Sergeant here.'

'No, I meant your name.'

For the first time in the past five minutes, the woman looked hesitant. He gave her the full benefit of the earnest stare which had previously melted so many female hearts.

She hesitated another second before replying. 'It's Starsky. Sergeant Starsky.'

'Starsky? As in . . .'

'Yes. That's right. The 1970s cop show. My father was a fan, changed our family name by deed poll. OK?'

He tried not to smile. 'It's lovely to meet you, Sergeant Starsky, but I actually meant your first name.'

'Don't patronise me.'

'I wouldn't dream of it, Sergeant.'

She snorted, pushing an imaginary piece of hair from her smooth forehead. 'Don't you still have a job to go to?'

'Of course, but you can't blame me for asking, can you? What's your first name? If I'm allowed to know.'

She sighed. 'It's Ophelia.'

'Like the Shakespearian character?'

The fight seemed to go out of her. 'Yes, that Ophelia. My father was a frustrated actor. Whenever I complained about it, he'd just say, "You're lucky your surname isn't balls".'

'Ophelia Balls.' Harry chortled, but he was swiftly cut off.

'I've heard it all, believe me. Now, if you don't mind, I have a million things to do, and I'd like to get on with at least some of them.'

'That's a shame, because I was actually hoping you might do me the honour of coming out for a drink with me, sometime?'

'Do you ever stop? No, Mr Hedges, I don't have the time to go out with you or with anyone and if you knew anything about the state of policing in Britain today – which I'm guessing, going on several reports, you very well might – you'd understand, wouldn't you?'

And she slammed through the kiosk door.

Well, thought Harry, *that's told me.* But he'd enjoyed the pursuit. And he'd seen the look in her eyes: she liked him despite herself.

* * *

He sauntered back to the office.

The door was propped open, and he quickly discovered the reason why. 'Poor' Ignatius was apparently not feeling well.

'I think we can all smell that,' said Harry, vigorously swatting the air with his hand. 'Where's Hattie?'

'Out on a job,' mumbled Ray, paying sudden attention to his screen.

'Good, because we need some copy and when she gets back, I'm going to set up an X feed.'

It was twenty minutes before she flew through the door, pink-cheeked and puffing.

'Good story?' He caught the look from Ray.

'Oh, yes. Yes, very good,' she said, moving into the kitchen. 'Tea? Coffee?'

He decided to let it pass. After all, it hadn't always been work every time he'd stepped out of the *Daily News* office. But he was the editor, and he knew that at some point he'd have to try to enforce some official working hours.

* * *

Setting up the social media feed was not as difficult as he'd imagined. If you discounted the fact that Ray's internet appeared to be still on dial-up. And the fact that his and Hattie's machines were stealing criminal amounts of bandwidth from the Life & Style Store. And the realisation that there was a spoof @PiddlingtonGazette feed re-tweeting racist memes and adverts for a soft porn site.

It was Hattie who saved the day, pointing out that they could just be @ThePiddlingtonGazette, and within two minutes they were ready to send their first official post.

'What about putting: "Hello, we're the *Piddlington Gazette* and we're on Twitter"?' volunteered Ray.

'I think they would be able to tell that because they will actually be reading it *on* X, won't they?'

'Good point,' Ray conceded, dunking a Hobnob into his drink.

If he could just block out the tea-slurping noises of Ignatius, it would be his most successful hour yet as editor of the *Piddlington Gazette*, thought Harry.

As he worked his way through the usable information from PC Collins, and scribbled down a few more ideas, he began to relax. Maybe this could actually work. Maybe he could make a success of it and somehow return to London, journalism and solvency on a tide of glory.

As his mind drifted, he found himself looking up Violett Travers on the internet.

His looks and charm had ensured that an endless string of Immys and Daisys, not to mention Sophies, Serenas and even a couple of Cressidas, had been thrilled to date him – until he'd fallen for Violett. He missed the time they'd spent bouncing ideas off each other in the newsroom: how clever she was, how intuitive. He loved the way she found the non-stop rollercoaster of journalism and news reporting as energising and thrilling as he did – that constant feeling of never knowing what the day would bring.

When he was first convicted, Violett had tried her best to keep in touch, checking in on his case, making sure he knew he had her support. It had been tempting to lean on her but, in the end, he couldn't quite shake the feeling that she was staying in touch out of guilt rather than the old feelings. Eventually, he felt so far from the man she had known, he found it easier to let the messages fizzle out and to nobly hope that, without him, her life would go back to normal.

Unlike him, Violett hadn't had to leave her job in a blaze of ignominy. Now looking at pictures of her showing a government minister round the *Daily News*'s newsroom, as Jasper's doorman bulk carefully shielded the rude doodles on the office whiteboard from photographic view, he couldn't help but feel a pang of nostalgia. And something else . . . as another picture showed her leaving a restaurant with a good-looking man. Harry sighed.

The latest image, on a gossip site, showed her at a reception aboard the yacht belonging to the *Daily News* proprietor, a florid Scotsman called Sir Jimmy Knox, upon whom everyone in his immediate universe paid terrified and fawning attendance. Violett was dressed in a demure white lace frock, clutching a champagne flute and gazing attentively at her boss, who was grimacing at the photographer. 'Never a dull moment' was the sarcastic caption.

With Violett there never had been. Her intelligence never ceased to surprise him, but it was her wit and, if he was being honest, how incredible she was in bed that had kept the flame burning so brightly. He loved how they would chat for hours, after a night of passion, about what they were working on. She had a way of making you feel like the most fascinating person in the room, and this vitality reminded him of his late mother, Isabella – you couldn't help but be swept off your feet by them.

There was only a brief Wikipedia page and a few paparazzi images of Isabella on the internet, mostly taken outside Annabel's and Le Caprice in the 1980s and uploaded after her death. Apart from the picture he always kept with him, there were no photos or even paintings of her in their family home; not even a copy of that coffee table book he'd been told about, which featured images of the 1980s glitterati. His poor father had found her loss so appalling that he couldn't bear to be reminded of her, as far as Harry could make out.

He was remembering Isabella's throaty laugh when he was jolted by a sharp rat-a-tat on the office door and an elderly, small-boned, agitated-looking woman with a helmet of grey hair strode smartly in, slamming the door behind her.

'I am here to see the editor. I have an appointment.'

Oh, no. The town busybody. Who, he belatedly realised, was also the mad placard woman.

'I am the editor, madam. May I help you?'

'Hmmm. You barely look as if you're out of short trousers, but I suppose you'll have to do.'

He let the insult roll away. As Hattie returned to her desk, he asked if she could perhaps get the lady a cup of coffee.

'It's Mrs Robarts. And it's tea. Darjeeling.'

Hattie looked nervous. 'I don't think we have that.'

'Perhaps you could try and get some,' asked Harry, looking around for a place to chat in private.

Hattie gratefully slipped out again and Ray announced he was going to the bathroom.

'How can I help you, Mrs Robarts?'

The woman started rummaging violently in a handbag that had a catch resembling a poacher's gin trap.

'It's all here, every single document. For the past few years, I've been conducting a campaign to have this town cleaned up, Mr Hedges.'

His mind began to whirr. Prostitutes in the Minster Walk? Gambling? Shebeens? Brilliant! Readers loved clean-up campaigns. They gave them the chance to simultaneously moralise, complain and relish the lurid details of whatever was causing the trouble.

'You must have noticed it by now?'

'Noticed what?'

'The way this town is falling to rack and ruin. Dog mess all over the streets . . .' Here, she paused to frown pointedly at Ignatius. 'That roundabout resembles the Amazon jungle, and the council does nothing.'

Gratified by Harry's assiduous scribbling, Mrs Robarts bulldozed on. The roundabout was a health hazard, and very dangerous. 'No one can see round it – some idiot nearly hit me yesterday – and it is a disgrace to the town, especially as we're trying to win the regional heat of Britain in Bloom next year and no one is doing anything.'

He stared downwards and scratched at his wrist. Then his ankle and then his head.

Mrs Robarts pursed her lips again. 'Could you stop fidgeting? I haven't finished yet.'

After sucking in enough air to fill the Albert Hall, she was off again. It wasn't only the roundabout – there was also *the house*.

'What house?'

'As you come in on the road from that roundabout. You can barely see it, it's so overgrown. It's infested with rats and must be a health hazard. They still have the plague in Africa, you know.'

'How exactly do you think we can help?' asked Harry, wondering this himself.

'Investigate it! Start a campaign to have something done. Call yourself a local newspaper?'

According to Mrs Robarts, a keen attender of local council meetings, the entire town was 'disgusted' with the sight of the roundabout, the 'danger' of the house and the smell from it.

The word 'smell' had a dreadful portent about it. In his new corner, behind the desk of the terminally absent Hattie, Ignatius appeared to have let off his worst fart yet.

Harry swallowed. His eyes were burning. Even Mrs Robarts faltered.

'Is there something wrong with your drains here?'

'Er, probably,' he gasped.

'I'm surprised you can work. It's as if something has died.'

He stood up, delighted that Hattie had not returned or produced any tea. They needed to get this woman off the premises and then open the door before everyone died.

In as grand a manner as he could muster, he told her: 'You have my best assurances that we will investigate.'

'Good,' said Mrs Robarts. 'Now, here's the paperwork – make sure you don't lose it.'

He gratefully accepted the bundle and stepped forward to open the door. *Please let her go. And please let this turn into a proper story.*

Chapter 4

Given the appalling nature of the smell from Ignatius, Harry decided to prop the door open, just as Ray stepped back into the room.

'Coast clear?' he chuckled.

'Do you know her?'

'Oh, everyone knows her. She's always moaning about something.'

He agreed she was a bit of an old harridan but felt constrained to point out that she had also brought in the first sniff of an interesting story he'd had in twenty-four hours.

'Anyway, like it or not, Ray, she's right about that roundabout. And that house she mentioned . . . I didn't realise there was one under all the mess. Pictures of overgrown houses do very well on social media and will drive readers to our site.'

Ray was looking puzzled.

'That's what I don't understand. If we put it all over our site, why would they buy the paper? They'll have got it all for free, won't they?'

Harry began explaining the labyrinthine relationship of online clicks to advertising, and the fact that clickbait stories may persuade people to buy the paper itself, even if they had just obtained everything for nothing on their mobile or laptop, but found himself petering out. Put like that, Ray's logic was hard to argue against. But he wasn't giving in that easily. It was his job, as editor, to talk up the great digital revolution.

'What we'll do is get an exclusive interview with whoever is living in that house and that will be the reason people buy the paper. "Piddlington Minster's house of mystery." Trust me, they'll love it.'

'Well, I don't know . . .' began Ray.

'That's the point. No one knows or appears to even *do* anything in this newspaper that might mark out to anyone caring to step in here that this is what we are about,' said Harry. 'We have dogs strewn about the place, computers out of the Ark, coffee that tastes like the stuff you find at the bottom of a radiator, and staff who spend half their time away from the office.'

'In my young day, they used to complain if you were in the office,' said Ray. 'The editors always thought you should be out on your beat, having tea with people and getting stories and such. Not sitting on your backside in the newsroom.'

'Yes,' said Harry, torn between pointing out that Ray's young day was possibly in the 1970s, and modern newspaper staff had to complete three times the amount of work, with half the staff and charging twice what the paper was probably worth.

Still, his was not to reason why, his was but to do. Or suffer the horror of never getting out of Piddlington Minster and back to big journalism, where he knew he really belonged.

'I'm going to send Hattie out on this job,' he said. 'I want you to send out a few posts, fire the readers up a bit, and I'll tackle the police.'

He pretended not to notice Ray shaking his head.

* * *

Walking through the town, he began to relax. He had some story plans, he'd managed to engage the staff – well, fifty per cent of them – with his ideas and he was pretty sure he could get Ignatius evicted, too.

The police station's blue main door was locked but that didn't bother him. The first rule of newsgathering is to go round the back, he told himself, walking along the building to the station's smaller, side door.

It was snatched open and he found himself facing an irritated Sergeant Starsky.

'What are you doing here again? You do know it's an offence to trespass, especially in the precincts of a police station?'

He didn't know any such thing but peered at her from beneath his fringe. 'I know, but there was no one in the front office and I wanted to ask for a comment on the situation at the roundabout.'

She looked at him as if he had just been declared insane.

'What *are* you on about?'

'The roundabout, as you come into town over the bridge. You know, the large, circular road feature that's rather overgrown.'

'Yes, thank you. What's it got to do with the police?'

Harry explained that there had been a complaint and that he had come to ask in person, from a road-safety angle.

'A complaint? No need to ask from whom, is there?' snarled Sergeant Starsky. 'If it's not the bloody roundabout, it's the house. If it's not that, it's dog poo. If it's not that, she's on about perverts. Or communists, or . . .'

She actually looked quite sexy when she was angry.

'Can I come in?'

Her mouth fell open. As she started to speak, there was a crackle and then a call signal over a radio further inside the room, on a desk. She strode towards it and Harry stepped in and sank into an office chair, trying to pretend he wasn't looking at the screen in front of him, which didn't fool Sergeant Starsky, who flung a hi-vis jacket over it.

'Yes? A body? Where?'

Harry couldn't hear the response, but Ophelia looked shocked.

She started scribbling on a pad. 'Yes. Yes. No. Yes, I'll go. Traffic? Yes, please. I'll secure the scene.'

He tried his best to look totally disinterested. A body! An actual dead body. He'd originally thought that the best he'd get in this place would be a neighbours' hedge dispute with, on a good day, a couple of punches thrown. Maybe London wasn't that far away after all . . .

'You! Out!' she said, yanking on the hi-vis jacket and pushing him with her free arm.

'Perhaps I can help,' he offered. 'We can—'

'There's no *we*,' she said, pushing him in the back. 'Move.'

As he stepped out of the door, and she slammed it behind them, he spotted a furry shape outside in the carpark. Sergeant Starsky bent down and swiftly kissed Ignatius's head. 'Hello, what are you doing here?'

The dog thumped his tail, looking adoringly into her chest. Harry was astonished. 'Do you know him too?'

'Everyone in Piddlington Minster knows Ignatius,' she replied, wrenching open the driver's door of a police Ford Focus. 'He's probably smarter than you.'

He was thrilled. For once Ignatius had come in handy. He'd distracted Sergeant Starsky so comprehensively that she'd given him no official warning about the body – so they could go ahead and report it, he reasoned. As she roared off, blue lights flashing, he started jabbing at his mobile phone, which had thankfully rolled onto the next month's data allowance.

'Ray? Listen, there's been a body discovered. Yes, here. In Piddlington Minster. No, I don't know exactly where but can you tweet to that effect? Something along the lines of: "Breaking news hashtag dead body found in hashtag Piddlington Minster. Follow for more".'

'Is it dead, then?'

Harry ground his teeth. 'It must be, otherwise why would it be reported?'

'Well, if you're sure.'

'I am. Where's Hattie?'

Ray explained that she had gone out to try and interview the owner of the overgrown house and take some pictures on her iPhone.

Hooray! Staff Showing Initiative alert! He felt like high-fiving someone but as the only someone available was Ignatius, he moved on, trying not to notice the Labrador plodding faithfully behind.

As he began to feel the old excitement of having a proper story to work on, Harry decided to race back to the office and get his car; it shouldn't be too long before he tracked down the site of the body.

* * *

The one-way system appeared to be flowing at a snail's pace, which was good news because he had long ago perfected the art of driving while looking at anywhere but the road. As the system started to peel away from the town, he saw blue lights flashing in his rear-view.

Muttering grateful prayers to the patron saint of news editors, Harry stopped to let the police car pass, so he could follow it to the body. It must be going there. Nothing else had happened in this town since the Domesday Book. As the vehicle overtook, he flicked the gear stick into first and nipped in after it.

He didn't have long to wait. As they approached the road out of town, he saw a row of red lights in front of him. He slowed and then stopped behind a giant pick-up, stationary behind a box van.

He jumped out and walked to the pick-up. 'What's going on, mate?'

'Don't know, looks like an accident or something.'

The hold-up appeared to be on the slipway leading onto the overgrown roundabout. In the distance, he could detect a police officer, spooling out incident tape. The officer appeared to be circling the roundabout itself.

He ran forward, swerving past the Ford Focus police car that blocked the road. PC Collins was in charge of the tape and Sergeant Starsky was nowhere to be seen. It was definitely the roundabout itself which was being cordoned off. As PC Collins walked round to the right, Harry dodged to his left and, dipping under a branch, pushed his way through what seemed like half of Sherwood Forest, towards the roundabout's centre.

He could hear voices.

'Didn't I say this is exactly the sort of thing that would happen?'

'Mrs Robarts,' came the weary voice of Sergeant Starsky. 'I have no knowledge of what you have or haven't said to the council or anyone else.'

'I told the young man at the newspaper.'

'I'm sure you did, but you may as well have told that dog they keep there, for all the use he is. Look, I'm treating this as a potential crime scene and if you don't move immediately, I'll have you arrested for police obstruction.'

He could see both women now: the grey helmet of Prudence Robarts and the short figure of the sergeant. Stealthily, he pushed forward. Just a bit nearer. He was concentrating so hard that he failed to notice a twig, which jabbed into his eye.

He let out a blood-curdling scream, whose sound only intensified as he realised he actually could not see out of his right eye.

'My *eye*!'

Clutching his head and staggering around in the manner of his namesake at the Battle of Hastings, he felt a hand gripping his shoulder.

'How *dare* you come in here, contaminating a potential crime scene,' growled Sergeant Starsky. 'PC Collins? Collins!'

Harry attempted to open his right eyelid. Or where he last remembered it being. Immediately, his eye swam with big, greasy tears and he started seeing everything in triple.

'Sorry, Ophelia, had a prang with a branch and I think I'm injured.'

'I'm sure. But not mortally, unfortunately. And it's Sergeant Starsky to you. Now, just get out before I do arrest you. Take this as God's way of telling you not to contaminate potential crime scenes.'

Feeling as if he'd undergone some sort of Tudor-style torture, Harry wandered into the road and felt himself being restrained by a large and gentle hand.

'Not so fast, Mr Hedges.' It was PC Collins. 'Come over here and I'll take a look at that eye.' Desperate to see what was going on, he craned his good eye and immediately cricked his neck. Letting out another yelp, he sat at an uncomfortable angle on the verge, while PC Collins rummaged in the boot of the police car, before bringing out a small first-aid case and putting on some plastic gloves.

'Now, careful.'

He was grateful for PC Collins's kind and seemingly expert touch. As if reading his mind, the officer said: 'Highest marks they've ever had on Bramshill's first-aid course. My mother was a nurse, came over on the *Windrush*.'

After a few minutes of blinking, dabbing and washing, an eyepatch was placed on him, and he was treated to a welcome sip of coffee from PC Collins's sophisticated stainless-steel flask. Harry felt composed enough to try and do his job.

'Thank you, PC Collins.'

'Call me Patrick. Except when Sarge is around.' He smiled.

'What do we reckon's happened here?' he asked. 'All off the record, of course.'

This produced peals of laughter. 'I know I may look young and immensely hip, but I wasn't born yesterday. A statement will be made, when it will be made.'

'But there *is* a body?'

'A suspected body.'

'A suspected human body?'

'Yes. Now go away before I tell you it was murdered.'

'Was it? Are there suspicious circumstances?'

'Plenty, if you ask me. Now, off you go.'

* * *

He strode off purposefully until he saw PC Collins walk into the roundabout's centre again. Then he looped back, fishing out his iPhone. He knew the body wouldn't be moved for a while, but he could maybe get some footage of the forensic teams arriving and put it on social media.

For good luck he snapped the roundabout and decided to send the picture to Ray. Could it really be true that today the *Piddlington Gazette* would post its first live blog?

As the activity continued, and PC Collins and two other officers set up a new road system to allow the traffic to flow again, Harry clocked the determined figure bearing down on him.

'Mrs Robarts! How are you, you poor thing? You must have had the most terrible shock.' The flattery worked. Within a few minutes, he had extracted information from the eager eyewitness who – unlike every other person who had ever found a dead body – was not out walking her dog, but had gone onto the roundabout to 'check if there was any fly-tipping'.

'How immensely public-spirited of you.'

'It was. Then I noticed it. There was a skeletal hand, protruding from the earth, for all the world as if it was pointing to me.'

He scribbled furiously.

'I couldn't believe what I was seeing, so I moved closer and within a few seconds there could be no doubt: it was the remains of a human arm.'

Mrs Robarts had then loosened the earth around the limb to satisfy herself 'it was a whole cadaver' and then had 'informed the authorities'. Not for the first time, Harry wondered just why people involved in an incident of this nature immediately lapsed into the kind of language that wouldn't have been out of place in *Dixon of Dock Green*, a TV police show which had ceased broadcasting before any of them were even born. Although, looking at Mrs Robarts, definitely not in her case – she looked ancient.

'How did you feel when you saw the arm, Mrs Robarts?'

She looked into the distance. 'I felt fearful. I felt sorrow for this poor, abandoned creature. Then I felt angry, very angry. In fact, I felt livid that the very thing I had said might happen had now actually occurred and if my requests hadn't been ignored, then an innocent life might not have been lost.'

'Are you saying you actually predicted a murder?'

'No, you stupid boy. But I predicted that because of the disgraceful state the roundabout is in, anyone – drug dealers, perverts, communists – could use it to hide anything, and no one would know.'

His phone pinged.

'I do think those things are intrusive,' she sniffed.

'Indeed,' said Harry, thrilled to notice that @ThePiddlingtonGazette had posted his pin-sharp image of police vans and the cordon at the roundabout captioned: 'Piddlington Minster – dead body found on roundabout. Follow #PiddlingtonRoundaboutBody for more'. And it had already racked up ten re-posts and twenty-five likes.

He called Ray. 'Great stuff, Ray, now can you put in something about the traffic chaos?'

'It says on the police website thingy that traffic's flowing again.'

'I know, I can see it, but there was traffic chaos, and that always attracts hits, and sales on the print edition, so can you just do it?'

With a mutter, Ray put the phone down.

Harry's phone buzzed again, and Mrs Robarts moved away slightly, shaking her head.

'Hello, Hattie – what have you got for me?'

She had gone to the overgrown house, which was creepy, like the worst horror film *ever*, and then battled her way up the garden path, like the prince in *Sleeping Beauty*, past all this horrible, overgrown lavender to the front door, which was brown. Not a nice brown, like Ignatius, but a sort of tired, *evil* brown, like the eyes of that dead horse in *The Godfather* movie – had Harry ever seen it?

He clamped his jaw. He didn't want to put her off, and her enthusiasm was refreshing, but could she just get to the point?

Anyway, she'd knocked, because the bell was long gone, and didn't get a reply and couldn't push open the letterbox, so she looked in one of the windows. Amazingly, the place didn't have curtains pulled across and she saw all this *stuff*.

'Like what?'

'Weird, horrible art stuff, like sculptures.'

'Sculptures are art, Hattie.'

'Yeah, but not like any stuff I've seen before. It was all kind of metal-box people with their heads missing and sort of industrial-looking fish welded to blobs.'

He wondered what she'd make of Epstein, or Moore, then.

'It was nothing nuanced, like Hepworth,' finished Hattie. 'Although I prefer Frink, I think.'

That told him. Hattie explained how she had tried to get round the back, but it was impossible, as the garden was so overgrown, you couldn't see the house.

'Anyway, I did what you told me national journos sometimes do, and put a handwritten note through the front door, saying how we'd like to help.'

'Good girl.'

'And I stepped back and looked up. I couldn't see anyone but, you know, I got the idea there was someone watching me. I felt it quite strongly.'

After instructing her to return to the office, Harry felt well enough to drive, even though the eyepatch was already driving him mad. He flipped it upwards and immediately tears began to gush from the injured eye. He flipped it down again and set off, more carefully than usual.

As he passed the overgrown house, he slowed. The sight really was incredible. Swiftly, he indicated and pulled up on the kerb opposite.

Either side of the giant green mess were two sedate Victorian villas, one 'improved' with plastic windows, giving the look of a man with his eyes punched out – something dead about modern glass, he concluded. This one had the traditional black-and-white tiled path, bun-edging and a small front garden with a diamond-shaped flower bed planted alternately with scarlet salvias and orange French marigolds.

The front door was red, too, and it suddenly opened as Harry crossed the road. A man – presumably the owner – looked at him.

'Are you from the council?'

'No, sorry. Is everything OK?'

'OK?' exploded the man, who then spurted a stream of invective: look at the mess next door, just look at it. Fifty years, to his knowledge, the place had been like that. Probably filled with rats and fleas and lice and God knows what else. A health and a fire hazard too, he wouldn't be at all surprised.

Harry let him finish. He had a point. Like the house where he stood, the property had a front wall. Only, that one was groaning under the weight of an assortment of laurel and other evergreens, whose branches were causing the structure to bow out towards the pavement. Despite the September sun, there was a pile of greasy black leaves underneath it. Behind the laurels were brambles which had grown up to half the house's height; some were spangled with orange and blue plastic bags, plus the odd Coke can which had been tossed in there. Scraggy lavender, all run to seed, was flowing over the front path, whose tiles were raised, jagged and forlorn.

'Do you know the owner?'

The man did not but he thought it was an old lady.

'Does she have cats?' Cats, as Harry knew, added greatly to eccentric old people stories.

'Matey, she could have a bleedin' T-Rex in there and no one would know about it. It's not right.'

He agreed. He decided not to tell the man he was the local newspaper editor; sometimes it was best just to keep things quiet, especially when no one had asked.

'I want it sorted,' the man continued. 'It's about time your paper did something about it.'

'Sorry?'

'Your paper. I've just realised. You *are* the new editor, aren't you? I hope you're better than the last one.'

He was beginning to wonder, with a grapevine like this, if Piddlington Minster even needed a paper.

The man was staring at him.

'I know your face from somewhere, don't I? Are you that bloke who—'

'No,' he said firmly, walking back to the car and pulling away. 'I was never that bloke.'

* * *

Arriving back at the office, having finally discarded the eyepatch, he felt better than he'd done since the arrest horror. Ray was at his desk, glasses on, tapping away at his keyboard. Hattie was at hers, the fairy lights twinkling. And if Ignatius was in the building, he couldn't see him or smell him, which was a giant improvement on the previous twenty-four hours.

'Everything OK?' he asked, for the sheer satisfaction of hearing a chorus of 'Yes'.

He logged back in and clicked on to the internet. The *Piddlington Gazette* Facebook page was humming along and so was the X feed. Time to crack on with his lead story.

Pensioner in roundabout body riddle

Exclusive, by Harry Hedges.

A leading community clean-up campaigner has spoken of her shock after discovering a dead body on Piddlington Minster's eyesore roundabout.

Mrs Prudence Robarts claims the cadaver's skeletal hand was 'pointing' towards her when she made the gruesome discovery.

He then left a space for police comment, before continuing.

Speaking exclusively to the Editor of the Piddlington Gazette, *Harry Hedges, Mrs Robarts, who has been campaigning to have the road feature tidied up, explained that she had visited it to check for fly-tipping.*

He added in her quotes about the potential age of the corpse and a few observations about the town in general.

And the Piddlington Gazette *can further reveal that this is not the only campaign which public-spirited Mrs Robarts has been spearheading.*

She is also fighting to get a clean-up for an overgrown property on Bridge Street which, she claims, is a 'health hazard' and a 'danger to life', as well as threatening the town's chances in next year's Britain in Bloom competition.

The story was shaping up nicely. Ray told him he'd laid out the sports pages – mainly jottings by meticulous and obsessive lovers of darts, carp fishing and Piddlington United FC, but Harry was happy to take everything he could get.

He showed them the layout of the front page and basked in their approval. Could it actually be working? Was he really an editor, earning his living from journalism once again?

He felt strongly that cakes were in order, having learned over the years that little else impressed seasoned hacks more than a fresh Victoria sponge, a tub of deluxe flapjacks or, failing that, expensive biscuits smothered in chocolate.

'Go to Brenda's,' said Hattie. 'Ignatius likes their caramel muffin.'

'I won't forget,' he said with a smile, which quickly faded as he wondered, yet again, how he was going to get through to Hattie that Ignatius couldn't live in the office. Why couldn't he live with her, if she was so fond of him? Or with Ray?

Making a mental note to find out more about his staff's private lives, he stepped into the courtyard, which was ablaze with sunshine. Even the dandelions looked cheeky, instead of a mess. A large, red admiral butterfly added to the gaiety of the scene.

The contrast to fume-filled London, where no space – even one as small as this – was overlooked by developers, struck him. *Get me*, he thought. *I could get used to this.*

Chapter 5

Harry strolled back to the office, juggling an array of yellow-striped paper bags. A Bakewell tart for Ray, a pink-princess, glitter-strewn cupcake for Hattie, an old-school iced currant bun with a cherry on top for him and the caramel muffin for Ignatius. Best of all, Brenda had made him a proper espresso. 'In one of those things.'

'A percolator, I think you'll find it's called,' he'd said and winked.

'I do know, Mr Smart Alec!' she said, rolling her eyes and pretending to be annoyed. He'd be going back there.

He pushed the office door open with his shoulder. 'Cakes are on me!' The excitement shown by all, including Ignatius, whose tail thrashed on the carpet tiles, made him smile. His staff. His little office. His paper. And now, a dead body. If it had been helpfully murdered, preferably by a town worthy or a serial killer – he wasn't fussy – they'd be living off it for weeks. A few months of sales-driving exclusives, plus a juicy investigation into the murder, would help his ultimate aim of getting back to London.

As he sipped his drink, relishing every single caffeine-laden slurp, he rolled up his sleeves. For some reason, his shirts and socks had started to irritate him. Probably the dust and filth in this place.

The post arrived and he ripped open the brown paper envelopes: a few court lists and the council committee agendas. Ostensibly boring, but he knew that many a great story had been dug out of a council document.

'Hattie, could you go through this?' he asked, chucking a clump of yellow papers onto her desk. 'I'll do the courts.'

Like most small towns, Piddlington Minster's magistrates' court list was groaning with defendants accused of minor criminal damage, common assault and drink-driving offences. He'd probably send Hattie to the sentencing of the man 'drunk in charge of a combine harvester', but he wasn't sure how their proprietor would want the unfortunate subject of the farmer and the goat dealt with. When it came down to it, most papers considered themselves 'family reading'.

That reminded him. He really must track down the proprietor. Idly, he wondered if Jasper Grant would know – after all, he'd put him on to this gig – but he didn't want to contact him if he didn't have to.

He just needed a few decent stories under his belt and offered up another silent prayer for the body on the roundabout to have been the victim of something truly bizarre, like Satanists or people who dress up as goldfish – anything suitably splash-worthy.

* * *

While Ray tapped away and gave the occasional chuckle, Hattie was running through her lists with a pink highlighter pen.

'Anything good?'

'Not sure yet,' she began. 'Sounds from this that the council might be making redundancies at the local museum.'

'Good,' said Ray. 'That's where that Robarts nuisance volunteers. Perhaps they'll up her hours and she won't have time to come here, complaining all the time.'

That woman, pointed out Harry, had given them their best story for weeks, possibly months.

They both agreed. 'But I still don't like her,' said Hattie.

'And I don't trust her,' said Ray. 'She's got funny eyes.'

Harry spotted some further pink sections on the agenda Hattie was reading and asked what they were.

'Strangely enough, there's an inquiry about Number 43 Bridge Street, the overgrown house. Looks like someone's asked the council to take out an order to have it compulsorily cleaned up, or something, probably because it's now affecting the street. No prizes for guessing who that came from.'

Great, thought Harry, picturing someone old and possibly deranged being extracted noisily from the property. Preferably with around twenty hollering cats. Another potential front-page splash. He should be so lucky.

Reminding himself to chat to Mrs Robarts about this, he announced he was off to the police again.

'It's 4 p.m., they must have got something on the body by now.' He felt convinced it was his lucky day. So convinced, in fact, that he bet himself he could get Sergeant Starsky to give him some additional information.

* * *

The police station's front office was open, and he found Ophelia alone in the reception kiosk.

'Yes?'

'Oh hi, I didn't mean to disturb anyone, but I thought it would be easier for you if we ran over the details of the roundabout situation in person.'

'That's good, because I was about to come and see you,' she snapped. 'I was about to ask you what the hell do you think you were doing, trespassing on a crime scene? You potentially contaminated the area, wasted my officer's valuable time when you injured yourself and, quite frankly, given your reputation, you're lucky I didn't have you arrested.'

Like a game of snakes and ladders, Harry felt the unwelcome downward slither. He tried another tactic.

'What can I say, Sergeant? My enthusiasm ran away with itself. I know I probably shouldn't have, but I do have another, very good reason for coming here just now.'

'And that is what, exactly?'

'I was going to ask you out.'

She blinked.

So did Harry. He was pretty sure he hadn't meant to say this. But looking at Sergeant Starsky, her hair escaping from that bun thing she wore, her eyeliner just a little smudged now, and her skin so luminously pale, the idea grew on him. Why not? She looked so neat and vulnerable, in a ball-breaking kind of way.

'Well, you've got a nerve, haven't you?' she snapped. But that voice seemed a tiny bit less sure of itself. And she appeared, suddenly, softer round the edges. She was looking up, peering from behind a strand of titian hair.

He took the chance and subjected her to the full force of his smile. 'Can it do any harm to get on better?'

'Plenty, I expect.' She sighed. 'But yes. A drink sometime would be nice.'

Now *he* was surprised. Had he just pulled? Too easy. 'There is something you have to let me do first, though.'

Her eyes narrowed.

'You have to let me call you Ophelia.'

And she laughed. An unexpectedly merry giggle, like fairies and elves dancing in the summer dew, he thought.

'Don't get any ideas, though, it's deffo a drink, not a date and . . .' She looked at her watch. 'I need to grab something to eat so you can practise not being an idiot by walking me there if you like.'

Thrilled, but trying to look merely rather delighted, he immediately agreed. Walking and talking evidently suited Ophelia, who asked him a string of questions about his job: how he'd heard about it, how difficult it had been to get things up and running after the sudden departure of the previous editor, what were his plans, and so on.

'Why are you so interested?' he joked. 'Are you looking for a new job?'

'Good God, no. It's probably because, like you, my job is about being interested in other people. For you it leads to stories, for me, well . . .'

She broke off as they entered Tesco and paused briefly beside the newspaper shelves which, Harry noticed sadly, were around fifty per cent smaller than they would have been ten years ago.

He watched Ophelia cast her eye over the nationals, which were reporting on a mixture of news about the new Crime Bill and an Old Bailey court case involving a beloved celebrity who had turned out to be a closet coercive controller.

'Duplicitous bastard,' muttered Harry, loud enough for Ophelia to hear.

She nodded, looking sad. 'Far too much of that about.' She seemed to be contemplating something, so Harry picked up a copy of *Private Eye* to give her space. It seemed to do the trick.

She turned to him. 'Anyway, about that drink?'

'Yes?'

'Tonight?'

'Amazing!'

'So long as you know it's a drink, not a date. It might be good to have a proper chat about stuff; we may need help in putting out appeals to find the family of the roundabout body, how they came to be there, that kind of thing.

Harry nodded eagerly. This would be a fantastic way of getting into her good books and impressing her with his journalistic prowess.

'We'd be delighted to help,' he said. 'I don't suppose there are any leads you're working on? Do you think it could be a local, or someone with a connection to the town?' It was a bit of a gamble, but you never knew . . .

'Maybe. We'll be looking at all mispers, people like your former editor, that kind of thing.'

'Do you think it could be him, then?'

Ophelia gave him a look. 'So, seven o'clock tonight at The Ball Inn? That's where you're staying, isn't it?'

'Yes, it is. But how did you know?'

She tapped the side of her nose. 'More than my job's worth.' She smiled, adding, 'Full disclosure: I heard Cassandra talking about it in the queue at the post office.'

* * *

He floated back to the office. Sorely tempted as he was to let the staff go home early again, Harry battled on until 5.30 p.m. For the sake of general good humour, he decided not to tell Hattie that Ignatius shouldn't be in the office tomorrow and ushered them out the door, locking up as quickly as he could.

He'd just have time to shower, grab a sandwich and be ready for Ophelia. 'Well done,' he told himself. It was nice enough to think he was stepping out again, but even nicer that he hadn't lost the old touch, even if this wasn't an official date, yet. And, better still, when she'd had a few, she might just spill a little more of the police beans on the body.

He whistled to himself as he splashed on the last, watered-down dregs of his almond body wash in the shower. All for a good cause. The scent reminded him of the good life, when times were fun, and money was plenty.

He dressed carefully, in a navy polo shirt and his best pair of jeans. It was just 6 p.m., so there was also time for a spot of dinner. He'd have to watch the pennies, but he reckoned he had enough money for The Ball Inn's 'Famous Fish-Finger Sandwich' – plus a half of Old Piddle.

The bar was cool and dark as he took a stool.

There was a clatter of high heels and Cassandra arrived. 'Ooh, my petal, I'm not ignoring you. I was just moving a bed around upstairs. What can I do you for?'

He ordered the drink and the food, enjoying that peaceful evening pub moment, as he listened to the beer chugging into the glass and Cassandra asking about his day and for gossip on the roundabout body.

She appeared to know Prudence Robarts – 'A bit stuck-up if you ask me.' – as well as the overgrown house: 'It's been like that for years, just like the roundabout.'

As she went off to make the fish-finger sandwich, Harry checked his phone. Lots of retweets on their stories. A text from his bank demanding to know when his next salary cheque would be paid in, yet miraculously extending his overdraft by another £500. And one from Jasper Grant, of all people, enquiring about how it was all going. He archived it for later.

'Busy m'love?' Cassandra's smile was dazzling.

'Just checking my emails.'

'I know, everyone's soooo on it these days.' She started telling him a story about a former guest at The Ball Inn, and a man who'd reported his wife missing and then found her in their own home. 'Men never look properly for anything.'

The talk of missing people reminded him to ask again about Kevin Fewtrell.

'Funny bloke. Nice, but skinny and sort of nervy-looking. Confirmed bachelor, I'd say. Slept with his window closed, which isn't healthy – addles your brain, if you ask me. He stayed here, just like you, when he first came; had your room, in fact.'

'Yes, I remember you saying. Didn't he have anywhere to live, then?'

'He was only here a month, barely enough time to unpack his suitcase.'

'Did he ever give any indication why?'

'No. He was the quiet sort. Just went. Mind you, before he did go, he got very tipsy one evening and just started rambling on. Kept saying he should never have come here.'

'Did he say what he was worried about?'

'Not really, m'love, but I remember him saying, "They can't force me," or, "He can't make me," something like that, when I asked if he was OK.'

He tried another tack.

'Did he ever mention the proprietor of the *Piddlington Gazette*? The owner? I really need to speak to him. Or her, if I'm being modern.'

She started vigorously polishing the pump handle. 'No one round here knows much about that side of the paper, except that it comes out every week. It was supposed to be owned by three men in London, wasn't it?'

What she did know was that Mr Fewtrell had become very excited to get an invite to visit the enormous country house that belonged to a man whom everyone described as the local hermit billionaire.

His ears pricked up. 'Everyone has known for years that he lives in the mansion in the Lost Vale, as they call it,' she explained. 'It's not really lost, though, because everyone knows it's there.'

To distract himself from her disturbingly rhythmic polishing, he asked for another half pint of Old Piddle.

'Coming up.'

'Then what happened?'

'Mr Fewtrell was very excited the night before; quite chatty, for him. Said the hermit man had wanted to give him an interview or something. But here's the thing. When he got back, he looked even more worried, if you know what I mean.'

He wasn't sure he did. 'Why was he worried?'

'Wouldn't you like to know!'

'I would. That's why I'm listening,' said Harry.

'Well . . .' She lowered her voice. He leaned forward expectantly, his elbow on the bar, hand under his chin. Maybe it was the drink, or maybe he was tired, but his elbow slipped, plunging his head forward into Cassandra's almighty chest.

She yelped and jerked backwards, and Harry tried to extricate himself. As he pulled his head back and attempted to sit upright, he was aware of another female presence.

'Oh, don't mind me.'

'Ophelia!'

'It's Sergeant Starsky to you. I suppose I should ask you if this man is harassing you, shouldn't I, Cassandra? But by the looks of things, at least one of you is enjoying it. Christ! Men! I don't know why I bloody bother. You're all the same.'

And she stormed out through the double doors.

'Oh dear,' murmured Cassandra. 'You've spilled your drink.'

There was no point chasing after Ophelia, Harry realised. No point in explaining it was all a terrible accident.

He let out a huge sigh, thanked Cassandra, put the money on the bar and walked out into the cool evening air.

* * *

Once you've eaten, had a drink and are watching the pennies, evenings can stretch. He'd have to go for a walk; no point in being stuck in that dark bar again.

He set off towards the river. Flowing water was supposed to be calming. He could just about remember dawdling alongside his mother beside the stream that trickled through the grounds of their old country home, as she pointed out the kingcups' brilliant gold against the darkening green of the water and the turquoise flash of a kingfisher. 'Look, Harry, there he goes!' As a painter, Isabella Hedges had always been captivated by colour, light and movement.

They say that time's a great healer but all it does is blur and fade the memories you do have, boiling them down into painful, disjointed little scenes, he thought. It was more than twenty years since she'd died, when he was just eleven, but the night of the accident was seared into his memory and the pain would never leave. He remembered waking up to the slow, heavy crunch of the strange car on the gravel drive. The police, a man and a woman, in the entrance hall after the housekeeper had let them in, their faces blank as paving slabs.

'Geoffrey Hedges? May we speak privately, sir?' His father, wearing a burgundy silk dressing gown, ushering them into the study and Harry into the drawing room, shutting the door, low voices across the hall, punctuated by that horrible, dry sob.

Then the drawing room doors opening, his father telling him to be very brave, because there was very bad news. Mummy had been in a 'terrible accident', hit by a motorbike, and died. Then crying. Lots and lots of crying.

Isabella was an artist and always going away for her portrait work so, to begin with, he'd coped by telling himself that she'd be home later that day or week – sometime. And because he hadn't seen her go, or attended the funeral – 'It'll scar him for life,' boomed Great-Aunt Maud – he'd never really believed she was gone, and had lived with the faint and ridiculous hope that one day, Isabella Hedges would just dance back into his life. When she didn't, he found that girlfriends and the relentless requirement to produce fascinating news stories took the edge off the pain.

As the river came into view, Harry turned away. Not now. Not tonight.

* * *

Wandering through the High Street, he forced his mind back to the present day. The body story was great, but he needed to know more and, unless he could travel back in time and undo what had happened with Sergeant Starsky, there wasn't much chance of that at the moment. And the *Gazette* couldn't live on one dead body forever.

There was the possibility of a few good council stories in the pipeline; the museum one had potential, too. But the public needed strong human interest. He reminded himself to try and entice the owner of the overgrown home to give him an interview. That might work. And this hermit billionaire. He liked the idea of that. If he hadn't heard of the bloke, then it was a cinch no one else had and he'd make an eye-catching feature.

He also had to increase circulation and get the website working properly.

Then there was his difficult financial situation and battered reputation. The key to it all was motivating his staff, he decided. If they produced more good stories and were more professional, things would improve by themselves, and he'd be able to plot his journalistic return to London. And this upward trajectory could all start, he decided, grimly, with that smelly old dog.

Unwilling to go back to The Ball Inn – it was only 9 p.m. and the square was lit with gentle old-school street lanterns – he flumped onto a wooden bench. 'In Loving Memory of Dot, a Lovely woman who loved this place.' He cringed. It wasn't just the random use of capitals for words that didn't need it. Like most journos, he had a congenital abhorrence of the 'second mention', the repetition of a word in a sentence, which generally resulted in news stories in which fires were later described as blazes, then infernos or conflagrations; and crocodiles were referred to as 'giant reptiles', 'cold-blooded creatures' and then, in one celebrated example, 'knobbly monsters'. The bench tribute sentence had three 'loves' in it. 'In Loving Memory of Dot', it should have said, which would have saved seven words, too. The brass plate was smeared with chewing gum. Absent-mindedly, Harry rubbed it clean with a tissue from his pocket.

A middle-aged couple walked by. A pigeon strutted in front of him, and a teenage boy idly showed off his parkour skills on the old mounting block. As the dusk began to wrap its way round the scene, he glimpsed a familiar figure walking through the square. Hattie!

She was dressed in jeans and a dark red hoodie. She was carrying a smallish backpack and was moving pretty fast.

He called out but she didn't appear to hear him, so he decided to try and catch her up. Perhaps he could persuade her to stop for a chat, find out more about her and Ray. Hattie walked across the square and cut into a side passage. The town's medieval footprint meant that many of the roads and lanes were interconnected and so he knew he could lose her quickly in the labyrinth.

At the end of the passage, she turned right, then crossed the road and took the path along the river, all the while maintaining a determined pace. He quickened his step; he could just about see her, when a large black car drove by, momentarily obscuring her from view. As he looked up, there were three pathways she could have taken. And he couldn't see her on any one of them.

He ambled back to The Ball Inn. Tailing young women was not a good look for any man, he decided.

As he prepared to step across the road, an ambulance, its blue lights flashing, streamed by and, in the distance, he could hear the faint wail of a siren mingled with the rumble of what sounded like a tractor. For a millisecond, he was back in London, before the scene returned to tranquillity – a small reminder that, despite its peaceful ambiance, life happened in Piddlington Minster, too. As he stepped into the bar, he saw that it was inhabited by a group of beer-bellied darts players, and Cassandra, thank goodness, was nowhere to be seen.

Sadly, he checked his wallet. No folding money, just a few coins. Sighing, he walked carefully up the stairs to his room.

Chapter 6

It was 9.15 a.m. when Harry arrived at the office. No Hattie. And no Ray. But the door was wide open, and Ignatius was staring at him.

'You, my old mate, shouldn't get too comfortable,' he told him. The dog settled on his bed with a loud sigh. *I may as well be talking to a brick wall*, he thought. Where was everyone? This persistent lateness and the random absenteeism were completely unacceptable.

Despite the crisper mornings, the room was warm, so he decided to keep the door open. Maybe it would stop his skin itching so much. He'd developed a strange rash and was beginning to fear that The Ball Inn had bedbugs.

The rush of air and light improved his spirits but highlighted everything that was wrong with the rancid little room. Harry was used to workplace assessments, footrests, posture-alignment chairs and lunchtime Pilates. Not this assortment of broken, stained, discoloured furniture and a carpet that stuck to his feet. He knew there was probably no hope of a cleaning lady but maybe he could polish the desks himself? He stepped towards the kitchen. Ignatius growled.

Childishly, he poked his tongue out at him; in the time it took his terminal to crank up, he reckoned he could make himself a triple-spoon cup of coffee. There'd been no time for Cassandra's West Country breakfast and he was already starving.

As he rummaged in the kitchen, he heard Ray arriving. 'Hello, Ignatius, how are you?' Through the wall came the faint thump of a tail.

Ray's gravelly voice, like the music from an old jazz club, filtered through, 'Just had a nice little win from yesterday. So, it'll be the best biscuits for you, won't it, old boy?'

Harry called out to ask if Ray wanted a coffee. Of course not, but a tea would be lovely.

'Where's Hattie? It's nearly nine thirty.'

Ray sounded shocked. 'Isn't she here?'

'No, Ray, she is rarely here, as far as I can make out.'

'I wouldn't worry, lad, she's probably doing a story, before she comes in. She is a reporter, you know.'

Harry frowned. 'I know, but I need everyone to be here on time.'

'Well, as you weren't here, I assumed you were out on a story too,' muttered Ray, making a great play of pretending he wasn't just turning on his machine.

Harry gave up. 'I think, since she's not here, I should go and try to interview the owner of the overgrown house myself – maybe a fresh approach might help.'

'Aye,' said Ray, through a slurp of tea. 'Lovely cuppa!'

* * *

After ten minutes, Hattie still wasn't there. 'I'm going out for the papers,' said Harry, deciding that he may as well get a proper coffee and something to eat.

'Right you are,' said Ray, not looking up.

As he arrived at the bakery, Brenda gave him a big wink. 'What have I done to deserve that?' he smiled.

'Ooh, you're such a naughty boy!'

'I'm sure I don't know what you mean!' he flirted. Maybe she would take pity and give him a free doughnut. Or an almond baton.

'Durrr, go on with you! Trying to get off with Cassandra in front of the sergeant!'

'Sergeant who?' he tried, playing desperately for time.

'You know very well who.' For once, Brenda looked serious. 'Don't you go breaking her heart now, will you? She doesn't deserve all that carry-on again.'

He smiled thinly and swiftly exited the shop, nearly colliding with Hattie, who was walking towards the office, wheeling her bike and looking as if she was about to burst.

'My bad!'

He had to move to keep up. 'You're late.'

'No, I'm not, I'm incredibly early. And you'll be very glad when you hear what I've found out.'

'What?'

'Police have found *another* body. On the roundabout!'

It took a few seconds for that to sink in. 'What? You mean in addition to the one that was already there?'

Hattie smiled, broadly.

'How do you know this?' They were now turning into the office's archway, and the delicious, familiar journo thrill was racing up his spine, even as his mind swarmed with various headlines containing the words 'roundabout' and 'ripper'.

It turned out Hattie had been to the police station. 'I didn't think you'd want to go there for a bit, after what happened.'

'What's happened, then?'

'Asking out Sergeant Starsky and then trying to pull Cassandra at The Ball in front of her. Honestly!' And she started giggling.

He decided to ignore the comment. 'I didn't try and pull anyone, actually, but never mind all that – what about this body?'

Hattie said she had intended to visit the police station anyway, explaining, 'PC Collins bakes soda bread every week and said he'd leave a small loaf for Ignatius. Turns out he's one of his biggest fans and I think it's good for his digestion.'

Judging by the aroma that frequently emanated from the creature, Harry thought not, but he was learning not to interrupt Hattie when she was in full flow, especially when that flow was about Ignatius.

'What did he say about the body?'

'He wasn't there – no one was, apart from the cleaning lady, who handed me the soda loaf. She said they were all busy at the roundabout, so I said "Still?" and she said yes, because they found another body while they were examining the scene of the first one! Can you believe it?'

Hattie had decided to cycle out to the roundabout immediately, where she had photographed the renewed police activity within the coned-off area closest to the traffic island and spoken to a dog-walker who had witnessed police rushing to the scene.

'Come to think of it, I heard sirens last night,' remembered Harry. 'Did anyone say who either body could be, or what had happened to them?'

Hattie shook her head. 'I asked the officer by the cordon but he wouldn't say anything.'

'You need to get back up there,' decided Harry. 'I'll keep an eye on the police feeds and pop round to the overgrown house.'

Hattie insisted that before she left, she had to give Ignatius his soda bread and launched into fulsome praise of PC Collins as she packed her rucksack.

Harry wanted to insist she got going but he knew it would never work.

Reverse psychology, that was the thing. While he busily refreshed the police's X feed, in case there was any new info on either of the bodies, he asked Hattie: 'Why is he called that?'

'PC Collins? I don't know . . . After the revolutionary and the saint, I should think.'

'No, Ignatius.'

She looked thoughtful. 'It was Arthur Conan Doyle's middle name. And because my name is Watson, I thought it was a good fit.'

'So, you knew him as a puppy, then?'

'Sort of.'

Getting rid of him was going to be very difficult but he had to plough on. His skin was starting to itch severely; probably he was getting asthma, too, and he felt sure Ignatius was the cause.

He now wished he'd never agreed to cover the overgrown house – he'd much rather cover the corpse-ridden roundabout. But Hattie had brought the second body in and it was only fair that she cover them both, he decided, instructing her to find out as much as she could and then place the story online. He could always jump in later, if it needed more kick.

In between refreshing the various feeds, and calling the police press line, Harry busied himself with flicking through the national newspapers, saving the *Daily News* until last.

It was filled with the usual fare: a large photo of an irritating celebrity with enormous hair outside the Nobu restaurant with only the letters 'Nob' visible; a photo of a politician dancing awkwardly with a half-clad influencer and the embarrassingly aged headline: 'Labour isn't twerking'; and a long and surprisingly erudite Q&A with an eco-artist who made sculptures out of abandoned festival tents, earning him the inevitable title of 'Campsy'.

He clicked on 'Newsdesk In' on his desktop file, showing the stories which had arrived for his inspection, and tried to damp down the irritation he felt at the virtual mess; it was riddled with files within files, the proliferating blue boxes adding to the visual clutter on the screen.

During one of his page refreshes, Harry was thrilled to see the Dorset Police Facebook page change. A new post explained that a second body had been found on the roundabout near to Piddlington Minster yesterday and police were investigating this matter, in addition to the body discovered on the roundabout earlier in the week. Neither body had been identified but the coroner had been informed. Traffic restrictions were expected to be lifted later that day.

Harry hastily bashed out and uploaded a story for the website and then prepared to leave the office, too.

* * *

He could have driven to the overgrown house, but he wanted time to think, and he had come to relish his little walks around Piddlington Minster. He was fascinated by the way the town centre, with its medieval and Tudor-beamed buildings, gave way to grander Georgian edifices, then Victorian and, if he'd spotted correctly, a collection of 1950s bungalows, ribboning away at the town's edges.

The overgrown house was on the north-facing side of Bridge Street, the road which led to the roundabout. He stood in front of the house and, now he had time to take it all in, he sympathised a little more with the irate neighbour and his pathologically tidy garden. The contrast between the two properties was shocking. Harry couldn't make up his mind whether it was worse to be right next to the mess or overlooking the leaves, brambles and neglected flora which exploded from the plot, shooting out over the bowing Victorian brick front wall.

He stepped across the road and shoved at the house's wonky metal gate. There was a path of sorts, trampled, he presumed, by the postmen who must occasionally visit. Shabby-looking lavender and brambles snagged at his trousers and by the time he was standing on what had been a step in the open porch, itself piled up with old newspapers, plastic bags and yet more leaves, he smelled like Great-Aunt Maud: of damp, and ancient lavender oil.

The door had been red or brown once, and possibly glossy, but now the paintwork was faded and peeling to reveal a dark blue underneath. The bulging, stained-glass panels had been partially covered from the inside, presumably to prevent them crashing inwards.

He cast a glance at the bay to the right. Had he imagined it or was there a movement at the filthy window?

Gently, he tapped on the door. Nothing. He rapped more smartly and stepped back a little, a trick he'd learned from Jasper Grant. 'Trust me, 'Arry, no one wants to open a door and find someone's boat three inches from it.'

Still nothing.

He knocked again and then bent to push open the letterbox.

'Hello? Is anyone there? Can I speak to you? Hello?'

Thanks to a lull in the traffic, he could hear a noise, which he was convinced came from inside.

'Hello?'

There it was again. A cat. Then a 'Shh'. Quiet, a small voice. But definitely a human noise.

'I know you probably don't want to talk to anyone, but I may have some important news for you,' he called. 'I'm not from the council.'

There was a rattling noise, then a scrape. It sounded as if someone was putting on a door chain. Harry's heart leaped. This was an improvement – maybe the person was going to open up.

More grunting and some quiet muttering. As the rattling got louder, he realised what was happening.

'I think the door's stuck. Do you want me to give it a shove?'

Stupidly not waiting for an answer, he braced himself and then thumped against it with his shoulder. There was a splintering noise, a shriek, and he fell forward to the floor inside the hallway, his face against an old newspaper which crumbled like stale toast.

'Burglar!' an ancient-looking woman was screaming and flailing at him with her walking stick. With every movement, more rubbish rained down from the skyscrapering old newspapers lining the entrance hall. Choking on the most appalling stench, he tried to stand up. The woman was about half his size and continued to flail at his chest.

'You have broken into my *home*! Get out! Get. Out!'

Chorusing, 'I'm sorry,' he attempted to move towards the door. But his way was impeded by piles of cardboard boxes filled with books that appeared to have been made of mould.

He started sneezing, wheezing and choking.

'Get out!'

Clutching at his chest, Harry attempted to speak. 'Mrs, Mrs . . . I'm sorry I don't know your name. Please stop hitting me. I was trying to help you get the door open and it must have broken. It's probably a bit old now.'

The battering ceased for a moment as the old lady herself started to choke.

'Look what you have done,' she said. Her long, straggly hair was wild about her shoulders, and she was badly bent over. 'You have destroyed my home. My home!'

'I didn't mean to,' he said. 'I've come here to help you.'

She looked up. Her eyes were bright, like a robin's, and despite the hairs sprouting from her upper lip and chin, she must have been beautiful once, he decided. True, the body odour was overpowering. But she was paying attention to him. Now was his chance.

'My name is Harry Hedges. I'm the editor of the *Piddlington Gazette*. And you are?'

She glared at him. 'Burge. Sadie Burge.'

'OK, Sadie.' He brushed his clothes down. He itched all over.

'It's Mrs Burge to you. Didn't your mother teach you any manners?'

'Yes, she did. Lots. Look, may I come in properly?'

'You are in, aren't you?'

He admitted he was. 'Shall I help you shut that door and then perhaps we can sit down?'

Surprisingly, she nodded, and he yanked boxes and newspapers out of the way to close the door.

'I think all that's broken is the chain, which I'd be happy to repair for you,' he said. What was he on about? The nearest he had ever been to a drill was when he reported on the Driller Killer of Kentish Town, an odd-job man whose jobs went very oddly indeed, what with his penchant for finishing off his customers with a Black and Decker through their ears.

Still, if it got him a few minutes . . .

'Mrs Burge.'

She looked up at him. 'You look like . . . someone.'

It was such a strange remark. Harry bit his lip. 'That's awfully decent of you to say, Mrs Burge.'

'I didn't say who, did I?' And she smiled, exposing a row of dark yellow teeth.

Her shuffling pace, plus the sheer and horrific amount of junk in the house, gave him time to glance around. It was a standard Victorian villa and must have been handsome in its day, home to a middle-class owner with a bonny family, perhaps. Now, however, the hall walls were obscured by the piles of papers and books in dampening cardboard boxes. Propped up on the piles were paintings, of a type Harry had never seen before – angular, mauve, orange and grey, all draped with huge loops of cobwebby dust.

There was a pile of letters, too, mostly unopened. 'The council,' sniffed Sadie. 'They are always writing to me.'

They turned right into what must once have been the drawing room at the front of the house, with the bay. He had never seen anywhere like it; there were bookshelves and more papers, and piles of old garments obscured what he surmised was the sofa against the back wall. An upright piano displayed a collection of grotesque-looking ceramics, twisted, daubed with violent reds and blues. There were other constructions: metallic shapes, like scythes and hammers, and blobby fish, as well as more anguished-looking paintings and threadbare, greying Persian rugs laid criss-cross over each other. The fireplace hadn't seen a living flame for the best part of twenty years, Harry reckoned, and in its place was a mean and extremely dodgy-looking two-bar electric fire that gave an ominous crackle. A pile of papers was perilously near. Beside the fireplace slumped an armchair which, he imagined, must once have been green. Now it was a dispiriting and randomised pattern of grey, brown and sludge, faded by years of sun damage. Upon it was an enormous ginger cat.

'Ah, Mr Chagall. There you are.'

The ginger cat appeared to smile at her. But, as it turned to Harry, it narrowed its eyes.

'Would you like to sit down?' she asked.

'Surely you would like to?' he said.

'No, thank you, I'll make you some tea.' And with that, the shuffling, scratching gait started up again and she moved slowly and painfully from the room, walking stick tapping.

He had no intention of sitting down. Apart from the evil stare of the cat – this place must be riddled with fleas and worse – he was too fascinated by what lay around him. The fireplace was black marble, veined with orange, with two columns supporting the mantelpiece, which was itself festooned with objects: ugly china ornaments of dancing cats, frizzled pine cones, a black-and-white postcard of London, and a tiny silver candlestick behind a small and fragile-looking animal skull, next to a cup of what must have been tea, around forty years ago, and was now coated with a delicate green fur. How could anyone live like this?

As Mrs Burge started shuffling back from the kitchen, Harry bent to touch the cat; people were more likely to warm to you if they thought you liked their pets. There was a rush of ginger and he screamed.

'Christ, it bit me!'

'What's the matter?'

Mrs Burge had shuffled back very smartly, and Harry had his finger in his mouth. The cat had now swelled up to twice his size and was hissing like a snake.

'I tried to stroke him, but he bit me.'

'What do you expect? Poor Mr Chagall is not used to men, even though I named him after the artist. I'll pour your tea.'

'Let me help you,' he said, carefully moving some of the papers on the table to make a space.

'You can see I don't entertain here very much,' she answered.

She busied herself pouring tea from a striped pot into two teacups, as stained as her teeth. Finally, she seemed to remember why he was there.

'You said you had something important to tell me?'

He explained that he had heard that she was to be subjected to some kind of council order to clear her house and possibly – he didn't know – undergo some 'help' in doing this.

'But this is my house. I own it. I live here.'

'I know, but apparently they can ask you, on environmental health grounds.'

'Who says I'm not healthy?'

He explained about the alleged rodent problem. She started to rock with laughter.

'Very funny. How can there be a rodent problem when I have Mr Chagall to take care of it all? I barely have to feed him because he catches so many.'

'But they think they come from here.'

'You, my dear boy, think too much,' she said. 'As a journalist, you should ask questions. And call me Sadie.'

'Right, Sadie. Can I ask why, I mean how . . .' And then he stalled. He had meant to say how did you allow this place to become such a tip. But his face had evidently given him away.

'Are you criticising the way I live? What business is it of anyone's?'

'But why do you live with all these things? And isn't it a bit dark, with all the vegetation outside?'

'No, it means I don't have to see the neighbours – miserable little people with their appalling suburban flower beds. Such dreadful use of colour, do you not think?'

He tried another tack. Was she worried about the council's possible move? 'No, it's my home, they can't make me leave it.'

But what would happen if she was made to change?

'I won't be. They can't just break into your home, and if they do, I'll be ready for them.'

And if not her, then that evil cat, he thought, as his slashed finger gave a throb.

'Have you always lived in Piddlington Minster?'

'Why do you ask?'

What could he say? Because she had the kind of cultured, bohemian air you wouldn't expect to see much round here?

'My voice gives me away, does it?'

'Yes.'

'I did use to live in London, mainly in the place called Spitalfields, which I understand has become very fashionable now. But after I married, my husband wanted to come back here to the county he was raised in, so we did.'

'What did your husband do?'

'He was an artist, like me. Surely you have noticed?'

The daubs and the sculptures. 'You made all these?' he asked, arranging his features into a look of sincere admiration. 'They are very individual.'

She smiled wistfully.

'He was the painter; I made the sculptures. So difficult to get a foundry after we left Spitalfields, and the costs are terrible. I had to scale down my work and he left me very little money.'

'This house is worth a bit,' Harry said, before he could think of anything else. 'You could sell up and live somewhere smaller and er . . .'

'You were going to say nicer, weren't you?'

He swallowed and nodded, sensing she would catch him out if he lied.

'Let me tell you, Mr Hoity-Toity newspaper editor who thinks he knows everything. This was the home where I lived with my husband. Then he died. I can still hear his voice and see his face when I am here. The only way I will ever leave or change things is if they carry me out in a wooden box.'

Sensing her melancholy tone, the ginger cat figure-of-eighted round her thin, sparrow-like legs and rubbed his head on her knee. She bent down to touch him and muttered something Harry couldn't hear.

'Would you like more tea? Or have you had enough?'

He'd had enough but felt unable to tear himself away. It wasn't going to make the kind of story he'd hoped for; frankly, she needed help more than anything.

'Would you like me to see if there's any support the council can offer you?' he asked.

No, she would not. 'They'll come in, tell me that I'm in danger, make me leave and put Mr Chagall in a cats' home before doing the same to me, and then taking my house and possessions to pay for it. I may be old, but I know what happens.'

She straightened up in her chair and pushed a strand of greasy hair aside from her face. Her arms were as thin as her legs, tracked with veins and sinews. For some reason, he could hear Ray's voice: 'There's nowt so queer as folk.'

'What are you thinking, young man?'

'That there's nothing so strange as folk.'

'Is that what I am? Strange?'

'No. Different. Individual.'

'Who would have thought you spend your whole day making up the right words to persuade people to buy your newspaper. What else were you thinking?'

He had been wondering what she looked like as a younger woman. The cheekbones, the flashing eyes hinted at a historic beauty beneath the shrivelled skin and the bent frame.

'Come on, I'll see you to the door.'

Harry raised himself and watched warily for the cat. But he needn't have worried; the creature had gone through the congested hallway towards the back of the house, where a bar of sunlight penetrated what he presumed must be the kitchen.

'Thank you so much, Sadie, for your hospitality. I'll probably put something in the paper to the effect of . . .'

She frowned. 'I don't want to be in your paper; I don't want to be in any paper.'

'So why did you invite me in?'

She smiled. 'As you can see, I am on my own. And I wondered what you wanted to tell me. Now I know. Anyway, if they try what you are suggesting, they will regret it. You can print that, all right?'

'It's a deal,' said Harry, his heart lifting a millimetre as he negotiated the matted path.

'Farewell, Harry; come again if you need another person to talk to.'

He nodded. He'd got his story. And right now, that was all he needed.

Chapter 7

Harry arrived back in the office eager for more body news. According to Ray, detectives were still at the roundabout and Hattie had written a small story to this effect, updating the website, before returning to the office.

Delighted by this development, Harry relaxed a little, refreshing the various feeds. He had been back at his desk for less than an hour when the phone rang. The voice at the other end sounded deep and educated.

'Am I speaking with the editor of the *Piddlington Gazette*? A Mr Harold Hedges.'

He was aware of Hattie's giggle.

'Yes indeed, how can I help you, sir?'

'It is madam, not sir, and I am calling on behalf of Mr Lionel Green.'

Harry got the feeling he was supposed to know who that was.

'Lionel Green, you say?'

At this point both Hattie and Ray sat up, and so did Ignatius.

'*The* Lionel Green?' said Hattie.

Harry flipped his hands up. How should he know? Hattie and Ray were now standing over him.

'He lives at Great Piddling, in the Lost Vale,' whispered Hattie.

'Lives there? Owns it, more like,' mumbled Ray.

'Would Mr Green like to talk to me himself? Does he have a story?'

'Indeed, he does. It is a story of great importance that he believes you will find extremely interesting.'

Not half as interesting as two bodies, thought Harry.

'Excellent! If you could give me an idea . . .'

'That is why we are contacting you,' said the voice. 'We were thinking you should arrive at 11 a.m. sharp tomorrow morning at The Grange in Piddling Vale, Great Piddling. And before you ask, it is Greta Sargent. Good day.'

Harry placed the phone in its cradle. Hattie looked excited. 'This is going to be immense! I know it.'

'I feel I should know him.'

'May I?' Hattie asked. As Harry moved back from his desk, she started typing on his keyboard, and Ray heaved himself into the office's far corner and started rifling through a shelf of dark brown box-files that looked as if they had last been in service in Churchill's War Rooms.

'Here's what we had in the past,' he said, blowing at the dust on them which turned the room's sunlight shafts into bars of solid gold. Ignatius sneezed so violently that he fell over backwards. 'Oh, poor Ignatius.' Hattie frowned. 'I think he's got asthma. Probably from your cologne.'

Unlike almost every other enquiry ever typed into Google, just one page showed up, including *Mail Online*'s 'Hermit billionaire buys silver collection', describing how a 'priceless' silver collection had been obtained by Lionel Green for an estimated £3 million.

The *Sun* online wanted to know 'Is this Britain's weirdest man?' It carried a blurred picture of an elderly, bowed gentleman learning on a stick, with what looked like a paper bag on top of his head and a suggestion that he may be 'reclusive billionaire, Lionel Green'.

Both stories were just shorts but the third, 'The billionaire who vanished', was more promising.

Harry clicked on the story, a badly copied PDF which had been published in an American magazine many decades ago. It contained more blurry images of Lionel Green at various locations: wearing a giant pair of sunglasses in a private box at Lord's, in the back of an ancient Rolls Royce, reading a newspaper, and trying to hide his face as a photographer ambushed him in a London street.

Lionel Green may be Britain's richest man. No one knows for certain, and possibly not even the man himself, because he has so much money. His fortune is understood to have been made via a series of audacious property deals, including the building of the infamous 'Chopstick' tower block on a back garden in London's Chinatown.

'So that's who built that monstrosity,' muttered Ray, who'd returned to join them in gazing at the screen. 'Caused a right fuss.'

According to the article, Lionel Green had been married very young to a beautiful woman who had died without having the child he was so desperate for, and he had 'turned away from the outside world, choosing to exist in what can only be described as Britain's most opulent hermitage, in the so-called Lost Vale near the Dorset market town of Piddlington Minster'.

The report's writer then went on to circulate what Harry guessed were well-worn rumours about why he had withdrawn from society: 'loneliness', 'hideous disfigurement' – a story, he noticed, which was attributed to the *Daily News* – having come under the influence of a cult, and suffering with a 'basket of mental health issues'.

Access to Mr Green is tightly controlled by his assistant, Greta Sargent, who guards his reputation and, one surmises, his money, with equal vigour. Mr Green has no known relatives, and his late wife was understood to have no close family.

The reporter then described how he had driven to, and approached, the enormous gates at the entrance to the parkland of the Lost Vale. 'The drive beyond suddenly bends, as if to shelter Green from the prying eyes of the world.'

So far, so clichéd, thought Harry.

The rest of the report consisted of more hackneyed speculation, a fleeting reference to priceless antiques and artworks, a rumoured colony of red squirrels and a 'tragic obsession', the nature of which went unhelpfully unreported. Presumably, he thought, because the journalist in question was too idle or useless to have discovered what it was.

Nearby villagers remained 'tight-lipped', perhaps because Green owned the homes they lived in, although it may be because they, like everyone else, knew little of the man in the Lost Vale.

Ray's dusty search produced little else, save a press cutting from a mother in 1982 complaining that she was threatened with trespass after her son's toy kite crashed into the grounds; it also mentioned that Green's home, The Grange, was Grade I listed and believed to house a magnificent art collection.

Harry continued reading, making notes and checking on the progress of his paper. Tomorrow was publication day, and he wanted the splash to be perfect. Would Hattie call or visit the police again and just ask them if they had any more on the bodies?

'If we can just get them to talk about suspicious deaths, that would be brilliant. I mean, two bodies, what the hell's going on?'

'I'm there already,' said Hattie, who was as thrilled as ever to get out of the office.

'And come straight back,' he called.

Ignatius groaned and started scratching again. 'Don't be daft,' Ray said to the dog. 'She'll be back soon.'

* * *

The old newspaper cutting had made Harry feel nostalgic for the London news scene again. He clicked on the *Daily News* site. Among assorted stories about bikinied women 'flaunting their beach bodies' as they lay blamelessly on a sunbed, there was an image of Sir Jimmy Knox, pictured with his fourth wife,

Lorford, a woman whose face had undergone so many lifts, she now resembled an orange Siamese cat.

Harry sighed. Ignatius waddled round and put his head on his knee.

'Get off.' The dog looked up at him with large, sad eyes. 'You heard what Ray said. She'll be back later.' He absent-mindedly gave him a pat.

A little trail of moisture trickled from Ignatius's nose, creating a large, round drip on Harry's moleskins. And what was that in the middle of it?

The black speck jumped onto his arm and then disappeared up his sleeve.

It was a flea. No wonder he couldn't stop scratching; the bloody creature must be riddled with them. He leaped up, scratching furiously and pulling up his shirt. Ignatius yelped in fear.

'Oh my God, it's disgusting,' cried Harry. 'He's got fleas.'

'It's probably the heat bringing them out,' observed Ray.

'That settles it. He'll have to be outside until we can get a vet in. Put his bed out there.'

'But Ignatius—'

'Will do as he's told. As will you,' said Harry. 'Get the Hoover and run it over these carpets. I'll spray some bleach.'

As Ray drew Ignatius outside with the promise of a cough sweet, Harry was shaking. Now he knew what those bites were. All over him. Jesus, he itched. He remembered a story the *Daily News* had published about some unfortunate soul who'd allegedly developed 'suspected plague' after being bitten by contaminated fleas. It later turned out the man was just suffering with acute hay fever, but inwardly, Harry shuddered.

Around ten minutes later, as they continued their cleaning, they were disturbed by a low howl.

Ray looked up. 'Not a *word*,' growled Harry.

Over the next five minutes the howl got longer and louder. Certainly, louder than the ancient Hoover, which wheezed its way round, creating yet more clouds of dust.

Harry cast his eye over the front-page template, then the clock. He called Hattie, whose phone went to voicemail. They didn't have much more time to get anything new for this week's edition.

The smell of bleach was now overpowering and even Harry started to cough. He heard a muttered, 'It's dangerous,' but ignored it. This disgusting, filthy hole had now turned into a bleach-soaked, flea-infested, overheated, filthy hole.

But one good thing had happened: the *Piddlington Gazette*'s front page was immaculate.

Scratching at his neck, Harry read through to the end twice, took a deep breath then pressed the enter key and watched his first edition of the *Piddlington Gazette* go to bed. In the past he knew that this momentous occasion would be marked by a session with the printers and staff down the pub.

Given that there were hardly any printers now, few traditional typesetters and just the mutinous Ray, he'd have to celebrate with a proper coffee.

He stepped out, studiously ignoring Ignatius and his hopeful tail-wagging, and when he returned, in better spirits, clutching a coffee from Brenda's, he found Hattie at her desk. Despite a few dark comments about asthma, lung cancer and the Hazardous Chemicals Act from Ray, the afternoon ambled along, punctuated by the sound of Ignatius scratching the office door.

But nothing, not even a plague of fleas, could dampen Harry's spirits. Within the next few hours, he knew the van would arrive, containing his first-ever copy of the *Piddlington Gazette.* A real newspaper. Edited by him.

* * *

Right on cue, two hours later, he heard the labouring of an engine and looked through the grimy glass to see a white Transit backing expertly through the archway.

'We usually go and pull our ones out,' said Ray.

Harry was already through the door. The small bundle he was handed was plastic-tied and had a chewy dog treat underneath it. Ignatius appeared, wagging his tail. Resigned, Harry pulled the treat free, threw it at him and bore in the four office copies, leaving the others for Bob, the town-seller, pretending not to notice as Ignatius slipped inside again.

There was, he thought, nothing that smelled and felt like a freshly printed newspaper. The silky feel of the unopened pages with their occasionally dragon-toothed edging. The sharp black of the gothic masthead script. The sweet scent of ink and anticipation. And his name, bang on the front and right above the all-important fold.

'Roundabout bodies riddle – police appeal for witnesses', by Editor Harry Hedges.

His story followed the standard procedure for when there isn't anything much to go on and only a limited amount that one could hint at. He'd remembered the old-school journo advice he'd heard someone quote: 'Shepherd the facts' when confronted with very few of the things and a front-page story to produce.

'Here we are,' he said, distributing copies to his staff.

'Yay!' said Hattie and jumped up to receive hers.

Aside from his front page, Harry wanted to check that everything else was in place: sport, crossword – never move the crossword – garden jottings and, of course, the weekly horoscope, written by the mysterious Madam Voyant, another correspondent he'd yet to meet.

Feeling he should try and tot up a list of everyone who was contributing to his newspaper and how much money they were receiving, Harry glanced at Cancer, his star sign.

You will make an enormous success of everything you do this week, Cancer. But only if you remember to care for all those around you, and to treat everyone, including pets, as you'd wish to be treated.

As if on cue, Ignatius dropped his head on Harry's leg. Absent-mindedly, he fondled his ear, the flea plague forgotten, and wondered again about the dog's peculiar living arrangements.

But he was soon distracted by the rest of the paper, which looked good, too: Hattie's stories were clean and clear; the local correspondents – enthusiastic members of the public who fancied themselves as journalists – had sent in snippets about jumble sales, parish council meetings and vandalism of the recreation ground's Silver Jubilee bench. The *Piddlington Gazette* didn't allow these people to upload their stories directly online. Harry had a fear of disgruntled correspondents publishing as fact their opinions on the way their local pub kept its beer or that the local MP was a closet Nazi.

But the use of more unpaid correspondents would probably come. Harry was not so naive as to believe that the cost-cutting which had laid waste to thousands of Britain's journalists wouldn't affect the *Piddlington Gazette* in time. Which is why the good stories had to come first. He clicked on to the website. His story was getting a lot of hits, which he could only hope would convert into advertising revenue. 'You're only as good as your last story,' he told Ignatius, who wagged his tail in agreement.

He sent the others home, relishing the peace it gave him to tackle some of the messy computer system. He was no geek but even the village idiot could re-categorise files within the correct area of the system, he felt.

He was amused by some of the catchlines – the story titles given to copy by the writer to help locate it in the system. Technically, these were supposed to be factual, such as 'SeesawAccident' to denote a mishap in a children's playground, but given how many stories journalists had to write in a day, they often had a bit of fun with them. He remembered reading about one hack at a coastal newspaper catchlining the story 'BellyDancing', for the naval movements that had to be reported every day.

He was particularly impressed with Hattie's effort, 'JointPain', about a man injured after his marijuana plant fell on him in the greenhouse. This was balanced by the number of stories that, on opening, were complete blanks and one particularly obstinate one that refused to disappear from the system, no matter how many times he pressed delete.

* * *

By the time he'd finished, it was nearly 9 p.m. He was still broke, but he was happy. Seeing his byline on a decent news story, in a newspaper edited by him, meant everything. After two years lying low, he'd secretly feared never being able to write again. Perhaps he could persuade Cassandra to make him a cheese toastie and then scrape up enough cash for a pint? He remembered dropping a £2 coin in the Cooper once – maybe it was still there?

His mind wandered to post-work evenings past. Everyone piling down the Ferret and Barnacle, or to the nearest cocktail bar, where Violett would be riffing on the story of the day. There were tales of upcoming splashes and the ongoing moans about Sir Jimmy Knox's latest diktat – usually formulated to flatter whatever prime minister or, God help them, royal, he was hoping to curry favour with that week.

Harry had only met Sir Jimmy Knox twice. Neither occasion had gone very successfully. The first was on his second day at the paper, when he'd come across a very disorientated elderly gentleman, slumped in the company elevator. Gently, he'd started helping the poor fellow back to the street again, before the then editor and his deputy galloped down the marble staircase, throwing murderous looks and bellowing: 'What the hell are you doing? That's the bloody proprietor, you imbecile.'

'I thought he was a drunk who'd got lost on his way back to Glasgow,' Harry had protested, receiving a painful shove into the entrance-lobby palm tree, as the executives vied to rescue their bibulous boss.

His second meeting with Sir Jimmy had gone a little more smoothly, probably because of the emollient effect Violett seemed to have on the old crust.

They'd been at the annual company party, which was being held at the Natural History Museum, where champagne flowed like the River Thames and the canapés outnumbered the exhibits.

'Sir James, I'd very much like to introduce our new special correspondent, Harry Hedges,' fluttered Violett.

'Aye, is this the one you're shagging?' came the reply in cut-Glaswegian, from a face that was Oxford blue from an aeon of drink.

Plastering on his widest smile to hide his surprise, Harry had shaken hands. He couldn't decide which was worse: warm, moist, flabby palms or icy-cold dry ones, like Sir Jimmy's.

'It's a pleasure to meet you, sir,' he'd began.

'You can cut all that crap,' Sir Jimmy had said, staring over his shoulder.

'Sir James is celebrating the purchase of another painting,' explained Violett. 'He was up against an anonymous bidder. All you need now is that Picasso, isn't it, to complete your collection?'

Sir Jimmy had stared at her. 'You're right. Why don't you get Lord Snooty here on the case? Get him off that posh Surrey arse of his.' Then he'd lurched off towards the back of the hall, crashing into a newly acquired stegosaurus as he went.

Violett had winked. 'I'll tell you more later.' But she never had.

* * *

When Harry arrived back at The Ball Inn, the bar was unusually quiet and there appeared to be no one around. He was starving. The kitchen hatch had been left open and he wondered how inappropriate it would be if he just sneaked in and helped himself. He could always ask for it to be added to the ever-mounting bill.

It was the work of a moment to slip into the bar and through the kitchen door. Still quiet. Harry opened and shut various cold stores and fridges, until he'd managed to assemble a few fillings. He wouldn't have had them down as Brie lovers here, but who knew? He cut a long, thin, bendy slice and added it to the growing pile of ham and lettuce on the baguette he'd found in the bread bin.

Not bad, especially if he could purloin a Scotch egg and perhaps a packet of crisps to go with it. He loved crisps, but especially the ridged ones, where the salt and vinegar coating felt like it was stripping the enamel from your teeth.

Humming as he worked, Harry decided he may as well help himself to a pint, too.

'What do you think you're doing?'

Cassandra's voice skidded across the kitchen tiles.

Best to come clean. 'Making a sandwich. I'm sorry, I couldn't find anyone and I was starving,' he admitted.

Cassandra tutted. 'Get out of the way. I won't have anyone saying they go hungry at The Ball Inn.'

Within ten minutes, Harry was tucking into the largest sandwich he'd ever eaten, with the most amazing pickled carrot, cauliflower and cucumber.

'Where'd you get these from?'

'Made them myself, didn't I? County pickling champion, four years running.'

'Well, they are bloody good,' munched Harry.

He listened while Cassandra rattled on about her day: out in the market, where everyone was asking about the bodies – 'Could be Lord Lucan!' – pulling pints all lunchtime and stopping a fight over the cribbage board. 'Next week it'll be the shove ha'penny, you'll see,' she warned, before humming tunelessly as she polished the already gleaming optics. Harry glanced at her hand. There was a tiny silvery ring with an emerald on the correct finger, but no gold band.

He realised he knew almost nothing about his landlady.

'Is there a Mr Cassandra, then?'

She looked up, sharply. 'Why'd you ask? Should there be?'

'No, I was just thinking that I'm surprised no one's snapped you up.'

'Are you offering, then?' She giggled.

'Er, not at the moment!'

She laughed. 'I'm used to it. And don't worry about the other night. You know, with the sergeant. If you know what's good for you, you'll give it another whirl. She's a good girl, that one.'

Harry glanced up at the clock. It was nearly 11.30 p.m.

'Time for your bed,' said Cassandra, stretching up to one of the top shelves.

He couldn't disagree. But he didn't feel tired.

'What do you do when you're not working?'

'I'm always working, m'love. Never stops.'

'But do you run the place on your own?'

'I have help,' she said, going into a lengthy explanation about George, a young drama student who needed to earn some money and was a godsend because he already knew how to change a barrel.

'Is it a tied house?'

'Oh questions, questions. We can all see why you went into your line of work, can't we?'

Harry smiled. 'I know, but most journos are like this; we're just interested in stuff and we can't resist an interesting story.'

Cassandra put her head on one side. 'You were in a bit of bother, weren't you?'

No point denying it. He admitted he had been. 'But I would hate anyone to think I'd done it on purpose, you know, to hurt people. It was a total, genuine mistake on my part. I know it sounds ridiculous, but I didn't realise that what I'd been asked to do was wrong. I didn't know the transcripts were from private voicemails and I took the blame because it would have meant even worse trouble for someone else. Someone I cared for at the time.'

She smiled and patted his hand. 'But it didn't work out as you'd hoped, did it?'

How did she know these things?

'Cassandra, was your granny a witch or something?'

She laughed. 'Don't be daft, she was Dorset's first-ever lady chimney sweep!'

Shaking his head, Harry walked upstairs.

* * *

It had been less than two years, but his old London life seemed to belong to another era. Had he really gone out nearly every evening, to bars and gigs, with his colleagues and with Violett, chasing the latest restaurant to eat at, the latest place to be? Life seemed so delightfully fast then, and the *Daily News* constantly changing, like an ever-shuffling pack of cards.

He got up. It was close and warm in his room. As he forced open the window, he heard a knock at the door.

'It's me, Cassandra. Don't worry.'

Oh no, she wasn't going to jump on him, again, was she?

'I thought you could do with some company,' she said, backing into the room while holding a bottle of Laphroaig, two glass tumblers and a bar of airport Toblerone.

He couldn't help smiling at the chocolate.

'That's the kindest thing anyone's done for me for a long time,' he said. 'My mum always used to buy it for me when she'd been away.'

'Ah.' She smiled. 'You looked like you need it. Still missing her, are you?'

He nodded and turned away as she settled the glasses down on top of the chest of drawers and began unscrewing the bottle cap.

Cassandra perched on the rickety wooden chair and snapped a few triangles off the bar. 'Always goes better with chocolate, I say.' She smiled. 'Down the hatch!' And she knocked it down in one.

Four glasses later and Harry couldn't feel his lower jaw. After quizzing him yet again for information about the roundabout bodies – 'They'll want to know all about it in the saloon bar tomorrow' – Cassandra had regaled him with tales of almost everyone who lived in Piddlington Minster. These included the naturist vicar – 'He had a cheek!' – and the hipster town gardener, who had got away with growing skunk in the municipal flower beds until a goat escaped from the petting farm and was discovered 'off its head' one memorable morning.

As he began to slip in and out of consciousness, he remembered what he really wanted to know.

'Cassandra, do you know anything about Lionel Green, the hermit, up the hill?'

'Now what do you want to know about him?'

'Everything,' he slurred.

'It's only gossip, mind,' she said and reeled off a list of details, relevant and irrelevant: the house was supposed to be stuffed with art treasures, Mr Green hadn't been seen in public by anyone in the area but was partial to the lardy cake from Brenda's Bakery; she knew this because Brenda had told her – 'It's top secret.' – and he was also said to have no family and made no will.

'What about his assistant?'

Cassandra hadn't seen her either, but she was known to be Mr Green's eyes and ears, and probably the person who was going to inherit all his money – or that's what everyone said. Mr Green was supposed to be raving mad and also very clever. He had been married but his wife had died.

So, asked Harry, with a superhuman effort at not dribbling, why was there so little about him on the internet?

Cassandra couldn't say. But she did know one thing.

'Lionel Green is supposed to have a secret. God knows what it is. But for years it's been said there is always something on his mind and it's nothing to do with the money.'

And with that, she left the room. He was asleep before the door closed.

Chapter 8

The long, vermillion laser of the rising sun was coursing through the gap in the curtains into his eyes. But, thought Harry, it was a good job it had, because he was already half an hour late and his head felt as if someone had filled it with painful rocks. The empty bottle told him all he needed to know and so did the Toblerone box. He couldn't believe they'd eaten the lot.

The shower ran unusually cold, and he could hear voices downstairs. Maybe there was a new inmate. He'd find out later. Grabbing his jacket and bag, he made a run for it.

Arriving in the office, Harry slopped down his Brenda coffee, grabbed on the go. 'You are quite late, actually,' said Hattie. 'And you've got your interview this morning.'

'I know.'

'I turned your machine on for you and I got you a pain au chocolat. They were selling them off cheap at the garage.'

The pastry tasted like dry paper bags and the chocolate inside was like two Rawlplugs. But he gave it a dutiful chew.

'Where's Ray?'

'Here I am, lad,' said the chief sub, stepping through the door, with some of the morning papers. 'Thought I'd check how our story's doing.'

There was a nib in the *Daily Telegraph*, and the *Sun* carried a downpage lead on 'Tragic Roundabout', so Harry guessed a news agency had picked it up.

'Good, eh?' Ray smiled. 'It was also on the local radio.'

Harry agreed it was great, saying that they'd try and sell the story on again and split the proceeds. In reply to Hattie's quizzical look, he explained that this was how journalists had traditionally made a little additional money in the past.

Remembering his conversation on the walk with Ophelia – probably the only walk he'd ever get to take with Ophelia, he concluded – he asked Hattie to start looking up missing people, paying particular attention to Kevin Fewtrell, even though he was not sure if he'd ever officially been reported missing.

At the mention of Kevin, Hattie looked shocked. 'You don't really think one of the dead bodies could be Kevin, do you? Has Sergeant Starsky said anything?'

Respecting confidences, Harry told her that Ophelia had not. 'But it's always good to get ahead of ourselves and maybe spot something the police have missed . . . And anyway, the bodies could easily be people who have no connection to this area.'

Hattie looked troubled. 'We never reported him missing. I mean, we talked about it but then, a few weeks later, we got this postcard from the Lakes, wishing us well, and Ray said he was probably embarrassed about everything and just to leave it. And we were really busy trying to keep the paper going by then.'

'That's completely understandable,' said Harry.

'But now I feel really bad that we didn't question Kevin's leaving more. It seemed to make sense at the time, because you couldn't tell if he was really happy here,' said Hattie.

Harry didn't want to distress her further and he also wanted to see some work done. So, to distract her, he asked her to get updates on the various stories and find out if the police were holding a press conference.

Hattie started dialling on the office phone and Harry began packing his phone and notebook, ready for the interview. Whatever Lionel Green said to him, he had a happy feeling this story would go far and make them all a desperately needed few quid on the side when he sold that, too.

Everyone assured him they knew what they were supposed to be doing, so he sailed outside and jumped into the Cooper, which started first time. It was going to be a good day.

* * *

Twenty minutes later, Harry was sweating profusely. The map he'd downloaded on the office Wi-Fi had taken him into the so-called Lost Vale, or Piddling Vale, and to a road blocked by what looked like a raging torrent, which the information had described as a 'gentle ford'. He'd driven round the alternative route at breakneck speed but then realised there was no other roadway to the house of Lionel Green and had to drive back. There was nothing for it but to drive through the water.

He looked at the old wooden depth-marker which showed a water height of eight inches. Shouldn't be too bad. He revved the engine, put it in first, released the handbrake and put his foot down. As the car darted forward, a giant swan landed on the water straight in front of him. Harry braked. The engine stalled. The swan floated to within inches of his open window and hissed.

There was a wet sensation by his feet. Oh, not now. Please, not now. He managed to push the door open, allowing what seemed like half the river to flow into his beloved motor. The swan hissed loudly at him again as Harry, now calf-deep in water, tried to wade to the bank. Bloody, bloody stupid country lanes. He was already on the hour. He *had* to get this interview. He waded back and began to push the Cooper towards the side. It weighed a ton.

Eventually, after what felt like half an hour, he'd managed to heave the car to the opposite side. It sat there, looking accusingly at him, water dripping from its sills. He looked at his watch. Then he looked at his trousers. They were now soaked up to the middle of his thighs, and a piece of waterweed had attached itself to his trouser zip.

He brushed it off, ran his hand through his hair and ground his teeth. He'd have to run, now. Or squelch.

Fifteen minutes' excruciating squelching later – and the realisation that he smelled faintly of pond water – he arrived at what he presumed was The Grange. Not that there was any sign, just a pair of gates which looked as if they had been designed by someone on an acid trip. The metal was nothing like the gates to his old school – elegant curlicues and rods topped with arrowheads – or the wrought acanthus of the gates to his childhood home. These comprised zigzags, starbursts and aggressive spikes. And they were shut fast.

As he contemplated the lost interview, there was a gentle whirr and a grinding noise, and the gates glided open. Harry nipped through and jumped as they shut with a resounding clang.

The Grange's driveway was ordinary enough, flanked with high rhododendron bushes, their blooms long gone. Pigeons occasionally rose from the glossy branches with a crack and a flutter. *Last night I dreamt I was back at Manderley again*, thought Harry, misremembering the first line of his mother's favourite book.

Unlike the one in *Rebecca*, however, this drive didn't twist and turn; it was straight, like a runway, with a sudden lurch to the right, meaning the house was invisible from the route. But there it lay, a statement to symmetry, nestled in its own private dip, a barrage of rhododendrons behind and to the side of it, and a view across stately parkland.

Harry trotted down the last part of the driveway, which was covered in tiny, sharp granite crystals that managed to work their way right into his brogue, adding to the general discomfort. As he approached the front door, he wondered if he was being watched but hadn't clocked any CCTV cameras around.

He lifted his hand to pull the dark blue rope, which he presumed must be attached to the summoning bell. As he did so, the door opened and he found himself standing opposite a very tall, narrow, elderly woman, who looked as if she'd been constructed from a series of rectangles.

'Good morning,' he began. 'I'm Harry.'

'We know who you are. You're late. And something has happened to your trousers, has it not?'

He admitted that, yes, it had, but only because his car had broken down in the ford.

'I don't think we need the full story,' rasped the woman. 'I am Greta Sargent. Please wait in here and I will see if Mr Green is ready to see you.'

For the first time, Harry was able to take in the space. He knew enough about old buildings to be aware that this was an extremely fine example of a Georgian property and that the entrance hall's serpentine pillars were probably almost priceless.

But it wasn't these which caught his eye. The walls were festooned with paintings – some with brilliant colours, and angry, angular images; others featured thin, nervous little lines and washed-out colour. But, he knew, these were not any old paintings.

He was dragged back to the time he'd spent with his mother, trailing round the world's great art galleries on their summer holidays. 'Look at that one – what is it, Harry?'

He remembered gazing upwards at the expanses of colour, lines, shades and curves he could not interpret. But he knew his Bacon from his Freud. And he was pretty sure he'd just seen one of each on the walls.

He turned, slowly. There was a Giacometti. A Modigliani and, tucked on a facing wall, a Warhol. And this was just the entrance hall.

There was also, incongruously, a suit of armour and a long-case clock, ticking the seconds away. Aside from that, there was complete silence. As he mentally tried to tot up the potential value of what was in this space alone, he gave up. Whatever else he was, Lionel Green was phenomenally wealthy. And he certainly liked art.

The tick of the clock was mesmerising, but Harry fought to be on his mettle. He needed to find out what Mr Green wanted from him and what he could find out from Mr Green. The art might be a good conversation starter.

There was the clack of a heel on the marbled floor and Greta Sargent drew up beside him. 'Before you come in, I am asking you to sign this,' she said.

It was a confidentiality document, running to three pages. As a visitor to The Grange, Harry agreed he would speak or communicate *nothing* of what he had seen or heard or observed there, on pain of litigation from Lionel Green or his agents from now until the end of time. He would also agree to make available to Green or his agents any copy he prepared before any publication that had been previously agreed could be published.

'Hang on a minute. You asked *me* here to conduct an interview and now I'm being told what I can and can't write in my own newspaper?'

'*Your* own newspaper?'

'The newspaper of which I have been appointed editor.' If this stringy old biddy could get on her high horse, so could he.

'Just sign it. Or you will leave immediately.'

Harry glanced round. The star-shaped grey and orange mouth of what he assumed must be a Dalí portrait that probably no one even knew existed gazed down at him. Of course, he was going to sign it. Who wouldn't want to meet this fabled recluse?

Greta Sargent took the papers from him and folded them onto the hall table.

'Follow me.'

They set off along a long corridor lined with traditional paintings and tapestries of hunting scenes, where everyone and everything looked the shape of a crescent. They were flanked with delicate-legged, glass-fronted cabinets containing silver and the kind of crockery he'd last seen in a TV programme about Versailles.

The floors were covered in a pale green carpet into which were woven dark footsteps. Harry was amazed. 'But I thought . . .'

'Yes, these are the other Footprints of Tilly Losch,' she intoned, referencing one of the world's most intriguing pieces of surreal art. 'There was another carpet in addition to the known one, which Mr Green procured.' Harry frantically tried to work out the worth of the surrealist icon upon which he was now trampling.

After several minutes, they stopped and she rapped upon a door constructed of dozens of pieces of finely veneered wood, like highly polished slabs of toffee.

'Come.' The voice inside was old and precise.

Greta Sargent turned the knob, and they stepped into the room.

'Mr Green, may I present Harry Hedges, editor of the *Piddlington Gazette*.'

If there was a Mr Green inside, Harry couldn't see him. The room was small by the standards of the property, with two enormous windows looking out over sweeping parkland.

There was a polished steel desk in the Art Deco style, with a large, black leather office chair in front, facing outside. It was only as the chair swivelled round that Harry caught sight of 'Britain's greatest living hermit'.

Except, he wasn't great. He was tiny, shrivelled and sunken – like an ancient fungus, clad in a dark grey suit. His hair was white and his skin had a sallowness that seemed to match the room's atmosphere. And, thought Harry, he had the look of a man who had seen enough.

For one so shrunken, he stood up surprisingly swiftly.

'Good morning, Mr Green,' said Harry, stepping forward to grasp a hand which felt cool and small, like that of a large doll. He decided against squeezing it too hard; he didn't want to fracture the old boy's mitt.

'Good morning. Coffee will be coming presently. Do you have a preference?'

'Black, please, dark as you like.' Hashtag winning at coffee, he told himself.

Lionel inclined his head and gestured for Harry to sit down. The chair he was expected to sit on was brown and carved like Medusa's hair, the wood snaking round, punctuated every now and again with what looked like fruits. It was deeply uncomfortable.

'It is understood to be the chair upon which King Charles I sat before he was beheaded,' intoned the hermit. Harry swallowed, glancing round.

'I see you admire my room.'

Admire wasn't quite the word but Harry nodded, hopefully managing to hide his astonishment. Georgian in arrangement, with a fireplace of the purest white marble, the rest of the space was painted in a violent blue-red, which clashed with a carpet of dull pink with lightning taupe zigzags across it and occasional blodges of hydrangea blue. 'Kahlo designed it for a European prince, but it was not quite what he was asking for.'

'I didn't know Frida Kahlo designed carpets.'

'She didn't, as far as I'm aware. This was the only one. I bought the design and had it woven in secret.'

They were interrupted by a whirring that got louder and louder, and then, from several clocks, came various crashing and ringing sounds as the half-hour was struck.

'Time waits for no man and certainly not for me,' said Lionel. 'I have asked you here after much thought because I cannot think of any other way to expedite what I want.'

Harry tensed. Something big was coming, he knew it.

Lionel looked at him.

'Ah.'

The door swung open, and Greta marched in, bearing a tray with the most exquisite coffee service Harry had ever seen. The spout on the silver Art Deco pot was so perfect that when Lionel poured it, the liquid emerged in a square-shaped stream. Harry was entranced.

'That's a great coffee pot.'

'So it should be, the money I paid for it. New York, 1972. I managed to outbid Getty on that one.'

Then it's probably worth more than my father's house, thought Harry.

As Lionel leaned forward to take his own cup, Harry glanced round the room again. It was festooned with artwork: what looked like a Seurat on the wall to the left, some Dalí-esque works either side of the mantelpiece, and one of shimmering gold squares next to it.

Lionel noticed his interest. 'To save you the bother, I shall confirm: that is a Klimt.'

Next to it, far lower down the wall in an ornate gilt frame was a smaller, darker work: black lines containing panel-like shades of blue, red, mauve and plum. Harry could just about make out an eye, marooned in the middle of the image and looking plaintively at him.

'*The Purple Child*, by . . .'

'Picasso,' finished Harry.

'Congratulations.'

On the mantelpiece, he noticed, were various maquettes, including one for a statue he was sure he'd once seen in the Bargello Museum. There was a bent silvery candelabra, a mis-shaped rock – 'A piece from a broken Michelangelo,' interjected Lionel – and what was, in all probability, a Fabergé egg in pale lilac.

'So, you like art, then?' began Harry.

Lionel looked impatient. 'Like? What does that mean? What sort of comment is that from a man of words, who claims to earn his living from putting them in the right order?'

'I was only—'

'You were making conversation. I don't have the time for it. I have asked you here because I need to trace someone, and time is running out.'

Harry straightened his face. A love child? Long-lost lover? A sledge named Rosebud? *Don't be daft*, he told himself.

'The person I need to trace is my younger sister. Her first name is Sarah, but I have no idea what her other name is now. I don't know what country she lives in or even if she is still alive. But if you find her, I want you to persuade her to come and see me.'

Harry's mind was whirling. Long-lost sisters were not as good as lovers or even a love child, but it was still pretty good. He could see the headline now: 'Find my lost sister – hermit's last request'.

He was puzzled, though. 'Why not just pay a private detective or a researcher, Mr Green?'

'I thought you'd ask that. I already have. I waited for many years to see if Sarah would get in touch. When Greta's enquiries produced nothing, I engaged the help of a private detective. He certainly spent enough of my money but the trail, as they say on the television, ran cold. I have a file detailing the enquiries he made.'

Lionel scratched at a wrinkle on the chair's arm and pursed his lips.

'Several years later, he – or someone in his office, I never did find out which – made public details of my life which appeared in a newspaper and then a magazine. I began to wonder if anything he'd told me was the truth, and I'm afraid it made me lose faith in such people.'

Harry nodded sympathetically.

'I can understand that. You want closure. I'll need to know a bit more than this, obviously. When did you last see her?'

Lionel made a cathedral with his fingers and looked up to the roof of his study, which was in gaudy competition with the walls and carpet, with its pink, orange and green starbursts. He appeared to be deep in thought.

'Do you mean when I last saw her with my eyes, or when I was last in contact with her?'

'Contact, please.' It would, calculated Harry, be far easier to trace her from their last meeting rather than going through some long and complicated childhood reminiscences.

'That's simple. The last time I was in contact with her was when she put the phone down on me in 1952.'

'Why did she do that?'

Lionel glared at him. 'Because she told me she was going to marry a man I had ordered her not to marry.'

To buy some thinking time, Harry sipped his drink. It tasted of little pavement cafés in Paris, of Roman and Milanese bars in the morning. It was probably one of the best coffees he'd ever tasted. To buy yet more time, he leaned forward and poured himself some more.

'So, let me see if I've got this right. You told your sister not to get married to this man. She did and in the last conversation you ever had, she banged the phone down on you. Where were you?'

'That is not relevant, and neither is anything else. I want you to find her and bring her back to me.'

'Mr Green . . .' began Harry, sensing that he wasn't a man who would take kindly to being told things he didn't want to hear. 'This is absolutely fascinating, and I'm so sorry you've lost contact with your sister, but it won't really make a news story unless I can have more background. And we're quite busy with other stuff just now.'

'Who said anything about a news story?' asked Lionel. 'I asked you to come and do this for me, and it will not appear in your paper unless I give my consent.'

'I'm a journalist, not a private investigator,' said Harry. 'What do I get out of it?'

'You are a journalist and, I should hope, will be good at finding things out. I have certainly seen good reports of your previous investigations, even if other parts of your career have not gone so well. You will have good contacts and, perhaps, the fresh eyes of youth, too. What you will get out of this is very simple – I am your proprietor. It will please me greatly.' The old man sat back in his chair as Harry nearly fell off his. Whatever he'd been expecting to come up on his daily bingo card, this hadn't been one of them. His mind started whirring.

'Can I ask you a few things about the *Piddlington Gazette*, then?' he started. 'There's the former editor, and we really should have a proper catch-up each week about—'

Lionel raised his hand. 'I am tired. And this is not an interview. Not everyone wants their affairs splashed all over the newspapers. Now, do we have a deal?'

'Yes,' said Harry, before realising that he was getting precisely nothing out of this one-sided bargain. 'Basically, you'd like me to help find your sister and persuade her to reconcile with you. It might cost money.'

'I'll have Miss Sargent authorise any legitimate bills. You can spend whatever is reasonably necessary to find Sarah.'

Harry opened his mouth to continue his quest for more information about the paper, but an old-school phone rang out somewhere in the cavernous building. Greta appeared at the door and summoned Lionel away.

'Will you excuse me for a moment?'

Harry stood up. He was starving and the still-warm home-made shortbread biscuits that had come with the tray were very tempting. The only reason he hadn't taken one earlier was because he didn't want to end up spitting crumbs on his interviewee. Cramming one in his mouth, he walked round the room again. In the grand tradition of great artwork, the Picasso with the eye appeared to follow him round as he moved.

He looked at the shelves of books – mostly legal tracts and mouldering classics, as far as he could see. The room smelled fusty; he guessed that Lionel didn't get out much and the cigar stubs in the heavy crystal ashtray attested to this. Fancy having everything in the world but having no one to leave it to, or to know what to do with it.

Outside, he heard the sound of footsteps and murmuring and quickly sat down.

'Admiring my taste in art?' asked Lionel.

'Yes, absolutely.'

Lionel looked at his watch. 'Time, as ever, is ticking, my boy. Is there anything else you need?'

How could he even begin? Photos?

'There are no photos now,' said Lionel. 'I don't have one of her, young or old.'

Her last-known address, then? 'London. In Kensington, I believe. That's where she was when she put the phone down.'

Fine. So, he was going to look for a nonagenarian Londoner – or ex Londoner, or dead Londoner – who once lived in Kensington, who had got married and annoyed her brother at some point in the middle of the last century.

'There is also this.' Lionel reached for a buff-coloured file, with a few documents in it. 'The investigator's papers. It has her old number and a few more details. You may spot something that Greta and I have missed.'

They were interrupted by the chorus of The Verve's 'Lucky Man' blaring out. Lionel looked terrified. 'Oh God, sorry,' said Harry, doing the mobile dance as he slapped each of his pockets in turn to locate the object.

'What is that abominable noise?'

'It's my phone. I'm sorry . . .'

It was Hattie.

Police think they may have identified one of the bodies!!!!

Infuriatingly, she didn't say who the body might be, and he guessed what Lionel's reaction would be, if he texted her back.

Still, it was a good point to make his exit. Not that he hadn't wasted a whole morning. There was no story to be had and only the very smallest and most withered of carrots dangling before him – the hope that Lionel would let him publish an interview.

As Harry bade his new boss goodbye, Greta entered the room, her chisel-toed patent courts shining menacingly against the carpet.

'This way,' she said, and Harry found himself returning down that long corridor and onto the steps of the mansion.

'Make sure you keep in touch,' she ordered, before closing the door.

Miserable old witch, he thought, as he trudged down the driveway, madly prodding at Hattie's phone number which went straight to voicemail. The gates swung open as he approached, and he stepped through.

* * *

Harry reached his car, which seemed to have got over its ordeal and started first time.

Once he'd detached some stray waterweed from the gearstick, he made his way along a lane which followed the estate's perimeter, before swinging him away from the property and towards the hamlet of Little Piddle. Suddenly ravenous, Harry parked, stepped into a shop that appeared to believe in selling proper pasties and bought two.

'Very popular, these are becoming,' said the store owner, sounding like a small character from a Star Wars movie.

'Sold three in the last hour. London types!' continued the shopkeeper.

Life was obviously quite slow up here.

Because he couldn't think of any other riposte, Harry said, 'Gosh!' and 'Thanks,' and inched towards the door.

'The editor of the *Piddlington Gazette*, aren't you?' asked the shopkeeper.

Harry nodded, dutifully. No point in denying it. 'Actually, is this the right way back to Piddlington Minster?'

The man looked horrified.

'Oh no. You need to turn round, and go back to Lower Gusset, then towards Upper Gusset.'

'Where, I presume, I'll then have to search for Middle Gusset.' Harry sighed. He was getting tired of all this rural smart-arsery.

'No, not at all. It'll be Gusset St Michael you'll be looking for. From there it's a drop down to town.'

Feeling mildly ashamed, Harry thanked the man and left. So that was Little Piddle Stores. And conversation of the type that Dalí could have painted; it was so surreal.

As he walked back to the Mini, along the pavement-less road, his elbow was nearly clipped by a shiny and very badly driven black Discovery. Wondering if a story about speeding in built-up areas was required, Harry bit into his pasty.

Chapter 9

The shopkeeper's instructions were spot on and, as he approached Piddlington Minster by the bridge – and was thus treated again to its 'chocolate-box view' – Harry decided to give himself a rare lunch break and eat the second pasty on one of the benches in the little public garden beside the river. He'd be busy enough this afternoon with all the breaking stories.

He called Hattie again but her phone went to voicemail. *Please can you get back to me ASAP, ref bodies*, he texted. While he awaited her reply, he gazed into the gin-clear waters. The spangled weed swayed hypnotically, reminding him of the ford episode and his trousers. Imperceptibly, a trout undulated in time with the plant. How soothing. A swan, looking as crisp as freshly fallen snow against the dark water, only added to the scene.

He began filming it with his iPhone. The swan, perhaps appreciating the moment, glided elegantly towards him. He slowly turned to film the street behind him, feeling it might do for the paper's Insta feed, then stopped. He knew that figure. In the distance he could see a girl on a bike. She was looking all around.

No wonder she wasn't answering her phone. Hattie was supposed to be in the office to accommodate Ray's lunch break.

Frowning, Harry shoved his phone in his jacket pocket, tossed the pasty corner to the swan and started to walk.

Hattie didn't cycle very fast and seemed to take a convoluted route across the town, incorporating walk-throughs and small side streets lined with well-kept Victorian brick cottages.

Harry walked faster. After eight or so minutes, sweat was pouring from his forehead, and he'd already got a funny look from two elderly ladies.

Hattie's route took her to the east of the town which, if the housing and surroundings were anything to go by, was far less prosperous than the more Victorian and Georgian west. Ribbon development of worn-looking 1930s semis abruptly gave way to grim 1970s terraces with mean, oblong windows, squatting in gardens, many of which had old mattresses, car parts or defunct children's bicycles abandoned in them.

As she slowed, Harry watched as she approached what was possibly the nastiest building in Piddlington Minster, on the town's far-eastern edge. It looked as if a bit of the Barbican had dropped off and been towed to this part of Dorset: slabby, graffiti-scrawled walkways and windows that peered hopelessly towards the back of what looked like a factory, all topped off with the pungent smell of chemicals.

Perhaps she was on a story, he thought. As a gaggle of aggressive-looking teenage boys pushed by, he began to wonder if he should hang around. This didn't look like a great area. He'd never considered that somewhere like Piddlington Minster would have a 'hood'.

He watched as Hattie started heaving her bike up the concrete staircase. He caught a sudden whiff of the urine stench, competing with the airborne chemicals, incongruous in what he'd thought was such a pleasant little town. There she was, wheeling her cycle along the walkway. He waited for her to knock at the flat she'd stopped in front of. But she didn't. She fished round her neck and then leaned forward as she used a key on a string to unlock the door.

He wasn't near enough to hear if she spoke, but he was puzzled. What was she doing here? At this hour? His phone bleeped. Damn! He'd left the car in a twenty-minute bay in town, and he was probably over the parking limit. Harry began to stride back, then run. He arrived at the river carpark to see a traffic warden the same size and shape as Henry VIII, slapping a ticket under his windscreen wiper with what looked like great alacrity.

'Am I late?' he gasped, turning on his most dazzling smile. If he really did look like a film star, now was the moment to find out. The woman stared at him.

'You're over the twenty minutes and I reckon you're lucky to get that. It's seventy pounds. Or thirty-five pounds if you pay within seven days. Your choice.'

She stalked off and Harry sighed. May as well go to the council and eat humble pie now.

* * *

Unlike the concrete horror Harry had just seen, the town council was housed in a splendid Victorian gothic edifice to the back of the minster. As he explained to the young woman on the desk: 'I'm sure it's a bit of a mistake, I was only there for ten minutes.'

She peered at him. 'Are you famous? You look just like that actor.'

Harry feigned astonishment. 'Come on! Which one?'

The woman pondered. Then she beamed. 'That bloke in *Love Actually*. The old one. The prime minister.'

'Thanks.' Harry handed over his credit card and prayed.

* * *

It was 2.30 p.m. by the time he returned to the office, where Hattie was tapping away furiously, and Ray was posting a biscuit into Ignatius's dripping mouth.

'How did it go?'

'Well, it turns out that Lionel Green is actually our esteemed proprietor,' said Harry, flattered by the genuine surprise on his colleagues' faces. Unable to supply much more information about that side of things, he began describing The Grange to a goggle-eyed Hattie. Ray appeared more interested in Miss Sargent. 'It was always said she was a former spy.'

'Who said that?'

'Everyone,' said Ray.

Harry glanced at Hattie. She typed innocently away, taking great care to stare closely at her screen. He cleared his throat. He knew he'd have to tackle the absenteeism problem but didn't feel like it. He knew he should also tackle the Ignatius problem. But he didn't feel like that, either.

Suddenly, Hattie banged down her hand. 'Oh yeah, I knew there was something I meant to tell you.'

He looked up. 'The bodies? That's all I care about right now.'

She shook her head. 'Nothing certain yet; we're just waiting on the official IDs. Wouldn't it be amazing if it was a serial killer, though? We've never had a serial killer before.'

He completely understood but felt relieved no one else could hear this conversation.

It was the bit of journalism he always found hard to explain to civilians. It wasn't that you didn't feel enormous sympathy and even outrage on behalf of victims or their families in any ghastly situation. God knows, he'd seen enough of his supposedly hard-bitten colleagues having a quiet weep, even as they banged out a particularly distressing tale. It was just the professional interest in working out the clearest and most humane way to present all the known facts in a story.

The first body on the roundabout had obviously been there for a very long time to have rotted into a skeleton, and he didn't know the timescale of the second body yet. On the other hand, he was hardly a forensic expert. Harry made a note to google decay times for a human corpse, just in case.

If a normal person looked at the average journo's internet history, they would wonder what was going on, he thought. Aside from frequent visits to the Sidebar of Shame, Harry's searches had, over the years, included everything from 'Confirmed UFO sightings in Northamptonshire' to 'How long would it take a python to digest a human arm' and, every month, 'The expenses calculator'.

'What was it you had to tell me, Hattie?'

'It's probably nothing but I've had a tip from a lady I know at the council who says that they are really under the shade at the town museum – apparently, they are supposed to be doing more fun and diverse things to attract visitors because it's too boring for the twenty-first century.'

Harry nodded.

'I thought we should maybe do an interview or a colour piece with them, go round there and check it out, see if it's all as boring as the council makes out. It's mostly run by volunteers, and they are all really hacked off.'

It didn't sound too bad, although Harry was no fan of local museums; too many fossils and pictures of tedious bearded aldermen. And spinning wheels. What was it with local museums and spinning wheels?

'Nice idea. One of us can go tomorrow if we have the time,' he said. 'Now, can you check with the police if they've identified either one of the bodies yet? You said you thought they had.'

He waited while she made the phone calls but there was still no official news.

As Ray typed away morosely, giving the occasional cough, Harry was able to attend to the admin that came with his job: time sheets, expenses, and calculating the replacement worth of the fixtures, fittings and effects in the *Gazette*'s office, for its annual insurance certificate. Given that you now appeared to have to pay the council to take old computers away, Harry reckoned the net value of the entire place was probably minus £400.

He was jerked out of these thoughts by the weight of Ignatius's head on his trousers and the dog's heavy sigh. Even he looked as if he was waiting for news, thought Harry. Giving him a momentary pat, he returned to his admin and passed the next hour checking early pages and trying not to feel annoyed by Ray's cough.

* * *

It was 4 p.m. when the statement arrived.

Dorset Police had identified the second of the two bodies discovered on the roundabout of the A350 south of Piddlington Minster.

The deceased was Mr Kevin Fewtrell, 48, of The Ball Inn, Piddlington Minster. The death was being treated as unexplained and investigations were ongoing. Dorset Police extended their sympathies to the friends and family of Mr Fewtrell at this very difficult time. Investigations into the circumstances surrounding the death of the other body found on the roundabout were continuing.

As he read it out to Ray and Hattie, they lowered their heads, and so did Ignatius. 'We should have tried harder to find him,' said Hattie, looking tearful. 'How dreadful to just die on a roundabout with no one coming to save you.'

'You weren't to know,' said Harry. 'No one was. All we can do now is our jobs, and do them well when we report this. I'll do a story for online.'

After typing it up, he decided to call time on the day – his staff had been through enough and he invited them to join him at The Ball for a glass-raising in memory of Kevin. As Hattie opened her mouth to ask, Harry smiled: 'Yes, of course Ignatius can come too. I'm sure Cassandra can find him a drink and a little snack.'

'He'd prefer a big one,' said Hattie.

* * *

Arriving at The Ball Inn, he was saddened to learn from George that it was Cassandra's night off – he could have done with a bit of her rhinestone sparkle tonight.

As they settled down at a corner table with their drinks, Ray proposed a toast to 'our editor, Kevin, wherever he is' and, solemnities over, they began discussing him, exchanging a few reminiscences.

'He always went out to the supermarket and bought the same lunch every day,' remembered Hattie. 'Pork scratchings and cheese and pickle sandwiches.'

'Aye,' said Ray. 'He got in a right pickle the day they didn't have that, and he had to have coronation chicken, instead. Said he couldn't concentrate properly.'

Harry smiled. 'What did he do when he wasn't at work? Did he have any friends, or hobbies or anything?'

They both shook their heads. 'I don't think he had a girlfriend but sometimes he'd go outside to take a call, so maybe he was just private,' said Hattie. 'Journalism seemed to be his life.'

Harry was beginning to see how Kevin had managed to fall off so many radars, but he still felt sad.

'What I don't understand,' began Hattie, 'is why he came back here after leaving like that? It must have been a pretty big decision to just go. So why return? Do you think he was coming to see us or to tell us something? He was kind enough to send that postcard. Maybe he missed us after all.'

'Do you still have the postcard?' asked Harry, thinking it would interest Ophelia. 'It might be evidence.'

'No,' said Ray. 'And evidence of what, anyway?'

'Evidence that he was alive at the time of the postmark,' said Harry. 'Also, evidence of where he was, perhaps, after he left.'

'Maybe,' said Ray, standing up. 'Probably about time we got going; you haven't had your tea yet.'

Harry escorted them to the bar door and then enjoyed a quiet pie and another pint before walking sadly up to bed.

Chapter 10

Friday morning passed surprisingly uneventfully in a town with two dead bodies on its roundabout. Ray had elected to type out some nibs – the little 'News in brief stories' that ran down the side of a newspaper – which always featured the name of some obscure village or town district, helping to reassure readers that their area was being covered properly.

Harry elected to google his predecessor. There was a short bit in the *Press Gazette* about his appointment as editor of the *Piddlington Gazette* and a list of his former and fairly unremarkable jobs in local journalism and the trade press.

No mention of family, though. Harry looked at the few online images. In one, Kevin was playing in a five-a-side game, eight years ago, for a team in Buckinghamshire. Another was of him in the *Piddlington Gazette* office, in a classic 'busy working editor' pose, sitting bolt upright, pretending to talk into a landline phone while fake-typing. Terrible shirt and haircut, not to mention the world's dodgiest trousers, thought Harry.

In his appointment interview with the *Press Gazette*, Kevin had spouted the customary pledge to champion local journalism and revamp the newspaper's website. But there was nothing about his departure, and nothing, anywhere, to suggest anything sinister had happened – apart from the fact that the man who occupied the very chair Harry was now sitting in had allegedly run off, before turning up dead on the roundabout. And, according to Cassandra, he had looked worried and nervy before he'd disappeared.

Harry did not enjoy the cold feeling that settled around him.

He was cheered a little by Hattie arriving back with a spring in her step. She'd shown commendable initiative by visiting the police station on her way back from the council meeting, to check if there were any updates, and was delighted when Sergeant Starsky produced a squeaky bone toy confiscated from an annoying member of the public at the magistrates' court that morning. 'They kept squeaking it when the prosecution asked a question,' explained Hattie.

'Did she say anything about Kev— I mean, the body?' asked Harry.

'Not as such but I think they are hoping to have more info later.'

The office chugged on, lunchtime passing in a waft of quinoa salad (Hattie), a ham, pickle and English mustard sandwich (Ray), and a yellow-sticker BLT for Harry.

As Ray prepared the late-afternoon tea round, Hattie started riffling through her notebook. 'I knew there was something!'

'What?'

'Sergeant Starsky said that if you went round, she'd explain a bit more about the investigation.'

Whatever else had happened that week, he wasn't expecting this. 'What time?'

'Around now, I think. Don't worry, we'll lock up.'

* * *

It was only as he entered the High Street that Harry realised that it was probably just their way of getting an extra half-hour off. But the news had raised his spirits so high that he ignored it and, pulling his hair into some kind of order and straightening his tie, set off towards the police station.

The building was in deep afternoon shadow and through the front door he could see a small woman in uniform, moving about behind the glass. The second police car was gone and there was no sign of PC Collins – maybe now was his chance.

As he walked through the door, he could see that a loop of hair had escaped from Sergeant Starsky's severe bun and trailed aimlessly over her forehead. It made her look quite sexy, Harry decided, wondering whether to tell her.

'Hello.'

She looked vaguely bored. Or maybe it was reproving. It was an instant reminder to up his game.

'I hope I'm not intruding, Sergeant, but a member of my staff informed me that—'

'Bit formal, aren't we? You can call me Ophelia. If you like.'

'Thanks. And Ophelia . . . is there any chance of a cold drink?'

'Ribena do you?'

He laughed out loud. 'We're a match made in heaven. Actually, it's my favourite soft drink. My mother used to . . .'

She shot him a look. 'Too much information.'

With two Dorset Police anti-burglary promotional glasses in front of them, filled with Ribena and ice-cubes prised out of the station's fridge-freezer, Sergeant Starsky got going.

'The reason I've asked you in – and this is all off the record, mind – is because I don't want a load of rubbish published about those bodies on the roundabout.'

He could practically feel the air escaping from his personal balloon of happiness.

'Why would we do that?' he asked. 'We only want to publish the truth. And good quality news, of course.'

'Of course.'

She was very good at blocking, he felt. But he hadn't been the star interviewer at the *Daily News* for nothing. Summoning the memories of *El Rato* and Princess Anne, he sat back, attempting to look urbane.

It was Ophelia who blinked first. 'OK,' she said, leaning forward. 'I know that finding two dead bodies anywhere is good news from your point of view. And yes, it will sell papers and get you clicks. And there is definitely a lot more to look into on Mr Fewtrell's death, which I'm guessing will interest you very much. But we cannot afford to have you lot going around Dorset, spreading rumours about serial killers and roundabout rippers and the like.'

'We do have freedom of speech in this country,' he argued, hoping desperately that he didn't look guilty as charged.

'I know, and of course you can print what you like in the end; this isn't an official warning, or censorship, don't get me wrong. It's more a personal plea. I want to be able to spend my time looking after these cases and getting answers for the families. Not attempting to bin off daft questions from all the bloody internet sleuths who will crawl out of the woodwork if they read sensationalised stories. Like the one I'm guessing you really want to write.'

She rubbed her face with her hand. When she was tired, he thought, she looked pretty, a bit vulnerable. Especially as quite a lot of her hair was falling out of that bun in the kind of way that hair does in films before it tumbles out and spreads over a pillow on a large double bed.

Harry mentally slapped himself. Ophelia looked up.

'Are you even paying attention?'

For some reason, even her disgruntled voice was attractive. Nicely authoritarian. He assured her he was, and to cheer her up, told her about his visit to Lionel Green and why he'd been summoned.

She was suitably fascinated.

Harry pressed home his advantage. 'Maybe you could tell me how to find a missing person like his sister?'

Ophelia sipped her drink, thoughtfully.

'Has she ever been registered as a missing person? That might be one way to get more information, but people don't always report this kind of thing – look at poor Kevin Fewtrell, he wasn't ever registered.'

Harry was surprised but Ophelia pressed on. 'Trouble is that this sister doesn't sound like an actual misper and there's no evidence that she's dead, is there? If you check out the Public Records Office, you could find if there's a death certificate – it would speed things up for you. It also doesn't sound like she's the victim of a crime, so police probably wouldn't be involved. If your boss is that rich, why doesn't he just hire a private detective? Why's he asked you?'

Harry explained about the previous failed investigation and Lionel's proprietorship. 'I helped solve a missing person's case when I was working in London, and I suppose I am the local newspaper editor and his employee after all.'

She laughed. He glanced at his watch, mainly to hide his delight, then had an idea.

'Look, I know it all went a bit wrong the last time, and please say no or give my head a wobble if you think I'm an idiot, but would you like to come out to dinner with me tonight? Just friends, no strings?'

'Dinner? Looking like this?'

'You could go home and change. But I do like you in your uniform.'

She pulled a face. 'I've got some civvies here and since you've asked me so nicely, and I'm too exhausted to cook, that would be very welcome. But I'll be paying my half.'

'Of course,' said Harry, a little too quickly. God bless feminism.

'Let me fix my face, at least.'

Ten minutes later, she looked fresher and brighter, her eyes lined with a dark grey pencil and her lips softer in pink, and they chatted as they walked towards the place where she said the best burgers in town were served, the Flying K Ranch House.

'Don't get me wrong,' said Harry, as they wandered along. 'The Ball has its good points and by that I don't just mean Cassandra, although she is, obviously, a fantastic asset, but the food is just . . .'

Ophelia looked at him. 'When you're in a hole, stop digging. All is forgiven. Or it will be if you stop going on about Cassandra and The Ball Inn. Look, we're here.'

Harry had to admit he hadn't noticed the A-board advertising the Flying K Ranch House, which was sited down one of the town's interminable passages that opened out onto yet another little courtyard square. He was amazed he hadn't also noticed the incredible aroma in the evenings: smoky chipotle and rich barbecue sauce.

'Glen, who runs it, is from Wolverhampton but he's just besotted with America,' said Ophelia. 'I recommend the dirty burger with Carolina sauce.'

And so, they ordered; Harry was almost delirious with excitement at getting a bottle of freezing craft beer. 'They're a microbrewery too,' explained Ophelia.

'Waddo, Sergeant!' winked Glen, emerging from behind the bar. 'Named after Glen Campbell I was, in case you was wondering!' he told Harry, who had not been wondering this at all.

Within twenty minutes, two towering burgers arrived, hand-made relish and melted Monterey Jack volcanoing down their sides. One bite and Harry was in burger heaven.

'Didn't I tell you?' munched Ophelia.

He managed to get her to open up, chatting about her work and the difficulties of running a small police station under the eternal threat of closure, with just PC Collins for company.

'He's a great copper, joined us a few months ago, but there's just the two of us and the odd visit from the PCSO,' she said.

No wonder she didn't want any further issues to add to her workload, he thought, and considered whether it was the right time to broach the subject of the bodies on the roundabout. Surreptitiously, he topped up her glass with the bottle of YeeHah pale ale.

'But don't think, by the way, that you're getting anything more out of me about the roundabout business,' she said, sipping furiously. 'Even though there's something fishy about it all.'

'Aren't murders usually fishy?'

She eyed him for a few seconds, in which he tried to look as reputable as possible. It must have done the trick, because she leaned forward and lowered her voice. 'Going forward, I need to be able to trust that if I talk to you about certain things, they will be off the record. Is that understood?'

He nodded.

'Now, I have not used the word murder for the simple reason that any family may need to be traced and that forensics are still looking at both bodies – I'm hoping for some kind of report back by Monday. But there's almost no doubt that Mr Fewtrell met his death in an unnatural way. In the meantime, I need to find out as much as possible about him, his life and what he was up to in the months immediately before his death.'

Harry nodded again, acknowledging the treasure she'd just brought him. But professional pride made him press on. 'Anything about the first body?'

'I will admit it's a weird one. We don't know if it was there before Kevin's body came to be in that location or arrived afterwards. Can't tell if it was dumped there or even how it died yet. We're still trying to identify it.'

And she took another sip of her beer.

To give her space, he thanked her and changed the subject. 'As our esteemed local law enforcer, is there anything more you can tell me about the town or the paper?'

'Er . . . you're its editor, shouldn't you be telling me? And why are you here anyway? You never really answered that the other day. Shouldn't you have been struck off, or whatever it is they do to journalists, for what you did?'

He explained as honestly as he could what had actually happened. 'I know it looks bad; it was bad. It was a crime and there's no excuse. But the explanation for what I did is that I had no reason at the time to think anyone had done anything wrong and, well, I'm not the sort of person to let others take the blame.'

As Glen arrived with the pudding menu, Harry took another slurp of YeeHah and Ophelia asked him about the office.

He felt happier describing his day: Ray and his betting, Hattie and her sudden and mysterious disappearances.

'How do you get on with Ignatius?'

Harry pulled a face. 'That dog is a flea-infested eating machine that farts continuously, but never more so than when I have just arrived in the office. I would like to stop him being there but it's proving rather difficult at the moment.'

'Oh. I think he's lovely.'

Damn.

'So, again, why here, Mr Hotshot Journalist? Why Piddlington Minster?'

He groaned again. Talk about Twenty Questions. But seeing as he had nothing else to do and she was now close enough for him to smell the scent of her perfume, he acquiesced.

He explained that, basically, after losing his job and his reputation, he was now in journalistic bargepole-territory.

'In other words, this was all you could get?'

'If you want to put it like that. But that doesn't mean I won't make a success of it, Ophelia. And I mean to. I need to. To get back to London one day, I have to show the world I can do this job, honourably and properly, and really make a difference to this town.'

She made a gagging gesture. 'Spare me the tabloid talk.'

'It's not, it's the truth. But why don't you tell me more about the town, then? Its good points. Apart from you.'

So, she started telling him about Piddlington Minster; how she'd been told she could be sergeant here or nowhere else, because 'nothing ever happens' and the former chief superintendent was a 'raging, sexist pig'.

According to Ophelia, the main problem in the town were the over-pampered 'coffin dodgers' who had little better to do than pick holes in everyone who lived there, but especially the younger generations.

'The times I've been called out to what we were told was a major disturbance and found it's a couple of kids kicking a Coke can around.'

Harry thought of Prudence Robarts. Maybe Ophelia could tell him something more about her?

'The woman who found the first body? If anyone in this town was going to find a body, it would be her, that's all I'm saying,' she said. 'Seems to spend her entire day faffing about with the Britain in Bloom committee or going on about people not keeping their front gardens tidy. Mind you, she's pretty good for her age, must be about ninety-something, I think.'

Harry was astonished.

As things were going so swimmingly and they were talking bodies again, he asked her what she knew about Kevin Fewtrell. 'Maybe I can fill in a few gaps for you,' he said, eager to help after her useful comments previously.

'You're the journalist, you tell me what you've dug up about him.'

Ignoring the unfortunate turn of phrase, he explained that all he'd learned was that Fewtrell had barely allowed the seat of his beige nylon trousers to connect with the fraying fabric of the editor's chair before scarpering. And Cassandra had said he seemed nervy. He mentioned the postcard, too, but Ophelia didn't jump.

'I'll make a note about that but it's probably hopeless without the original item,' she said. 'When he left, I just assumed he'd offended the owner of the paper or something, or got bored. No one officially reported him missing and there was nothing to suggest he may have been the victim of a crime. As far as I know, he'd never committed a crime but maybe he was breaking the law too,' she said, looking pointedly at Harry.

He bore the disgrace. This was probably always going to be his lot. To distract her, and because he was fascinated to know, he asked her why she'd accepted his invitation to come out.

'You've seen this place for yourself,' she said. 'People, well, most of them, are lovely but in my job it's not easy to step out, and I haven't always had the best time, if you see what I mean.'

He didn't, really, and wondered if there was more behind her comment, but Ophelia had started rummaging around in her handbag. He knew the signs. 'Shall I call for the bill?'

'Yes, but I told you—'

'You're paying your half,' he said, a little too quickly.

'Yes. Because otherwise I will probably have to register this somewhere and can't be arsed.'

'Can I walk you home, Ophelia?'

He could not. 'See you tomorrow,' she said.

He watched her walk to the end of the road, before turning round for his journey back to The Ball.

It was nearly 10.30 p.m. Time for bed.

* * *

As he had to go through the bar to reach the staircase, Harry decided to have a nightcap to top off what had easily been not only his best evening in Piddlington Minster but, indeed, the best evening of his life since the Awful Day.

The room was pleasingly full, with people at the tables and on the bar stools. Three oldsters were arguing over a game of shove ha'penny and two men were leaving by the propped-open saloon door.

Harry ordered a pint of Old Piddle from George and reached into his pocket for his notebook.

On Monday he would send Hattie to the museum to chase up the possible story there. And, he thought, he'd get back to Ophelia and see what was coming out about the body on the roundabout.

As he stood up to pay, George smiled and Harry nodded.

'Busy night?'

'Yes, it's the good weather, brings them out.'

'Yes, I'm sure.'

George turned away and then turned back, frowning slightly. 'Have you ever heard of the old billionaire guy up in the Vale?'

Harry was jerked out of his mental slumber. 'Why d'you ask?'

'One of the customers mentioned it, that's all, and I thought it was odd. I said there were a lot of rumours, you know . . . that he was rich and liked a bit of art, that kind of thing. Just wondered if you knew him?'

'Who? The old billionaire?'

George nodded.

'Not really. But I understand the house is really beautiful and unusual inside. Did the man who came in ask about anything else?'

George considered. 'I told him that if he really wanted to know about the area, he should read your paper!'

'What did he look like?'

'Don't know, really: middle-aged, dark T-shirt and jeans, baseball cap, that kind of thing.'

'Thanks, George,' said Harry. 'If it happens again, can you let me know?'

Chapter 11

He awoke on Saturday morning at five o'clock. He tried all the usual tricks to get back to sleep, but nothing worked. To distract himself, he contemplated the forty-eight hours of – technically paid – freedom ahead.

In the old London days, it would have been so easy. Waking up with a girlfriend, a shower so powerful it would feel like he'd gone a couple of rounds with Tyson Fury and then an amble off for a breakfast that would probably include everything from bacon sandwiches to smashed avocado. The only smashed avocado he'd find in Piddlington Minster would probably have fallen off the back of the indecently priced fruit and veg stand in the town square and then been run over by a skateboarder.

The thought of breakfast began to grow on him. He racked his brains to remember if he'd spotted any decent places. He was still contemplating it as he drifted along the corridor to The Ball Inn's bathroom, which remained untroubled by anything that could be categorised as 'other human life'.

As he dried himself and pulled on jeans and his only other T-shirt, he smelled a delicious whiff of bacon. He yanked open the curtains – being in his room was like being able to touch the 1950s. He eased open the window and a cloud of cool air billowed in. And he realised the scent of bacon was coming from downstairs.

Stepping into the bar, he was amazed to find a pile of small, triangle-cut, exquisitely cooked bacon sandwiches, butter dripping from the sides.

The kitchen doors burst open, and Cassandra tottered out, wearing what he presumed was her weekend outfit – a bright-pink checked shirt that made her look like Dolly Parton.

'Macchiato espresso, wasn't it?' she enquired, pouring it into a small china cup.

Harry was speechless. 'And the sandwiches?'

'Who else would I get up this early for?' She winked. 'I'm guessing you don't eat ketchup?'

He shook his head. He couldn't stand the stuff. But he already knew enough to realise he'd never find out how she knew that.

As he munched the delicious sandwiches, he contemplated the day. After checking all the news feeds, he should really ring his long-suffering father, Geoffrey. His last words and gallant hug before Harry had set off for Piddlington Minster were: 'Take care, dear boy.' Meaning, Harry guessed: 'Don't mess it all up again now, will you?'

He straightened his shoulders. OK, it was only a week but, so far, he reckoned, he'd been reasonably successful, so he should ring his dad and let him know about it. Reassure him that all the efforts to secure his freedom had been well invested. But really, he fancied a walk on the Downs, a chance to clear his head a bit and contemplate the week to come.

Cassandra bustled back in. 'Now, I don't have a lot of time, what with it being the weekend, but if you're stuck for places to go, I'd suggest the ridgeway on the Downs – it's beautiful up there, give you time to think and have a nice relax.'

'Cassandra, how do you *know*?'

She laughed. 'Don't ask me any questions and you'll get no lies. I just do, that's all.'

He asked her a few more questions: what was the best bit to visit? 'Well, if I were you, I'd go up to the High Downs. The view from there is beautiful, like a living map, and it gives you a right proper perspective. On a clear day . . .'

'You can see forever,' he finished.

'Oh no, on a clear day you can see the oil refinery at Southampton. And a bit of Wiltshire.'

How could he resist? Tapping into The Ball Inn's Wi-Fi, Harry plotted a route to the ridgeway, which would allow him to walk along it. As he strolled through the bar to leave, Cassandra handed him a packet of sandwiches: 'On the house.' He wanted to kiss her.

* * *

In the still-gentle morning light, the ridgeway resembled a Ravilious painting: soft colours, reassuring lines and a soothing otherworldliness. He parked in a deserted carpark and began to walk westwards.

As he loped along, he spotted the flash of toadflax, the tiny yellow and orange snapdragon wildflower. Their sunny faces reminded him of cowslips, his mother's favourite flower – he used to bend down to sniff them, enjoying the feel of the downy stalks. He remembered his mother picking one for him as a tiny child. 'Smell it, Harry. It's the smell of spring.'

That season was a long way off, and before it, they would have to go through autumn and the dark of winter, the season in which Isabella had died. He was glad the only living thing that could see him brush away a tear was a red kite, which rocked and dipped overhead.

He shivered. Clouds had crept across the sky, and he felt cold. Time to go back to the car.

* * *

The Downs walk had had a good effect and after agreeing to stand in for a missing player in the evening's snooker competition, then scoring the winning point in spectacular fashion – with a trick he'd learned from thrice world champ, Lenny 'Whirlwind' Wiggins – Harry wandered up to his room. Pleasantly tired from the day's activity, he clambered into bed, where he slept deeply and well.

He was woken by the minster's bells and, on a whim, decided to attend morning service. Good to be seen around the place, and going to church was technically free.

Belting out 'Praise My Soul', he felt his spirits rising, especially when they came to the bit about being ransomed, healed, restored and forgiven.

He felt slightly less certain when the prebendary reminded the congregation during his sermon: 'There is joy before the angels of God over one sinner repenting,' while looking straight at him, but the man was cordial enough as he shook Harry's hand as he left, and welcomed 'the new editor of our local paper'.

After buying a packet of supermarket sandwiches, Harry decided to walk east along the Downs, parking in the same spot as before. There were supposedly the remains of a chalk figure carved into the hillside after around two miles and he wondered if he'd still be able to see it.

After a peaceful hike and much searching, he concluded that if there had ever been a chalk figure, it had succumbed to the tufty grass a long time ago. But the view was just as beautiful as yesterday's – far better than anything he'd encountered along the tourist-encrusted King's Road – and some kind soul had decided to place a rustic bench for people to enjoy it. Harry sat down. He couldn't put it off anymore. He called his father.

'Thank goodness, I was really worried – you could have texted or something.'

Harry grimaced. It wasn't that he didn't love his dad. God knows, he'd helped him out of the worst hole he'd ever fallen into. But, despite his kindness, Harry had always found it hard to fathom Geoffrey. Being more similar to Isabella, he'd found it easier to open up to her; they spoke the same language. She had been so affectionate, funny and spontaneous; his father was seemingly more watchful and distant.

He dutifully told Geoffrey about his first edition, his colleagues and The Ball Inn. 'Excellent. That all sounds most satisfactory.'

He assured him it was.

'And there's been no, er, *difficulty*?' His voice sounded slightly strangulated, and Harry knew why. The embarrassment of the legal proceedings – 'Royal waste bin son's court shock' – had nearly finished the reticent, proper Geoffrey.

'No, Pa, nothing like that.'

'Oh good. Good! Marvellous!'

Harry was silent as he tried to think of something else to say. 'Everything going OK with you?'

Geoffrey hesitated for a microsecond, before replying: 'Yes. Yes of course.'

Harry sat up. 'What's the matter?'

Geoffrey sounded even more strangulated. 'Nothing. Nothing at all.'

'You're not ill, are you?'

A nervous cough. 'No, nothing like that.'

Harry remained silent. As an interview tactic, it usually worked, prompting the interviewee into saying the first thing that came into their head to fill the void.

It didn't work.

'C'mon, Pa, what's the matter?' Perhaps it was something trivial, like being defrocked as the Croquet Club captain?

'Nothing. Probably just missing you – empty house and all that. You know.'

Harry didn't really, but went along with it. They had just spent the best part of two years together, with him doing very little work and his father slaving at the luxury wastepaper bin business to keep the income flowing.

'Where are you?'

He explained he was on the Downs and turned to look at the landscape around him.

'It's really lovely here. Ma would have loved it.'

Geoffrey agreed. 'Of *course* she would.'

It seemed like the right time to ask the question he'd often wondered: 'Do you still miss her?'

There was a slight pause. 'Of course I do. Who wouldn't?'

Harry murmured his agreement. No point in mentioning the lack of photos of Isabella in their house now.

'How's that car running?'

He assured him it was as temperamental as usual but still going.

'Ah. Excellent news. Splendid.'

As he bade his father goodbye, Harry reflected on Geoffrey's stoicism in the face of widowhood and public disgrace by association.

But he still wasn't sure he understood it – or even him.

Chapter 12

He woke early on Monday and was thrilled to notice an email announcing that a police press conference was being held at 11 a.m. in the old library. As he quietly let himself out of The Ball Inn's side door to drive to work, a voice called out: 'Nice early start for you?'

Cassandra was dolled up in a tight, pink minidress and swinging a giant bunch of keys.

'Just had a great night's sleep so I thought I'd crack on,' he said.

'No breakfast?'

He patted his extremely flat stomach. 'Very kind but I'm trying to lose weight.'

'Get away with you,' she teased.

* * *

The short drive in was peaceful and gave Harry time to appreciate the way the light prodded through the housing and business premises at the different hour, spotlighting different features to those it caught later in the day.

His mind was buzzing. What to do first? He still didn't know if the police would be revealing any more information about the body.

Then there was the digging to do at the local museum.

And Sadie Burge, who was about to be subject to a council order and whom he'd promised to help. And then there was his pledge to Mr Green about the search for his sister.

He put his foot down. Really, there weren't enough hours in the day.

As he sped past Brenda's, he noticed the shop was open. And there was no queue. He braked, waved cheerfully at the vehicle behind him, pulled up on the pavement and dashed in.

Brenda was delighted. Yes, she would do him a coffee – and she'd had a delivery from a new supplier of 'Danish cakes'.

'I'll have two of those,' said Harry, pointing to the glistening cinnamon rolls.

'Right you are.'

As Brenda grabbed them with the tongs, Harry looked into the street. A shard of sunlight was cutting through the gap between the old record shop and one of the endless charity shops. A small figure was passing through.

Mrs Robarts. She was pushing a large, tartan trolley of the kind that usually annihilates the ankles of the unwary in supermarkets. It reminded him of a story he'd once done, where the murderer had used much the same conveyance to move the body parts he'd hacked from his victims. Tartan shopping trolleys may look innocent, but they always gave Harry the creeps.

'That'll be six pounds fifty,' chirped Brenda.

He fished out his last few coins and stepped out to notice a new traffic warden bearing down on his car at warp speed.

'They've got to catch you first,' he muttered as he leaped in and pulled away, without even putting on his seatbelt.

He liked to see himself as someone who always found a parking space and always avoided a parking ticket. In his mind he liked to attribute it to his mother looking down, like an angel, bringing him luck.

Thinking about Isabella dampened his spirits a little, but they rose as he arrived at the office to find it open, and with Hattie seated and typing furiously.

He opened his paper bag and proceeded to tear off a strip of cinnamon Danish as he flicked his machine on.

As if by magic, a brown panting shape appeared in the office doorway.

'Oh look, Ignatius wants some of your bun.'

'A, it's not a bun, and B, that dog gets quite enough food as it is,' said Harry, tearing off another strip.

She pursed her lips and stared at him. Ignatius, tail tick-tocking wildly, approached Harry's desk. 'Go away,' he said, refusing to look into the beseeching brown face.

The dog moved closer, as Harry stared at his screen, then placed his head heavily on his lap and sighed.

'He won't go away unless you give him some,' said Hattie.

Harry glared. Ignatius blinked and pressed his head down more firmly, spreading drool down both sides of his thighs.

'Oh, for pity's sake,' he said, ripping off two inches and dropping it into the dog's mouth. He was rewarded with a tail thump and Ignatius sitting there, with his ears cocked.

'See, he does love you.' Hattie beamed.

Harry snorted and realised that the pattern left by the slobber looked very much again as if he'd suffered an unfortunate accident in the gents.

He started checking the opening times of the town museum. He should send Hattie there; after all, she'd tipped him off about the possible story and it could be a good one. He started explaining to her what he was hoping to find. 'I'm there already,' she cried, grabbing her notebook.

'Not too long,' Harry warned. 'We've got a lot on.'

Ignatius leaned his entire body weight against Harry's leg and looked as if his heart would break. 'She'll be back later, you silly thing,' he said. The dog thumped his tail and moved a little closer to the side of the desk where the other cinnamon Danish lurked in its bag.

Idly, Harry started searching again for Fewtrell, trawling Facebook, X and even Instagram. The man appeared to have no internet footprint at all, unless you counted the account he'd opened on Twitter to re-tweet *Gazette* stories, which had stopped being current at around the time he'd disappeared.

* * *

At ten minutes past nine, Ignatius heaved himself over to the door. It's either the postman or Ray, thought Harry, and smiled, as he realised he was starting to know everyone's habits.

Ray shuffled in. He looked terrible: pallid, coughing and with watery eyes. He smelled as if he hadn't had a bath, and his shirt,

Harry noticed with concern, was the one he'd worn on Friday and, come to think of it, the day before that.

A waft of sweat streamed over to him. It wasn't too bad, thank God, but Harry decided to tread carefully.

'Are you OK, Ray? You don't look too good.'

Ray glanced over. 'I'm fine, thanks, no one's to go worrying about me.' He then added even more of the brown liquid from his desk-drawer bottle to his tea, Harry noticed. He really needed to get on top of this.

He looked at his watch, wondering if it was too early to check on the bodies.

What about Hattie? He texted her.

Five minutes later, his phone rang.

'It's me! I've found out something interesting.'

* * *

Hattie had arrived at the museum five minutes after opening time and charmed the curator, Mr Prentiss, into fishing out a book of old maps of the area while it was quiet.

'Such a pleasure to help someone who wants to look at real history,' he'd told her.

She had asked him what he meant, and he told her the rumours were true; in order to get a new maintenance grant, the local council were demanding an updated diversity and inclusion action plan after the scrutiny committee had 'audited' the museum. This plan would have to show how they intended to attract more of the Chinese locals to the building, as the council's survey had shown they had 'a significant Chinese population in the town'.

'Probably the Cheung family, who used to run the Chinese restaurant,' Hattie said. 'I went to school with Liam Cheung. They've been here forty years and own a cider farm now, so they're actually more Dorset than I am.'

The museum also had to formulate a policy on adapting and interpreting their displays 'for other marginalised populations'.

'I would be quite willing to do that; we *should* do that,' the distracted curator had told her. 'But to make the changes they want, I'd need to have secured the grant first and, without it, we may have to close.'

Hattie could see that trying to make the displays interactive – council-speak for touchscreen-based to interest children with the attention span of a small insect – would take thousands that the museum just didn't have.

'The museum's great – it's got displays on the old, one-armed Hangman of Piddlington Minster, and some really cute stuffed weasels, although one's gone a bit mouldy and—' Harry cut off the lava flow of information.

'Is there enough for a page lead?'

Hattie thought so. 'Maybe we could run an appeal in the paper for marginalised people to come forward or visit, so we can keep the museum open . . . or start a campaign or something?'

He foresaw plenty of trouble that way, even if it was true, and pointed out that what was happening was newsworthy enough.

'We'll play it with a straight bat but get on to the council about it, too.'

'I wouldn't be surprised if they wanted to close down the building and sell it off for flats or something,' said Hattie. 'Councils are always doing stuff like that.'

He couldn't disagree.

'OK, but if you're going to the council, come back soon and we'll carry on.'

She replied but her words were drowned out by Ray's coughing fit.

Harry grimaced. He hated germs, and Ray looked like the sort whose body might brew the kind as yet unknown to science.

For want of something concrete to do, he asked Ray if he'd like a cup of tea.

The man's subdued gratitude told him something was just not right.

Chapter 13

He was far too early but Harry hurried along to the press conference, keen to get a good seat and, if at all possible, to have a quick word with Ophelia beforehand.

There were two extra cars in the parking spaces, and he saw PC Collins placing bollards in two others. 'In there!' he called, gesturing to a side door which Harry hadn't noticed before. It led to the library side of the building which, a notice said, would be closed for half an hour while the conference took place.

At one end of the book-lined room, Harry saw a table with three chairs and three glasses of water. Facing it were ten chairs, with only six occupied, by journalists he'd never seen before.

Probably news agencies or someone from the local evening paper, way down on the coast. He decided not to sit but to lean on one of the bookshelves, giving him a better chance to keep an eye on everything. At 11 a.m. precisely, three people, two of whom were Ophelia and PC Collins, walked in.

'Good morning, ladies . . .' There were none. 'And er, gentlemen,' said Ophelia, looking immaculate in her freshly pressed uniform shirt.

'I'm here to update you on the discovery of human remains on the roundabout at Piddlington Minster.'

She proceeded to read from a piece of paper produced for her by the force's press officer.

According to the statement, Kevin Fewtrell's post-mortem report had revealed that the body had suffered blunt force trauma to the head – at this point all the journalists leaned comically forward – but Dorset Police were keeping an open mind as to how this injury had occurred and were treating the death as unexplained, rather than suspicious. There were other unexplained injuries to the body and so there would be further forensic tests as well as investigations.

Ophelia went on to the second page of her statement.

The force were appealing for anyone who had witnessed 'activity' of an unusual nature on the roundabout or near it on or around the date of Tuesday 25 March, when Kevin was last seen, to contact them on a special number which had been set up by the investigation team.

She then sat back and invited questions.

'Can the force tell us anything about the body that was initially discovered on the roundabout?' asked the BBC's correspondent.

'And are the two connected?' interrupted a bright young reporter who Harry presumed was from the local news agency.

According to Ophelia, Dorset Police were conducting two separate investigations and keeping an open mind as to whether the bodies were connected, either to each other or by the circumstances of their death.

'Several lines of inquiry are being pursued,' she said, but Dorset Police could not go into details about them. Nor, in answer to the news agency question, could she say if they had identified the other body and if it was true that its skeletal hand had been 'pointing accusingly', as described by the original witness. Yes, they were looking at all missing persons from the area from the past thirty years, dating to the time of the roundabout's construction. And no, they certainly would not be commenting on whether either body was connected to the rumours of witchcraft which had 'plagued' the area for centuries. This enquiry had come from the local evening newspaper reporter, Barry Hands.

'We won't be commenting on that for the simple reason, Barry, that it's your paper which has tended to promulgate this nonsense for as long as most people can remember,' said Ophelia.

But Barry would not be put off so easily. 'Well, that's what *you* say, Sergeant,' he began. 'But I think our readers would be fascinated to know why your force is spending so much time trying to dampen down this story when we only need one more stiff to make it the work of a serial killer – the Roundabout Ripper. Are people actually safe round here?'

Ophelia looked livid and Harry drew breath to bowl her an easy question but, as he opened his mouth to speak, the room was invaded by a small elderly woman, upholstered in pink and grey dogtooth tweed.

'If *I* may be permitted a question?'

'No, you may not, Mrs Robarts,' said Ophelia, firmly. Harry felt proud of her composure. 'This is a police press conference and is only open to accredited members of the press. Not the general public.'

'Press? They couldn't run a whelk stall. The real story here is the criminal neglect of this town by the council. For years I've been trying to get something done about that roundabout and the other abominable messes in Piddlington Minster and no one has listened. Not a soul. Now look where we are!'

The other local newspaper journalist stopped filming Ophelia on his smartphone and started filming Mrs Robarts.

As if to the manner born, she turned to the camera.

'It wouldn't be so bad if it was just that roundabout, which is littered with dead bodies. But the fact is,' she said, leaning forward so the hairs on her chin prickled menacingly, 'there is that house of horror on Bridge Street. Who knows what's going on there?'

Barry was looking even more interested. Houses of Horror would definitely be up his boulevard. *I'm going to lose yet another exclusive if this goes on*, thought Harry. *Not to mention any chance I've ever had with Ophelia.*

As Mrs Robarts continued her rant, Harry noticed PC Collins slide from his seat and begin advancing towards her. But he was beaten to it by someone else. Delighted to find so many of his fans gathered together, Ignatius trotted confidently towards the table and stopped as he reached Mrs Robarts's leg. He then lifted his and urinated copiously upon her.

She screamed and tried to slap his nose. Ignatius yelped, jerking backwards into Harry, who was moving forward to try to grab him. Once again, he experienced the sensation of tripping over Ignatius, this time toppling a bookshelf full of brightly coloured crime novels onto the miserable old bat.

'Murder!' screamed Mrs Robarts, as a hefty hardback bounced off her head. 'They're trying to silence me.'

What else she was going to say was stifled as PC Collins sidestepped Harry, the books and Ignatius, before gently but firmly escorting her from the room.

Ophelia looked aghast. 'What the hell is your dog doing here, Mr Hedges?'

'He's not mine,' moaned Harry, a bruise forming on his shin.

'Yes, what *is* he doing in here?' demanded the police press officer. 'Really, Sergeant, it's imperative that you take into account the security of the room for occasions such as this.' Ophelia looked ready to commit murder herself.

She swiftly handed out the press release to the assembled hacks and the group started to leave.

'Ophelia . . .' began Harry.

'It's Sergeant Starsky,' she growled, as the officials left the room.

* * *

After helping to re-shelve the books which had fallen upon Mrs Robarts, Harry decided to creep round to the police station's official entrance and try his luck again. When he arrived near the front door, he was relieved to see through the open back-office entrance that the press officer was leaving.

He waited a second and then went up to the booth. He couldn't see or hear anyone.

'Can I help you?'

He spun round. It was PC Collins. For such a tall man, he could certainly move very delicately.

'You still here?' asked the officer.

He explained that he wanted to ask a bit more about the process of the investigation and how the second body had been discovered.

PC Collins pursed his lips. 'Not sure what more I can say about that on the record just yet – you heard the sergeant just now.'

'I know,' sympathised Harry. 'I'm so sorry about Ignatius, he's a force of nature.'

PC Collins smiled. 'These things happen.'

Harry didn't think police pressers were often interrupted by incontinent dogs urinating on elderly ladies but kept quiet; PC Collins looked as if he was weighing something up.

'What I can tell you – all off the record – is that the body of Mr Fewtrell was discovered as part of the investigation into the first body,' he said. 'As you've seen for yourself, it's like the Amazon jungle on there and we had to get a landscape gardener in to give us a hand with some cutting.' The wider search of the roundabout had come later in the day and on to the evening, when the second cadaver had come to light.

Harry longed to ask him a string of follow-up questions – did they think Kevin had died on the day of his disappearance? Was he identified by his dental records or by the fact that he was wearing indestructible beige polyester trousers? – but realised he could only push it so far.

PC Collins looked up. 'Can I ask you a question now?'

'Of course!'

'We've been getting reports that a black four-by-four has been seen in the area, hanging around north of Piddlington Minster. You know what people are like . . . They worry that it's criminals checking out places, that kind of thing, and then it's all over WhatsApp, although we've had no reports of any crimes connected to it,' he said. 'I just wondered if your newspaper had had anyone calling in about it?'

Harry was sorry to tell him they hadn't, but he would let the officer know if it happened.

'Look, PC Collins, I really appreciate your help on this roundabout thing. Is there anything else you can tell me?'

The officer looked into the distance. 'Not now. But you get around, Mr Harry. Let me know what you see. Deal?'

'Deal!'

* * *

He arrived back in the office to find Hattie enthusiastically writing up her museum story and Ray looking reasonably alive.

He decided to ignore the now wide-ranging smell of Ray's shirt and bang out the latest from the press conference. He added in a few details about the town's road system, after learning that the roundabout had been deliberately built to an extra-large size to accommodate the road from a proposed housing estate and industrial park on either side, which had never been built. For good measure, he alluded to the witchcraft yarns which had indeed been peddled by Barry Hands in the *Wessex Post* newspaper for at least the past twenty years – without a shred of evidence, as far as he could see, that they were true.

Even though he said it himself, it was a good read. He decided to put it up on the website – hopefully, there would be more information by the time of the next paper edition to refresh it all.

The tapping sounds on the computers were only punctuated by the occasional sigh from Ignatius and the odd buzz of a trapped fly.

Harry stood up to prop open the door.

'Use this, lad,' said Ray, handing him a hideous Perspex object. 'It's the award we got for Weekly Newspaper of the Year in 1980.'

Did Perspex even exist then, Harry wondered.

He turned his back to return to his desk but was stopped short by a bellow from the courtyard.

'Mr Hedges! I want a word with you!'

He sighed. 'Mrs Robarts?'

She stepped into the newsroom, mercifully without the tartan trolley. 'I hope you're not going to be fooled by that farce in the library?'

'I'm not sure what you mean?'

What Mrs Robarts meant was that the whole thing was a cover-up and a 'despicable whitewash.'

'They know quite well that the body I found has been there for donkey's years. They don't need tests to tell them that.'

Harry wondered what to do to get her out of the office more quickly. But he was saved by Hattie.

'Excuse me, Mrs Robarts, but how can you say that?'

Mrs Robarts glared. 'I came here to see the organ grinder, not the monkey.'

Now it was Harry's turn to glare. 'Please don't insult my staff like that, madam. Miss Watson is our senior reporter and will be handling this story along with myself.'

'Senior reporter? Don't make me laugh. We all remember what happened to her fa—'

But she was cut off by a blushing Hattie. 'I'm trying to help you, Mrs Robarts. My questions are perfectly reasonable. You seem very sure that the body you found is very old and has been there for a long time. Is there any reason you can say this?'

Mrs Robarts snorted. 'It stands to reason, doesn't it? If the council kept this town properly then surely it would have been discovered ages ago. I always said that roundabout was a death-trap. Same goes for that disgusting house. The place is ridden with vermin, the woman who lives there is a danger to herself and others, and I've been complaining about it for years. Mind you, they're taking notice now, aren't they? I wouldn't be surprised if there were a few dead bodies in her garden, too. It's simply disgusting.'

Hattie scribbled something in her notebook and looked up. 'You were the person who found the first body, weren't you, Mrs Robarts?'

'Yes, I've told you that, you stupid child.'

'Why were you on the roundabout?'

Mrs Robarts stared. 'I was investigating.'

'Investigating what?'

'The mess on that roundabout!'

'What made you want to go there?'

'I told you, the mess.'

'Can I ask you, who do you think that body could be?'

Mrs Robarts put her head on one side. 'Probably a tramp who thought it was a clever place to live without being discovered and then died before anyone noticed. Let's face it, Lord Lucan could be living there and no one would know, would they?'

Hattie looked uncomprehending. 'Who's he? Are you saying you blame the council?'

'I certainly do. If they kept this town properly, we wouldn't be facing murders on the roundabout, and we wouldn't be in danger of losing our place in Britain in Bloom.'

Hattie asked Mrs Robarts some more questions: her address, her age and, 'Is there a Mr Robarts?'

She looked astonished. 'Of course there was, you idiot child. I'm not one of these modern feminists, you know.'

Hattie pulled an exhausted face. 'And how old are you?'

'I'm ninety!'

Ignatius, who appeared to have had enough of the conversation, started scratching himself assiduously, his chops making a slapping noise against his teeth.

'Is there something wrong with that creature?'

'Yes,' said Harry, who'd had a sudden brainwave. 'He's riddled with fleas. And ticks, I shouldn't be at all surprised.'

She looked horrified. 'Get him away from me! Tick bites can kill. What about health and safety?'

Panting heavily, Ignatius moved closer to her. Mrs Robarts stepped backwards through the doorway. 'Shoo! Go away!'

As he wagged his tail, she stepped from the room and moved across the cobbles. Harry let out a little cheer. 'Ignatius, old boy, sometimes you really have your uses!'

He then looked up to smile at Hattie and congratulate her on her handling of the situation, but she looked pale and nervy and was typing furiously at her keyboard.

Chapter 14

The day continued more peacefully, punctuated by Ray's cough and Ignatius's scratching.

Hattie had started hammering out story after story. Harry took another moment to consider Kevin Fewtrell. He'd visited Lionel Green, hadn't he? And hadn't Cassandra said he looked frightened after going there?

He made a note of both facts. *Need to check them out.* He also added Sadie Burge to his to-do list. Her notice-serving date must be nearing. Maybe he needed to check with the council on that. And of course, he had to start searching for Mr Green's missing sister.

He wondered idly about contacting Jasper. The man was dodgier than Kevin Fewtrell's trousers, but he had tipped him off about this job and, as the *Daily News*'s news editor, he'd handled a lot of missing-people stories so might be worth a punt.

'I'm just stepping out!' Harry said to the other two. Ignatius plodded after him.

He pressed Jasper's contact number.

''Ello 'Arry! Long time, no speak. How's it all goin'?'

Jasper had actually attended St Basil's in the year above him and was the son of a very wealthy businessman, but he'd studiously perfected his Essex credentials since leaving their old alma mater.

Before Harry could reply, Jasper was off. 'It's mental here! Old Sir Jimmy's going off his rocker. We keep 'aving to interview all these artists who he reckons are going to be big, because he's bought their work. He went and bought a see-through crystal glass toilet the other day. Crystal balls, more like. Three mil! But he reckons it'll soon be worth six million and wants us to do a *tasteful* story to impress the Tate Gallery; he's got this campaign to make them name their new extension after him. Hopefully, the bloody toilet block, if there's any justice. It's doing my head in.'

Harry laughed, hollowly. It would amaze him if such an ill-educated old philistine as Sir Jimmy Knox knew one end of a painting from another. But he knew that once he became obsessed with something, he was relentless.

'Jasper, can I ask something?'

'Fire away, old boy.'

'Someone's asked me to trace a family member – sort of a story, that kind of thing. But apart from Google and the obvious places, I've no idea where to start. It's a bit out of my wheelhouse. I've got a name – Sarah – and a rough age. She is in her nineties, or would be, if she was still alive.'

'Where do they live?'

'Last heard of in London.'

'Good luck with that one, mate. I wouldn't know where to start. Sally Army? They do missing persons, don't they? Look up death certificates? Anything else?'

It was like he had a sixth sense.

Harry hesitated.

'How's Violett?' 'Doing very well, as it happens. Our paths do cross but I'm running the desk most of the time and she's floating about above it all, working on strategy.'

'Does she ever say anything about what happened?' He was definitely sure he hadn't meant to say that.

'Er, sorry, mate . . . call from Sir Jimmy coming in, got to fly. Stay in touch, yeah?'

The line went dead before Harry could even agree.

He decided to try and contact Greta Sargent. Perhaps she could confirm that Fewtrell had been up to the house and also shed some light on his disappearance.

He punched in Lionel Green's number and braced himself for the Dalek voice, but was amazed to hear a gentle Dorset burr and the words, 'Good morning, and how may I help you?'

Harry explained who he was and said he'd hoped to speak to Miss Sargent. 'She's not here, sir, just me, Elspeth, the cook. Can I help?'

He hesitated, but decided that the woman could only say no.

In his best voice, he asked if she'd heard of a man called Kevin Fewtrell, the former editor of the *Piddlington Gazette*, visiting The Grange.

'Actually, I remember it quite clearly,' said Elspeth. 'He turned up and I'd just prepared the coffee and a Viennese whirl for him and Mr Green, when Miss Sargent called down to say it wouldn't be needed. Then I looked out and saw him walking down the drive, very fast.'

'I don't suppose you know why?'

The cook hesitated. 'I don't know. I think perhaps Mr Green just wanted to talk to him . . . as I think he spoke to you, didn't he? Now, if you don't mind, can I take the spelling of your name and I'll pass your details on to Miss Sargent.'

Harry thanked her and rang off. He stepped back into the office, sat back down and contacted Piddlington District Council about Sadie Burge.

* * *

Naturally, they couldn't discuss personal cases, an official advised him. However, any proposed civil action or otherwise against any party would be dealt with by way of a notice, which legitimate parties would receive. Other actions may be private.

Harry loosened his tie and leaned back in his chair. Time to put the pressure on.

'We're talking about a very senior lady here,' he told the official. 'And if she is made to undergo the forced cleaning and clearing of her home, I can promise you, it will be a front-page story in my newspaper.'

'I'll put you through to the press office,' she muttered. He grinned. Worked every time.

But the press officer, Gemma Edgerton, was just as unhelpful.

'Just so you know, I have an interview with the elderly lady in question and it will be my front-page splash this week,' fibbed Harry. 'This is your chance to rebut any allegations she makes about heavy-handedness. And cruelty.'

The last word seemed to galvanise the woman into action. She promised a statement by 'close of play'.

'Make it one o'clock, please.'

'Go Harry!' cheered Hattie. 'They really are such bullies. Always evicting people and being horrible and totally inhumane, and I bet they break the Human Rights Act, too.'

'Aye,' agreed Ray.

After putting out a few tweets and Facebook posts about the week's sports offerings, he decided to try and tackle the missing sister.

The private investigator's file was indeed painfully slim. It revealed an address in Kensington and a phone number. Harry rang it. The line was dead. He tapped in the number online to see if it was connected to anything now, but it appeared to be defunct.

He looked up the address. Going by the image online, it was now a block of smart apartments that had been built in the 1970s. There was a newspaper cutting in an envelope about a street party held for the Coronation of Queen Elizabeth, featuring a line of blurry, paper-crowned children and adults. Harry stared at the fuzzy picture. The reproduction was so bad that the new queen herself could have been in it, and he wouldn't have been able to make her out. He suspected it had been put in merely to help justify the investigator's fee.

For want of anything better, he googled Sarah Green, together with the ages ninety, ninety-one and eighty-nine, in London. Lists and lists of people came up. As he'd suspected, it was hopeless; he couldn't think she was any of them and, anyway, if she had married, she would almost certainly have changed her name. Various genealogy sites were similarly fruitless.

* * *

Two o'clock arrived and with it the total non-appearance of the council's statement. He put in another call and got Gemma Edgerton again, sounding flustered. 'You know it's got to receive three ticks,' she said. 'All press statements have to go to the portfolio-holder in question.'

Portfolio-holder, my backside, thought Harry. More like elderly dignitary who'd got lucky enough to chair a committee with the welcome uplift to his income that such a position entailed.

Harry told Gemma he didn't know anything about their tick system. But there was no point in riling her.

'Look, I know the lady's house is on the grim side and that something really needs to be done about it. But does the council have to be quite so heavy-handed? Because it just looks like bullying from where I'm standing.'

Gemma sighed. 'Do you really think we need all this grief? I can't say this officially, but unofficially, Miss Burge's home has been the subject of a file that's a good . . .' He heard her counting. 'Five inches thick, I would say. This has been going on for years. I know you won't believe it, but we've exhausted every informal route and tried to engage with her in every way we can think of. We can't let a rat infestation take hold, can we?'

'Would it help if I had a word with her? Try to make her see sense and come to an agreement?'

'Really? I mean, yes. Anything would help, that would be fantastic. Unofficially, of course.' Her enthusiasm burned down the line. 'Like I said, no one wants to be horrible, and no one wants to hound her, but we have to think of other residents in that area, don't we?'

He ignored Hattie's snort.

'I'll see what I can do. Now, can you do something for me?'

'I'm listening,' said Gemma.

He outlined his efforts to track down information on Kevin Fewtrell.

'That poor man who was found on the roundabout?' She told him she couldn't look up any private details, but she remembered him very clearly.

'What was he like?'

'Ordinary. But he wore beige polyester trousers, which I thought was a bit off.'

'Was he scared of anything?'

'What a question! I only met him once, at a council reception, and he seemed fine, especially when he started – very positive, with lots of plans for the paper and everything. But the second time I spoke to him, on the phone, he was different, quite jumpy and talked very fast. Then he just left and that's the last I heard of him.'

'I thought you'd say that. What did he want on the phone?'

Gemma couldn't remember clearly. 'Something to do with that big house . . . The Grange, is it?'

In an effort to be conversational, Harry told her it was where Kevin's boss lived and, after a few more comments, he ended the call and started writing, soothed by the clack and rustle from his colleagues, although Ray's cough was beginning to worry him.

As the day wore on, Hattie finished her list and headed off home, and Ray pottered idly round his desk.

'I'll lock up,' said Harry.

Ray looked up. 'Don't you worry, I'm perfectly capable. I've got to finish a few bits.'

'But you've been here a whole hour over and there's no need.' Was it his imagination, or did Ray look a bit furtive?

'Look, I'm fine. But only if you're sure?'

Harry said he was sure.

The sub-editor spent an inordinate amount of time opening and shutting the drawers of his desk, rattling coins in his pocket, patting Ignatius and hunting around for his bag, which was actually hung over the back of his chair.

Harry pretended to concentrate on his screen.

Eventually, Ray left, as Harry had hoped, because he'd decided to follow him to his home and see if there was anything he should know about.

A small whine changed his mind. Ignatius! What happened to him at night? The dog was looking longingly at the door Ray had gone through. Harry peeked into the kitchen. Hattie had filled his bowl with water and topped up his biscuits.

There wasn't time to do anything now.

'You be a good boy,' he said, closing the office door on Ignatius and stepping out.

He'd seen Ray's departing back go right, towards the river. He remembered Hattie and Ray joking at one point in the week about 'down by the riverside'. Maybe that was where he lived.

* * *

The path alongside the river stretched the entire length of town. He enjoyed himself, striding along, noting the way the water lapped up against the very walls of some of the properties. This was a proper, old-style town. In another world, he'd have been fascinated by its history. But his aim, he reminded himself, was to do a great job here so he could get back to journalistic civilisation.

As the path meandered along, Harry noticed a swan gliding by and a small, Thames-style eyot, where the splashing of water indicated children playing. He was getting out of the town centre by now and there was still no sign of Ray. He marched past a row of cottages, painted in pretty pastel pinks, blues and yellows.

Abruptly, the town and its buildings seemed to end, and Harry found himself wandering along a water meadow, spangled by yellow and purple flowers. Over his head, a late swallow swooped and screamed.

A herd of Jersey cows flicked and chomped at the top half of the field, while Harry felt the path becoming ever boggier. At the far end he could just about make out a small building.

A few minutes later he realised what it was: a very ancient caravan, almost hidden behind a twisted colony of brambles, halfway up the field. The caravan was in bad repair and covered in a green film of mould and, as he slowed, he could just about make out that the rear window was open. Maybe the farmer used it for something, although, given its shape – the kind of rhomboid effect that square things become before they collapse entirely – it didn't look long for this world. Harry walked nearer. Then he heard a female voice floating out of the structure.

'Quick, before anyone sees us. Have you got everything?'

Hattie!

Harry went and stood next to an alder and strained his ears. More talking – a low, male voice and then Hattie's again.

'You'll have to. When it's dark. Don't be daft, he won't notice.'

Harry felt very strongly that the 'he' she was referring to was him.

She was talking again, 'Look, I've got to go, I'm late already. Just do what I say, OK?' Then she slipped out of the caravan's door and towards the path, near to where he was hiding.

He really didn't want to be discovered there, spying on his staff. Carefully, he retreated towards the river and the cover of some willows. Broken and muddied by the Jersey cattle, the bank was very uneven. Harry gritted his teeth. In order not to be seen by Hattie, he'd have to go even deeper into the mud behind the trees. He prayed it wouldn't squelch.

She was walking straight towards him now. He wondered if he should think up a convincing excuse, in case he was spotted. But he needn't have worried. She was phoning someone.

'Hi! Yes? Sorry I'm late, I'll be home in a minute. Yes, of course. Love you.'

Keeping a careful eye on the caravan, after she had passed, Harry decided it would be a good idea to extricate himself from the mud. But the mud had other ideas. As he pulled and wrenched, he felt his brogue slipping off. He managed to pull it out, but it was filled with the stuff. As he pulled out his other leg, the other shoe slid off too.

Great. His only shoes. He had meant to go up to the caravan and speak to whoever was inside. But the window was closed now, and he knew that he would look a complete idiot trying to speak to anyone in no shoes.

As he began the long journey home, gingerly holding his shoes away from him, he was aware of two blonde children and a nervous-looking mum in a garden on the opposite bank, staring at his appearance.

'Mummy, why has that man got black legs and no shoes?'

Harry raised his hand to wave and smile, but was greeted by the sight of the mother wrenching the kids back towards their house. Perhaps it was best not to draw any more attention to himself just at that moment.

He managed to navigate the town centre with as much dignity as he could muster, ignoring the teens on skateboards who started laughing and photographing his shoeless appearance on their smartphones.

The Ball Inn was cool and dark as he arrived, and he wiped his feet on the scratchy doormat. He'd managed to wash his muddy legs and brogues off in the river, while chatting to one of the more credulous townsfolk about how it was lovely to paddle 'on a day like this'. Never mind, he could have a shower and change in a moment. The brogues were probably doomed. As silently as he could, he started the journey upstairs.

'Who got stuck in the mud, then?'

He looked down the stairs, then up. Cassandra was on the landing, laughing.

'How do you know what I've been doing?' he asked her.

'Ha! Word gets round fast, Harry. Very fast indeed round here.'

'Cassandra . . .' He sighed. 'Are you sure you're not descended from witches?'

'It has been said. Look, give me those,' she said, nodding towards the brogues, which looked as if they'd been retrieved from the Grimpen Mire. 'I'll get them clean for you.'

Back in his room, Harry shrugged into his bathrobe and decided to run a bath.

'I've already started running it,' said Cassandra, materialising in the doorway.

'Thanks,' he said. Maybe they should be doing a story about her . . .

Chapter 15

Harry awoke the next day to the sound of dripping. It was incessant. After ten infuriating minutes, he decided to get up and investigate. After opening the curtain, he saw why – rain was pouring down, clattering onto the roof tiles and rattling at the window.

Silently cursing, Harry stared at his phone – it was 5 a.m. He knew he couldn't get back to sleep and the Wi-Fi was so bad that – coupled with the lack of decent coffee at this hour – he couldn't work in bed. He needed to order some new shoes, trainers and perhaps some more trousers. Aside from the brogues, the only other footwear he possessed from his old life were a pair of unravelling navy-blue espadrilles.

He remembered that the town garage was open twenty-four hours and they did hot drinks. Maybe a croissant, too. He showered, dressed and slipped on the espadrilles. What had looked so chic on the Croisette at Cannes, as he covered the film festival, looked ridiculous when paired with his work trousers and perennial tweed jacket and tie. Especially with the rain pouring at this rate.

He hopped into the driver's seat of the Cooper, which provided a pleasant respite from the downpour, although it always made the interior damper. He often wondered why his mother had been so attached to this truculent old heap, which had been stored in a barn on the family grounds following her death. But, despite the smell, the dashboard lights and the thrumming noise every time he cornered, he would never give it up – he'd spent too many hours just sitting in it when the loss became overwhelming; one day he'd found one of her favourite earrings, lodged in the rusty floorpan, and that had made him feel she was nearby. Driving it made him feel closer to her.

After shuffling across the garage forecourt, earning a puzzled look from the assistant, who told him the coffee machine was broken and their bakery supplies were delayed, he pulled in to the *Gazette*'s courtyard, carefully closing the door to his car out of respect for those living in the area who were still fortunate enough to be asleep.

'It's nice to be nice,' he told himself, before locking the vehicle, shuffling across the cobbles and unlocking the door.

He was greeted by a terrible sight.

A tramp appeared to have broken in during the night and died amidst a heap of damp bedding. He could just about make out the shape of the man's head, covered with a Union Jack blanket. He'd obviously been sleeping on Ignatius's bed. Harry pushed the door open further.

The noise caused Ignatius to come waddling out of the kitchen area, barking. The dead body moved.

'Blimey, Ignatius, what's wrong with you now? You nearly gave me a heart attack,' said the voice coming from the tramp's bedding.

'Ray?'

The figure started to struggle up to a sitting position, coughing violently.

'Oh no, I said this would happen. Sorry, Harry, lad. What's happened to your feet?'

Harry looked down. The espadrilles appeared to be leaking a puddle's worth of water onto the carpet tiles. Ray wheezed and Ignatius pressed himself into his side, as another coughing fit took hold.

Harry kneeled down. 'Ray – why are you sleeping here? Has something happened?'

He tried to speak again but his words were consumed by another bout of coughing. Harry went to get a glass of water. When he got back, the old sub was sitting in his office chair. Pale, sweaty and with bloodshot eyes, he shook his head.

'Please don't be cross, lad. It was only for a few nights, till I can get on my feet.'

'I don't understand; I thought you had a place in town.'

'I did. Nice little caravan. Until the farmer told me he wanted it back – or wants the site back, anyway. Wants to put a little Airbnb *shepherd's hut* there instead. All the rage, apparently, these days. So, my caravan has to go. I was told to leave by yesterday.'

As if reading his mind, Ray continued: 'Accommodation isn't cheap in these parts. I'd had a bit of bad luck and the old farmer – I knew him from years back – said I could stay, but the young lad – his nephew or something – just wants to make money, so I had to go. Occupying a prime spot, I was, apparently.'

'I'll make us some tea,' said Harry. As he filled the kettle, his mind raced. Was it his job, as editor, to get embroiled in his staff's troubles? It probably was. But what could he do? He wasn't in a position to house Ray.

He brought the tea in and, in solidarity, braved the office coffee. The colour was returning to Ray's cheeks, but he still looked sweaty and shaky.

'Look, Ray, you can't stay here at night, but I'll think of something,' he said. 'I also think you need to see a doctor today, that cough sounds terrible.'

Ray grimaced. 'I don't want to be a trouble to anyone. I can do me job and . . .' He was interrupted by Hattie, arriving dripping and breathless through the door, which blocked her view of Harry at his desk.

'Ray, are you OK? I came as quick as I could. Mum's a bit—' A look from Ray silenced her and she spun round. 'Hi, Harry!'

He sighed. 'How long has this been going on?'

Hattie and Ray started at once and Ignatius whined.

Harry put up his hand. 'Look, Ray can't sleep here, it's a newsroom, not a hotel. For a start, we won't be insured for that kind of thing. Suppose there was a fire?'

'If there was a fire here at night, Ray could put it out,' said Hattie. 'Our insurance bill might even go down. You should tell Mr Green.'

Inwardly, Harry groaned. 'Hattie . . .' He rummaged in his wallet for his overwrought credit card. 'Please go to Brenda's and get me a proper coffee before I die. Get yourself and Ray something proper to eat, and me a cinnamon Danish. Or almond. And get Ignatius a muffin.'

She thanked him and rushed out. Ignatius put his head on Ray's knee.

'Why did you have to live there in the first place?'

Ray looked troubled. 'Stuff happened; I lost quite a few bob a while ago now. It was the gee-gees. But then I had a tip and a win enough to buy the caravan, and I'd helped the old farmer with a few stories in the past, so he let me stay there . . . until now. I've been saving up to rent a little place and I was owed some money for something, but what with one thing and another . . . You know.'

'I think the best thing for you is to go to The Ball Inn, tell Cassandra I sent you and ask for a room for the night. Then get a shower and get cleaned up, and come in when you're better. Right, where's Hattie?'

Ray pretended to look around. 'She'll not be long. She's a good girl. Give you the shirt off her own back, she would.'

'I don't want her shirt; I want her to actually stay in this office and do some work for a change.'

'She really does work hard,' Ray insisted.

When Hattie materialised with the food and drink, Harry felt better and, after gulping it all down, made a swift decision.

Leaving instructions for Hattie to contact the police for more information on the possible identification of the first roundabout body, he stepped out to his car, trying to dodge the giant drops of rain that were still exploding on the cobbles.

* * *

Parking outside Sadie Burge's house was non-existent. Cursing, Harry settled for a spot round the corner and pulled out his ancient, partially destroyed umbrella which resembled a one-winged bat. He then dashed quickly to her gate and waded up the path, where giant boughs of lavender slapped extra water on his trousers, which gleefully soaked up the liquid, along with the espadrilles. He banged on the door and then banged again.

This time there was no twitch from the downstairs nets. He stepped back to look at the higher windows and bumped into a person.

'Arrggghh!' shrieked Harry, jumping as Prudence Robarts's face glared at him, framed by an over-large tartan sou'wester.

'I saw you come in here and I wanted to ask you when you are going to have something done about this frightful mess, young man. And about that roundabout. You'd think, after everything that's happened, they would have cleared it by now.'

As rain began to cascade onto his shoulder from the broken umbrella, the God of news editors briefly decided to smile upon him, and he noticed the house's front door opening.

'Quick, Harry, come in,' croaked a voice. 'And you,' it growled, 'get off my property. You are not welcome here.'

Mrs Robarts, who was further insulated from the downpour by a large, grey mac, pushed her head past Harry.

'You should be ashamed of yourself, you dirty old woman.'

'Now come on,' said Harry, trying to edge himself towards the door. 'Please let's not forget our manners, Mrs Robarts.'

Sadie Burge emerged and smiled. 'Ha! You should be ashamed of *yourself*, Mrs Robarts. You come to this town from London and then try and impose your values on everyone. No one likes you; they think you are bourgeois.'

The insult didn't quite hit its mark. Probably because, thought Harry, Mrs Robarts would take it as a compliment and no one under the age of seventy would understand what it meant. But her hesitation did allow him to advance to the door and he stepped quickly inside. Sadie shut it with a dull thud and then they both began the process of inching past the piles of newspapers and towering cardboard boxes into the sitting room. It appeared even more crowded than before.

'Tea?' she asked.

He nodded. Anything, really, to speed things up. He heard a rustling noise and looked round, hoping against hope it wasn't one of the fabled rats.

A large, ginger form appeared from behind a pile of boxes.

'Hello, Mr Chagall,' said Harry. The cat moved its head forward, appearing to want a pat. Harry decided to risk it, before it swiftly sank its fangs into his hand. Again.

He screamed and flicked the creature off, just as Sadie was re-entering the room with a cracked teapot and two of the filthiest mugs he'd ever seen – and he was used to the mugs in a newsroom.

'What did you do to Mr Chagall?'

'He bit me,' said Harry, busily wrapping his handkerchief round his thumb.

'You shouldn't annoy him, he's a very sensitive cat,' said Sadie, laying the tray down on the edge of the filthy wooden table.

'Look, Mrs Burge . . . I mean, Sadie. I've come to tell you that they are planning to serve you with a notice imminently, to order you to get your home cleared. I've looked it all up and if you don't do as they say, they reserve the right to do it themselves and charge you for it.'

She shrugged and reached for the teapot, pouring the black liquid into each cup.

'I don't care.'

'You have to,' he said. 'It's serious. Someone at the council has told me about your file.'

She looked up at him.

'I've seen off far worse than a few officials with clipboards. They don't scare me.'

Patiently as he could, Harry tried to explain about the notice and the implacability of councils, plus the health hazard her hoard was probably creating.

'Can I ask, Sadie, why you don't want to live in a house that's a bit more, you know, tidy?'

She laughed, sloshing her tea. 'Tidy? You think I care about tidy? Do you know how much more to the world there is? Like the sun on your face, and the wind in your hair as you run down a hill. Like the freedom to choose what you want to do.'

He nodded, but it wasn't relevant. No one could choose to live like this, surely.

'Sadie,' he said, bringing out his notebook. 'Can I ask you, on the record, if there is any reason we should know of, for you not to want to clear the hoard or leave here?'

'This is my home. No one can take it from me or make me live in it in any way other than that I choose.'

She may be tiny, but she was fierce, thought Harry.

'Can I ask you a question?' she said.

'Ask away.'

'Why do you think that dreadful Robarts woman is so concerned about keeping this town all neat and tidy? If she didn't want to live in a place with wild plants and houses that are not all the same, why didn't she move somewhere dreadful, like Milton Keynes? Why did she come here?'

It was a bit unfair on Milton Keynes, but she had a point, even though, he thought, it was hardly relevant, either.

His phone beeped and Sadie tutted. 'Those awful things. They are eating your very soul.'

It was Hattie. The first body on the roundabout had been sent off for further tests but they could confirm that it, too, was the remains of an adult human male.

Hurrah!

Sadie sipped noisily and Mr Chagall reappeared, winding himself round her legs.

After tapping a quick text to Hattie, he looked up. 'Do you know much about Mrs Robarts, then?' May as well find out a bit about his constant adversary.

'I know she is what you'd call the town busybody – never stops poking in her nose where it's not wanted.'

'She's quite old, isn't she?'

'She's ninety,' said Sadie. 'I had to go into town once to buy some fresh chicken livers for Mr Chagall and I overheard her boasting about her age in a shop. She didn't see me and I was glad. I can't stand the way she won't leave people alone; if it's not the Flowers in Bloom, it's the football team kicking their balls. She should have stayed where she came from.'

'London, wasn't it?'

'Yes, she came from London and, if you ask me, there is a reason for that!' she said. 'I had heard there was some difficulty or unpleasantness with her husband, or about him. It was said they left the city in a hurry, but it would have been a long time ago. Perhaps he was sensible and had an affair with someone more pleasant? Or maybe they didn't pay their taxes? I never gossip so I never got to the bottom of it.'

Trying to hide his smile, he asked her for a quote.

'I need a statement from you regarding the council and this house, then I can write a story about it,' he said. 'Whatever you think, the council are serious but they will relax a bit if they can see you are tidying up. What about starting with the front garden and getting that cut down? Then people could see you are making an effort.'

She banged her cup down. 'No! I've told you; this is my home. I am hurting no one and this isn't a mess, it's a lifetime of work. Here's a statement for your newspaper. Let them do their worst. An Englishman's castle is his home. Now, if you don't mind, I have things to do.'

He knew when he was beaten and thanked her, then stood up and inched glumly towards the front door, trying not to breathe in the damp, solid air. He'd done his best. But he felt a pang of worry for the old lady and what he felt must be awaiting her. Assistance operations for the unpersuaded were rarely a happy affair, in his opinion.

As he left, she slammed the door and he shuffled down the treacherous path. A bullet-headed man walking a bullet-headed dog along the pavement stopped.

'Been in there, mate? You must be mental. One day she'll wake up eaten by rats, you mark my words.'

Harry opened his mouth to defend Sadie. But one look at the dog told him it was the stupidest idea he'd had since making the decision to open the envelope filled with phone-call transcriptions that had arrived on his desk in London.

Chapter 16

The rain had eased off as Harry made his way back to the Cooper. Miraculously, given the damp – a small puddle had formed around the passenger-seat sill – it started first time. He pulled away, doing two rights to get him back on the road and facing the right direction.

As he moved into the one-way system, he decided he could do with a sandwich, especially after the Sadie Burge tea horror. He knew there were a small amount of twenty-minute parking stops further along from Brenda's and, now it was dry again – although the streets sparkled with excess water – it was easy enough to walk to.

He pulled into a space and as he stepped into the road to avoid a twin buggy, pushed by a woman whose ear appeared to be surgically attached to a giant smartphone, he stopped.

He must be hallucinating. Because he was pretty sure he could see Violett Travers looking at her mobile phone in the entrance of a shop across the road.

His heart gave a thud. Her dark hair flowed down her shoulders, its shine enhanced by the sunlight that was bobbing in and out from behind the clouds. She was wearing an immaculate, stone-coloured trench coat belted over black trousers and was talking into her phone, head nodding every now and again, her back turned towards him.

Harry crossed the road, moved into the wide entrance of the nearby bicycle shop and listened discreetly.

She seemed to be agitated by something, shaking her head. He inched nearer. Thanks to the street's medieval acoustics, he couldn't hear the conversation.

The next part, after which she frowned and started wildly jabbing at the end-call button, was drowned out by a motorbike, which ripped the air around both of them, causing her to glance up. And to spot Harry.

'Oh my God! Harry? It's you!' Her face lit up and so did Harry's heart – he missed the way her eyes had always sparkled when she looked at him.

Within a few seconds, she was by his side; up close, she was as petite and perfectly formed as ever. 'Well, hello, my soggy-espadrilled stranger!'

He nodded, warily.

'What are you doing here?' she asked

Now it was his turn to be surprised. 'Didn't Jasper tell you? I got the editor's job at the local paper here.'

'Yes, now you mention it, I do remember him saying something. I just didn't realise it was this town, that's all. Didn't I read that they'd found a dead body on the roundabout here?'

'Two, actually,' said Harry.

Violett's jaw dropped. 'God, how awful. I mean, fantastic for you, news-wise, but those poor, poor families. Sounds like a serial killer.'

Harry reminded her there would have to be three bodies for that to happen.

'Of course – have they identified them yet?'

'One of the bodies was my predecessor. Grim, eh?'

Violett's eyes widened, then she frowned. 'Must be scary. How did they die? They both can't be accidents, surely?'

'Blunt force trauma to the head for the second one, but they aren't sure yet – or at least that's what we've been told,' said Harry, enjoying his chance to be the imparter of news.

Violett shivered. 'You'd never think it in a place like this, would you? It's really great to see you, you know . . . I've missed you,' she said, as she leaned into him, the familiar scent from her hair and her skin cream stealing about him like a spell.

Memories of their brief liaison started flooding back. As Harry straightened up, his phone pinged.

'Work?'

He nodded.

She smiled. 'I'm really happy for you! I mean, I know things have been difficult and I'm so pleased it's all worked out for you.'

Had it? Visions of the public trashing of his reputation and the loss of his dream job careered through his head.

But Violett was looking up at him, her sapphire eyes rapt and admiring, and he was suddenly overcome by an alternate vision: of days spent chasing fantastic stories, world-class craic and the salary to pay for it.

'Look, I know you are busy but can I take you for a coffee?' she asked. 'Or early lunch? Whatever you have time for, it's just so good to see you again.'

His first instinct was to say no. It was also his second instinct. But there was also another instinct, which he couldn't ignore. Apart from the one dinner with Ophelia, the last couple of years had been fairly lonely ones. Most of his social life had revolved around the *Daily News* and although he'd caught up with a few old school friends, they all seemed to be starting businesses or families, or giving up alcohol and taking up meditation, which didn't make for much of a fun evening out. What harm could a quick chat do?

'OK, but I've got to go off pretty quick.'

She was looking around. 'Do you know anywhere that actually serves proper coffee in this place?'

There was Brenda's but he couldn't face the questions. And there was no seating. There was also The Ball Inn, but he'd never hear the end of it from Cassandra. And there was the Ball Hotel. It wasn't exactly the Ritz but he reckoned there would at least be some privacy for them among the Tudor timbers and the ancient wooden booths.

'Come on.'

* * *

They walked down the imaginatively named Side Street and entered the hotel's sunless bar. Violett gestured for him to take one of the cosy booths at the end of the room and he was only too pleased to see her paying for their coffees.

As she returned, he started asking her about the news scene in London, and Violett obliged, explaining that her new associate editor's job meant strategising and managing stories of personal interest to Sir Jimmy Knox, on top of keeping an eye on Jasper and the newsroom and all its works. In addition to this, she poured out premier gossip about superinjunctions, royal indiscretions and who was really pulling the levers of government.

He'd forgotten how fun it was to have her around and for a minute he found himself transported back to his old life: the pace, the fun and the non-stop entertainment. Before she was promoted, they had worked on a few investigations together and he remembered thinking then how much fun it had been. Working in a busy national newsroom had been like living on a giant merry-go-round in the centre of the universe and he felt an enormous stab of longing. Piddlington Minster was like the moons of Jupiter. You may have heard of them, but when it came down to it, no one really gave a monkey's.

As he sipped his coffee, Violett fell silent and examined her manicure. Then she started talking again.

'You know, I've got a bit of a confession to make.'

'Go on.'

'You might have guessed already, but I did actually know you were working here and that's one of the reasons I came. I understood why you stopped replying to my texts but I wanted to tell you how sorry I am about everything that happened. *Really* sorry. I still can't understand how it turned out like that. Jasper told me that he'd sorted it all and I believed him.'

She looked up at him, eyes catching the light from the bar's dim lamps, and he tried to remain dispassionate.

Harry muttered a hasty, 'It's fine,' but Violett had started talking again.

Work was 'manic', the paper was 'not the same' without him and Sir Jimmy Knox's demands were getting even more erratic and unreasonable.

'In what way?'

She leaned forward, her hair caressing Harry's outstretched hand. He felt a jolt of that old chemistry.

'You remember he'd got into art collecting? Well, he has become totally obsessed. To the point of mania, I'd say. To him, they are a bit like those Pokémon cards, you remember, that all the kids used to collect way back – he's got to have the full set. And . . .' Here she dropped her voice, so Harry had to lean forward even further, his head now practically touching hers. 'He's trying to obtain two particular paintings.'

'Which are?'

'The first one is a Jackson Pollock, which he insists you can see the image of his face in. That belongs to an American tech billionaire who thinks it also depicts the image of *his* face, so not much will happen there, because he's worth about three times as much as Sir Jimmy, if you can believe that. But the one he really wants is this Picasso. It's so special that no one even seems to know what it actually looks like.'

'How does he know he wants it, then?'

'He heard about it on the grapevine a few years back and you know what he's like. I'm not kidding, it's literally all he goes on about. Even when I'm supposed to be working, he's on at me to try and find out where it is and how he can get hold of it.'

He could imagine. Sir Jimmy was well-known for playing his employees off against each other, and over the years, his random enthusiasms had struck terror into the hearts of his staff, who lived in fear of being forced into supporting them. Known as the Twelve Labours of Jockules, for their hopeless impossibility, they ranged from his campaign to prove some lunatic academic's theory that the Lost City of Atlantis was really off the coast of Blackpool, to his strenuous attempts to have Glasgow declared the new capital of Scotland.

Harry remembered the rare Scotch phase – all the newsroom had to do was produce endless articles about the very expensive hard stuff and how it was going to replace Bitcoin as a valuable investment. Which it possibly was, until Sir Jimmy had consumed his entire cellar in a rage, when his prize racehorse had run off the track at a major meeting, escaped into a traveller settlement and got pregnant by a sturdy piebald.

'That's the other reason why I'm here . . .' said Violett, holding his gaze.

'In Piddlington Minster?'

'Well, yes.' She looked down at her coffee. She seemed to be weighing up something.

'I understand there's this old billionaire bloke who lives in this area and collects art, and there is a strong rumour that he has this painting Sir Jimmy is after.'

'Do you mean Lionel Green?'

'Do you know him?'

'I wouldn't say know, exactly.'

'Do you know he is an art collector?'

Harry calculated. She'd mentioned rumours, so more than a few people must know about Lionel and his extraordinary art collection. He wouldn't be infringing anything by going a little further, surely?

'I do.'

Her face lit up. 'Wait, have you been to his house? You have, haven't you?'

'Maybe.'

Violett sat back and batted her eyes. 'I knew it would take no time for Harry Hedges to charm everyone in a ten-mile radius. Did you see any Picassos?'

Enjoying the moment, he leaned forward. 'It's not that easy. I've signed an NDA. You can't just break those. You should know that.'

She touched his hand. 'Of course! I completely understand.'

Violett sipped her coffee and Harry finished his, relishing the quiet moment.

She carefully placed her cup in its saucer and stared at him. 'You haven't asked me about my other reason for coming here.'

'Go on, then.'

'I'm not just here to say I've missed you. I really want you to come back to a real newsroom, where you belong. London . . . or something even better? I want to help you, after everything you've had to go through.'

He laughed. 'That sounds like a nice dream, but how? Not sure I could believe it, who would take a chance on me now?'

Violett looked at him knowingly. 'Sir Jimmy is more obsessed with getting this Picasso artwork than anything else. It's called

The Purple Child. If I let him know you were the one who helped bring it to him, I can't think of much he wouldn't do for you. Even after all the . . . difficulties.'

'Hang on a minute. Even give me my old job?'

'Or the New York job. If you'd prefer. Selfishly, I'd rather have you back in London . . . but I understand if you'd want a fresh start.'

Harry hoped his jaw hadn't fallen open. The New York job was the most prized on the entire paper, coming as it did with a comparatively gargantuan salary, an even more gargantuan expenses account and a corner office. Far more important, however, was the fact that Manhattan was a whole ocean, a six-hour flight and an entire time zone away from Sir Jimmy Knox.

'It's confidential at the moment, but the New York bureau chief has had some kind of mid-life crisis – went on a holiday to the Far East, decided to become a soothsayer or something, and is planning to live in a cave with a yak.' Violett sighed. 'We've kept it under wraps, but he'll be leaving at the end of the month. All I have to do is put in the right word and it could be yours.'

'Really? Sir Jimmy did say I had no place in any newspaper, if you remember.'

'Oh, you don't want to pay any attention to that. Yes, really. I have some powers to hire and fire these days.'

He didn't know what to believe and decided to play for time. 'What exactly would all this entail?'

'Well, first of all I'd need to know whether your Mr Green actually does have this painting,' began Violett. 'Then, if he did, ideally, I'd need you to ask him if he'd sell it.'

Abruptly, she stood up. 'I'm going to the ladies'. Please have a think about what I've said. It would be so good to have you back.'

As she disappeared into the hotel's hallway, Harry thought quickly. Violett's idea that Lionel Green would give up one of his precious artworks was ridiculous. But he was fascinated to know more about the whole thing. It must be pretty important for her to have decided to come to Piddlington Minster in person, although, he knew of old, it was often easier to acquiesce to Sir Jimmy Knox's demands than reason with the old crocodile. And he was pretty sure that more than a few people knew of Lionel's collection.

Violett had certainly mentioned rumours circulating about its existence and even who owned it. What about Kevin Fewtrell? He'd been to The Grange, hadn't he? For all Harry knew, he was the source of those rumours. Or what about workmen over the years, or former staff? Pub gossip? Local gossip? Internet gossip? Put like that, any number of people must have seen *The Purple Child* and the other works and spoken about them. He really wouldn't be breaking any confidences.

Swamped in a swirl of possibilities, Harry decided to play along, telling the returning Violett, 'Actually, there was one painting which was a lot of squares and circles, and another was sort of a giant eye on a stalk, all mauve and black and blue.'

Her face lit up. 'Wowsers, Harry, I really think that could be the one Sir Jimmy wants! It would be amazing if it was and if you could ask Mr Green if he'd sell it.'

Harry laughed. 'He loves his paintings and he's a very private person.'

But Violett persisted. 'Of course, I completely understand, but could you try? Just once? Or be a sort of messenger? Don't worry, in a way, it's absolutely fine if he says no. I'd totally expect him to. But if you ask him, I'll be able to tell Sir Jimmy quite honestly that we've all done our best to track down and obtain the painting for him and it's no dice, then recommend you for the job and tell him you've gone the extra mile. He'll listen to me.'

It certainly was tempting; could he really get his old life back? As easy as that? He agreed to think about it.

Violett squealed. 'Thank you, Harry.' Then she leaned forward to kiss him. Surprised by the move, he closed his eyes for a millisecond.

When he opened them again, Violett had moved back into her seat and was looking startled at an irritated Sergeant Starsky.

'Oh, hi, Ophelia,' Harry stammered.

Violett smoothed her mac down as they both stood up.

'Don't get up on my account,' said Ophelia, looking Violett up and down.

'You must be the local copper,' said Violett, flashing her brightest smile.

'Ophelia, this is Violett Travers, and Violett, this is the town's top law enforcer, Sergeant Ophelia Starsky. We were just catching up.'

Ophelia ignored him. 'I came in here because Brenda wanted me to let you know the warden's just slapped you with a ticket on that heap.'

She turned on her heel and walked out. Violett looked concerned.

'Have I caused an upset?'

'She's not my girlfriend, if that's what you mean,' said Harry, quickly. 'We have a professional relationship and there's been a lot to discuss, crime-wise, around here recently.'

'I bet. So I haven't just witnessed a lovers' tiff, have I?' she said, looking pensive.

'God no, we had a drink once.' He shoved the memories of the Flying K burgers to the back of his mind.

'Well, she'd be a lucky lady if she was.' She flashed a megawatt smile and started fishing in her handbag.

'I've changed my number so here's my new one,' she said, pulling out a plain white business card.

He still wasn't sure how he'd approach Lionel Green about the painting. But he was fascinated by Violett's eagerness. And he'd enjoyed the glimpse back into London life.

When he reached his car, even the presence of the ticket couldn't daunt him. He removed it, chucked it into the small puddle in the passenger footwell and drove back to the office.

Chapter 17

Hattie was typing demurely as he walked through the door; Ray's seat was empty. The half hour he'd spent with Violett made him view the distinctly provincial room more critically. Not only did it smell of mould, but it also smelled of old, wet dog.

'Would you like a coffee?' asked Hattie.

He thanked her but said no, pleading busyness.

'How was Mrs Burge?'

He explained the situation. 'She won't do anything; I fear they'll just kick her out.'

'That is so cruel, how can they?'

'Well, to be honest, the place is disgusting – it just smells. Which, I'm sad to say, is something that applies to in here too.'

Hattie looked astonished. 'I could buy us a scented candle? They have some really boujee ones at the minster gift shop.'

He shook his head and took the plunge. 'I'm sorry to have to say this, but it's Ignatius. Not only does he smell, but he really has no right to be here, as I keep telling you. He's also an insurance risk.'

She shook her head as Ignatius emerged from the kitchen, water dripping from his whiskers. He put his head on Hattie's knee.

'He knows you're being horrible about him. And, anyway, what rule says we can't have a guard dog here?'

He ignored the challenge.

'If he hadn't been here, poor Ray might have frozen to death. He cuddled up with him to share body warmth.'

'It's September,' said Harry. 'No one freezes of anything at this time of year.'

'They might.'

The mention of Ray reminded him that he needed to check on him, and he called The Ball Inn.

Cassandra's voice purred down the phone. Yes, Ray was fine, she'd fed him a steak and kidney pie. The hot water had been on all morning and she'd put some of her own scented oil in his bath, so he was nice and clean. He was now enjoying a nice drink in the bar and then he'd go up for a nice nap. She'd send the bill to Harry.

He sighed. He'd have to ask Greta Sargent and pray Lionel Green would be kind enough to pay up.

Cassandra started laughing.

'Glad someone's happy!' he said.

'Judging by what I've just heard, it sounds like you're the one who should be happy. Didn't fancy bringing your young lady to my little inn, eh?'

Oh no. Bloody town gossips. He didn't want to fall out with her – best to brazen it out. 'I don't know what you mean.'

'I think you do! I hope she was worth getting that ticket for.'

* * *

Hattie pretended to type very fast while peering at her screen.

'Ray's OK,' said Harry, unnecessarily.

'Yes, but he'll soon need somewhere proper to live, won't he?'

'I'm sure the council will do all they can to help him when the time comes.'

Her mouth hardened. 'I've lived in this town my whole life. They don't help anyone. They are a bunch of cold-hearted bastards. It'll be Sadie Burge, next, you see.'

He opened his mouth to protest and remind her about the dossier of discontent at the council but realised it was pointless.

He emailed the council about Sadie and stared into the middle distance, wondering how Violett would go about securing the painting for Sir Jimmy Knox. He could imagine her going up there herself. Door knocking had always been one of her specialities.

His thoughts were interrupted by a bang on the office door and a be-gloved Prudence Robarts stepping through.

'I've come to see how you're getting on with everything.'

Harry sighed. 'Mrs Robarts, we are a newspaper. I've told you that when we have news, it will be in the weekly print copy and on the website. Now, if you'll excuse us, we've got work to do.'

He looked down and began to type. The old lady remained obstinately in position.

'I know you went round there this morning. What did she say?'

He stood up, startling Ignatius, who yelped.

'Mrs Robarts. Please, will you stop barging into my office and disturbing my staff. I am running a newspaper here, not a personal news service for you or anyone else. I suggest you buy the paper, and that will tell you everything we know. Now, if you'll excuse me, goodbye.'

'Not until I get any answers. Keep Britain Tidy are coming in three weeks. What is it going to look like if they see that disgusting hovel and that roundabout? What are they going to think of us then?'

'I don't know,' he said. 'But what I can tell you is that if you don't leave, I'm going to have to use force.'

He was aware of Hattie quietly stopping her work. He walked over and opened the door. Mrs Robarts appeared to press her block-heeled shoes more firmly into the rotting coir doormat.

'I demand satisfaction.'

He placed his hand in the small of her back and leaned forward to pull the door open.

'How dare you, this is common assault,' she screeched.

As Harry walked her out onto the cobbles in what he hoped was a humane manner, he was aware of one of the owners of the Life & Style Store staring disapprovingly at the spectacle as she took a bag of rubbish to the communal bin.

'Thank you, thank you, Mrs Robarts,' he said, preparing to let go and nip back inside before she could put another scary foot in the door.

He needn't have bothered. She strode across the cobbles and out under the arch in deadly earnest.

'Brace yourself for a visit from Sergeant Starsky,' predicted Hattie when he returned to the office.

* * *

They didn't have long to wait.

Within fifteen minutes, PC Collins had arrived in the courtyard, unfolding his limbs in a precise manner as he exited the police car, and putting his hat on.

Angrily, Harry pressed his terminal's sleep button and awaited the tirade.

While Hattie hid in the kitchen, pretending to make tea, and Ignatius enjoyed the officer's affectionate pat to the head, he tried to explain what had happened. Even he had to admit that attempting to bundle a tiny nonagenarian from the premises of the local newspaper was not a good look.

'We've received a complaint,' began PC Collins, outlining a potential list of crimes against the person.

'I'm really sorry, PC Collins,' Harry said, hoping he sounded sincere.

'I'm not sure that I'm the one you should be apologising to.'

'Would it help if I apologised to her, then?'

PC Collins nodded. 'Very much so. I'm also sure that if you promised her a nice, double-page spread about whatever she's on about this week and let her go on a bit, you'd find that all this would probably melt away.'

'So, I should choke on humble pie, just because she's an interfering old biddy who makes accusations and threatens people whose mess she doesn't like? I bet she's racist too,' he added, hoping to hit a raw nerve.

'We're not here to discuss unfounded allegations of racism, though, are we?' said PC Collins. 'And, with respect, I think I'd know a lot more about racism than you. What with being Black *and* Irish.'

Harry knew when he was beaten.

'Sorry, PC Collins. It's been a bit of a day. Don't worry, I will publish something substantial. If it'll help?'

'It will. And apologise. Like you mean it,' said PC Collins, brushing off the hairs and drool that had transferred from Ignatius to his trouser leg.

'Excuse me?' Hattie's voice piped up as she entered the room. He smiled at her.

'What can I do you for?'

She smiled. 'Nothing. Actually, that's not entirely true. I just wanted to say thanks for the soda bread and ask if there's any more news on the bodies?'

He shook his head. 'I'm sure we'll have something new soon but there's a lot to look into.'

'Any details?'

'More than my job's worth.' He smiled. 'Now, if you don't mind, I'd better be going, and, for the sake of peace and quiet, I'd like to know this apology piece will be published in your next edition, Mr Hedges?'

He agreed it would.

'Better get going on it today, hadn't you?'

He nodded. There was nothing else to say.

Chapter 18

It was only after PC Collins had left that Harry realised he didn't know Prudence Robarts's phone number or her address.

Hattie said she could help with that.

'She lives in one of those prissy bungalows on the east side of town, Godolphin Court. I bet you could guess which one was hers from the outside – it's all covered in baskets, with those creepy-looking flowers that never seem to die, but it's actually Number 13.'

Harry swallowed. 'Look, I hope this doesn't sound strange.'

He stopped himself. Actually, he was the editor and could do what he liked.

'I'm afraid I'm rather busy and I'm concerned there'll be another incident if I go, so please can you do this interview and make our apologies?'

'I thought PC Collins said you should go round?'

Harry shook his head. 'I'm not sure that was the agreement at all.'

Hattie considered. 'OK, I'll do it. But I need to have the rest of the afternoon off. And tomorrow afternoon, too.'

'What?'

'You heard. I need that time for something important, thanks.'

Harry nodded. He was too busy to care. 'Fine, just don't mess it up.'

'That's not very nice, considering you caused it in the first place.'

He sighed. Hattie, Ray, being an editor . . . It was all very nice and had fitted into his career rehabilitation plans very well. But the pay was a pittance, and he was beginning to feel strongly that despite his initial hopes, he wasn't really built to live in a backwater like this. Seeing Violett had been like glimpsing a tiny fragment of what he still regarded as his proper life, and he realised how much he missed it.

'Look, sorry, it's just been an annoying day. Mrs Robarts would test the patience of anybody. Of course you can have the afternoon off.'

'Afternoons.'

'Of course. Have a good time.'

Ignatius whined as she left the dingy room but, with no one to hear, Harry told him to pipe down and get on his bed. The dog glowered at him for a full five minutes, before turning round and round on the bed six times, and then loudly and thoroughly washing his doggy bits.

Lovely.

Still, it gave Harry time to think about how he could trace Lionel Green's sister. It would be a nice thing, to be able to reunite the two of them if, by some miracle, she was still alive. Something Prudence Robarts said had stuck in his mind. She was ninety and had lived in London. It was quite possible there were a fair few sprightly ladies like this around the nation.

Maybe that would narrow it down a bit. There couldn't be that many ninety-year-olds who fitted the criteria.

And then there was the sister's name. Would it be hard to run a check of all the UK's Sarahs of that age, he wondered. A quick bit of research showed that if he joined one of the heritage tracing websites, he might be able to narrow things down far more. Fine. He'd borrow the office's ancient laptop and do that this evening.

He texted to ask Hattie how the interview had gone, although he knew he'd have to wait a while before she replied. He wondered what her 'important' task must be. For someone he saw every day, he realised he knew very little about her, yet she had lived in this town all her life, apparently.

He considered her living circumstances. It was odd she never talked about her family, although there had been that moment when Prudence Robarts had been about to mention her father, and she'd looked very agitated.

He googled 'Piddlington Minster' and 'Watson'. And then kicked himself when pages of Hattie's name came up, because of her bylines. Nothing useful there. He should have realised. He wondered if she was estranged from her family and felt a pang of sympathy before remembering she'd mentioned her mother. He also wondered where she lived. He hoped it wasn't that godforsaken estate at the crummy end of town.

* * *

He banged out a few more stories and made some adjustments to the website.

A text pinged onto his phone from Hattie.

You owe me. Old bat spent ages going on about how bad the paper was. But I've got the stuff you need and said how sorry you were. See u tomoz and don't forget about Ray.

Yes, yes and yes, he replied.

Harry hoped Ray wouldn't expect him to sit and drink with him all evening. He'd just have to tell him he was busy.

The phone pinged again.

Don't forget to feed Ignatius and change his water.

He'd do it now, before he forgot. For once, Ignatius seemed very grateful, wagging his tail and appearing to smile.

'Why can't you live with Hattie?' he asked him. Ignatius looked doleful. It wasn't just him, was it? Keeping a dog in an office was just weird, thought Harry. It wasn't as if he could catch rats or anything, although Hattie had told him that Ignatius had once chased an enormous spider from the room. 'I think he must have eaten it,' she'd concluded.

He glanced at his watch. 'I'm the boss of me,' he said to Ignatius, and decided to leave.

* * *

Reluctant to return to The Ball Inn so early, he decided to take a drive round, checking out some parts of the town he hadn't seen yet, while he thought about Violett's request and the bodies on the roundabout.

As he set off into the one-way, instead of continuing round, he turned off to the right and ambled through a few streets of pleasant 1920s semi-detached residences to the town's south. He passed a short parade of shops with a little service road in front of them. Attempting to turn left to go north, he found himself travelling down the road beside the hideous block of flats where he'd seen Hattie. Harry stared at the building. With the sun off it, it looked even meaner: grimy and graffitied. Funny how Hattie hadn't suggested they do a story about that.

He watched as a boy wearing a hoodie spat on the ground close to an abandoned stripey mattress.

At the top of the block's outdoor concrete staircase, he saw what looked like an elderly woman in a wheelchair. Another, younger, woman came out of a door and joined her. Hattie! She hauled the older woman to a standing position and helped her to hold on to the metal stair rail while she folded up the wheelchair.

She then clambered down the three flights of stairs, wielding the chair and opening it up when she reached the bottom. Then she ran upstairs again and wrapped her arms around the woman, whose head was bowed. Harry felt nervous. She wasn't going to help this person down the concrete stairs, was she? He was a grown man, and he'd have found it difficult enough.

As Hattie helped the woman manoeuvre first one leg, and then the other down the flight of stairs, he realised the spitting youth was approaching the wheelchair. The grey hood slipped down and he could see a cruel, hard little face, grinning. As the boy grabbed the chair and started pushing it away, Harry leaped from his car.

'Oy! Yes you, you little scrote. Bring that back! Bring it *back*.' He caught up with the youth and grabbed his hood, swinging him round. The boy screamed: 'Get off me, you old perv!'

Infuriated by the 'old' reference, Harry yelled back, 'Put that down.' Whipping out his press pass, he waved it in the brat's direction and let go of the hood.

'I'm an undercover police officer, OK?' The youth looked deeply underwhelmed as he sloped away. Harry tried to look threatening and when he looked up, he could see Hattie's head poking over the railing.

'Harry? What are you doing here?'

He couldn't think what to say.

'I was just, er, passing and then I saw this little toad trying to take a wheelchair and . . .'

He could tell by her face that she didn't really believe him. The woman was leaning heavily on Hattie's slight frame and, from what he could see, she looked exhausted.

'Are you all right?' he asked the both of them.

'Yes,' said Hattie, faintly.

The woman did not look fine, thought Harry. Locking his car, he moved towards the concrete staircase and walked up the stinking flights of steps.

As he rounded the corner, he could see a defiant look on Hattie's face.

'I'm fine. We're fine. We can cope.'

'Whoever said you couldn't?'

'People.'

'Aren't you going to introduce us?'

The woman looked up and Hattie looked down.

'This is my mother, Barbara. Mum, this is Harry Hedges, my new editor.'

Barbara looked grey and whispered, 'Pleased to meet you.'

Hattie shook her head. 'I'll explain it all in a minute, although I don't see that I have to. Can you help me get Mum downstairs?'

He leaped forward, but assisting Barbara was difficult.

'Wouldn't it be easier to live on the ground floor?'

'You have to have what they give you,' said Hattie. 'And you're supposed to be grateful.'

Something was going badly wrong here.

As he grunted and shuffled, he asked, 'Are you going anywhere?'

Hattie explained that she liked to be able to take her mum for a walk when she finished work. 'I have to check on her in the day, too.'

As she settled Barbara in the wheelchair, the older woman seemed to regain her energy and the three of them chatted about the town and the weather as they set off.

'Hattie's such a good girl,' said Barbara. 'She never thinks of herself. I'm always telling her not to worry about me, but she does, you know.'

There was such love in her voice that Harry felt tearful. 'Has it always been like this?'

She laughed. 'No, I was diagnosed with MS ten years ago, not long after Des – that's my ex-husband, Hattie's dad – went to prison for fraud. It happened in the same month. Found out he'd stopped paying the mortgage because of his gambling debts and my name had never got on the deeds, even though he'd said it had. Anyway, we lost the house and got rehoused here.'

Hattie nodded, looking stricken.

Harry glanced at his watch. He'd been so taken up with this story that he'd forgotten about Ray.

'Will you be OK getting back?' he asked, realising they'd walked quite a way.

'Of course, I've done it every day for years. Why do you think I have to keep leaving the office?'

He could have kicked himself. He should have guessed there was some reasonable explanation.

'Look, I have to go now but tomorrow I want to hear more, Hattie. Lovely to have met you, Barbara.'

'Yeah right,' Hattie muttered, and Barbara waved as Harry walked back to his car which, miraculously, still had all its wheels.

As he unlocked the vehicle, he glanced up at the graffitied staircase, imagining it in the rain and covered in ice. This was no place for two vulnerable women.

Chapter 19

Harry went straight into the bar at The Ball, where Cassandra was nowhere to be seen. George the barman smiled over to him as he shoved his phone in his pocket.

'All right, Harry?'

'All right, mate, thanks. Can I have a gin and tonic?'

'Ooh, bit of a change for you?'

He admitted it was, but he wanted something cold and sharp. He decided not to mention that crunching up and swallowing ice was also one of his favourite sensations.

'Good day?' he asked George.

It had been. Loads of people in, a couple of tourists down for the day, business people stopping off.

Harry nodded. He let his mind wander. It alighted on the conversation he'd had with Violett. Whatever he thought of her and her request, he couldn't help pondering the idea of working in New York. Maybe one day . . .

Turning his attention back to the present, he decided that the best way he could accelerate his prospects was to do a great job for Lionel Green and discover what had happened to his sister.

He guessed Greta Sargent would have already gone through the public records but there was no harm in doing so himself.

He glanced at his watch, then at George. 'What's the special tonight?'

'Artisan sausages, celeriac mash and you can probably guess the rest.'

'Peas and *jus de gravy*?'

'*Petit pois* to you!'

He ordered his meal for 7 p.m. and enquired after Ray.

'He's a fascinating old boy, isn't he? We were chatting away earlier about all your work on the paper, but he's gone out for a walk now, I think. Cassie's been fussing round him all day.'

Harry could imagine. At least it would cheer Ray up.

* * *

There was a bit of time and instead of wasting it, he decided to remain in the bar and try to do some online research about the Sarah Greens of this world, using the antiquated office laptop. If Lionel's sister was dead and he could prove it, it would be very helpful in bringing some kind of closure and the man's gratitude, he thought.

An hour later, after joining two heritage websites, he'd located several potential leads. Most Sarahs had married once, a few had married twice. There was even a candidate in London itself, which he favoured. Perhaps he could apply for her birth certificate? Then he noticed something else. A Sarah Prudence Green, from Ealing, who had become a Mrs Roberts. Who had an address in Dorset.

True, the address wasn't Piddlington Minster, but then he noticed something else, and a tiny shiver rattled his spine.

As was the case with documents produced before digitisation, the writing on the online certificate was almost impossible to decipher. The person who had filled in the new Mrs Roberts's name had an infuriating habit of slanting their words to the left, instead of right, offending Harry's public-school ideal that all handwriting should slope forward.

As he squinted at the certificate, he called to George for another gin and tonic.

'Coming up.'

The way the word had been written looked different every time. Harry stared. Yes, her new name was initially given as Roberts, this Sarah lady. But on the certificate of marriage, it looked distinctly like Robarts.

It was a very unusual name. A very unusual name, right here, in Dorset . . .

Could it be possible that the woman he was searching for was the appalling Prudence Robarts?

Of course, he told himself, she was called Prudence, not Sarah. But people often changed their names without changing their documentation, especially in the past, when there were far fewer checks, and if the certificate could be believed, it was this woman's middle name.

He gulped down his gin. There was nothing for it. He'd have to go round to her bungalow himself. He had to know if, by some almighty miracle, Prudence Robarts was actually Sarah Green. Put like that, it didn't sound likely. But it might be an enormous help in convincing Lionel Green that he was at least trying to assist him with the search for his sister.

He decided to make the gin his last, eat dinner and go straight to bed.

* * *

He awoke in pitch darkness. The light was glowing from his phone. It looked as if his father had tried to call. Knowing the technophobic Geoffrey, he'd done it by accident, but by then Harry was wide awake. *Wouldn't do any harm to check in on him.*

He pressed call and was shocked to find the phone picked up immediately.

'Pa?'

'Oh! It's you!'

Who had he expected it to be?

'Is everything OK?'

Silence.

'What's the matter?'

'Nothing, I'm so sorry, I must have pressed the wrong button. Very fiddly things, these phones.'

Given that Geoffrey was not the kind to call anyone in the middle of the night, Harry didn't believe him.

'Look, Pa, I'm getting worried now. Are you ill? What's happened?'

Geoffrey let out a long, wobbly sigh. 'I had hoped not to trouble you with this, but I'm going to have to put more of my own money into the company to help with the cashflow.'

'How bad?'

'I'm selling the house. It's the only thing left, really. If I can't pay off the debt, I'll lose the company and it'll get in the papers. We can't afford any more . . . *unpleasantness.*'

Harry closed his eyes. Their home was as beautiful as it was valuable. He knew his father loved it and that it must be the last link for Geoffrey with Isabella.

His father was talking again, more easily now, as if the burden had been slightly relieved by his admission. 'It would be entirely natural for a man of my age and circumstances to downsize to something more suitable. I don't think it would attract attention in the papers, would it?'

Once again, Harry felt the sadness coursing through him.

'Pa, I'm so sorry. Is there anything I can do?'

Geoffrey's hesitation told him everything he needed to know. Unless he could magic up the cash to secure the company, the answer was: nothing. And given that he had been the cause of so much stress to his father on top of it all . . .

Geoffrey was talking again. 'I shouldn't have called now, but I was trying to text because I didn't want you to find out about the house from anyone else. Anyway, how's that car running?'

Harry assured him it was as temperamental as usual but still going.

'Ah. Excellent news. Splendid. Well, you go off to sleep now, or you'll be fit for nothing tomorrow.'

As he bade his father goodbye, Harry reflected.

If only he could get him the money. Visions of New York and dollar signs drifted into his head.

He looked at his phone again. It was 3 a.m. He hated 3 a.m. That was the time he'd awoken to the sound of the police arriving.

The memories came flooding back, pooling dark and cold in his mind. He'd been eleven when Isabella died. She'd taken to going out in the evenings a lot by then, as his father toiled at the business. At the beginning of this phase of her life she'd come home smelling of Mitsouko perfume, wine and a faint whiff of cigarettes, and she would kiss him while she tucked him in. He'd felt safe and warm and loved.

But, gradually, she'd come home later and later. Occasionally, he'd heard raised voices in the small hours – hers husky and monosyllabic, his father's louder and then more pleading. He'd never tried to make out what they were saying, he didn't want to. And during the daytime they seemed happy enough – she pottered around their enormous house, producing the occasional portrait in her studio, while his father went to and from work.

Just as his eyes were closing, his phone lit up again.

Violett.

Can't sleep and was thinking of you. So glad we talked. The offer's still on, if you're interested.

Harry groaned. Getting involved with anything to do with the *Daily News* was a mug's game. Sir Jimmy Knox even more so. But: money. Also: kudos.

He was desperate to drift off, but his mind kept jerking him awake. If he could clinch the New York job, the generous salary that came with it would mean he could pay off his overdraft and offer a few quid to Geoffrey. It would also mean the kind of high-octane work life he was used to and still hankered after in his dreams. And all he had to do to be considered for the job, it appeared, was ask Lionel about the painting. Given that quite a few people seemed to know about the artwork, that wouldn't be so bad, would it?

Better still, if he could find the sister, maybe Lionel would be so happy that he would consider selling the painting.

He lay on his back, staring upwards. He mentally road-tested a few scenarios. None seemed to work, and most ended with Ophelia arriving with a pair of handcuffs and a sorrowful-looking PC Collins.

He sighed. There was one possibility, however. He could visit Lionel Green and mention that he was on the trail of his sister, show him a copy of the online certificate and then stall for time while he tried to persuade him to at least consider selling *The Purple Child* to Sir Jimmy. As a strategy, it was flimsier than a butterfly's wing, but it would have to do.

Before he could talk himself out of it, he texted Violett.

Maybe.

She texted back a series of hearts and kisses.

* * *

He wondered if he dared tiptoe downstairs to the pub's kitchen and raid it for a cup of hot milk – Isabella had always made this for him when he couldn't sleep – and maybe a cheese sandwich. He suddenly felt starving.

Popping on his moleskins and a grey sweatshirt, he quietly let himself out of the room and began his progress towards the old and slightly lopsided staircase. Each tread produced its own different squeak and at the bottom step, he turned and made his way towards the kitchen.

Gently, he pushed the double doors and felt around for the switch. A second later the room was flooded with a spooky blue light. He opened the fridge to see a giant block of cheddar and three pints of milk.

Fantastic! He got a knife and chiselled off a large hunk of the cheese, fetched a slice of granary bread and wrapped it round the piece, before pouring the milk into a pan and setting it to boil.

The crackle of the milk heating filled his ears. So much so that he didn't hear the sound of a person entering the room.

'And what do you think you're doing?'

Cassandra was standing there in a pink negligee, her platinum hair wrapped in a pink scarf. And she was holding a large shotgun, pointed directly at him.

'Bloody hell, Cassandra! You scared me! What the hell is that?'

'My old hunting rifle.' She sniffed, breaking it and putting it on the kitchen's stainless-steel island. 'You scared the lights out of me, walking around in the dead of night.'

He apologised and explained about being unable to sleep. And then thinking about his mother, and feeling hungry.

'Thought as much,' said Cassandra, indicating they should move into the bar.

'How can you know any of that?'

'Seventh child of a seventh child,' she said. 'I've got the powers.'

'What powers?'

'You'd call 'em the smarts, or something like that. But it's the powers. It means you know what people are thinking before they tell you . . . sometimes even what they're going to do.'

'So, what am I going to do?'

She looked wistful. 'Apart from raiding my fridge? You're going to make a decision soon. This decision will have a big impact on the lives of others, as well as your own, and you're secretly wondering if it's worth it.'

Maybe she was a witch, then. 'And supposing you're right, Cassandra. Supposing I do have to make a big decision soon . . . Any advice?'

For the first time ever, she looked sad. 'I could offer advice. But I think you've already made up your mind on what you're going to do. For your sake, I hope it ends up worth it and no one gets hurt. But nothing's a given. Now, if you don't mind, I've got a pub to run and no one's going to come in here if I look like the back end of a sheep through lack of sleep, are they? Night night, and don't forget to turn the lights off.'

* * *

By the time he had climbed the stairs, he could see the grey dawn starting to seep from behind the curtains.

If this were London, he could have got up and dressed and found breakfast somewhere. But it wasn't, so he'd have to lie in bed until later. And think about what Cassandra had told him. Unexpectedly, he drifted off.

Chapter 20

He was woken from a deep sleep by his phone alarm, which sounded like a NASA warning of impending doom. And on press day, too. Feeling half dead, he dragged himself to the bathroom. No sign of Ray anywhere in the building, which probably meant he was asleep and wasn't coming into work again. Hopefully, it was aiding his recovery.

He schlepped himself to the office and was met by an ecstatic Ignatius. Dutifully, Harry filled his bowl with the Premium dog food, changed his water and promised him something nice from Brenda's.

He worked productively for an hour, finalising a tasteful but dead-body-heavy front page until Hattie tiptoed in. Quietly, she made herself a tea and handed a biscuit to Ignatius. Then she sat down, slipped off her shoes and tucked her feet underneath her.

'Harry?'

'Yes?'

'Thanks for yesterday. I never meant for you to find out like that. It's just that Mum gets so embarrassed about how she is now. She hates people seeing her at home. Where we live . . . Well, you can see for yourself.'

'People aren't always kind or understanding?'

'Very much so. Don't get me wrong, there are loads of nice, friendly people there, but they are all scared of the local yobs, too.'

He could easily imagine the particular kind of terror that people must feel when forced to live in a neighbourhood patrolled by feral youths and over-large men with vicious dogs in tow.

'Do you have to live there?'

'Yes,' she whispered. 'Unless we were to win the lottery, we actually do.'

Then she started describing how she, her dad and her mum had been living peaceably in the old Railway Cottages, not too far from Sadie Burge's home on the other side of town.

They had been happy there, until her father had defrauded his firm to try and support his secret gambling habit, in the same year Barbara had been diagnosed with multiple sclerosis.

'We would have been OK, but then we lost the house.'

'That's awful.'

'I know. We had to be rehoused by the council and the only place they had with two bedrooms at the time was a flat on the Thomas Hardy Estate. Up three flights of stairs. Mum was OK at first but now she can hardly get out and that's why I work in this town and never went away to train, so I can go back home in the day to check she's OK. She's very independent and always trying to do stuff for herself, but sometimes she falls over.'

He tutted sympathetically and Hattie's eyes brightened.

'You don't understand. If this happened and social services found her, I think they'd say I can't look after her properly. They might even say she should go in a home and the only home she could go to is down in Bournemouth and I'd hardly see her. And if that happened, I'd be homeless, because they'd take the flat back, wouldn't they? She's the tenant with the needs, not me.'

He didn't know what to say. His own family home was so big that he'd once got lost in it.

Hattie picked at her nail. 'I'd read about those assistance dogs and put our name down for one, but it can take years. Then I saw a story in the *Piddlington Gazette* about an abandoned Labrador, so I decided to see if he'd do the job instead. You know, train him up.'

'That's a good idea – did it not work out?'

Her eyes dropped to the faithful Ignatius, whose head was now on her knee, looking adoringly up to her.

He could have kicked himself. No wonder she doted on him. But something still wasn't right.

'So why can't he stay with you at the flat?'

'When the council put us in there, they said it was a no-dogs policy – mainly to stop the drug people and their horrible Bullies and pit bulls, I think,' she said. 'I pleaded and pleaded with them to let Ignatius stay. I said I'd take him on a dog training course and all the rest of it, or pay extra, but they said no. It was brutal. I thought I'd have to send him back to the dog charity. Then Ray had a great idea and said that no one ever bothers with the newspaper or comes here, so he could live at the office. So that's what we did. I couldn't bear him to go away.'

Harry sniffed. 'Something in my eye,' he said, turning away.

'Do you really mind him?' Hattie asked.

'No, of course not, not now I know. Ignatius can stay as long as he likes. I can't see Lionel Green being bothered and, if he does ever come, we'll say a random stray paid us a visit, won't we, Ignatius?'

Ignatius looked towards Hattie and then at Harry, before thumping his tail.

'There's just one condition.'

'What?' she asked, looking worried again.

'He's got to have a proper flea treatment. From the vet. Can you book him in sometime?'

'Oh Harry!' She flung her arms round his neck, hugging him tight. Instinctively, he hugged her back, deciding the occasion warranted this kind of comradely gesture. Too late he noticed an all too familiar figure glowering by the door.

'Please don't mind me. Just go ahead. Who will it be next? Brenda at the shop? The church warden? You're lucky that you're a dog,' said Ophelia to the startled Ignatius. 'Otherwise, he'd probably be groping you, too!'

Then she stared at Hattie. 'Is he attempting to harass you? Because . . .'

Stifling a giggle, Hattie assured her that he was not.

Ophelia scowled and then made a bad job of slamming the office door before stalking across the courtyard. Harry rushed after her.

'Ophelia! I'm sorry. But it's not what it looks like.'

'It never is,' she said. 'I was actually coming here to let you know that we're having a press briefing this afternoon at 4 p.m. to update the media on the latest developments in the body on the roundabout.'

He tried to put his hand on her arm, but she flipped it off.

'It wasn't like that. Honestly. It was Hattie who hugged me.'

'Seriously? In truth, I can see why you were all over that woman in the pub the other day, if you like that sort of thing, but Hattie Watson? She's only a kid, for God's sake. And she's a member of your staff. You should think yourself lucky you're not being arrested for sexual harassment.'

Did she have a point? Perhaps he really was suffering with some kind of unconscious and deeply un-woke sexism problem? On the other hand, Hattie was twenty and quite capable of making her own decisions, and wasn't Ophelia being a bit unfeminist about Violett? He wondered whether he should point this out, but her thunderous face told him otherwise.

'Just try and behave yourself at the press conference, will you? For all our sakes.'

He promised that he would, and returned to the office to reluctantly send the newspaper to bed – why couldn't the press conference have been this morning instead? Then it could have gone on the front page too.

Ray's absence reminded him that he needed to sort out his situation. Filled with gratitude, Hattie offered to try and come up with a few ideas.

'Ray is constantly broke,' she said. 'He always needs money; he bets on the horses a bit too much. We tried to keep it from you.'

Harry explained that this wasn't his main concern, but Ray's reduced circumstances had led to ill health, and they needed him back. 'Could we ask Mr Green to pay for his room at The

Ball for a longer while?' asked Hattie. 'Or maybe he could lend Ray the money?'

He nodded noncommittally; he didn't really want to ask him this on top of the painting, but Hattie had made a good point. As he tried to consider what would work best, he found his resolve trickling away. There was the press conference this afternoon, but he had a few hours to fill before then and the paper had already gone. The thought of approaching Prudence Robarts about the sister situation made his teeth itch, so he decided he'd have to try Lionel Green about the painting and slip in a quick request about Ray.

* * *

His journey to the Lost Vale was uneventful and, miraculously, he was admitted via the gates after claiming to Greta Sargent, through the intercom, that he'd got some useful news.

'This is most unorthodox, but Mr Green is at home and has graciously agreed to see you.'

Harry swallowed, wound up his window and trundled up the driveway.

The Grange was as beautiful as ever and the interior just as unnerving. He noticed a lot more artwork: a Pollock, two Klees and a spidery Nicholson, looking incongruous beside a solemn long-case clock.

Greta Sargent escorted him to the study, announced his presence and then moved out, leaving him alone with Lionel

Green, who was standing by the window. He looked even smaller than before.

'What information do you have for me?'

Harry swallowed. *Here goes.* 'I-I think I may be on the trail of someone who could . . . might be . . . the person you're looking for.'

Lionel's face changed and, for a second, Harry glimpsed a very different man: eager, with a future.

'There is a "but", however?'

He agreed there was a 'but'. 'I need to speak to the person, establish a few more facts, but I thought I should let you know.'

'And this you couldn't have told me on the phone?'

Harry shook his head. Playing for time, he mentioned Ray's plight.

Lionel looked irritated. 'I have already told The Ball Inn I will pay for his stay until the man can get on his feet again. I hope you do not see me as a person who would allow a man to become homeless if I could prevent it?'

Harry agreed, then took a deep breath. 'The thing is . . . I also wanted to ask, um, have you ever thought about selling any of your paintings?'

Lionel looked puzzled.

'Pardon? What do you mean? What paintings should I sell? And what has this got to do with my sister?'

He can see inside my head, thought Harry.

'It was just a thought. I mean, I don't know. That one?' he said, pointing to *The Purple Child*.

Lionel stared at it and then back at him. 'Why that one?'

He felt like a blind, one-legged kangaroo in a minefield; one false move and it could all go up. He urged himself to get a grip. It was not against the law to ask people if they wanted to sell something.

'Right. Well, if you did ever want to sell it, I may know of someone who would like to purchase it. You know, for the right price?'

His voice tailed off. He couldn't blame Lionel for looking at him as if he had been declared insane.

'Shall I tell you what the right price is?' asked Lionel, moving nearer. 'That painting is worth more than this house to me, more than anything I have ever owned. I will never, ever sell it. And you,' he said, prodding Harry's chest, 'will remember that you have signed a non-disclosure agreement. No one but me, Miss Sargent and you know it is here. And, let me tell you, she is a crack shot!'

Harry ran his hand through his hair, which felt incredibly sweaty – how had they got on to shooting? 'Of course, I totally understand your position, Mr Green. Absolutely. But unfortunately, someone else does know it's here. Sir Jimmy Knox. The newspaper magnate. He collects Picassos and I have heard that he's really, really taken with this one.'

'But how does he know it is here?'

He didn't like the way the old man's eyes were narrowing. But he'd come this far and knew he had to lay it on the line.

'He just does, OK? People like him have a way of finding out stuff.'

The silence in the room was overwhelming. In the far distance Harry could hear a plane. Soaring over this was the yelp of a buzzard.

Lionel turned to him. 'You just find my sister. Find her. And forget about that painting. It's nothing to do with anyone but me.'

'Well,' said Harry, 'that's all I came to tell you. I have to go now.'

'Yes. And don't bother coming back unless you can tell me something useful.'

Lionel pulled the bell beside the fireplace and, like a spectre, Greta appeared at the room's polished wooden door.

'Goodbye, Mr Green.'

'Goodbye,' said Lionel, turning towards the window. Harry was marched down the tiled corridor and into the main hall.

'He's quite right,' rasped Greta.

'About what, Miss Sargent?'

'Me being a crack shot,' she said.

He smiled wearily and thanked her. What else was there to do? Now for the press conference.

Chapter 21

Once again, the presser was to be held in the town library, but this time, a PCSO was guarding the door and demanded to see Harry's credentials.

The usual media crowd was there, including Barry from the *Wessex Post*. 'What d'you reckon on all this, then?' he said to Harry, leaning precariously on the back legs of his moulded plastic chair, which wobbled threateningly under his considerable weight.

Harry wasn't going to be caught like that. 'Have to see, won't we?'

'Aren't you the one from the court case?'

Harry pretended to be fiddling with his phone which, given the circumstances surrounding his disgrace, was probably not the best move.

'Practising your technique?' snorted the odious Barry. 'Fair play to you, mate,' he said, tipping forward again and letting out an onion-laden belch.

His thoughts were interrupted by a stir at the end of the room as Ophelia, flanked by PC Collins and the force press officer, walked in.

She looked so professional and determined, thought Harry, noticing that her hair had been cemented into the world's harshest bun. PC Collins looked as loose-limbed and relaxed as ever.

The press officer was looking at her watch.

'Right,' said Ophelia, staring at the five hacks who sat before her. 'We have called this press conference to inform you of the progress that has been made in the ongoing investigation into the human remains discovered on the roundabout intersecting the A350 to the south of Piddlington Minster.'

She repeated the order of discovery and looked up. 'As you know, the second body has been identified and the post-mortem has revealed that death occurred following a blunt force trauma to the head. We can now also reveal that the body appears to have suffered other trauma, which will be further investigated.'

There was a satisfying collective forward lean from the assembled hacks. This was new.

'It is now believed that Mr Fewtrell may not have died instantly from this catastrophic injury, and investigations are ongoing to determine exactly how he came to be on the roundabout,' continued Ophelia. 'While no exact date of death has been established, Dorset Police are extremely keen to speak to anyone who saw or spoke to Mr Fewtrell in the days leading up to his sudden disappearance from his job as editor of the *Piddlington Gazette* on the twenty-fifth of March this year.'

'Can you tell us what this actually means?' enquired the young journo from the local news agency.

Ophelia looked annoyed. 'I don't understand?'

'Well . . .' said the young one. 'Do you think the injury to Mr Fewtrell was caused deliberately? Have you established if he had any enemies, or people who would want to hurt him in this way? In short, is this a murder investigation?'

All eyes were on Ophelia; she looked to the press officer, who nodded imperceptibly. 'We are still keeping an open mind as to how the injury occurred,' she said. 'Of course, we can't rule out the possibility that he was deliberately harmed, although there is no evidence yet to show that the injury was done on purpose. That's why we are making further inquiries and asking people to help us establish a picture of Mr Fewtrell's life, in the weeks leading up to his untimely death.'

Everyone sat back.

The bright young journo put his hand up again. 'Can I ask again, if or how the death of Mr Fewtrell is linked to the other body discovered on the roundabout?'

'We cannot say yet if it is linked, but the first body had been on the roundabout for far longer than that of Mr Fewtrell.'

'So, some kind of slacker serial killer, then?' snorted Barry Hands. 'Too bone idle – ha! – to go and commit a third one?'

The collective glare from the police bench would have frozen hell, thought Harry. Unfortunately, Barry was made of sterner stuff and started chortling at his own feeble joke.

The press officer indicated PC Collins. 'Now we come to the second part of our conference, where PC Collins will update you on the inquiry into the first body.'

The officer picked up a piece of paper and began speaking.

'As you know, the first set of remains were sent for forensic testing, as there was some dispute as to their origins and their potential age. I am now in a position to confirm that these are indeed human remains These remains have been subjected to . . .' And here he listed a slew of tests. 'What I can now say is that the human remains belong to a male person. From the bones we can ascertain that he was around five foot six and had suffered no serious injury to his frame. However . . .' At this point everyone in the room leaned comically forward again. 'We are still investigating issues around the age of the remains, which I am not at liberty to disclose, and our investigations are continuing. There are several unexplained matters, including how he died and how he came to be in the location he was found.'

'Are you saying that someone moved him there, after he was killed?' asked Harry.

'Like a serial killer?' persisted Barry.

'For the record, I have not said anything about the cause of death and nor have I speculated about any other aspect of this case. Dorset Police are not saying anything further at this stage.'

'Have you been checking names of mispers to see if he matches anyone's description?' asked Barry, in a rare show of initiative.

'Of course, and we are pursuing a number of lines of inquiry.'

This was the cue for the assembled journalists to fire a barrage of questions at him, which he skilfully avoided answering.

After a few minutes, the press officer stood up. 'I'm afraid we have to wrap it up now. Thanks for coming and, of course, you can find out more on our website and . . .' But she was drowned out by the mass scraping of chairs as everyone scooted off.

* * *

Harry wandered back to the office and relayed all the news to Hattie.

'It's all so weird.'

'What, the Kevin business?'

'Uh-huh. Ray and I racked our brains when he left, in case it was anything we'd said or done. But he seemed really nice, worked hard and even seemed to like Ignatius.'

'Did he mention anything at all about being threatened?'

Hattie considered. 'Nah, I don't think he was the sort of person to have any enemies, although he did get quite a few calls on his mobile, which he just rejected, as far as I could see. But everyone does that. We didn't socialise outside the office or anything.'

'You and Ray definitely need to tell the police all that,' said Harry. 'Anything might help.'

* * *

Ray's absence meant a long afternoon, going into the early evening, and he felt exhausted as he fed and watered a grateful Ignatius, before locking up to return to The Ball.

His phone pinged.

How's it all going?

Violett. The message was accompanied by an x and three hearts.

Work in progress

Harry was stalling.

When he arrived at The Ball, he was greeted by Ray and Cassandra, who were enjoying what looked like a giant cocktail each. 'Never 'ad a pina colada before,' slurped Ray. 'Bottoms up!'

Cassandra winked. 'South-West champion cocktail maker, three years running, 2013 to 2015, as I'm sure you wanted to know. Want one?'

Normally, he'd never have turned down the offer of a free drink, but, despite the news excitement, he felt curiously flat. Perhaps it was the glimpse he'd had of life as it used to be. Or perhaps his idea about assisting his father by getting the New York job was as rickety as a two-legged table. He could imagine the look on Geoffrey's face if he were to learn that his son's vague plan would mean being in Sir Jimmy's orbit once more, even if it actually worked out. But did he really have a choice, if he wanted to move his career and his financial dial on?

He looked up as Ray, very spruce in a clean, new shirt and a pair of trousers that Harry hadn't seen before, started talking.

'Cassandra here's very kindly said I can stay until I'm back on my feet again, so I'll be able to come back to work tomorrow.'

'That's great news,' said Harry. Evidently, Lionel had been true to his word, then. 'Sorry to be a party pooper but I'm just going to pop out for some fish and chips.'

They both nodded.

The Chippy-In-The-Square was quiet. Harry joined the small queue and savoured the delicious tang as he waited. Across the square a small flock of pigeons rose, the sound of their beating wings echoing against the old buildings.

You could get fond of a place like this, he thought to himself, but Cassandra was right: he did have choices to make.

The pigeons fluttered again, disturbed by a woman walking past them. He knew who that was. Prudence Robarts. Minus her tartan trolley. Maybe now was a good time to approach her, on neutral territory.

Leaving his place in the queue, he strode across the square as Mrs Robarts disappeared down one of the town's myriad twisting alleys. Harry followed. She was clearly a faster walker than he'd anticipated, because he couldn't see her, yet this part of the route was straight enough. He quickened his pace, passing a boarded-up shop and a defunct red telephone box.

As he approached the end of the alley, there was a metal fence, blocking off a road. But no Robarts. He slowed.

'Thought you'd lost me, didn't you?'

She stepped out of the shadow cast by a deep shop doorway.

'No.'

'You are almost as unaccomplished a liar as you are a newspaper editor.'

'Actually, Mrs Robarts, I wanted to ask you something,' said Harry, hoping to turn the tables. 'Were . . . I mean, did you ever have a brother?'

She looked nervous.

'What an extraordinary question.' 'It's just that I did a court case years ago and the judge looked just like you,' he lied.

He deserved the look she gave him; as fibs go, this one could easily find a place in the *Guinness World Records*: Worst Lie Ever, it was so feeble.

'What are you talking about, you stupid boy? What does my brother have to do with anything?'

Harry's heart gave a tiny flip. She may have a brother, then . . .

'Did you ever live in London? I mean, did you live there a long time ago?'

She looked furtive. 'Who says I did?'

'No one. Well, quite a few people seem to think you did, so I just wondered. Because—'

She cut him off. 'Instead of behaving like a stuffed owl, why don't you do your job properly and support the important work people are doing in this town? You haven't found out anything about those bodies on the roundabout; bodies, I might insist, that wouldn't even be there if this town wasn't a disgusting mess. What about their grieving families? And as for that house and that filthy woman – why aren't you campaigning to do something about that? Instead, you choose to stalk me round the town, harass me and waste my time with pointless questions. Get on with it.'

The words were spat out and her face was twisted. If she really was the sister of Lionel Green, Harry would actually start to feel sympathy for the man. Fancy being related to someone like her.

'As a matter of fact, I did live in London, many years ago. But I came here after I married. Satisfied?'

Harry blinked.

So, Prudence Robarts had lived in London, was the right age and didn't want to confirm anything about a brother. True, he was too cowardly to ask if her first name was Sarah, but all this meant that, *technically*, she could be the sister of Lionel Green. As evidence of anything, it was thinner than his bank balance but, thought Harry, it was good enough for what he planned next.

Chapter 22

Delighted to have a very chipper-looking Ray back the next morning, Harry popped out for some Danish pastries. Hattie had, for some inexplicable reason, brought in fresh orange juice and, together with tea and coffee from Brenda's, they all breakfasted together, al desko.

Harry then made the last checks on the paper: crossword, gardening, horoscope. This week's predictions from Madam Voyant seemed extremely fulsome.

Cancer, your kindness and understanding will result in unexpected rewards. Always stay true to these ideals and you will do no wrong.

They spent the morning writing, and Harry urged Hattie to take an early lunch and check on her mother.

Ray went to Tesco and arrived back with a very passable hoisin duck wrap for Harry and a ham sandwich for himself. Harry propped the door open and smiled as Ignatius carefully dragged his bedding onto the cobbles to bask in the sun.

The peaceful scene was shattered by the sound of a bike rattling into the yard and then being flung on the ground.

'Harry! Quick!'

He leaped up. Hattie looked distraught.

'It's the council, they are trying to get into Sadie Burge's house or something, and it's just horrible, she's screaming out of the window and there's an ugly pitchfork mob—'

'In my car!' he ordered.

She wrenched open the Cooper's door and strapped herself in as Harry crashed the gears and drove off, narrowly missing Ignatius's tail.

They could see the crowd before they even arrived. Harry recognised the aggressive neighbour, plus a few of what looked like the local yobs, gleefully anticipating the spectacle to come.

'We'll stop here,' he said, parking the car on the double yellows that ran along Bridge Street.

As they approached the scene, Hattie started filming on her iPhone and Harry noticed Ophelia and a PCSO hastily spooling incident tape at the entrance to the overgrown front pathway.

A man with a clipboard and wearing a hi-vis jacket was talking into his phone. On the street were three more men in luminous jackets with hard hats, and yet more be-suited people, their faces grim and determined.

At the top of the house, he could just about make out a shape at the filthy window. Sadie must be upstairs.

She had managed to open one of the ancient sashes and was screaming invective through the narrow gap. It was a depressing sight.

'Ophelia, is this really necessary? I mean, couldn't someone speak to her?'

The officer stared at him.

'I don't have the bandwidth for this. This is a council operation – a civil matter. We're only here at the council's request to ensure that a breach of the peace is not occasioned and to ensure the occupant's rights are respected.'

'That's right,' said Hattie. 'Just doing your job, aren't you?'

'Yes, I am. And you'd better make sure you're doing your job too, Miss Watson. Obstructing an officer in the course of their lawful duty is an offence.'

Hattie pulled a face and Harry indicated for her to move away. No point in provoking a situation and, it was true, Ophelia was only doing her job. He tried to smile at the beleaguered officer, but she stared straight through him.

He marched up to the official with the clipboard. 'Harry Hedges; I'm the editor of the *Piddlington Gazette*,' he began.

'I don't care if you're that bloke off Watergate,' said the official, displaying a stunning knowledge of heritage journalistic endeavour. 'We have done everything we can to avoid this. All we'll be doing today is trying to access the property, assessing what is there and gauging the alleged rat problem in the back garden. No one is going to hurt or evict anyone.'

'Don't believe a word of it, Harry, they just want her out,' said Hattie. 'It's mob mentality.'

'They only want to get inside and talk to her. I don't think they're trying to evict her or anything.'

'Yeah, right.'

Harry stood in front of her.

'Stay here and no backchat. These people are only doing their job.'

He turned to the official. 'I'm going to try and talk to Mrs Burge.'

'I am duty-bound to warn you, sir, that this house is potentially dangerous and a health hazard and that you could be at serious risk if you chose to enter.'

Harry nodded. 'Thanks, but I've been in before, I think I'll be OK.'

Under his breath the man muttered: 'Thanks, mate.'

Harry stood directly under the window.

'Mrs Burge? Sadie?' Silence.

'Please, Sadie.'

The thin, tired voice floated down. 'Go away!'

'Perhaps I can help. The people here only want to help, too.'

He dodged as an old book was projected from the upper window and narrowly missed his head.

'Go away!'

He moved towards the front door. It was wedged tightly shut. He poked open the letterbox. The hallway was as crowded as ever. 'Sadie? Mrs Burge?'

Silence. He waited a few seconds before calling to the council team: 'I'll try the back.'

The council official moved back a few steps. 'I'm not sure that's wise, sir.'

Harry quietly assured him that he thought he could help.

Sotto voce, the man said: 'Anything really, we would be grateful, sir. We don't want to upset the poor lady.'

'Bit late for that, isn't it?' snapped Hattie.

Ophelia raised her voice. 'Could you please come to this side of the cordon?'

Harry nodded in Ophelia's direction.

'Go on.'

He waded along the path then set off to the left, hoping to find the back entrance to the lane at the rear of the houses. As he moved along, he heard Prudence Robarts from the other side of the cordon.

'Are they getting rid of her? Good riddance. This town will be better off without her!'

The woman was vile. Not trusting himself to speak, Harry nodded and walked onto the stony lane which ran alongside the giant, overgrown hedge that surrounded the rear of the Burge property.

He'd never seen the back garden before. Unlike its neighbours, which were home to various colourful blooms, with bland patios and the occasional trampoline and garden pond, Sadie Burge's was filled with old mattresses, twisted pieces of metal, bedsteads, forlorn chairs, broken tables and what looked like an old motorbike – all festooned with plastic bags and wreathed in brambles like razor wire. Something moved ominously across the ground beneath the bushes. As Harry's eyes adjusted, he realised that, whatever Sadie liked to think, even a dozen cats couldn't keep this nest of rats in order. The place was positively rippling.

Trying not to worry about Weil's disease and the bubonic plague, he took a deep breath and attempted to scramble across the festering piles.

As he got closer to the back door, he realised there was a tiny space in front of it. So perhaps it did open, then. The back door was half glass and, even though shut, hung at a desperate angle. He tried the knob. It turned and within seconds Harry was in a space he imagined must be Sadie Burge's kitchen. If the smell of rotting food wasn't bad enough, the flies and the ominous rustle were worse.

'Sadie?' he called. 'Mrs Burge? Please answer. It's me, Harry Hedges.'

He managed to battle his way to the back of the room and through the door into the hallway.

'Mrs Burge? Please don't be angry, but I'm sure I can help.'

The house was deathly silent now, despite the commotion at the front. She probably couldn't hear him.

He inched past what must have been a dozen papier mâché sculptures, plus some in clay, all piled on top of each other, all covered in patches of sinister mildew.

The smell and the dust were beginning to irritate his nose. As he crept forward, he could see the front door. Perhaps he could open it, and the official could get in and take over? But once he came parallel with the bannisters, there was a sudden noise and he felt a blow to his head.

'How dare you?' raged the voice of Sadie Burge. Harry, who had fallen forward into a pile of clothing that smelled of urine, coughed and sputtered. As he turned to get his face away from it, he could see halfway up the stairs, where the woman was standing, her face contorted with rage.

'Burglars. Liar!' she screamed. 'Get out of my house. Get *out*!'

As she raised her stick, he saw sense and scrambled to his feet, making a sideways dash, so as not to upset the papier mâché sculptures, to the front door. As he opened it and fell outwards, he was aware of a small crowd and noticed Ophelia Starsky staring at him.

'You really are hopeless, aren't you?'

Fortunately, his fall had been broken by a particularly substantial lavender bush. Standing up, he realised he was now freckled with the seeds. But at least he smelled acceptable again.

The council official moved towards him, looking nervous.

'Probably worried you'll sue,' said Hattie, throwing many shades of hatred at the man.

'No harm done,' said Harry. Then, turning to the official, he added, 'Afraid it's no dice. She threw a book or something at my head and she's very upset. What happens now?'

The official explained that they would be back soon with an order and reinforcements, including a social worker.

Harry felt depressed. 'I'd better go and write this up.'

He beckoned to Hattie and, as he trudged away, he saw Ophelia herding the little crowd.

'Move along, nothing to see here,' said Hattie.

He got into his car, and she slipped into the passenger seat. His phone pinged. Violett again.

And???

And what?

Aware of Hattie trying to look at his phone, Harry tapped quickly.

Can't discuss now, call later.

* * *

He drove them back in silence at a sedate pace and parked quietly, in order not to disturb Ignatius, who was still snoring in the sun. He asked Hattie to update the website while he settled down to subbing the nibs and the sports reports from 'One-eyed Norman'.

'He is an old mate of Ray's who played county cricket once for Dorset but got hit in the eye by a ball and became an umpire,' explained Hattie.

'But isn't calling him One-eyed Norman a bit un-woke?'

'Not really – it's to distinguish him from Norman who writes the darts column. He lost his foot in a farming accident.'

Harry shook his head.

He waited until Hattie set off to visit her mother, then stepped out and marched swiftly round the block to a bench by the river.

He started pressing the keys on his phone. It was now or never. Violett answered immediately.

'So?'

'He won't sell the painting. No way – I asked him straight out.'

Silence.

'Oh no, how disappointing. I just don't think that's going to be good enough.'

'Sorry, but you did say that all I had to do was ask. Well, I've asked. Short of stealing it, there is no way you'd get that painting away from him. Now, about the New York—'

He was swiftly cut off. 'There is another way, actually. I've just had the best idea! We'll go there and explain in person. I'm sure that once he understands, he'll see sense.'

Harry started explaining again that Lionel Green didn't want to sell the painting but was silenced, mid-flow.

'Every man has his price, Harry, even your Mr Green. Time's ticking on. There must be something that means more to him than that painting. What about his lost sister?'

Now Harry really was astonished.

'How do you know about Mrs Robarts?'

It came out before he could stop himself.

She laughed, lightly. 'Well, I didn't know about *her* before, but I do now.'

There was another second's silence, when he could almost hear the clicking of her brain cells, before Violett's voice danced down the line.

'You think this Robarts lady could be the missing sister, don't you? Fantastic! We'll go up to the old gentleman; you can introduce me as an investigative journalist, explain how we used to work together and say that I've been helping you find this sister. I'll tell him he can only know our information if he signs a document to sell the painting for its established worth and that we'll facilitate an introduction to this woman and he can take it from there. Boom!'

Harry swallowed. As plans went, on the terribility factor, it was right up there with Napoleon invading Russia, or the Archbishop of Canterbury telling children there was no Father Christmas on Christmas Eve. He remembered her being determined in pursuit of a story but not actually deranged. Which this idea most certainly was. 'Listen to yourself, Violett, not only is it utterly absurd, but it's also verging on fraud. We don't know if the woman I mentioned actually *is* his sister. And we don't know that, even if she was, she'd want anything to do with him.'

For a merciful two seconds, Violett was quiet. Then she started again.

'I'm guessing there isn't any written requirement for this long-lost sister to want to see Mr Green – just for you to locate her, or find out what happened to her,' she said.

Silently, Harry had to agree.

'Look,' she continued. 'I know this is a sweet little town, but do you really want to spend the rest of your days writing reports on giant vegetables and attending mayor-making ceremonies? Because that's what you're looking at, and if you were being honest with yourself, you'd know it. You used to be a great operator, Harry, but you know what it's like, word gets round the industry pretty fast, and you might not get a second chance ever, if you don't take this one. And then how will you help your dad?'

His silence must have registered his shock.

'Please don't be cross, but Jasper told me about your dad's company – that's why I thought this idea about the painting and the New York job might help. It's a legitimate way to get money into your pocket, don't you think?'

He wondered if working in the upper echelons of the *Daily News*'s shiny Canary Wharf tower had addled her brain – maybe the London pollution was worse on the twenty-seventh floor? The only thing he could do was stall her, until he thought of a way out. Like joining the French Foreign Legion.

'OK,' he lied. 'I'll see about making an appointment.'

'Oh, don't worry about all that, we'll just go up there.'

As he started to protest, the line went dead.

Mentally slapping his own face, Harry sloped back to the office.

* * *

As Ray typed smartly and whistled, Harry felt a headache coming on. He was too dispirited to even mind as another of Ignatius's fleas hopped onto his wrist – a black, insolent shape, next to his watchstrap.

'All right, Harry?'

He nodded, trying to look amenable. It was good to see the improvement in Ray; even his moustache seemed to have perked up.

Ignatius embarked on a long scratch and just as Harry was about to tell him to stop, Hattie whirled round.

'Hey, guess what?'

'What?'

'No, guess.'

He couldn't.

'Mr Prentiss from the museum has just emailed to say they are launching an inquiry into "certain missing items". Good story, eh? Shall I do it for the site?'

Harry nodded. His head felt as if large rocks were rolling around inside it, and his temples throbbed.

'Are you all right, lad?' enquired Ray.

'I don't know. I think I may have a migraine or something,' croaked Harry. 'Look, can you two cope with the last few bits? I think I might need a lie-down.'

They assured him they could, and Hattie offered him a herbal headache-relief tablet.

'No, but that's really kind, thanks,' he said as he set off, slowly, his jacket over his shoulders and his phone in his hand. He felt too ill to drive – he'd have to leave the Mini there overnight.

He arrived at The Ball and told George what had happened.

'Go straight upstairs; I'll make sure you're not disturbed,' he said.

Harry could have kissed him.

He went straight to his room, gulped down some aspirin, pulled the curtains, removed his clothes and slid into bed, his head pounding. Before closing his eyes, he switched the phone to airplane mode and sank gratefully into sleep.

* * *

It was pitch dark when he awoke, disorientated. The ChickinBiteTonite sign must have finally broken. He switched on his own light. It was 2 a.m. He'd been asleep for eleven hours. On the dressing table there was a Tupperware box. Inside it was a sausage roll, a Penguin biscuit and a short note: 'Thought you might fancy a little snack! C x'. Bless her. Migraines always left him ravenous. He gulped the food down and drifted off again.

When he awoke, it was sunny and light and his phone said 7.30 a.m. His headache had receded but was still squeezing at least fifty per cent of his brain in painful, merciless waves. As he showered, he ran the conversations of yesterday through his tired and painful mind.

He'd dodged Violett and her barmy plan for the time being. But he knew there was no way she'd be put off for long. It was only a matter of time.

Chapter 23

Harry's prayers for a quiet and peaceful Friday were answered. He felt pathetically grateful for the lack of drama, as his head was always fuzzy after a migraine and on several occasions he found himself typing whole sentences that looked like a Russian code, as his confused fingers had hit the wrong part of the keyboard.

He struggled on until 4 p.m. and then told everyone they could go home. Thank God it was the weekend. Cassandra, concerned about his indisposition, ordered him to turn his phone off and spend the evening in bed. When he finally emerged into the bar on Saturday afternoon, she made him a coffee and a cheese sandwich. Feeling too ill to drive anywhere, Harry decided to take a walk round the town, hoping it would clear his head.

His wander took in Bridge Street, where he felt a terrible sadness for Sadie Burge as he passed her neglected house. He then continued on to the public gardens behind the minster, which were home to a splendid rockery and, to his delight, a small Japanese garden. The air, and the peace of the tiny pond and red-painted bridge above it finally chased away the migraine and, by Sunday morning, he was well enough to join the crowd in the bar watching the rugby.

* * *

He arrived at the office on Monday to a scene of unaccustomed industry. Ray was typing away, nodding and smiling at his own screen, while Hattie was scrolling slowly through a huge slab of copy. Ignatius was sitting patiently at her feet, occasionally snapping at one of the flies which seemed to infest the building.

According to Hattie, he had received his flea treatment from Rudd's, the town vet, on Saturday morning and was now officially flea-free.

'You're going to love this,' she said, describing how she'd been back to Mr Prentiss at the museum to get more info about the thefts. They'd all been reported to the police but, she explained, 'Here's the strangest thing. None of the items seems to be at all valuable. They are, like, totally random.'

Harry wondered how people could just steal things from a museum but, he quickly learned, all the thefts were from the 'secret' stores, which were actually in the building's basement. 'They just tell people it's elsewhere to put potential thieves off the scent,' explained Hattie.

'That obviously worked well, then.'

Hattie ignored the intervention. She had managed to blag a list of the missing items so far determined and they included: the dog collar which belonged to the former Lord

Piddle's Dalmatian, a thimble that was said to have belonged to Queen Victoria's niece, part of a chastity belt – 'Don't ask me which part!' – a stuffed horseshoe bat, a mummified cat and a fake love letter from Oscar Wilde.

Harry smiled at her enthusiasm.

'Don't you think it's weird?'

'What's weird? Museums are full of stuff like that.'

'Given that they could have taken . . .' Hattie referred to her notes. 'A ruby ring that was part of the ancient Piddlington Hoard, the papers of Sir Gresby Bibb – "man of science" apparently – or an actual real letter sent by Oscar Wilde to Lord Piddle, back in the day. It seems strange that someone has taken such pointless stuff.'

'Yes, why would they?'

'Find that out,' said Hattie, 'and you'll solve the case!'

'Why don't you?' he replied. 'I bet Sergeant Starsky could do with the help.'

'I'm not working with her, she's a complete face-ache. Anyway, I thought you should know. The best bit is that there might be even more stuff taken – Mr Prentiss has to go through the whole store now to find out.'

* * *

As the day hummed along and he watched his little band at work, Harry felt alternately hopeful that things might spontaneously work out in his favour, and then mystified at the thought of Violett trying to make her ludicrous idea into reality.

What had possessed him to agree to any of it? His mind went into panicked overdrive.

Perhaps he could fling himself on Lionel Green's mercy, mention his father's financial plight, admit he couldn't find the sister but explain again about the painting's importance to Sir Jimmy Knox? Realistically, there was probably more chance of landing a spacecraft on Mars, with Ignatius at the controls.

He began to wish he could go back in time and give Picasso a broken arm, so he couldn't paint, or that he could prove Lionel Green's sister was six feet under – anything to stop this nightmare. His mood was not helped by the image of their family home on the website of an upmarket estate agent's, describing the place where Harry had grown up as 'a unique opportunity to acquire this historic property with royal connections'. Poor Geoffrey. And poor him. It was like losing another little bit of Isabella. Sensing his melancholy, Ignatius padded over and placed his head carefully on his knee, while eyeing the uneaten end of a Crunchie bar that lay on his desk.

As Hattie prepared to go home for lunch, Ray looked up. 'Penny for them, Harry.'

'I wish.'

Ray asked what was worrying him. He explained that he had been tasked with trying to locate Mr Green's missing sister but the best – indeed, the only – lead he had was Prudence Robarts. Hesitantly, he outlined his evidence, cringing as the words made it into the light of day.

'Stranger things have happened, lad.'

'Really? It's not as if she'll even tell me anything I want to know. She's not exactly an accommodating person.'

'Aye. But you can only try, can't you? And, you never know, it might even make her happy if you help her reconcile with her brother. Why don't you pop round there now? No time like the present. If our job is about anything, it's about the one per cent.'

'You mean the one per cent who turn out to be axe murderers or secret billionaires?'

Ray meant exactly that. 'When I think of the court cases I've been to, not to mention the stuff you hear at inquests and the people who used to come in the old front office . . .'

Harry understood. Nothing struck doom into a journalist's heart more than hearing the magic words: 'There's someone in the front office.'

And Ray was bang on the money – very few of these individuals ever had a coherent story, let alone a printable one, as far as he could remember. The rest appeared to be people who were plagued by satellites hovering over their home, embroiled in interminable neighbour disputes, or who wanted a judge-led public inquiry into why their conservatory extension plans had been turned down.

'Ask her outright,' said Ray. 'Then at least you'll know.'

Harry sighed, thinking back to his last conversation with Mrs Robarts. He tried to summon up the enthusiasm, remembering his mother's encouragement when he had to reluctantly return to boarding school each term. As he'd sit there crying on the bottom stair, desperate not to go, Isabella would list all the positives: his friends, the tuck box, the extra tenners she'd hidden for him in various bits of his suitcase.

He still missed her, even though he'd been alive more years without her than with. Isabella had always been so perceptive. Geoffrey, while well-meaning, had always seemed vague and preoccupied.

But Ray was right. There was no time like the present and one way or another, he had to know.

He decided to drive – you never knew when you'd need a quick getaway – and by way of encouragement, the Cooper started first time. Harry patted the dashboard as the vehicle ambled from the courtyard and into the one-way system.

Prudence Robarts's bungalow was exactly as Hattie had suggested: a begonia-hanging-basket-encrusted horror, with a fearsomely square front lawn edged with a border in which red salvia, purple aubrieta and stripey French marigolds alternated with migraine-inducing intensity. As the last vestiges of his headache gave a throb, he decided not to park on the little concrete drive and instead put the Cooper under a lime tree, its leaves like giant gold pennies, further up Godolphin Court.

He walked carefully towards the Robarts driveway and up the concrete path to the front door. He pressed the doorbell and, from within, came a faint tune. On the step was a pristine doormat – obviously not too many visitors here, then – and a resin Scottie dog statue. Harry pressed again. Nothing.

Looking about, he decided to go round the back, experience having told him that it was easier to find people in their kitchen or garden, especially if they couldn't hear the bell.

The wrought-iron gate clicked open, and he walked down the side of the little building until he could see a picture window into a small dining room. He peered in. Apart from a few items wrapped up in newspapers on a traditional gateleg table, and some tired-looking wooden chairs, there was little else by way of furniture. Harry knocked gently on the glass.

Silence.

He continued to peer in as he waited to see if Mrs Robarts would appear. Copper warming pans hung on the walls, surrounding a little, brown-tiled 1950s fireplace with an electric fire and a mantelpiece on which he could see a model of the Eiffel Tower and a couple of diminutive-looking candlesticks. In the middle was a photograph in black and white.

It appeared to be a young woman standing in front of the Tower of London. In the background was an old newspaper billboard. Harry couldn't read what it said but the billboard had a large 'V' on it. Could it be VE Day? If so, and if that was her, it put Prudence Robarts in London at that time, which might be helpful.

True, it wasn't 1952, the last time Lionel had heard from his sister, but it might come in handy. Trying to square his conscience – after all, if she did turn out to be the sister, it was all in a good cause – Harry fished out his phone and quickly snapped the image. He had to hope it would pique Lionel Green's interest enough for him to plead his case again. He didn't have much else.

He gave the back-door window one gentle knock and called her name but there was still no reply. Feeling ashamed at the relief he felt in not having to face her, he walked round the building, back to the Cooper and got in.

A text flashed up on his phone. Hattie.

Huge news!!! Would need firming up, but people saying on Rumours of Piddlington Facebook group that Kevin F hit his head on a pavement.

Harry decided not to risk a mental episode by enquiring how anyone on that particularly lunatic outpost of social media would know this, and tapped back: *Interesting, keep an eye on it* and added *!!!!* to acknowledge Hattie's enthusiasm.

His phone lit up again.

OK for this evening?

It was Violett. She didn't wait for a reply.

Walk to the mini-roundabout near the station and I'll pick you up there – 6.30 p.m.

Harry flicked the key and the Cooper started first time again. Slowly, he drove back to the office and spent the afternoon working on his next edition, more as a distraction to stop his mind from spinning off into orbit. It actually looked really good, and Harry felt a tiny swell of pride, which he decided to try and quell. He'd made his decision. Finance- and, sadly, career-wise, London was where he belonged. New York even more so. Piddlington Minster was just an enforced interlude, for now. He'd have to do his best and hope everyone would understand when the time came for him to leave.

As he locked up for the evening, Ray asked him if he felt OK.

'Fine, thanks.'

'So long as you are,' he said, giving him a long look.

* * *

After eating the dish of the day – Cassandra's Champion Homity Pie – Harry wondered what to do. He'd already changed into dark jeans and a black jumper, with his trusty brogues, which Cassandra had had cleaned for him.

The dark clothes darkened his mood. There was absolutely no way Lionel Green would sell that painting. But he was in too deep, now. Best go through with things and then try and retrieve what he could from the situation.

George the barman gave him a sympathetic smile. 'Busy, Harry?'

'Not really – I'm meeting an old friend for a drink.' The lie stuck in his throat.

'Anywhere nice?'

'Round and about. You know. Might strike out to one of the villages.'

George nodded.

At 6.20 p.m. Harry walked to the mini-roundabout near the entrance to the train station. A dark Range Rover was parked on the verge. As he approached, the driver's window slid slowly down, revealing a man wearing a baseball hat and a pair of sunglasses.

''Ello, 'Arry!'

'Jasper? What are you doing here? Where's Violett?'

'She's busy! And I'm here for the same reason as you! We can't afford for this to go wrong. Sir Jimmy's off his head with excitement about getting *The Purple Child*. If he doesn't, it'll be a disaster.'

Harry felt sick. 'Hang on a minute. It's not a done deal, Jasper. It's not even half a done deal, in fact . . .'

Jasper laughed, coldly. 'In his mind, it is. Ours is not to question why; ours is but to do or . . . you know. Look, just get in. Why are you dressed like that?'

Harry tried to explain that this was his off-duty look. Jasper looked disbelieving. 'You look like a criminal.'

The journey to The Grange was far too short and uneventful. If it had been in a movie, there would have been lightning bolts and swooping dragons, portending the doom Harry felt washing over him. As it wasn't a movie, all they had to contend with was a pack of luminous Lycra-ed cyclists and a young woman on a pony, who thrashed the car with her crop as Jasper nearly took the creature's ear off.

As they arrived at the gates, Harry trudged round to the intercom.

'Er, hello. It's me, Harry Hedges. I've come to see Mr Green.'

The voice of Greta Sargent rasped out, 'This is most irregular, as I have already warned you. What time do you call this? Why didn't you make a proper appointment?'

Harry looked at Jasper. 'Sudden development, Miss Sargent. Could be helpful news about Mr Green's sister. I wanted to tell him immediately.'

A few seconds later the gates glided open.

'Good boy,' murmured Jasper, as the Range Rover crunched forward.

Like a sentinel, Greta Sargent was standing at the open front doors when they arrived.

'Who is your friend?' she asked, nodding towards Jasper.

'Someone I used to work with,' admitted Harry. 'Just seeing him for a drink.'

She looked incredulous. 'Well, he can wait in the anteroom.'

Jasper hauled himself out of the driver's seat, impervious to Greta Sargent's withering look, and followed the pair inside.

'In there,' she said, deftly opening a tall door and waiting while Jasper ensconced himself in the square room, whose walls were covered in large, multicoloured spots.

'Nice bit of Damien Hirst, unless I'm much mistaken,' chirped Jasper.

Greta Sargent shut the door on him and turned to Harry.

'You are fortunate that Mr Green is so keen to hear what you have to say. He has cut short his dinner. You are to meet him in the library.'

Harry walked along beside her. They were passed by a homely woman carrying a half-empty tray of food. 'Thank you, Elspeth,' said Greta.

'Right you are, madam,' she replied.

The library was in stark contrast to the rest of the house, its high walls canyoned with leather-jacketed books and carved wooden pillars. There was no modern art anywhere in this room.

Lionel was sitting on a red leather Chesterfield. He sprang up as Harry arrived.

'What have you got to tell me?'

Nervously, Harry explained that he believed he had found a possible match for Sarah, living nearby.

'But I can't give you the details, Mr Green, until you at least entertain the idea of selling *The Purple Child* to Sir Jimmy Knox, who has been crucial to this process,' he blagged, crossing as many fingers as he could.

Instead of exploding, as he'd imagined, Lionel laughed.

'I summon you here to help me, nothing happens and all you do is try to strike a bargain? Did you know I could buy out your Sir Jimmy ten times over? I was in business with him years ago, until I realised what he was like when I bought the *Piddlington Gazette* from him. I gave you a job, after your precious Sir Jimmy sacked you. And you insult me like this. Despite everything I read about your disgrace, I thought you deserved a second chance and when I engaged you, I thought you might be able to help me trace Sarah, as well as run my newspaper. But you come here and insult my intelligence. You throw away your chances. You will tell me the name and location of the person you say is my sister and I will decide whether or not I should sack you on the spot.'

Harry swallowed. 'I've fulfilled my part of this bargain over your sister and all I'm asking is that you just entertain the idea—'

'There is no bargain, you idiot. Have you ever stopped to think just why I won't sell *The Purple Child*? Why I won't even put it on public display?'

Harry shook his head.

'Because it is a painting of my sister! *She* is the Purple Child! She sat for the artist and that painting is the last image I have of her. There are no photos, no drawings, just this. And you expect me to give it up to a drunken bully who wouldn't know his backside from a Botticelli.'

And then he started weeping. 'Get out. Just get out. You're fired.'

Harry felt nauseous.

'I am so sorry, Mr Green, I would never have asked if I had known the painting was of your sister, truly. But I was trying to help you because the thing is, I know Sir Jimmy Knox, too. Maybe better than you do. He's absolutely awful and if he wants something, he just won't stop until he gets it. I was trying to protect you.'

Lionel was dabbing his face with a large green handkerchief. As he blew his nose, the double doors opened and Greta Sargent swept in.

'You! Out. Now.'

'I'm so sorry,' mumbled Harry. 'I didn't mean to upset anyone.'

Greta stepped forward and grasped his bicep. Despite her age, she had a grip like a Rottweiler.

'Out! How dare you behave like this?'

She started marching Harry down the corridor, her feet smashing on the cold, hard stone.

'You have behaved unforgivably,' she said. 'Mr Green gives you a job when no one else will and this is how you repay him. Don't you dare show your face here again.'

And with that, she shoved him onto the steps, and he ran down them and jumped into the Range Rover, where Jasper was waiting.

It was only when they were out of the gates that Harry noticed Jasper smiling.

'Well done, 'Arry,' he said. 'Nice little distract-a-thon!'

Harry stared at him, but Jasper was wearing his Ray-Bans. He didn't speak again until they swept back into the town. Pulling up on the double yellows on a side street, Jasper nodded.

'Out you get. I'll be in touch.'

Chapter 24

Harry slunk into The Ball Inn. He felt as if everyone in the bar had noticed him and could smell his shame.

'Penny for them?'

Cassandra was in tight, stonewashed jeans with a rhinestone pattern over the thigh and wearing high-heeled, white cowboy boots.

'Can I have a large vodka, please?'

'Are you sure? Headache gone?'

He nodded. Well, the physical one had . . . He just had to manage the giant one that Jasper had landed him with.

'Coming up.'

He sipped the drink, relishing the lime slice and the ice. Right now, he felt he could down a whole bottle.

'It didn't go well, then?'

Harry shook his head.

'Another? On the house?'

I don't deserve this, he thought.

Both glasses quickly hit their mark, and he walked light-headedly up to his bedroom. He wondered if his dismissal would get into the *Press Gazette*: 'Hedges fired again!' He'd lose his entire career – he wouldn't come back from this, unless he could persuade Violett to honour her New York job promise. If he couldn't work as a journalist, he'd have to swallow his pride, move back in with his father, probably, and get a hideous proper job, involving never-ending Excel spreadsheets and excruciating team-building days at motorway hotels with people called Brandon.

He lay down. He'd get undressed in a bit.

* * *

He must have dozed off, because he was awakened by The Verve's 'Lucky Man'.

''Arry? We're going back to the house. Tonight.'

'What? Why?'

'To get the pissing painting, of course, why else would we?'

Harry's head spun. Had he missed something? Suffered an episode or amnesia? 'What are you talking about? How? Who?'

'Never you mind. Possession is nine-tenths of the old proverbial and all that bollocks, isn't it?'

'You're going to break in and steal it?'

'Break in? Don't be daft. Technically, it won't be breaking – just entering.'

'But it *is* stealing,' groaned Harry, wondering if he should call Ophelia. 'You must be mad.'

'It won't be the both of us. It'll be you. While you was talking to the old boy, I nipped round and got the pantry window open. It's not too high off the ground. All you have to do is get in there, get into that study room and get the painting. The alarm system is mental, covers some bits of the house and not others, and everyone'll be in bed. By the time any alarm does go off, you'll be long gone.'

Ignoring Harry's hesitation, he continued, 'Look, there's nothing to worry about. The police will reckon it's some antiques gang; there's always one somewhere that's all over the shop, nicking stuff. It won't be traced to you or Sir Jimmy, guaranteed.'

Harry felt faint. 'Your guarantees are worth nothing. What makes you think I'd get involved in something like that? It's criminal. I agreed to ask a question on Violett's behalf and now, thanks to you, I've lost my job again. The answer's no.'

Jasper chuckled darkly. 'Get that painting and your problems are all over, old boy; New York and enough moolah to help your old man and buy a decent pair of shoes for yourself.'

'Well, I'm not doing it. I'm going to the police. And anyway, after everything that's happened, Sir Jimmy is the first person they'll suspect, gang or no gang – how does he think he'll get away with it?'

There was a heavy, dark silence, before Jasper started speaking again.

'No one ever has *anything* on Sir Jimbo, I can tell you that for starters. But it sounds to me like you need something to help you make up your mind?' He didn't wait for an answer. 'After your little bout of trouble—'

'I was only doing what I thought was my job. You set up me and Violett, and you know damn well I only agreed to carry the can because you said you'd sort it,' Harry cut in.

Jasper gave another low chuckle. 'It matters not. The writs are still coming in and Sir Jimmy needs a fall guy, especially if the politicos start whingeing on again. All sorts of emails and documents show, or they will show, that you authorised payments to various scrotes and took part in all sorts of other illegal surveillance and spying activity. Substantial and compelling new evidence, I think they call it, under the Criminal Justice Act. It means you can be tried again and, believe me, we'll see to it that you are. So, if you don't want this new material coming to light, I suggest you play ball now.'

Harry felt murderous. He had never done any of these things and there wasn't a shred of evidence to suggest he had.

As if reading his mind, Jasper continued. 'Remember that internet hacker you did the splash on a few years back? It turns out he told you a load of porkies about going straight and instead has become very interested in faking documents and email trails, and he has been extremely helpful. What with one thing and another . . .'

Harry knew then, he was beaten. Jack 'The Hack' McQuitty was a sneaky, two-faced genius bastard who had simultaneously infiltrated the Pentagon and the Kremlin and played both sets of spooks off against the other. If he was on board for Sir Jimmy, it was hopeless – his e-forgeries were an artwork in themselves, and no one had ever managed to lay a legal finger on him.

Jasper knew he was on the ropes, unless he could think of something. And fast. As Harry tried to rev up his horrified mind, Jasper started talking again.

'So, we're on for eleven p.m. Be there, but don't be in the square, too many cameras around. I'll see you at the end of the alleyway behind that dump you're staying in.'

And the call ended.

* * *

At 10.50 p.m., dressed in his darkest office trousers and an old, black hoodie, Harry crept down the stairs, glad of the cover that time at the bar offered. He moved quietly through the back door and through the yard, before walking down the alley, all the while urging his shivering brain to come up with a solution. Should he call the police now? Should he call Violett? He *had* to think of something to put a stop to this.

As he emerged onto the backstreet, the Range Rover glided up like Dracula's carriage and he went round to the side and got in.

'Good man. You know it makes sense.'

Harry felt as if he was going to be sick. Perhaps he could feign a heart attack, or something? Or maybe a stroke?

As journeys to somewhere horrible have a habit of doing, it seemed only a matter of minutes before they were fording the river, water spraying up from the car sides like giant wings in the deepening darkness.

As they sailed up the narrow lanes, Jasper, who was chewing gum, ferociously, swore under his breath when they nearly took the wing mirror off of a car speeding the other way.

Harry sank down in his seat, terrified of being recognised. He idly hoped Jasper might choke on the gum or suffer some trauma that left him in a coma – or at least a full-body plaster cast – for the next year. As he shifted, he felt his mobile in his pocket. A hope sparked. It was fifty per cent charged. If he could just manage to put it on record, he could use it as evidence to show Ophelia. Maybe even Lionel, if he had to.

It was worth a shot. Slowly, he began to ease it out of his back pocket.

'What are you doing?' snarled Jasper.

'It's your bloody driving, it's doing my back in,' lied Harry, quickly shifting and pretending to massage his left hip. He'd nearly got the thing out of his pocket.

'Christ! You always were a great wet lettuce, weren't you? I remember you in rugby – they only picked you because you were tall.'

'That's not true,' protested Harry. 'I was the best lock St Bastard's ever had.' If he could just keep up this manly banter, it might distract Jasper enough for him to try and turn the recording app on.

As they approached the turn-off for The Grange, Jasper wrenched the steering wheel to the right, and they started bumping down a rough track. There was a horrific noise from the front axle and Jasper stopped and jumped out. Quickly, Harry pressed record, put the phone on silent and settled it in his pocket again.

As Jasper got in, he grinned. 'Best of British engineering!'

Harry smiled weakly.

They arrived in a small clearing; Jasper turned the engine off and gestured to Harry to put on a pair of black gloves he produced from the side-pocket.

'We're more or less at the back of The Grange and the window is here,' he said, pulling out his phone, which cast an eerie blue glow in the vehicle. It had an image of the pantry window on it, seemingly taken earlier.

'Turn that off – someone will see us.'

'Don't be ridiculous, we're the only people here. I was just showing you. I don't want any cock-ups.'

Harry looked at the window on the screen; it appeared to be positioned among a jumble of add-on extensions at The Grange's less elegant rear. This was not going to be easy.

* * *

As he and Jasper crept towards the estate's perimeter fence, Harry asked him how they would get through. 'That's it, the security fence looks wired, but it isn't and this bit's the most secluded,' whispered Jasper. 'I've already cut a hole big enough for both of us, and the painting.'

As the chain-link fence came into view in the deepening gloom, Jasper ducked down.

'How do you know it isn't wired?' demanded Harry, imagining himself frizzled like an escapee in a World War II movie.

'Friends in low places,' chuckled Jasper as he pushed through, waiting for Harry to follow.

The Grange was shielded by colossal rhododendron bushes, but Jasper seemed to know the way to go and, as they circumvented one particular monster, Harry gaped. They were within twenty or so metres of the pantry window, a small, square sash affair.

'Right, in there,' indicated Jasper. 'Get in, then go to where the painting is and get it off the wall. You should be able to open the study window and pass it through to me before getting out. Don't worry about the gravel noise – I've checked, and we can walk on grass until we get round here again, and I know they all go to sleep early in there.'

'What about security lights and the alarm?'

'The old boy doesn't appear to go in for security lights, and the alarm that covers the pantry door is on a different circuit,' said Jasper. 'If it goes off at all you'll be well away, up the corridor, before all the major alarm is triggered. Go on! Quicker you go in, quicker you can get out and get to New York.' He ducked behind the rhododendron and gestured Harry to go forward.

Pouring with sweat, Harry approached the old pantry window. A plan was forming in his mind. Like most of his plans, it was rubbish. But it would have to do.

As Jasper disappeared from sight, Harry, instead of going towards the window, crept carefully round the curved side of the bush, out of view of the house – and of Jasper.

The plan was beginning to take shape.

He calculated that if he could just make it look as if he had attempted the break-in, and trigger or raise an alarm while not actually committing the crime, he could keep Jasper off his back for a few hours more and stay one millimetre on the right side of the law. The recording, he hoped, would prove his intention to foil the theft but, for good measure, he murmured, 'I've got a plan to stop all this,' and prayed the microphone had picked it up.

To make this work, he needed to set off the house alarm without physically entering the property. But doing that would require the ability to instantly grow an arm that was about two metres long, so he could reach from outside the pantry window to the pantry door, and poke through its lock to disrupt what he guessed were the corridor beams of the security system. What he needed was some kind of big stick. Given the spartan nature of the garden at that point – just giant bushes, basically – the big-arm thing felt slightly more viable. Desperately, Harry craned his neck to each side, perspiration pouring down the inside of his T-shirt. He caught sight of the corner of what looked like a walled garden or something. There might be sticks for beans. Harry tiptoed towards the structure, hoping Jasper wouldn't see him.

He stopped. There, against the wall at the far end, was a pile of spindly bamboo sticks. All about one metre long. But if he could tie two together . . .

Hardly breathing, Harry tiptoed in and gathered up the two longest ones. Then, looking around, he approached the cover of the bush again, wondering how he could tie them together. As he looked down, he saw the cord from his hoodie. Perfect!

With an almighty yank, he pulled the string out, nearly strangling himself in the process as the fabric bunched. He then removed the string, winding the two sticks tightly together and tying them.

Darkness was cloaking that part of the garden and as he set off the few paces towards the pantry window, he prayed Jasper still couldn't see what he was doing.

On the bright side, Jasper had been as good as his word and the window was at least two inches open. Gently, he pushed it upwards and it went with surprising grace on its Victorian sashes. Harry stood on tiptoes and looked in.

The room was pitch-black. He knew he had very little time to locate the pantry door, which, he hoped, had a handle of the push-down variety. He picked up the stick and pushed it through the window. It stopped. Had he hit the side? For a split second he wondered idly about just knocking some stuff off the shelves. But that wouldn't do. For his plan to work, Jasper had to hear an alarm being triggered.

He fished out his phone and turned on the torch. And nearly screamed.

A giant brown bear on its hind legs was snarling down at him. It was accompanied by a fox, whose black eyes glittered, sightlessly. And a peacock. Taxidermy. This pantry room wasn't used for storing food but old items.

His eyes adjusted and, swallowing, he realised that at the end of the space he could see a pinprick of light. He surmised it must be the door. Shining the phone's torch higher, he saw the door lock. With a round handle. Which meant he had no chance of pressing it down and triggering any alarm.

As his mind raced again, he realised there was only one thing for it: pray he could poke the stick through the keyhole and somehow trigger the alarm system that way.

Instinctively, he grasped the stick with both hands, like a garden gnome with a fishing rod. But it was still a few inches too short.

As his mind scrabbled around for a solution, an image came into his head. It was of a short, tubby Bristolian wearing an orange waistcoat: Lenny 'Whirlwind' Wiggins, three times world snooker champion, whose capacity for drink was slightly less than that of an oil tanker. Despite imbibing solidly for the excruciating three days of their interview (it was only meant to have lasted an hour), Whirlwind Wiggins had taught Harry how to play his signature long shot and had been suitably impressed that he'd got it right, first time.

Right now, it was Harry's only shot. Carefully, he placed his left hand on the window ledge and angled the stick in his right, ready to glide over it.

As he pulled the stick backwards to line up the shot, a piece of bamboo sliced through the glove and into Harry's hand. He bit his lip and carried on. He could scream later. Narrowing his eyes, Harry drew the stick back as far as he could, then fired it forward towards the door and its light.

It took him a few seconds to register a terrible ringing in his ears before realising he'd done it. There was an alarm! And he'd only gone and set it off!

Hastily withdrawing the stick and javelining it high into the rhododendron bush, Harry started sprinting across the lawn, the way he'd come. As he moved, he was aware of a huge, World War II-style searchlight coming on from the roof and a commotion near the front of the building. The light raked the grounds just as he managed to dive behind another giant rhododendron.

'Stop, whoever you are!' came a voice from on top of The Grange's roof. 'I have a firearm and I'm not afraid to use it.'

Greta Sargent let off what sounded like a shot from an elephant gun and Harry made a run for the fence. Where the hell was Jasper?

As he reached the gap and squeezed through, he flung himself to the ground. There was faint shouting and the roof-light appeared to have stopped arcing. As he crawled into the clearing, he saw it was empty. No car, no Jasper. That double-crossing bastard.

He was about to start running down the inky track, when he saw blue flashing lights moving rapidly towards him. Oh God no, please no, not Ophelia. He needed to explain all this to her calmly and clearly, then hand over the recording. Not looking as if he'd been in cahoots with the Kray twins. Harry launched himself into a patch of bracken, their musky fronds sheltering him from the sight of the vehicles, which thankfully sped right past.

Shaking with relief, Harry got himself upright. Glancing at the cars in the distance, where they appeared to have stopped, he could hear urgent male voices, the men's shapes silhouetted against the headlights as they walked round their vehicles.

'Oy, guv, over here. Look at the fence.'

There was the sound of cracking twigs as another person approached the fence.

'Good God.' The voice was low and strong with a faint London edge to it. 'You know what this means, don't you?'

The other officer didn't answer.

'It means,' said the London voice, 'that the person they clocked at the back of the house was probably some kind of decoy – there's no way they could get anything out of that old pantry window.'

Harry stood stock-still.

'Look, sir,' said the first officer. 'Our intel was that there was going to be a raid on this house directly to the room where he keeps his most valuable paintings. There was nothing about this pantry business.'

The London voice replied, 'Agreed. But they appear to have got off with the Picasso and there may be other works.'

The other officer made a sympathetic noise. 'Who bloody knows, sir. I haven't had time to check it against the messages. What we do know is that if we don't sort this soon, there'll be trouble. You've spent enough time on this one already – time you were back at the Yard.'

'Thanks for your support,' said the London voice. 'But this is *not* the outcome we were looking for.'

He stopped again, as his police radio crackled into life.

As he walked towards the car's headlights, Harry was finally able to see the man's outline and his thoughtful face.

The officer in charge was PC Patrick Collins.

Chapter 25

It was a long and exhausting walk home, not made any easier by getting lost and walking in a circle for part of it. Harry's clapped-out phone had run out of battery, and he was fast running out of hope. Despite his best endeavours, it appeared he'd still managed to help Jasper commit a serious criminal offence and it wouldn't be long before Greta Sargent put two and two together and came up with half a million. He just had to pray that the recording would help establish that, whatever else he'd done, he had not had any part in physically removing the painting from The Grange.

The sun had risen over the Piddlington Downs by the time the minster hove into view. The early-morning light made the town look even prettier than before. Harry's heart ached at his own stupidity. Too embarrassed to go to The Ball Inn, he quietly let himself into the office. Ignatius danced heavily around him, thrilled to see someone so early.

'I'll feed you in one minute.' Ignatius let his head droop so low that Harry didn't have the heart to make him wait any longer.

'OK, here you go.' He may as well make someone happy.

Harry shuffled into the kitchen and fished out a Premium dog biscuit. Ignatius's tail thumped with pleasure. He put on the kettle and rummaged around in the kitchen cupboard, finding an ancient bar of soap.

Checking the door, he carefully stripped to his underpants and quickly washed himself, using handfuls of scratchy paper towels to dry. He wiped the mud and twigs off his trousers and hoodie and raked his fingers through his hair before dressing again. His eyes felt sore and gritty, and his hand still sported a nasty gash from the bamboo snooker cue.

He was starving, but it was far too early for anywhere decent to be open, and anyway he had no money on him. On the off chance, he stepped into the newsroom and opened the office cupboard. Nothing but 'Premium Dog Food' and the dog biscuits. He reached into the box, drew one out and bit into it. Not too dreadful, considering. This was what his life had become. Eating Ignatius's biscuits.

Making a weak, grey, instant coffee, Harry contemplated his alternative futures. Waiting in the office until Greta Sargent arrived to bodily remove him, following his sacking? Or leave immediately – but only after he'd asked his father if he could return to live with him *and* settle this bill, too, from the proceeds of their family home?

More likely, there was the potential arrest and prosecution for being an accessory to the theft of a Picasso from an elderly gentleman who had done him no harm.

Or Jasper producing 'evidence' of crimes he'd never committed but which would be difficult to disprove, causing eternal public humiliation and no journalism ever again. Except running the prison news-sheet, probably.

He wondered idly if he should contact Violett. She had said she wanted to repay him – now would very definitely be the moment, he felt.

The only thing that could possibly save him was the recording, which would prove that he had had no intention of helping to steal the painting. He plugged his phone into the charger and watched as it slowly flickered into life again.

He put his head in his hands.

* * *

He didn't know how long he'd sat like that but was jolted by the sound of the door.

It was Ray.

'Harry, lad, what are you doing here? Are you OK?'

Summoning every ounce of his energy, Harry replied, 'Just got up early. I couldn't sleep and, er, fancied a little walk but I had a bit of a mishap, so I thought I'd come here to get myself sorted. You know, make an early start.'

Ray stared.

'What's the matter?'

'Why are you eating dog biscuits?'

He hastily brushed the remains onto the floor, where Ignatius devoured them in one gulp.

'Didn't realise,' he said, shakily.

Ray looked concerned. 'Shall I go and get us something nice to eat? And a bit of that funny coffee you like? Won't be a minute.'

Harry could have wept. He didn't deserve such kindness. 'Yes, please.'

'Come on, Ignatius,' said Ray. 'Do you good to get some air.'

When Ray arrived back, with the drink and a bacon roll, Harry could have kissed him. He'd already managed to place a few stories online but was unprepared for Ray's animation.

'Meant to say, there are loads of police all over the town – Brenda said there's been a robbery or something.'

'Robbery? Where?'

'Up at The Grange – something to do with a painting. Inside job, people reckon. We should call Sergeant Starsky and get a bit more info.'

Harry felt sick. This was deadly serious. What the hell had Jasper done?

'Maybe I'll take a walk round there, try and find out a bit more.'

Ray nodded.

He stepped out. He needed time to think.

He'd intended to take the recording straight round to Ophelia. But he had no intention of visiting the police station until he could work out how to bring Jasper down and extricate himself from this giant mess. Ophelia was scary enough when she was angry and as for PC Collins . . . He wondered if Ophelia knew her PC was so important that everyone called him 'sir' and that he wasn't even Irish?

Wandering carefully away from the police station area of town, he stepped into Tesco and bought two small Toblerone bars with some coins Ray had given him. By the time he'd arrived back in the *Gazette*'s courtyard, he'd eaten them both.

Chapter 26

As Harry stepped back into the newsroom, he could see immediately something was wrong: Hattie and Ray looked stricken.

'Is anything the matter?'

Hattie looked at Ray. Ray looked at Hattie; Ignatius looked at his two front paws. *Even he can't meet my eye*, thought Harry.

Ray cleared his throat. 'We've just received a letter, Harry. On paper. Dated yesterday. It says you're no longer the editor of the *Piddlington Gazette*.'

'And you have to leave the office, otherwise you won't get your pay,' said Hattie.

Ray shuffled some of his desk papers around before saying: 'It said something about a gross breach of trust. Have you done something?'

Harry didn't have a clue what to do. Tough it out? Or go like a good boy? Before he could say anything, Hattie cut in.

'Oh yes . . .' she said, carelessly. Harry knew enough to know that he should listen very carefully to what came next.

'I'm really sorry, and it shouldn't be a problem but . . .'

'But what?'

'Well, very unfortunately, poor Ignatius got tangled up in the charging cable while you were out and accidentally pulled your phone into his water bowl, so I'm afraid it might need to dry out for a while. It's OK, I've dropped mine in all kinds of places and it's fine, you just have to put them in the airing cupboard or a box of rice or something,' said Hattie brightly.

'But I need it! It's got the recording . . .' he quickly tailed off.

Fortunately, Hattie wasn't paying any more attention because Ignatius had let out a huge cough and then stared at the carpet tiles, as something that looked distinctly like a fly crawled around on it.

The ghastly interruption focused Harry's mind. He wasn't gone yet and if he could just get the phone dry and the recording to Ophelia, he could prove he had nothing to do with planning the robbery and would be in the clear. Well, nearer to the clear, anyway.

'Look, I can't explain now but I think I should just get on with it for the moment – we've got some good stuff for the next splash and the website, haven't we?'

They both stared, but news values took over.

'Actually, we have,' said Hattie. 'There's a press statement coming about the museum – apparently, they have discovered more thefts; that would be a good one.'

'There's all the painting stuff and the eviction of old Mrs Burge,' said Ray. 'We ought to do something about that and get the latest on the bodies.'

'I'll cover that,' said Harry. It could prove a good excuse for getting out of the building.

As they all started to write, the silence was shattered by the office phone.

'Harry?' Ophelia Starsky's clipped tones snipped down the line. 'I'm calling to let you know that we have a press briefing taking place at noon sharp.'

'The bodies on the roundabout?'

'Yes. And the theft of an extremely rare and valuable painting from The Grange.'

He made surprised noises.

'Noon. And I warn you, Harry, we've got an officer coming from London for this, so don't let me down. PC Collins hasn't shown up yet and I'm trying to track him down.'

Harry told the others he would be attending the press conference. 'Even though you're not supposed to be here?' asked Hattie.

'Ophelia doesn't know that.'

'Ophelia! Ooh!'

'Please, not now.'

He quickly left the office after that, hopped into the Cooper and careered towards The Ball, rejoicing that Cassandra didn't appear to be about. After a quick wash and clothes change, he drove to the police station. Aside from its regular Ford Focus, he saw a black Audi sports job parked there.

As he walked round and into the main library room, the usual press conference suspects were in attendance: Ophelia, the force press officer and a second, more sharply dressed, man studying a shiny new iPad, who Harry assumed was the Met Police press person.

The Met man looked edgy and kept checking his watch.

'Detective Chief Inspector Hayden Martin is due here now, Sergeant Starsky,' muttered the press officer.

On the dot of noon, Chief Inspector Hayden Martin strode in.

He was clad in a Belstaff leather jacket, an immaculate white T-shirt and the kind of jeans that cost half a week's wages and, as he strode by, smelled like the perfume counter at Harvey Nichols.

Sergeant Starsky's jaw fell open.

'PC Collins? What are you doing here? Where's your uniform?'

DCI Martin smiled kindly.

'Please excuse me, Sergeant, and,' he said, turning to smile briefly and dazzlingly at the room, 'apologies to anyone here who has met me in my undercover guise as PC Patrick Collins. I actually work for the Met's Serious Theft Squad.'

As everyone wrote this down, he turned to Ophelia, and Harry could hear a muttered: 'Sorry, Sergeant, no time to tell you before.'

As his strong voice filled the room, a strand of hair broke free from Sergeant Starsky's perennial bun and coiled over her forehead. She impatiently wiped it away, her face flushed – probably with embarrassment, Harry thought. His heart went out to her. All that time she'd been working with an undercover chief inspector and never known.

DCI Martin outlined the 'serious' theft of a Picasso painting from a 'property near Piddlington Minster', which had taken place the previous night. He described *The Purple Child* but refused to put a value on it, instead emphasising that it was unique and needed to be found quickly.

'I also have to tell you that the owner of the property, who is an elderly gentleman, was verbally threatened by the robber, or robbers, as he tried to prevent the theft of the artwork and potentially other valuables. He has not been admitted to hospital but, as you can imagine, he has been left very shaken.'

The local radio reporter asked if there were any other people in the house.

DCI Martin nodded. 'Yes, the cook and the other resident of the property, who acts as a secretary and personal assistant to the owner. She attempted to track a man we now believe was acting as a decoy, at the rear of the building. The robber was able to enter from the opposite side of the property during the commotion.'

Harry stared at his feet. This was horrendous.

Barry swung forward on his seat. 'Any descriptions of anyone?'

'Not as yet, although we understand that the decoy would have been a tallish man, as the window he used, before the house's alarm was set off, was fairly high off the ground and there were no ladders or other items to facilitate entry from this point.'

Harry quietly sank lower in his seat.

'We are still looking into the manner in which the thief was able to enter the other side of the building. I don't need to tell you that an item as valuable as this painting can generate a crime response all of its own,' he said, gazing upon Sergeant Starsky, who appeared to have shrunk. As you would, thought Harry, when you found out your deputy is really much higher up the greasy pole than you.

He tried to catch her eye, to give her a reassuring smile, but Barry was talking.

'So, how come you're undercover, then, PC Collins? Did Sergeant Starsky here know anything about it? Why was it all kept under wraps?'

DCI Martin smiled apologetically, as a cloud of exquisite aftershave wafted away from him and into the room.

'If you don't mind – Barry, isn't it? – I think we'll leave that for another day. I'm sure I don't need to tell an experienced reporter like you that sometimes police officers have to work undercover. Sergeant Starsky has done an impeccable job of investigating a number of important issues at the same time in this area. By contrast, my squad have only got the one: a person or persons who steal valuable artworks.'

Harry had to hand it to him – he was as smooth as silk.

There was a rasping noise as Barry absent-mindedly scratched his polyester-trousered bottom and DCI Martin winced and looked away.

'I would like the assembled members of the media to help us in returning this painting to its rightful owner, and catching those responsible for this crime,' he continued. 'If you'd be willing to put out an appeal to that effect, we would be very grateful.'

He explained that his office could provide images of the painting and a rudimentary timeline of the theft. 'We really appreciate your assistance in this,' he concluded.

The bright young agency reporter thrust up his hand. 'This is the third serious crime reported in Piddlington Minster this week – is it a coincidence or can any of it be put down to lack of policing caused by government cutbacks?'

DCI Martin hesitated for a second then smiled broadly. 'That's a very good question and my answer is that nothing's off the table.' And then he stood up, posing for a few pictures which, Harry guessed, Barry would caption: 'Very *Hot Fuzz*!' He then wrapped up the press conference by thanking everyone for coming and politely escorting a deflated-looking Ophelia out of the library and back into the police station. As they left, Harry heard her calling him 'sir'.

Chapter 27

Harry got back into the Cooper. He needed to call Jasper but there was no way his phone would have dried out yet. And he was now terrified that, somehow, his calls could be connected to that awful man. As he wondered what to do, he felt thirsty and rummaged around under the seat for the bottle of water he usually kept there. It tasted like it had come out of the River Thames, but he swigged a mouthful, desperately willing his exhausted mind to think what to do next.

He drove slowly back to the office and was just about to swing into the cobbled yard, when he saw a delivery van there. Spotting him, the driver smiled and walked towards his stationary car, waving a small white package.

'Parcel for Mr Hedges?'

Surprised, Harry thanked him and, while waiting for the delivery driver to back out, he pulled open the packet and the small box inside.

It was an old-school Nokia. With a text from an unknown number saying:

Been a hitch

He parked, picked the parcel up again and walked into the office.

He needed to call Jasper. He'd always known his old news editor had sailed close to the wind. But it had never occurred to him that he would deliberately employ criminals to expedite Sir Jimmy's crazy plans.

As he entered, a sepulchral form moved up from his chair.

'Mr Hedges. What are you doing here?'

Out of her firmament, Greta Sargent was even more terrifying. Her pallid, skull-like face was immobile.

'I've come to ensure that, as per Mr Green's instructions, you leave these premises. You are no longer the editor of the *Piddlington Gazette* and I expect you to immediately hand over the offices of your trade.'

Harry looked blank.

'Keys!' she snapped. 'Computer passcodes.'

'I've got those, Miss Sargent,' said Ray, his eyes firmly averted from Harry's.

'Good. Well, you and Miss Watson can run things between you until we find another editor. If, after all this, Mr Green can be bothered to carry on with the publication. He has suffered grievously thanks to you, on top of his ordeal last night.'

Harry felt appalled.

'How is he?' But she just pointed to the door and snapped: 'Out!'

'Can I just say goodbye?' pleaded Harry.

'You have precisely two minutes.'

She swept out of the door, leaving Hattie and Ray staring.

'Harry, what's happened? I don't want another boss, neither does Ray. They might not love Ignatius like you do. Can't you do something? It can't be that bad.'

Harry shook his head. 'I can't say right now. But maybe here wasn't ever the best place for me. Maybe I really do belong somewhere else.'

'But who's going to employ you after, you know, everything?'

'Maybe I'll get lucky and get my old job back. Or something.'

Her face turned to horror. 'What? Working for that old fascist Sir Jimmy Knox? What's wrong with you? I thought you liked it here? I thought you liked *us*.'

'And Piddlington Minster,' added Ray.

'I do but . . .'

Greta burst through the door again.

'You've had your two minutes. Out! Mr Featherwaite and Miss Watson – get on with your work.'

As they subsided into their seats, Harry walked out.

Greta stalked away and while he fiddled with the lock of the Cooper, Hattie shot out of the office and picked up her bike.

'Just got a call about the body on the roundabout!' she said to him.

'What?' He was keen in spite of himself.

'Call me!' she shouted over her shoulder.

'Out!' yelled Greta, turning round.

Harry got into the Cooper but it wouldn't start.

Then the Nokia rang.

He pressed the button to accept the call.

'Hello?'

'Good. It is you. From now on you're to use this,' said Jasper's voice. 'Burner. Untraceable.'

'Seems like you managed to get the painting, then,' said Harry, cutting to the chase.

'Do me a favour. Utter dog's breakfast; there were cops everywhere, so I ended up driving into town and shoved it in a bush. On that bleedin' roundabout. Went back early doors but couldn't find it where I thought I'd put it, and there are police all over so it was too risky to stay. Fuck knows what's happened. Looks like someone else found it first.'

Harry was astonished but kept his cool. 'Well, that's your problem. Mine is that you owe me. New York, wherever, I'm not fussy. Thanks to you I'm finished here.'

Jasper gave a low chuckle. 'You're finished everywhere, mate. Do you really think Sir Jimbo is going to give you your job back, or any job? From what I've heard, that stinking mutt in your office would be more use to him.'

'We had an agreement! Violett said—'

'I don't think so. We don't have that painting and, even if we did, do you really think the Knoxter would have someone like you back? You're a cock-up merchant, like that idiot Fewtrell, and if you carry on like this, you'll end up like him.'

Harry was astonished. 'You knew Kevin Fewtrell?'

''Course I did, we worked together years ago on the *Bucks Bugle* and when he was made redundant from his job on some trade mag, I tipped him off about the ed's job at the *Piddlington Gazette.* I knew Green was a collector who had loads of old paintings, and I thought it would be handy to have someone who could get into the house legitimately and find out if the rumours I'd heard about that Picasso were true. My mistake, big time.'

'Why?'

'Apart from the fact he didn't seem to know a Picasso from a pork pie, he only met Green once. I asked him to try and interview him and find out a bit more about the paintings, but he was rumbled by that scary old bird, who threatened him for snooping. Next thing I know, he's just run off, the big girl's blouse.'

'You said "end up like him". Care to elaborate?'

Jasper barely skipped a beat. 'Turn of phrase, mate. He died in an accident, didn't he? At least that's what your crummy paper's been saying.'

'Blunt force trauma to the head doesn't sound very accidental.'

'Stuff happens.'

Harry felt enormous sympathy for the nondescript Kevin. He could imagine what it would be like to be on the sharp end of Jasper's bullying. But he was also confused. 'Did Violett know any of this?'

'Don't be daft. She's madder than a box of frogs as it is – seems to think you can sweet-talk anyone into doing anything. My way is best.'

They had moved quite a long way from the matter of the job, Harry felt.

'Where does all this leave me? Whatever so-called evidence you bring about the phone hacking won't change what I can tell the police about what you've just admitted.'

'Admitted? What are you on about?'

Harry boiled. 'Fuck you, Jasper. Because of you I've been sacked from here and basically lost everything *again*. I'm calling Sir Jimmy now – maybe when he realises the truth about you, he'll see sense.'

'I wouldn't if I were you.'

Furiously, Harry stabbed the button to end the call and then fished around under the passenger seat until he found a filthy notebook, with half the pages hanging out. His old, paper contacts book which contained Sir Jimmy's private number. He'd managed to charm it out of his PA at some dreary modern classical concert the company had sponsored.

It was a risk but one worth taking, he thought. He dialled the number, and it was picked up within two rings.

'Yes?'

'Sir Jimmy? Hello, it's me, Harry.'

'Harry who?' He sounded like a Glaswegian car engine whose big ends were going.

'Harry Hedges.'

'And what the fuck are ye calling me for?'

Harry faltered, wondering exactly why he was calling a global media magnate who despised almost all living things. It was one thing to threaten Jasper, quite another to attempt to menace Sir Jimmy Knox.

'I want to talk about the New York job that was offered to me in return for my help to negotiate over a painting that you've tried to have stolen.'

There was an exploding noise at the other end.

'How dare you mention that to me, you strip of English dog piss? What painting? I don't know what you're talking about.'

Harry swallowed but pressed on. 'Yes, you do. I've already risked everything to protect valuable members of your staff and your reputation in the past, and look where it got me. Now your employee has been trying to blackmail me into committing a crime.'

For a few seconds there was a blessed silence.

'Your. Fucking. Job? Christ, you're as entitled as your tart of a mother, aren't you?'

'I beg your pardon. What's my mother got to do with this?'

A soft chuckle came down the phone.

'You mean you didn't know?' 'Know what?'

'Your mother was the same as you, some posho thinking she could throw her weight around and tell everyone what to do; in her case just because she'd dropped her fancy knickers for them.'

'Sorry, but I'm not following.'

'Try this, then! Isabella Hedges! I had a few laps with her, back in the day.'

Harry felt a black, rushing sound in his ears. 'What are you saying?'

'What I'm saying is that your mother was a slapper and when it came to delivering, she was about as useless as you and that soakin' blanket of a father of yours. No wonder she was always playing away from home!'

A sick feeling swept up from Harry's stomach. Flashes of those overheard conversations – muffled, desperate, loaded with anger – came back, with a new, horrible clarity.

Oh God no, it couldn't be, could it? A vision of Isabella danced before him: dressed up to the nines, humming little tunes, staring at her beautiful face in the mirror as she applied eyeliner to those huge, dark eyes.

'Worked it out yet?' rasped Sir Jimmy. Then, not waiting for an answer, he finished the call.

As his mouth filled with saliva, Harry opened the door of the Cooper and was sick onto the cobbles. The vile, bitter taste wouldn't go. Tears squeezed from his eyes. He rubbed furiously at them.

Not Isabella. And Sir Jimmy. That ignorant, vicious, thieving bastard. As he glanced back into the Cooper's shabby interior, it seemed to mock him for the idiot he was, thinking he was somehow in control of anything.

Harry put his head in his hands. A lifetime seemed to pass before he looked up. Hattie was standing nervously outside. 'Harry? Are you OK? You've been sick. What's happened?'

'Nothing. It's nothing. I've really got to leave now, so can I ask you to chuck a bucket of water over this?'

'Please don't go. Please. I'm sure we can work something out. It's been so great with you here.'

He felt the tears prickle again and he looked down, trying to hide them. The peace was shattered by the sound of Ray bursting out of the door.

'Harry! Quick!'

He looked up.

'It's the council – someone's called in to say they've gone back now to try to get into Sadie Burge's house and apparently it's even worse this time.'

Harry felt exhausted. 'Look, what's the point? If they don't do it today, they'll do it tomorrow or some other time. And what can I do? You both heard, I'm not even the editor of this paper anymore. I'm not sure if I'm even a journalist,' he said, biting his lip as the enormity of the situation rose up like a tsunami.

Hattie looked disbelieving. 'Honestly, what are you on about, Harry? You're the only person who can stop this happening to Sadie now. You can *do* something. Are you really going to chicken out?'

He looked at her face. And then at Ray's.

He'd failed at everything. But there was one thing he didn't have to fail at.

'In the car!'

Hattie flashed him a huge smile, wrenched open the door and strapped herself in. As, miraculously, the car started, Harry crashed the gears and drove off.

Chapter 28

The officials' presence at Sadie's was even bigger than the last time. All for one tiny old lady.

Something snapped.

Yes, he'd let everyone down; he'd been sacked, he was going to lose his career and everything he'd ever worked for, and nothing could prevent that now, but he *could* try and stop Sadie Burge being carted away from everything she cared about.

He was aware of Hattie pulling his arm. 'For God's sake! It looks like a war zone.'

He looked from her anguished face to the determined ones of the officials in the front garden.

They were in a huddle. As he and Hattie stepped forward, a police officer he didn't recognise put up his hand.

'Please step back, sir.'

Harry flashed his ancient press card. As he did so, the older official stepped towards the door and poked open the flap, intoning what Harry assumed must be the law relating to situations like this. Then the man screamed and jumped backwards. Sadie had evidently poked something in his eye through the letterbox.

The burly police officer tried next, pleading with Sadie to come out and talk.

Silence. As the council officials moved forward again, he nodded.

They knocked on the door.

Harry could hear a shriek of what sounded like genuine terror from the inside.

Breathing hard, he decided what to do. Remembering his old rugby lessons, he lowered his right shoulder and charged forward, shouting. The startled officials leaped out of the way a millisecond before he slammed into the door, which gave way under his weight.

Once again, he fell into the hallway, which, along with the usual mountains of rubbish, was now bedecked with what smelled like pieces of rotting food.

As he landed, he felt a stinging blow on the back of his head.

'Take that!'

Harry managed to twist himself round.

'Sadie, don't hit me! I've come to help. I won't let them move you out, I promise. Let me stay here with you and help.'

Her face peered over him, silver hair flying wildly.

Struggling to his feet, with a particularly pungent piece of cheese squashed into his right shoulder, Harry flung his arms round her as two officials staggered into the hall. Sadie pulled herself up and started screaming and hitting them with a rolled-up newspaper, dust particles clouding the air. One started coughing and fell over onto what looked like a fifty-year-old piece of cake, as Sadie kicked up dust and more paper. The other attempted to step forward.

Harry drew Sadie to him, but he needn't have bothered. The man yelped and fell sideways as Mr Chagall sank his fangs into the exposed, beefy calf and hissed like an anaconda.

'Good boy.' Sadie laughed. The standing official managed to shake the cat off which, Harry thought, was a huge mistake as it then bit into the cheek of the prone man. Sadie grabbed Harry's hand and pulled him into the sitting room, jamming the door shut and flicking a key in the lock.

'Quick, help me put the sofa in their way.'

Feeling strangely exhilarated, he did as he was bidden, trying not to contemplate what lay under the frankly disgusting piece of furniture, which weighed a ton.

'Horsehair.' Sadie nodded. 'Very good quality.'

She stood, panting. 'You have surprised me. You are a man of the angels, I think.'

He shook his head. 'I'm not great really, Sadie, I just wanted to do what was right. For once.'

She patted his arm. 'It is an adventure, no?'

'Funny sort of adventure.' He grinned, aware of how bad both of them must look. And smell.

'Would you like a biscuit?'

His face must have given him away but hers flickered with amusement.

'Don't worry, I know what you are thinking. Every week I get a fresh packet of Penguins and leave them in there,' she added, indicating a drawer in the side table next to the mantelpiece. 'Then I don't have to go out to the kitchen if I want one. It's hard to find things in there.'

As Harry rummaged in the drawer, he found two biscuits left and handed her a blue-wrapped one.

'So what do we do now?' she asked.

'You tell me.'

She looked thoughtful. 'I know they will come in here eventually, because I do know that I can't keep my home like this forever.'

He tried to hide his surprise.

'If you know that, why have you resisted it? Why did you let it get like that in the first place? You could have avoided all this.'

She sank into the ancient leather armchair, which let out a puff of dust, and started unwrapping her biscuit.

'It's a long story. A very long story. But first, tell me, if you had been made to leave your home a long time ago, in fear of your life, what would you have done?'

He couldn't think.

'Wouldn't you see your home as a sanctuary? Somewhere that should be safe, where only you can decide who does and does not come in? Somewhere you can keep all the things you love? Unfortunately, where I came from, that courtesy was not always extended.'

The noise in the hall was getting louder as the officials moved around, and he could hear voices outside and see shapes on the other side of the filthy windows.

'I don't think we have much time before they lose patience. Shall we try and come to a compromise? I think they really only want to help you and do something about the rats.'

She got up and went to the mantelpiece. 'There are no rats. I keep telling you. But yes, I know you are right in what you say. I think I just wanted to prove to myself that I still have the fire.'

She turned and looked into the dust-covered mirror above the mantelpiece, a ghost in her own home and time. Then she turned to Harry, rolling up the worn sleeve on her left arm.

'Look,' she said, indicating the thin, veined limb.

Apart from wrinkles and the odd liver spot, there was nothing.

Her eyes were deep and still.

'If I had stayed, I would have ended up with a tattoo there. Or worse.'

She leaned on the mantelpiece again, her hair touching the tiny, worn arm of a silver candlestick, its bent, exhausted limbs echoing hers.

As he contemplated what to do next, there was a hoarse shouting noise from the hallway.

'Mrs Burge, Mr Hedges. Please come out. We don't want any more upset. We only want to help.'

Then the owner of the voice started coughing, which stopped with what sounded like a loud vomiting noise.

Harry looked at Sadie. She seemed calmer and was smiling.

'I put the contents of my fridge out there so they would get it all over them if they came in. Some of the food is a little bit old. Do you think it makes me a bad person?'

'Of course not. You're actually a much better person than I am.'

As the officials moved around outside again, Harry put his hand on her arm.

'I'm going to open the bay window and speak to them all. Then, I think, it will be time to start a dialogue about what we can do here.'

A few heaves later, Harry had managed to dislodge the side sash and was speaking to Ophelia, with his head thrust into the blessedly fresh air. He assured her Mrs Burge was happy to comply with any order but needed to make some arrangements first.

'She has a cat, and we need to ensure that other issues regarding her property are resolved,' he said.

Ophelia sighed. 'Of course. It was never about kicking her out, it was about helping her – this is her home. Perhaps I could come in and explain a bit more?'

'Are you sure? It's a bit ripe in here.'

Sadie looked at him. 'I'll go out.'

Which was how Harry found himself listening to Sadie describe her artistic work to an enthusiastic Ophelia, before they agreed a temporary resolution – a council worker would be allowed round the next day to discuss her needs, the clearing of her hoard, and possible alternative temporary accommodation for her and Mr Chagall.

As they walked away from the house an hour later, Ophelia smiled at Harry. 'Well done, that's a great conclusion. I mean, I'm still worried about her health but if we can get things tidied up, maybe we can have a whip-round, get her a new fridge and some bits or something.'

She looked tired.

'Are you OK?' asked Harry. He realised he was going to miss her.

'I'm fine, just the theft of a valuable painting to worry about and a couple of bodies on a roundabout, but yeah, just fine! This was the one I was dreading and thanks to you, it's gone far better than I could have hoped.'

As Harry walked back to the Cooper, he knew what he must do.

He'd remembered where he'd seen Sadie's tiny candlestick before. Turning on the ignition, he decided to risk one more visit to The Grange.

Chapter 29

He was just pulling out of town, his heart soothed by the timeless spectacle of the Piddlington Downs, when he realised he'd left Hattie behind.

Pulling up, he used Jasper's burner to call the office number. Ray answered.

Yes, Hattie had returned but gone off immediately to the police station.

'How are you calling me, when your phone's here?' he enquired.

'I've got an old Nokia in the car,' Harry busked. 'Forgotten the number – don't suppose it's come up on your screen?'

It had. Ray read it out and Harry scribbled it down, before adding, 'She can call me on this number.'

A few minutes later a text came through.

Breaking news!!!!!

He forced himself to carry on driving. He wasn't getting into all that.

The phone started ringing. The noise was incessant, so Harry pulled over and answered.

'Yes?'

'There's no need to be rude,' said Hattie. 'Where have you been? Why haven't you got your phone? I've been trying to speak to you.'

'I'm going to see Lionel Green; I've got something to tell him.'

'If you do get past Gestapo Sargent, could you mention my office chair to him? It's the most horrible colour and Ignatius has chewed—'

'I am not going there to ask him about your office chair. I'm—'

It was Hattie's turn to cut him off.

'Look, it can't wait any longer.' She paused dramatically. 'I've found out about the first body on the roundabout.'

'What about it?'

'It's not real.'

'What?'

'It's not real. I mean, it is real but it's not a real person. I mean . . . it was real once but not anymore.'

'You're not making any sense.'

'I know. But it's so exciting!'

Hattie explained how she'd cycled to the police station and, while she'd stopped to take off her bike helmet, which had got stuck in her hair, she'd overheard a conversation in the entrance to the building.

'Sergeant Starsky had got back from Mrs Burge, and from what I could hear from what she was saying on the phone, it looks like the body on the roundabout has been dead for about a hundred and sixty years.'

'Eh?'

'Exactly! But get this. The person she was talking to was Mr Prentiss. I heard her use his name.'

Harry looked at his watch. He really should be getting on. 'Look, can this wait until I get back to the office? I've got to clear my desk, and I wanted to say thanks properly to you and Ray.'

'Must you?'

'I must,' he said, quietly ending the call.

He was about to pull away, when the phone rang again.

'Harry?'

Violett!

'Jasper gave me this number,' she said, reading his mind. 'I thought we had an agreement?'

'Agreement?'

'Yes, you were going to help me get that picture. And you haven't. For everything to work out for you, we have to facilitate it for Sir Jimmy.'

'I won't be coming back. Thanks to Jasper, I've lost everything. Again. And if you knew what Sir Jimmy was really like, you wouldn't go within a mile of him and neither would anyone else. He's disgusting.'

Violett was silent for a few seconds. 'My God, he hasn't threatened you, has he?' She sounded genuinely alarmed.

'Who? Sir Jimmy? He's just one giant threat factory, as far as I can see.'

'Not Sir Jimmy,' said Violett. 'Jasper.' She lowered her voice, so Harry had to strain to hear. 'Can I trust you with something really important, Harry? Like, *really* important?'

Harry agreed that she could.

'I've just found out that Jasper was trying to blackmail that Kevin Fewtrell. He told me it was the best way to find out about the painting, then we could make a legitimate offer to Lionel Green off the back of the information.'

'Jasper would blackmail his own granny if he thought it would benefit him,' muttered Harry.

'I know, right? But that's not the worst thing, and that's why I'm scared.' She hesitated. 'It's not just the blackmailing. I'm beginning to think he had something to do with Kevin's death. He's out of control.'

'Well, if he was blackmailing him, then he certainly would have terrified the poor man,' said Harry, wondering if Jasper's 'box of frogs' diagnosis of madness in Violett was actually correct.

'But that's it!' persisted Violett. 'Don't you see? Everyone on the local Facebook seems to think the blunt force trauma came from being struck with an item or an implement. Or a fist. But what if it was something else? What if Kevin fell or was pushed so forcibly that his head struck something really hard?'

Harry glanced at his watch. He needed to get to The Grange and Lionel Green.

In an effort to get rid of her, he conceded that Violett may have a point. 'But do you have any actual evidence that Jasper hit or attacked Kevin? Because without that . . .'

'Why would he have to? What if he deliberately ran Kevin over or rammed into him or something? You've seen the way he drives – it's terrifying.'

'Look, Violett, I can't deal with this now – if you're worried, you should go to the police. Or tell Sir Jimmy – he is Jasper's boss.'

'Harry, Jasper scares me. That's what I'm trying to tell you. You know how upset I was when you had to leave after all the transcriptions stuff?'

'I suppose so.'

'Well, I was. But he was the one who forced me into making you take the blame. I didn't think it was fair, and I told him, but he told me you came from a wealthy family and you'd be fine. He knew you were a decent person and would feel sorry for me. He said it would all blow over, and I believed him, like you did. We're both victims here. I don't trust him and neither should you.'

After reminding her that he actually didn't trust Jasper anymore, Harry gently urged her to contact the authorities. 'If you're still worried you can call me again, but now, I've really got to go,' he said and ended the call.

Then he fired the engine and took off for The Grange.

The gates when he arrived seemed as implacable as ever, and he got out and pressed the intercom button.

'Miss Sargent? I've come with some vital news.'

Her voice crackled from the intercom's polished silver box. 'What are you doing here? You're fired. Or haven't I made it plain enough?'

'I know. But this time I really think I could be on to something crucial. Please, can I come in and see you? One last time? I give you my solemn promise that this is the last you'll ever hear from me.'

'Don't think you are going to trick your way in like that! I'll come to the gate and see *you* instead.'

Five minutes later, a low-slung and familiar-looking silver car appeared from the bend in the drive.

'Yes, it's a DB5,' she snapped, as she sprang from the driver's seat. 'And yes, it's one of the ones they used in the James Bond films. Next?'

As swiftly as he could, Harry explained about Sadie: her house, the artwork and her story.

'I need to know, Miss Sargent, is Mr Green Jewish?'

'Why do you ask that?'

'I noticed when I came to see him that he has one of those little candlesticks. With the arms.'

The change in her face was extraordinary. Softly, she replied: 'They are called menorah, Harry. They are lit on the first night of Hanukkah.'

'Great. I mean, I probably did know that about them. But the thing is, I noticed this Mrs Burge, the town hoarder, has a tiny one that looks almost exactly like it. From what she said, I think she is Jewish, too. She's an artist, too, and I thought . . .'

Greta looked thoughtful. 'I have never seen him use his menorah. I asked him about it once, and he wept as I have never seen a man weep before.'

She looked into the distance, then turned back to Harry.

'He said they had been made for him and his sister as a twin pair by their father, who died after a beating by some Nazis. His mother had heard about the Kindertransport so she got them ready, I think she must have hidden the menorah with them, but they were split up and ended up on different trains. It was only later, in England, that he discovered his sister was there too, and he contacted her, but you know what happened then. He told me he could only light his menorah when it was back with its twin.'

She looked at him more closely. 'Describe the menorah to me again. Especially its size.'

Harry did and, slowly, Greta nodded.

'God help me after everything that you've done, but I am going to speak to him. Wait here.'

Then she stepped back into the sports car, executed a perfect three-point turn and roared away, rear wheels machine-gunning gravel through the gates and all over Harry and the Cooper.

It was around fifteen minutes later that the intercom buzzed again, and he noticed the gates start to whirr and glide.

'You may speak to Mr Green.'

Harry sped up the driveway, startling a giant pheasant. As he arrived at the house, he saw the double doors were open. Greta stood in the entrance hall and beckoned him to follow her.

Instead of going to the room filled with pictures, Harry found himself in what he concluded must be the drawing room. It was formally designed, with old masters and classical sculptures on the many marble and marquetry tables, and he spotted what looked like an enormous Rembrandt above the white marble mantelpiece.

The Louis-style chairs had a chilly, unloved air and were upholstered with faded pink-and-yellow striped silk. Nestled in one of them was Lionel Green, clad in a heavy mauve satin dressing gown, a red tartan blanket over his knees. He appeared to have shrunk even more, to no more than the size of a child.

'Tell me,' he whispered.

Looking around, Harry spotted a pink velvet button-backed footstool. He dragged it nearer to the proprietor and sat down so that he could speak to him at eye level.

He outlined the story of the town hoarder, her age, lifestyle, and the few scraps and clues he'd gleaned. It was only when he outlined her interest in modern art that Lionel looked more animated, nodding at Greta Sargent.

'Tell him what you saw,' she prompted.

'On her mantelpiece she has this tiny silver candlestick, with the nine arms, and I remembered you have one very like it.'

Lionel froze.

'Go on!' instructed Greta.

'It's a menorah, isn't it?'

Lionel nodded, his eyes now misty as if he was staring somewhere no one else could see.

He whispered something.

'Sorry, sir, couldn't catch it.'

'He says it's still not enough,' said Greta.

She spoke briefly to Lionel in a language Harry didn't understand, then turned to him again.

'Is there any way this woman could have acquired the menorah? Could she have bought it?'

'I don't know, I didn't speak to her about it.'

Lionel slumped and Harry leaned back.

'Isn't there anything else?' demanded Greta. 'Look at him!'

Harry wished fervently that a giant sinkhole would appear under Lionel Green's drawing room, allowing him to fall into it and never have to see the poor man's tortured, broken face again.

'That's it . . . I mean, Mrs Burge did—'

'Say her name again,' Greta interrupted.

Harry swallowed. 'That's the really sticky bit. Her name isn't Sarah Green, at all. It's Sadie. Sadie Burge.'

He bowed his head, unable to meet their eyes.

'How is it spelled?'

Carefully, he spelled it out.

When he looked up, to his amazement, Greta was smiling and Lionel looked a shade younger.

'Would it interest you to know that Mr Green was originally Mr Greenburg?' she said. 'When he started in business, he shortened it. And did you also know that Sadie is what you would call a nickname, or diminutive, for Sarah? Sadie Burge, eh? Sadie Greenburg perhaps? I will make enquiries.'

As she escorted Harry from the room, he could hardly believe it. By a small miracle he may possibly have done something worthwhile.

Chapter 30

He crept quietly into The Ball Inn, relieved to hear from George that Cassandra was giving a talk on 'Pickling for Champions' to the evening WI in Gusset St Michael. He couldn't face saying goodbye to her, too.

As he got ready for bed, he looked upon his room with a fresh eye, noticing the old photograph of The Ball Inn as it was being built, and the fact that there was a slight bald patch at the top of the bed cover. He wondered again about that poignant sense of perspective that is conferred when you know you have to leave somewhere or someone permanently.

He wished he'd been more aware of his good fortune in the past: his education, his home and his job. He wished, too, he could remember more of Isabella. He didn't have proper memories, more a montage of images which, thanks to Sir Jimmy, had joined up in ways he didn't want them to.

He got into bed and wondered about his conversation with Violett. He could imagine Jasper berating Kevin and, if he had tried to blackmail him over something – although God knows what – he could imagine the nervous-sounding Kevin becoming highly distressed. Could he have suffered a heart attack and fallen over and hit his head, or something? But why would his body be discovered on that roundabout? It didn't make sense.

As the washing machine of thoughts tumbled round, he fell asleep. Only to be woken a few hours later by yet another swarm of unwanted images, crowding out sleep like so many vindictive bats.

For Jasper to have pushed or hit Kevin so badly that he'd struck his head and suffered a serious injury, he'd have had to have been very close to him. And probably in a rage. So far, so believable. On the other hand, Violett could be right. One nudge with a car would probably do it, if the head had connected with something unyielding. Like a kerbstone. He wondered if the pavement theory being bandied about on Rumours of Piddlington had some truth to it. And it would certainly explain Kevin's proximity to the roundabout.

* * *

The next day he awoke late and managed to leave before Cassandra spotted him. He'd say his goodbyes properly and settle the bill later, after he'd handed over his phone and the recording to Ophelia. If it still worked.

As he drove past a woman walking the world's biggest Great Dane, Harry's Nokia went off.

He braked and groaned. Not Jasper again.

But it was Hattie's happy voice that floated out. 'Guess what? I've just found out that the body on the roundabout belonged to the museum! One of Ray's betting-shop squad knows Mr Prentiss.'

'What?'

'It was the museum's skeleton! That Gresby Bibb bloke. He called himself a "man of science" and left his papers and his body to put on display but, presumably because he was a sexist loser who kept trying to prove women were an inferior species, they never did. But that's not all . . .'

According to Ray's acquaintance, a lot of 'totally weird' additional items were stolen, along with the skeleton, but no one knew what had happened to those.

His interest was piqued but subsided just as quickly. He wasn't the editor of the *Piddlington Gazette* anymore. He probably wasn't even a journalist, really. Or he wouldn't be when Sir Jimmy Knox and his demented acolytes were finished with him.

'Honestly, I think it's really a matter for you and Ray now, but it sounds really promising. Well done.'

The call ended. Harry stopped at Brenda's and bought coffee and a bag of goodbye cakes.

As he was pulling away, the phone went off again. It was an almost incoherent Hattie on the line.

'Harry! You *really* won't believe this!'

'What now?'

'Rude! So, I thought I could make a little video with a voiceover for the website about the dead bodies, now that the police lines have gone and anyone can go on the roundabout. So I went on it and you'll never guess!'

'What?' Harry inched the Mini past a cyclist who seemed determined to meet his Maker.

'Are you driving?'

'Yes. Get on with it.'

'You do know that's against the law? Harry, guess what.'

'Just tell me.'

'You have to pull in first.'

Harry indicated left and pulled up, but Hattie couldn't wait.

'I've only gone and found it!'

'Found what?'

'That painting! *The Purple Child.* The police didn't clear all the vegetation so I was hacking through the undergrowth and, because it's so thick, there's quite a bit of litter on there – Mrs Robarts was kind of right—'

'Get on with it!'

He could almost hear her smiling.

'OK! I saw this huge bramble bush with this sort of black bag thing and a little glint of gold poking out. So, I went to have a better look and got scratched to pieces, but I managed to yank the bag out and pulled the cover off . . . and there it was.'

Harry swallowed. The thing was easily worth £30 million, probably more.

'What have you done with it?'

'Don't worry, it's not that big, so I wrapped it up in the plastic again and carried it back to the office. I had to wheel my bike so I didn't drop it. Ray helped me prop it up on the metal shelving so we could look at it. I can't think whether I really like it or not, although there's definitely something about it. Ray says he wouldn't buy it, even if he could afford it, so there you go.'

Harry asked carefully: 'It's not near Ignatius, is it?' It would be just like him to lift his leg on it, or eat it, or something.'

'Of course not. Why ask that? It's not like he eats paintings, is it? Anyway, he's not even here at the moment, he's gone out.'

'Look, can you just keep an eye on it?' asked Harry, propping the phone under his chin. 'I don't want to worry you but the painting's probably worth thirty million at least, so please don't let something happen to it.'

'I'm not stupid, you know,' said Hattie. 'I just gave it a quick scrub off with the sink cleaner.'

His screech of terror made her laugh. 'Don't be silly! I'm just joking. It's all fine, just come back quickly.'

Ramming the gear stick into first, the Cooper took off, and within a few minutes he was back in the office.

* * *

The Purple Child was indeed propped on the metal shelves but, Harry felt, it was dangerously near the edge, and he carefully eased it backwards. Up close, he could see the angles and how the thick strokes of paint had been urgently applied. He tried to see Sadie Burge in the face of the child but gave up. It seemed to represent all children, everywhere, reminding him of the universal agony he'd glimpsed in the artist's *Guernica*.

'Something to see, eh?' said Ray, staring at the artwork.

'Think how many dog biscuits you could buy if you sold that!' Hattie giggled.

'Look,' said Ray. 'We need to contact Greta Sargent.'

'Sergeant Starsky, don't you mean?' said Harry. He'd had an idea. 'We . . . I mean – you will need a good lead for next week.

If I contact Ophelia and tell her we have something of interest, I'll try and blag some more out of her about that first body. Then you'll have two good stories, which should keep you going for a few days until, you know, you get a new editor.'

Hattie flung her arms round him. 'We don't want a new editor. We only want you, even if you keep putting your foot in it all the time.'

'Let me call her,' he said, dialling on the office phone.

Now she had lost her PC, it was Sergeant Starsky herself who answered the station's private line.

'Hello, Ophelia . . .' began Harry. 'I've got some important information for you but – and this is a big but – we need some information in exchange.'

'I'm listening.' Her voice sounded flat.

'We need an official comment about the first body on the roundabout; specifically, what the police are going to do about it.' He ignored Hattie's scowl and her muttered comment: 'We know it's not a real body – tell her that.'

'And what can you tell me?' demanded Ophelia.

'*The Purple Child*.'

'What do you know about that?'

'Plenty. But it's not what you think. Now, that body.'

'Look, you don't cut the deals here, Harry.'

'Ophelia, I know I don't. But I have the best news you've heard all day and all I want is something for my colleagues in return.'

'Well,' she began. 'I could do with something useful myself. Right. This is all totally off the record, and I'll deny it all if you attribute it to Dorset Police, but we are in the process of making an arrest for wasting police time and, possibly, other offences too, over the first roundabout body. On the record I can confirm this is no longer an investigation into a suspicious death and we are making no further inquiries in that direction.'

Harry shook his head. 'Not good enough, I'm afraid. Who are you arresting and why?'

'I can't tell you that. And I'm tired of your games. What do you know about that painting? If you don't answer sharpish, I'll arrest *you* for wasting police time.'

In the background he could hear her police radio: a faint crackle and a male voice, reading out an address. Instinctively, Harry switched the phone to speaker. 'Right – are we ready to go?' asked the voice on the other end.

'Time's up,' snapped Ophelia to Harry. 'Any more and I'll be round to arrest you – I presume you're in that office of yours? For the time being, anyway.'

'OK, fine,' he said, pressing the button to end the call. 'Hattie, did you get that address?'

She had.

'I reckon she's going round to arrest the person responsible for the body now. Let's get round there, too.'

Ray looked up. 'You know where that is, don't you? It's where that bloody awful woman lives. Old Robot.'

'Mind that painting,' Harry yelled at him, as he and Hattie scrambled to the Cooper.

* * *

Within six minutes, they were pulling up in Godolphin Court. Sergeant Starsky's car was already parked on the road and Harry could see the front door of Number 13 was open.

'Come on, this'll be fun,' he said. Beckoning Hattie down the side passage, they were able to peek into the back room where Prudence Robarts was standing, arguing loudly with Sergeant Starsky while another officer looked on impassively.

No one appeared to notice them and, fortunately, one of the room's windows was slightly open.

'How *dare* you accuse me of this crime?' thundered Mrs Robarts. 'I'm a respectable member of this community.'

'Madam, the evidence is there on the table in front of you,' said Ophelia, indicating the selection of items wrapped in ageing newspaper and tissue. From one, a rancid-looking furry paw protruded.

'The stuffed animals!' exclaimed Hattie.

'What are you doing here?' said Ophelia, spotting them in the back garden.

'How dare you trespass on my property!' said Mrs Robarts. 'You should arrest him, not me.'

'Mrs Robarts, can you give any reasonable explanation as to how the museum's property has ended up in your home – and how you managed to find that skeleton on the roundabout?'

'Yes, I can. I've volunteered for years at that museum, and no one gives a damn about any of it,' said Mrs Robarts. 'Prentiss is an absolute fool. You could hide the Elgin Marbles in there and he wouldn't notice. For years I've been trying to win Britain in Bloom for this town. And all the council does is ignore me and my efforts – look at that filthy house . . . They still haven't evicted that dirty old woman, have they?'

'Her name is Sadie Burge,' said Hattie, stepping into the room through the French doors from the garden.

'So, I thought that if I could prove how neglected this town was – if, for instance, a dead body was found on that roundabout – and get that in the local paper, it would shame them into doing something. But look at you.' She gestured towards Harry. 'You're about as useful as a chocolate teapot.'

Wordlessly, Ophelia shook her head.

'What about the other stuff?' demanded Hattie.

Mrs Robarts sniffed. 'I knew I'd have to make it look as if a number of items were missing, otherwise people might just wonder about that skeleton and put two and two together. So, I purloined the taxidermy and a few other things, and moved them in my trolley bag. It wasn't stealing, because I always intended to give them back – I'm not a thief, you know.'

Ophelia started to draw herself up and straightened her hat. 'Prudence Robarts, I am arresting you on charges of theft and wasting police time. You do not have to say anything but it may harm your defence if you do not mention, when questioned, something which you later rely on in court. Anything you do say . . .'

'Will be taken down and used against you!' finished Hattie, triumphantly.

'May be given in evidence,' finished Ophelia.

'Come on,' said Harry, seizing Hattie's shoulder and propelling her from the room before Ophelia arrested her, too. They stood and watched as Mrs Robarts was manoeuvred gently into Ophelia's car, the sergeant ensuring her belt was correctly fastened. As Ophelia moved around the vehicle, she stopped and walked towards the two journalists.

'Right, you've got your story. Now I want my information.'

It was Hattie who spoke first. 'You'll have to give us an exclusive statement that we can use in the paper. Please.'

Ophelia glared. In the car, Mrs Robarts was shouting again. Several people were now standing at the ends of their driveways and staring.

'An arrest has been made relating to the issue of the first body on the roundabout and I can confirm we are no longer looking for any other suspects, and it is not a murder inquiry. A number of items have been recovered and will form part of our investigation into allegations of theft at Piddlington Minster Town Museum. Will that do?'

As Hattie scribbled, Harry looked at Ophelia.

'Thanks, Ophelia. Our news is this: we have *The Purple Child*.'

'Where?'

'It's in our office. Ray's looking after it.'

'What? Really? You do know how much that painting could be worth, don't you? It's probably worth more than the minster.'

'You're the only person other than us who knows,' said Harry. 'You can recover it and claim the credit.'

Ophelia's broad smile said it all.

'Thanks,' she said as Harry smiled back.

'Come on, Dr Watson, you've solved the mystery and now you've got a major splash to write up!' he said.

* * *

They returned to the office and spent a few more moments gazing upon *The Purple Child* until Ophelia arrived. She walked towards the painting, open-mouthed. Then she and Harry wrapped and positioned the artwork into the well of the police car's front seat, carefully packing Ophelia's police jacket round it.

'Thanks for this, guys,' she said. 'I owe you.'

Chapter 31

Harry elected to help bang out stories for the website for the rest of that afternoon. Anything to avoid him having to walk round to Ophelia with the recording, confess his part in the robbery, pray she believed him, then clear his desk and say goodbye to journalism forever. He hadn't heard anything from Lionel Green and he guessed it meant that Sadie wasn't his sister after all.

He felt low. He was stupid to even have thought that he could find the long-lost sister. As his fingers crawled over the keyboard, he reflected on how much he'd miss even the press releases from the Piddlington afternoon WI who, despite the seemingly eternal 'inclement weather', managed to enjoy 'demonstrations' of various skills and crafts, visit fancy gardens and thank almost everyone who'd attended every meeting.

He'd miss it all – even the occasional rows about dog poo, which erupted with a regularity that would put Yellowstone Park's Old Faithful to shame.

He looked round, trying to breathe it all in – the smell of damp, stewed tea, dog, and old paper – and closed his eyes for a second to hear Hattie's tapping and Ray's mouth-breathing. Perhaps he wouldn't miss that.

He caught sight of Ray giving him a sympathetic look as he started laying out the pages on screen. 'I'm just clearing off some more of the old files and then I can help you, if you need a hand with anything?'

'Er, no, I'm fine thanks,' said Harry, aware of how thick his voice sounded.

As two flies began circling the fluorescent strip, like neutrons round an atom, Hattie looked up.

'Ignatius is a bit late back, isn't he? He should be here to say goodbye to Harry.'

He forced a smile. 'Shall we go and look for him?'

Hattie agreed. 'I'll do the High Street; you do the square.'

* * *

As Harry walked up to the square, he tried not to notice how beautiful the town suddenly looked. The tips of the minster towers were glowing gold in the sun, which had peeked out from behind a rain shower, and the beginning of a rainbow was forming. As he turned into the High Street, he could see a crowd along from Brenda's. Crowds meant stories. Harry instinctively moved forward to the front of the gathering. And then stopped.

Lying on the road was a brown, furry shape. Kneeling over it was a young woman. She was crying and stroking the dog's ear, saying, 'Please don't die.'

Hattie's face was almost unrecognisable with distress. 'Some bastard's run over Ignatius. I think he's dying. Oh Harry, do something, please. Please don't let him die.'

'I've called the police,' said one grim-faced bystander. 'Whoever did this wants shooting.'

Harry dropped to his knees beside the sobbing Hattie, the damp from the tarmac soaking into his trousers. He didn't have a clue what to do. Ignatius's eyes were rolling and he appeared to be shaking.

A man leaned over. 'It was a black car. Going too fast as usual. Ignatius was walking across the road and they went straight into him, didn't bother to stop or anything.'

'How can anyone be so cruel? Oh, God, Ignatius, please, please don't die.' The sound of Hattie's voice seemed to rally the dog. He whimpered and raised his head. Harry quickly pulled off his jacket and put it under the injured hound.

He gingerly stroked him, trying to instil a feeling of calm and peace. 'Stay with us,' he said, remembering all the hospital dramas he'd ever watched.

Hattie started sobbing quietly but, as Harry put his arm round her, he realised that the tears that were cascading on Ignatius's thick, brown fur were coming from him.

As he gently stroked the dog, furiously wondering if there was anything else he could do, he felt a strong hand on his shoulder and looked round.

It was a ruddy-cheeked man in a tweed flat-cap, carrying a large, leather case.

'Mike Rudd, local vet,' he said, in a broad Dorset accent.

Harry's heart leaped.

'Can you do anything?'

The man nodded. 'Looks bad but I'll give it a try. We can't lose this one, can we?'

As he bent to his task, Sergeant Starsky arrived, moving townsfolk carefully away and establishing a small cordon as the vet inserted tubes into the quivering Ignatius.

'Thanks, everyone, thanks for helping, we'll take it from here.'

He had never seen Ophelia look more enraged.

'We'll get the bastard who did this, don't you bloody worry,' she told Harry. 'I'll ask DCI Martin, or whoever he is, to call in all the CCTV in the district and pull a few strings. I just need to get out a description of that car.'

Hattie continued to sob.

'Can you take her somewhere safer than the middle of the road?'

'Yes, of course,' he said, moving her to the pavement where Cassandra was now standing with a bottle of brandy and two glasses. As Hattie started weeping afresh, Cassandra clutched her to her bosom, all the while telling her, 'Hush, my lovely, hush.'

'He's the most beautiful dog in the world,' Hattie wailed. 'Who could do this to him?'

Who indeed, thought Harry, grimly. A dark car had hit poor Ignatius and he knew at least one person whose driving was so bad, they'd clip an animal and decide not to stop. Especially if they were crazed with worry about losing a £30 million painting.

Seeing Hattie settled, he sipped a small brandy before stepping away, pulling out his iPhone and dialling.

It rang and rang. Suspecting he'd been blocked, Harry yanked out the Nokia, which went straight to voicemail.

'Jasper? I know you're there. I'm giving you one last chance to tell me the truth about something. Did you run over a dog in Piddlington Minster today? If you didn't, you can call me back. If it was you, then I'm warning you now – the police are getting the CCTV footage and I'll be making a statement. You won't get out of this one.'

Quickly, he pressed the button to end the call and looked nervously in the direction of the accident scene.

Ophelia was talking to Mike Rudd.

She came over to Harry and pulled him aside. 'It all looks a bit bleak but he wants to take Ignatius to the surgery and try an operation, just to make sure Hattie knows we've done everything. You know . . .'

As Harry's face brightened, she shook her head. 'Not a hope, I'm afraid. I heard Mike say Ignatius has got internal injuries, and look at his back legs . . . I think it's the end. That poor kid,' she said, indicating Hattie, who was still being comforted by Cassandra. 'I'll tell her what we're doing but can you look after her for a bit? Try and prepare her for bad news.'

As Ophelia started explaining the next steps to Hattie, an ambulance arrived and two paramedics gently manoeuvred Ignatius onto a stretcher trolley.

'He's a very special dog,' said Cassandra, firmly, catching Harry's surprise.

He told Cassandra he'd be taking Hattie home – 'You can't hang around at the vet's.' – and as he walked her through the town to his car at the *Piddlington Gazette*, she looked up. 'Can we get my bag? It's inside the office.'

Remembering how many of Ignatius's pathetic collection of chewed toys were in there, Harry asked: 'Are you sure? I could get it instead?' She shook her head.

As he stepped forward and touched the handle, he was surprised to feel the door open and see Ray and Greta Sargent, who appeared to be enjoying a glass each of Ray's brown alcohol.

'Hello, Miss Sargent. Hello, Ray.'

Greta stepped forward, coral lipstick standing out in her gaunt face. Must be a special occasion.

'I'll get straight to it,' she began, looking at Hattie, who had moved inside, too. 'Mr Green has heard what happened today. I am so very sorry, my dear. He wants to let you know that he arranged the ambulance and will personally pay for Ignatius's care and, er, any other services that are needed.'

Harry desperately hoped that Hattie hadn't fully understood – Greta was probably talking about the disposal of the unfortunate dog's body. He was also quietly relieved. He had been thinking that maybe he should sell the Mini to pay for Ignatius's medical and funeral bill.

'That's so kind. Thanks, Miss Sargent,' whispered Hattie.

She nodded. 'Mr Green has a message for you, too, Mr Hedges.'

Harry bowed his head. More fresh humiliation.

'He thanks you profoundly for what you have done for him, in finding the woman who we have indeed ascertained is his sister. In recognition of that, he has decided to re-appoint you to the editorship of the *Piddlington Gazette*. If you would like that?'

Despite everything, Hattie gasped and flung her arms round him. Ray started bashing his metal submarine against his metal desk.

'Gosh, I mean, I never thought. Yes please, of course. Thank you.'

Hattie was looking puzzled. 'But what does that mean?'

'Sadie Burge is Sarah, Mr Green's long-lost sister,' confirmed Greta. 'I will tell you this – but I don't expect it to leave this room: Mr Green had made contact with her by letter and phone after the war ended; they had been split up as the Nazis took power, but both had gone to London eventually. By the time they were in contact again, she was determined to marry this young artist and they rowed over her fiancé. The pair of them left the city and never spoke again. Extraordinary to think she's been living here under his nose all this time.'

Ray sniffed. 'There's a little more, isn't there?'

Greta looked at Hattie. 'I understand from Ray, young lady, that your and your mother's situation on the Thomas Hardy Estate is not entirely suitable. So, when it has been renovated, Mr Green and his sister would like to invite you both to live in Sadie— I mean, Sarah's house. Would that be acceptable? If we were to refurbish it properly?'

Hattie's open mouth gave her the answer.

'You need time, I understand,' said Greta, standing up. 'Finally, apart from the sad news, I think everything is well here. Don't forget to lock up.'

As Ray saw her to the door, Harry was rewarded by Hattie's watery smile.

'Wait till I tell Mum.'

'Sadly, you'll have to tell her about Ignatius, too,' Harry pointed out. 'I'll drive you home.'

* * *

Harry deposited her at the footwell of the Thomas Hardy Estate staircase. He offered to come upstairs with her, but Hattie shook her head. She told him she would tell Barbara herself and didn't need help.

As he drove off, he decided he was hungry and fancied a pint. Which he could now afford, along with his Ball Inn bill, given that he was once again a proper journalist. As he parked in the small space at the pub's rear, the Nokia rang.

''Arry?'

'Did you get my message?'

'No! What message?'

'Don't lie. About the dog. You ran over a dog today, didn't you? If you'd listened to my message, you'd know the police are getting CCTV of the incident and it won't be long before they catch up with the person who did it. Who was you.'

Jasper was silent for a second.

'I don't know what you're on about.' Harry had to admire his nerve. He sounded genuinely surprised.

'Really?'

Jasper paused, then dived back in. 'Apart from last night and early this morning, I haven't been anywhere near the town.

I actually do have a newsdesk to run, you know, so you're barking up the wrong tree, mate. Or maybe just barking.'

'I'm not your mate. I was with you when you nearly hit that kid on a pony so don't tell me you wouldn't drive over a dog.'

'How dare you accuse me of such an evil thing? My auntie's got a Chihuahua.'

'Stop changing the subject; you ran over Ignatius and you know it. Just admit it.' Then he ended the call, before striding into the pub's saloon bar – to see DCI Martin standing there, talking to Cassandra.

'Ah, Harry, I'd like a word. Can you step over here,' he said, indicating an empty corner.

He looked relaxed enough, but Harry felt nervous. Cassandra disappeared into the kitchen.

'I understand you have paid a few visits to Mr Lionel Green up at The Grange?'

Harry cautiously admitted he had.

'Ever seen this lady around the place?'

He showed Harry a picture on his phone of an older, homely-looking woman.

'She's Elspeth, Mr Green's cook,' said Harry. 'She makes the most fantastic shortbread biscuits.'

DCI Martin grimaced. 'I'm sure she does. But it's not her biscuit-making abilities we're interested in – I need to ask her a few questions about the theft of Mr Green's painting.'

'What? Elspeth must have worked there for years – why would she suddenly steal his painting?'

'We don't believe she did. But we have enough evidence to show she was probably the insider who helped the real thief get in.'

Harry's brain hurt. 'But why? It doesn't make sense.'

'I'm guessing her story will be along the lines of her being blackmailed into helping this person, but we don't believe that's true,' said DCI Martin. 'There's been no evidence of financial inducement; no additional money in her accounts, nothing stashed away that our forensic examiners could find and, while she may have a comedy Dorset accent, we know she actually hails from London.'

Harry wanted to point out that this was hardly indicative of a criminal nature but felt it would not be a good time to discuss the ins and outs of criminal natures, and how you could discern them.

The officer pulled a much-folded newspaper cutting from his pocket. 'Recognise this story?'

Harry didn't. It was from the *Daily News* in 1984; the reporter had interviewed people who had 'had their lives destroyed' by the building of Lionel Green's so-called 'Chopstick' tower block, on a back garden in the middle of London's Chinatown.

Within it was a boxout section which outlined the 'heartbreaking tale' of a Mrs Lil Parker, a housebound, elderly lady who 'lived only for the plants that graced the bright, sun-filled balcony' at her rented flat. According to the story, Mrs Parker had not lived for a year after the finalisation of the Chopstick, which had 'blocked every inch of light to her home, killing her plants and her reason for living'. This quote was attributed to her daughter, who was photographed, in dramatic form, pointing accusingly up at the tower block, which did indeed leer over their property like a vicious concrete Colossus.

'The man who built this monstrosity has ruined our lives. My mother didn't live for a year after that tower went up,' said trainee cook, Elsie Parker, 16.

'That's her?'

DCI Martin nodded.

'So, she got a job at The Grange and just bided her time until she could find a way to get back at Mr Green?' asked Harry.

'Pretty much, we think. She's been there for at least fifteen years so she would have come to know that the painting meant everything to him and used that knowledge against him.'

Harry felt sad. She really had made the best shortbread, and he felt Lionel would be very distressed about the betrayal. But why was DCI Martin telling him all this?

'We have someone arresting her now but what we really want are the people behind this. And we think *you* can help with that.'

Chapter 32

Harry looked at the round glass marks on the wooden pub table. He heard the thrum of the dishwasher behind the counter and inhaled the faint scent of beer-soaked carpet.

DCI Martin was just sitting there, looking at him. As an interview technique, it could rarely be beaten – but Harry knew it couldn't go on forever. He sat back and looked at the officer as he tried desperately to think of what to say.

It was the sound of Cassandra, singing along to Dolly Parton in the kitchen, as she started preparing for the evening session that decided it. If he wanted to stay in Piddlington Minster – and be able to look the townsfolk, and especially Cassandra, in the eye, ever again – he had to play a proper part in the community. And that meant explaining everything. And letting the chips fall.

He cleared his throat. 'How do you think I can help you?'

'It's like this.' DCI Martin leaned forward. 'For a while now my team and I have been interested in Sir Jimmy Knox and Jasper Grant, who I believe is the news editor of the *Daily News* and your former manager. We suspect he's been involved in varying amounts of criminality: blackmail, theft, communication crimes, that kind of thing. He's always used burner phones and been very smart about his moves so there's never been anything to connect him directly to Sir Jimmy, crime-wise, and for most of the time, he really is running that newsdesk. But, a while back, we had a tip that he was trying to uncover information about *The Purple Child.* I knew Mr Green owned it and so I managed to get myself in undercover here, a few months ago, to try and see if we could firm anything up.'

Harry hoped he looked as honest and innocent as possible.

'I've long wondered if Grant had something to do with the disappearance of Mr Fewtrell. But all the time we had no body or any inkling that he was dead – his cards were used a few times but we now think that he must have dropped his wallet and someone felt they got lucky – there wasn't much we could do, apart from keeping our ears up. Now, however . . .'

He looked directly at Harry again.

'Have the extra tests on Kevin's body shown anything more?' asked Harry, wondering about Violett's theory.

'In what way?'

'Could he have been the victim of a hit and run? Bashed his head on a kerbstone, or something?'

'You think Grant ran him over on purpose?'

A lorry chose this moment to stop outside the pub, its airbreaks letting out a deafening hiss.

'It's got to be a possibility,' stammered Harry.

'Has it?' DCI Martin leaned back again and folded his arms.

Oh God, what to do? It was now or never, wasn't it? 'Can I tell you something?'

'If you're going to confess to serious criminal wrongdoing, then no. There are proper procedures.'

'Actually . . .' began Harry. 'I don't believe I am; I mean, I hope I'm not, but you'll have to be the judge of that.' Then, feeling strangely relieved, he started to recite the whole, sorry saga, from the day the brown envelope arrived on his *Daily News* desk, to the attempted blackmail and the appalling evening at The Grange. 'There's also this recording. Or at least, I think there is.'

When he explained what had happened to the iPhone, DCI Martin said he would take him back to the office to download the recording himself. 'If it pans out, you may be in the clear,' he explained. 'I'll drive you round.'

* * *

As they arrived, Ray was circling the newsroom, turning off the terminals, and he looked astonished to see DCI Martin.

'We've come to get some info off my phone,' said Harry, very much hoping he was not giving off big helping-the-police-with-their-inquiries energy.

'Right you are.'

Annoyingly, as Harry patiently sent three copies of the recording to the DCI's various email addresses, Ray hovered by his desk.

'It's OK, Ray, I'll lock up.'

'If you don't mind, I wanted to ask you something.'

'Can it not wait?' Harry sighed.

It couldn't. Ray had been valiantly attempting to spring-clean the computer system, building on Harry's earlier efforts. But, as he was attempting to expunge one file, the whole system had locked up.

'Excuse me,' said Harry to DCI Martin. He sat at Ray's desk and tapped more confidently than he felt at a few keys. The machine gave an encouraging whirr, but the file wouldn't budge and it wouldn't open.

'See,' said Ray.

Harry tapped again.

'Can I help?' asked DCI Martin, indicating the chair, whose grubbiness contrasted embarrassingly with the officer's immaculate clothing. As he fiddled away at the system, fingers flying over the keyboard, the file miraculously opened. To reveal another twenty or so files. 'It may be that there's something wrong with one of the documents within all these files, a virus or something,' he said.

'Thanks,' replied Harry, eager now to get the recording sorted and the DCI off the premises. 'We can look at them later – don't want to take up more of your valuable time.'

But the DCI remained seated. 'Are these all stories for the paper?'

'Yes, they're ones that haven't been used; sometimes you just keep them in case you need the info or for background. They just remain spiked and slow down the operating system until we can get rid of them. Looks like no one's ever done it before.'

DCI Martin moved the mouse around to click on some very aged stories about pantomimes and the Piddletrenthide ploughing match. Some had been written by Kevin, and he carefully considered them before clicking on to the next file.

'Thanks, DCI Martin,' said Harry, more firmly, hoping he'd take the hint.

The officer ignored him. 'What's this one?' he asked, pointing to another file. He clicked it open, and another three files appeared on the screen. He clicked them open to reveal yet more files. Within the fifth file of the third file there was just one story, written by Kevin, catchlined: 'MauveOffspring'.

'Someone having a joke,' said Harry, preparing, yet again, to explain journo humour. 'You have to write so many of these things every day that sometimes, you end up giving them silly or cryptic names just to amuse yourself.'

'Look at the date it was written,' said Ray. 'It says the twenty-fourth of March. Must have been one of the last stories Kevin ever did.'

'Open it,' instructed DCI Martin.

This time it was Ray who right-clicked the mouse, and the three of them watched as the document opened up.

It was a complete blank. Harry looked at Ray and DCI Martin. 'Looks like a story someone created but never wrote on. That happens quite a bit.'

'Hang on a minute,' said Ray. He began scrolling down. It was nearly thirty seconds before, at the bottom of the document, some words in minuscule American Typewriter font appeared.

'Quick, expand it,' said DCI Martin. Ray rapidly increased the font size until they could see the words.

I'm writing this in the hope that someone more courageous than I will be able to make use of its contents. The facts are these: I took this job as editor of the Piddlington Gazette in good faith, after a tip-off from a former collegue called Jasper Grant.

'He's spelled colleague wrong,' said Ray, instinctively moving to correct the word on the screen.

DCI Martin tapped his hand away. 'He was probably very stressed when writing this. Please don't touch – this could be evidence.' The document continued:

JG is the news editor of the Daily News in London but, as I found out to my own detriment (later explained) he is mostly a fixer for Sir James Knox, publisher of the aforesaid newspaper.

The document outlined how Jasper had contacted Kevin, asking for his help after tipping him off about the *Piddlington Gazette* job. He'd been told to help acquire the painting, in much the same way as Harry had been asked, by pressuring Lionel Green, and then later threatened with 'cruel exposure'.

'Exposure for what?' asked Harry. Crimes against fashion weren't really a thing.

DCI Martin looked angry. 'We believe, following our inquiries, that Mr Fewtrell may have been gay. Our preliminary investigations have shown that a few of his former colleagues in Buckinghamshire felt this may have been the case, but nothing was ever said and they rightly felt his private life was his own affair.'

'That's just awful,' began Harry.

'I know.' DCI Martin sighed. 'As we understand it, he was a very private man. His only real hobby was walking – there's an online picture of him playing football with his newspaper colleagues, but that was just a charity match. He had suffered severe bullying while at school, so perhaps it took a long time for him to feel safe around new people or perhaps he hadn't discussed things with his family, although he doesn't seem to have much family that we can trace.'

'That's made me all upset now,' said Ray, stopping to blow his nose. 'It's bullying plain and simple.'

DCI Martin was scrolling down the document again. At one point he stopped, where the date of 25 March had been added. Against it, Kevin had written:

Summoned to midnight (12am) meeting with JG on Commercial Road, Piddlington Minster. Not sure what my response should be. I know what will happen if I don't go, the man will do as he threatens. But if I do go, what am I getting myself into?

'This date correlates exactly with the last day he was seen, doesn't it?' said DCI Martin. 'If we can place Grant and his motor in Piddlington Minster on that day, we can examine it – see if Kevin was ever in it. Or was hit by it.'

He leaped up and walked into the courtyard, where Harry and Ray could hear him talking on his phone.

'I hope they crush him,' said Harry. He quickly scrolled down the document again but there was nothing else there.

Ten minutes later, DCI Martin walked back in.

Ray and Harry looked up, expectantly.

'No dice,' he said. 'We can't triangulate Grant's work phone or any relevant CCTV of his car on that night. We can't even place him here today, at the scene of Ignatius's accident. Are you sure he only drives the one car?'

Harry was not sure at all. But he was pretty sure that hiring untraceable cars was not beyond Jasper.

'In a way it doesn't matter,' said DCI Martin as he put his phone away and made for the door. 'Jasper Grant remains my only suspect for the painting robbery, and everything I've heard today makes him a prime suspect for the murder of Kevin Fewtrell. If you'll excuse me, gentlemen . . .' he concluded and stepped into the courtyard.

'DCI Martin has left the building,' said Ray.

'Yup,' agreed Harry, relishing the idea of Jasper's imminent arrest. 'Look,' he said. 'I think we're both knackered. Can you get back to The Ball and ask Cassandra if she can do us some dinner?'

Ray gathered up his belongings and left. As he went round ensuring everything was turned off, Harry felt exhausted. He really wanted to check on Ignatius and Hattie, and desperately hoped that no news was good news. However, as DCI Martin hadn't produced any handcuffs, Harry felt he had achieved some kind of personal victory over the day.

* * *

He started gathering up his bag and notebook and switched off the main office light, when he heard a tiny rattling sound. He glanced around but could see all the machines had now shut down.

The sound came again from the direction of the door. Someone was trying the handle. Harry yanked open the door. Thanks to the atrociously wired outdoor lamp, which refused to come on, the courtyard was shrouded in gloom.

But there was enough light to make out the person who was standing there.

Violett! This time she was wearing a dark-coloured trench and grey trousers, and she looked terrified.

'Are you OK?' She really did look scared.

'Sorry, Harry, but I was hoping to find you here. Jasper has gone crazy, he's beside himself. He's guessed the police are on to him for the painting robbery and he's said that unless I fess up that it was my idea, he'll make sure I'll regret it for the rest of my life.'

'Jesus, Violett, that's insane, I can't believe—'

She cut across him. 'You don't know him like I do – I've seen the way he reacts when he doesn't get his own way. You don't know what he is capable of . . .'

Harry was about to assure her that he did indeed know what Jasper was capable of, but his phone blared out the chorus of 'Lucky Man'.

'Don't answer it!' she instructed, looking round, fearfully.

'It's Hattie, I've got to take this. Hello, Hattie?' His stomach churned. Please God, don't let Ignatius have died.

'Harry?' Hattie's voice sounded faint and wobbly. 'It's Ignatius.'

He swallowed. 'Is he, I mean . . .?' He couldn't even say the words.

Hattie broke into sobs and Harry screwed up his eyes. Furiously, he bit his lip. This was terrible.

'He's alive! Harry, the operations were a success – they've saved him!'

He could hardly take it in. 'He's alive? Oh, thank God. Oh, Hattie, I am so, so happy,' he said, feeling the boulders of tension rolling from his body.

'He's alive!' He beamed at Violett.

She smiled, impatiently.

Hattie continued. 'But guess what, Harry?'

'What now?' He laughed and smiled at Violett again. She did not smile back.

'Sergeant Starsky went to the vet's and took Ignatius's collar and a bit of his fur away for forensic tests, but get this – she told me a few minutes ago that one of the CCTV cameras got a shot of the car and driver who they believe hit him. They could see damage on the passenger's side light and the driver was wearing a dark baseball cap with a kind of logo, like a ship or something, but . . .'

Harry was aware of Violett starting to turn away.

'Hang on a minute, Violett,' said Harry. 'Look, Hattie, I've got to go, but that's the best news ever. We'll speak tomorrow. I am so glad.' His mind was racing – baseball caps were Jasper's trademark headgear and the one Hattie had described sounded exactly like the design that Sir Jimmy Knox insisted visitors to his superyacht always wore when they were aboard. Surely this would nail the bastard?

Violett was beginning to stride through the archway. Harry called out to her again. 'Violett! What's the matter? Wait! It sounds like they've got CCTV of Jasper in the car that hit Ignatius.'

As she turned left, she broke into a sprint. Instinctively, Harry chased her.

Along streets lit by the glow of the town's old-school lanterns, he ran, shouting her name. But Violett kept on running.

She dodged into one of the little side streets and Harry attempted to increase his speed, his brogues clattering on the pavement. He'd lose her if he wasn't careful.

He followed her left, then right, and found himself in one of the town's smaller carparks. In the furthest corner was a small dark hatchback. She was running towards it.

As she urgently started pressing her key fob, he managed to grab her arm, the momentum swinging her round.

'Violett! What's got into you? What were you saying about Jasper? Has he threatened you, too? Because, if he has, we can do something about that right now; we can call the police. DCI Martin will—'

Violett tried to wrench his hand off, still desperately pressing the fob. 'Get off me!' As they scuffled, something fell to the ground from her mac's pocket.

Deftly, Violett flicked the object under the car with her foot. But thanks to the streetlight, Harry knew what he'd seen. It was a black baseball cap. With a white logo of a superyacht on it. And, as he looked towards the vehicle, the same streetlight flickered on the shards of glass, clinging like shark's teeth round the smashed passenger-side headlight.

Violett looked up at him. Her face was as devoid of emotion as those of the coppers who'd come to him that fateful night of Isabella's death. And now images began flying into his mind, like a jigsaw exploding in reverse: Jasper racing round the quiet lanes of Dorset; Ignatius, shuddering and bleeding on the damp road; Kevin, crumpled on the roundabout, a catastrophic wound to his troubled, harmless head. And Violett wearing a dark baseball cap driving manically through Piddlington Minster's peaceful streets.

'Did *you* run over Ignatius?' demanded Harry.

She didn't reply.

'Answer. Did you run over that dog?' As she moved, he seized her arm.

'Get off me!'

'Violett, I am trying to understand what happened here. Why would you hit a dog and not stop? Why? What were you even doing here today?'

Her cold laugh silenced him and she stopped pulling, although Harry maintained a firm hold – she wasn't going anywhere until he'd heard the truth. She seemed to be thinking and when she did start speaking, her voice was eerily low. 'What would *you* understand about any of this? You with your fancy mansion and your posh school and your idiot father who pays to get you out of every mess you've ever made.'

'Hardly every . . .' he began.

'Do you know what it's like to go to school terrified that people will say you smell, because your mum's run off and your dad is too drunk to wash your only set of school clothes? What it's like to go to sleep hungry every night, to the sound of sirens, and never need an alarm clock because there were so many drug raids in the mornings?'

Harry felt forced to admit that he didn't.

'So, when someone like Sir Jimmy offers you a chance to earn big and earn fast, and get away from all the crap, by sorting all the things he can't be arsed to sort for himself, like acquiring stupid paintings that are worth more than the entire block of flats you grew up in, you take it. And I'm telling you, Harry, you *never* look back.'

He could barely take it in. Was this the woman he'd been so close to? Who'd made him his coffee just the way he liked it, who'd looked at him as if he was the only person in her universe? 'But what about me, Violett? What about us? Didn't that mean anything?' He knew he sounded like a small kid again but he hadn't been able to stop himself.

She looked bored. 'Oh, Harry. For once, can you just work it out yourself instead of expecting someone else to do it for you? When you've been trampled on and overlooked all your life and you get the one opportunity to move up, you'll step on anyone and everyone to make it work. Sorry, but that's the way it rolls.'

'You were just using me, then?' He swallowed, unable to see the edges, trying to take in the enormity of what this all meant. 'Who else have you lied to and stepped on and used?'

Her mouth twitched. A tiny movement, but enough for the final piece of the jigsaw to fly into place. He didn't know how, and he wasn't sure he really knew why, but he now knew who. 'It was you, wasn't it? You killed Kevin and you came back here to try and pin it on Jasper.'

'If you say so.'

Harry jerked her arm. 'Not good enough. Why?'

'I told you – when Sir Jimmy tells you to jump, you say how high. All he cares about is the end, not the means – and he pays, big time. He wanted that painting and asked me and Jasper to get it for him. Jasper said he could menace Kevin into helping and I was stupid enough to believe him. Next thing I know, Jasper's telling me that Kevin's threatened to go to the police.'

Harry felt sure Kevin hadn't threatened anything of the sort – Jasper had been trying to stall Violett. Had he guessed what she might do? 'So?'

'So I got one of Jasper's burners and sent a message to Kevin to meet me in Commercial Road – that disused road off the roundabout. He didn't know who I was but I tried to reason with him, said Jasper had sent me along to work something out. But then he must have got scared and he started to run off. I followed him in my car but he ran across the road in front of me towards the roundabout and that's when I clipped him. He went down hard and I could see he must have hit the kerbstone but when I looked back and couldn't see him, I reckoned he must have got away. I couldn't hang around . . . After, there was nothing in your bloody paper about an accident and nothing about a death, so I figured I could get away with it.'

He opened his mouth to speak again but no words came out. Partly because he was in shock about her callous attitude to the stricken Kevin. But also because Violett had delivered him a baroque knee in the groin. As he staggered backwards in agony and shock, she took her chance, and wrenched free of his grip, yanking the car's door open, before leaping in and firing the engine.

She started crashing the gears ready, he guessed, to make for the carpark's exit. As she gunned the engine and moved forward, Harry knew what he had to do.

He ran into the car's path. Mercifully, it slowed, and then came to a stop, the streetlight illuminating the steering wheel, the bone-white of Violett's hands, her face a pale mask. Relief washed over him. Thank God, she was seeing sense at last. He started to walk towards her.

'Violett, whatever you've done, whatever threats have been made, it can be sorted, I promise. It's over, you don't have to . . .'

As he neared the vehicle, its engine roared and the car shot forward. She was driving straight at him. Now he knew why she'd told him everything. Harry yelled in shock and dived out of the way, crashing painfully onto his right arm, which made a horrible cracking sound as he thumped to the ground.

He turned his head in time to witness the car lurch right, out of the carpark, and then left onto the main road, its tyres giving a triumphant scream as they made the corner and it disappeared from view. Seconds later, there was the sound of an almighty impact followed by a hideous silence. Then, lying on the tarmac, as the pain swept over him, he could just make out the cold wail of sirens before everything turned dark.

* * *

It was forty-eight hours later, and Harry had been pronounced fit enough to receive visitors.

He was bracing himself for the front page in a special edition of his own newspaper – in hospital with a broken arm and a bandaged Ignatius sitting proudly next to him, under the Hattie-written headline: 'Hero hack and hound solve roundabout bodies riddle'.

The story had already gone gangbusters online, with the most-liked image being one of Ignatius eating the jumbo caramel muffin Brenda had specially baked for him.

Harry was thrilled to find that his first official visitor was Ophelia, who'd brought in a cream tea with a hefty side-order of news about what had happened following the accident.

Following Ophelia's courageous hard-stop of Violett's stolen vehicle – 'She'd learned how to nick cars from the villains she knocked about with in her youth.' – Violett had tried to escape, but had been apprehended close to the *Piddlington Gazette* office.

'I wondered why she wanted to hang around the town, with so much going on, but someone like her would only take such a risk if there was a big reward in it.'

'Which was?'

'Your office. Or, rather, something in your office.'

'Unless she has a secret fetish for mildewing newspapers or disgusting swivel chairs, I can't think what it was.'

'I can,' said Ophelia. She fished out her phone and called up the camera roll. 'Look.'

It was a black rubbish bag, neatly tied up in the *Gazette*'s office kitchen.

'I thought that had been chucked away,' said Harry, remembering his first day as editor.

'I'm glad it wasn't,' said Ophelia. 'Among all the crap – those pork scratchings were gross by the way – were two ancient phones. We managed to get them working and their data is fascinating. Forensics are still combing through it but thanks to what you told us, we were able to confirm that she and Jasper were in it together on the painting front. Sir Jimmy Knox is well-known for treating his staff like chess pieces and using them to sort things out for him, legally or otherwise.'

She believed that Violett panicked and decided to act alone.

'She came down here that night to deal with Kevin herself. He really did believe he was meeting Jasper and probably didn't know about her – one of the many burners she used had a text on it purporting to be from Jasper. It's the one Kevin wrote about in that document.'

'So, when she turned up instead of Jasper . . .' began Harry, attempting to apply clotted cream on an obstructive fruit scone with his left hand.

'Our best guess is that Kevin either worked out their game or threatened her back, maybe he even mentioned the phones? Who knows? He was probably so frightened by her response that he tried to get away from her – and that's when she drove at him with her car. It was no accident, the other injuries on his body prove that. You've seen how she drives when she's lost it.'

At this point, Ophelia had gently taken the knife from his hand and expertly added jam to the scone, before the cream. 'It's against the law in Dorset to eat cream teas any other way!'

According to Ophelia, Kevin's fatal head injury was almost a perfect match for one of the damaged kerbstones on the empty road by the roundabout. 'She must have thought her ship had come in when everyone assumed he'd just left, which is why we're pretty sure she organised for the postcard to be sent from the Lake District, just to keep everyone off the track. You said she has a good reporter's instinct for reading people, and she was spot on, guessing Ray and Hattie probably wouldn't be able to do much to find out about Kevin. But when the body was discovered, she needed to be sure that nothing we were looking at could lead to her.'

Ophelia also believed that Violett had returned to Piddlington Minster independently, following the theft of the painting, to try and find out how the Kevin investigation was going, as well as to try and ascertain if there was anything relating to Kevin that would incriminate her. Distracted, she had probably hit Ignatius by mistake.

'It pains me to say this,' Ophelia had added. 'Because I think she's a sociopath. But there's no way she would have wanted to draw attention to herself, especially as, by then, she was trying to pin it all on Jasper. I think she went to your office that night, hoping to get in and have a look round but she could have heard your conversation with DCI Martin, and Hattie's call would have sealed it.'

Harry shook his head. 'It's hard to get your head round.'

Ophelia agreed. 'I think they both had their reasons – which probably made sense to them. Did you know that Jasper had lost a lot of money gambling on the stock market?'

'No, he never said.'

'We believe he was doing it purely to keep his job and salary but for Violett, it was more a fear of going back to her roots. We don't think she could face losing what she felt was hers.'

He had to agree. Both had been remanded in custody; Violett on a charge of murder, as well as failing to report an accident, and Jasper on a slew of charges including robbery. Following their arrests, police had started digging into all their crime-related activity and, as Ophelia explained: 'There will be plenty more where that came from.'

But there was one thing Harry didn't understand. 'How did you know Violett was in Piddlington Minster that night?'

'I didn't. But you didn't end the call, so Hattie heard her name and some of what happened, and called me to say she was worried about you, that you didn't sound right. I was driving over to make a check, and that's when I saw the car. The driver was really caning it, so I took the decision to hard-stop, but she went into me.'

'That was incredibly brave,' said Harry. 'Thanks, Ophelia, I owe you.'

'Well, you did help a bit,' said Ophelia, pointing out that he had managed to transfer his precious recording to DCI Martin, as further proof that Jasper Grant had been involved in attempting to steal *The Purple Child*. 'And I'm sure you want to return the compliment by taking me out for a bang-up dinner!'

* * *

Two months later, Lionel Green had been as good as his word; following extensive surgery on his back legs and insides, and a two-week sojourn at Britain's top doggy spa, Ignatius had gone to live with Hattie and Barbara at Sadie Burge's old house, which had been cleaned, redecorated and adapted for them. Ray had been promised a cosy council bungalow, after officials had conceded that his caravan was indeed unfit for human habitation.

Harry was happier than he had been for years.

The last he had heard about the case was that Jasper's brief was trying to argue that he'd had an anonymous tip-off about the painting's whereabouts and was going to hand it in. 'They can all fight it out with the CPS,' was DCI Martin's cheery response.

When Harry had asked nervously if he would be facing any charges, the officer had laughed out loud. 'No, and for the simple reason that I told them you were an utter klutz who couldn't even make a clear recording of it all, never mind help steal a painting, although, as you know, we did manage to get enough useful material from it. We've got your statement, made some sterling arrests and my guv'nor is pretty pleased with how the undercover operation went.'

Chapter 33

As Harry, Hattie and Ray sat bashing out stories, there was a knock at the office door. At least it wouldn't be the ghastly Prudence Robarts, thought Harry – she had an upcoming date with the magistrates' court. He looked up to see two small shapes: Lionel and Sarah.

Out of her home and dressed in a new lime green artist's smock and purple beret, Sarah cut a tiny, almost elegant figure. Lionel was sporting a dashing purple silk cravat.

'Mr Green, how lovely to see you,' said Harry. 'And you, too, Sarah.'

She nodded and smiled.

Lionel looked round and smiled at Hattie. 'Everything going suitably, young lady?'

She nodded and rushed forward. 'We've written to say thanks, but I can't tell you what it all means,' she said. 'You saved Ignatius and I'll never stop being grateful. And Mum's like a new person – it's a whole new life for us.'

'Good,' said Lionel, smiling. 'Now, we have come to make an important announcement.'

Harry stiffened. He knew that sales had dropped off, mainly because Bob, the town newspaper seller, was off work with a bad leg.

'Don't worry,' said Lionel. 'It was Sarah's idea, but I said we should ask, first.'

Sarah touched Hattie's arm. 'You said you were very grateful about dear Ignatius. Well, I was wondering if you would now be prepared to do something for me?'

'Of course. If I can. But what?'

Sarah stepped outside and returned with a large cat carrier. 'While it is lovely to now be with my brother, we have made the terrible discovery that he is, in fact, a sufferer of allergies. So' – and here she deftly opened the box – 'I wondered if you would like to keep Mr Chagall as your office cat, perhaps?'

Hattie gasped and Mr Chagall stretched towards her, rubbing his head on her outstretched hand. She picked him up and buried her face in his ginger fur. Mr Chagall let out a sumptuous purr.

'I think we can take this as a yes,' said Lionel. 'Now, of course I will be paying for his upkeep and, in gratitude for looking after Mr Chagall, I'm going to give a pay rise to everyone and commission a new sign. One with the editor's name on. That is, if you still intend to stay with us?'

Harry nodded. He had been offered two new positions, both in London, by editors keen to have the man of the moment working for them. But he'd turned them down. Firstly, because Geoffrey had called after his accident to tell him the 'marvellous news' that following a bidding war, the family home and estate had been sold for three times its actual worth, which meant he was able to shore up the company and buy a pied-à-terre in Chelsea. And secondly, because Harry had realised that despite its filthy floor, eccentric colleagues and farting dog, this newsroom and the town that supported it really was his home.

He shook hands with Lionel. 'Thanks, Mr Green.'

'Thank you, Mr Editor.'

As they said goodbye, escorted out by Ray, Mr Chagall jumped on to Harry's desk and proceeded to arrange himself into a Sphinx-like posture, while fixing him with a glittering eye. Harry didn't have the heart or the nerve to shift him.

He was still lying there when Sergeant Starsky popped by. 'A little bird told me you've got a new office assistant. I've bought him these.'

As she pulled out a bag of luxury cat treats, she looked up at Harry. 'I didn't know you were a cat lover. He's gorgeous, isn't he?'

Harry was about to put her right about his opinion of cats, when he caught sight of Hattie's frown.

'Yes, he's wonderful. I absolutely adore cats. Do you know much about them?'

'We always used to have one at home,' she said, fondly scratching Mr Chagall's head.

'Then perhaps you could give me a few tips on caring for him?' he asked.

'Perhaps I can. You free at seven p.m.?

'Yes,' said Hattie quickly, 'he is.'

'Saloon bar, The Ball Inn, then?' said Ophelia. 'Your treat.'

Harry nodded, trying to hide his delight.

As the sergeant dropped a kiss on Mr Chagall's head and waved goodbye, Hattie punched the air.

'At last! Get your coat, Harry, you've pulled!'

Acknowledgements

No woman is an island, particularly one who takes up novel writing her fifties. At times, some of the lovely people mentioned here may have felt that they too were being forced to live in Piddlington Minster with me. My grateful thanks go to all the following, without whom not one page of this novel would ever have been written.

First and foremost, thanks to the wonderful Ashley . . . for all the meals cooked, fires lit, holidays organised, constant encouragement and endless, loving patience with me and my ways. A book dedication seems a very small way to say this, but it's true.

Many thanks to Dr Helen Lynch, Reader in Early Modern Literature and Creative Writing at the University of Aberdeen, who has helped hundreds of writers over the decades but unlike them, I've been privileged to know her since I was four. She continually encouraged me to believe I could write a book and wrote the academic reference that helped me to get on the Novel Writing MA at Brunel University. This led to my friendship with the wonderful Ronali Collings, novelist and writing maven, whose generous advice, constant cheerleading and gracious, thoughtful and very funny emails and lunches helped keep the flame alive. Profound thanks also to my marvellous MA supervisor,

Professor Bernardine Evaristo OBE, for her generous encouragement and meticulous assistance with the first book I ever wrote, her continued encouragement of my writing and also for her support of all writers, but especially women.

Thanks, from the bottom of my heart, to the best agent a girl could have: the wonderful and wise Caroline Montgomery of the Rupert Crewe Ltd literary agency. Your belief in my book and your hours of hard work to help make it happen were everything. I will never stop being grateful for all you have done and continue to do for my writing.

Huge thanks, too, to everyone at Embla and Bonnier books, especially my fabulous and brilliant editor, Martina Arzu, for buying my novel and then being so patient and kind when helping me whack it into shape. Profound gratitude, too, to my eagle-eyed and patient-with-rubbish-punctuation copy editor, Daniela Nava, proofreader, Lucy Littlejohns, my audio editor, Chelsea Graham, Lisa Horton for the beautiful cover design and the excellent Katie Williams and Vishani Perera for weaving their marketing magic. Thanks too, to assistant editor, Danielle Clahar-Raymond and managing editor, Emma Wilson. You are the people who have made my lifetime's ambition come true and I can't thank you enough.

I'd also like to thank my beloved former colleagues at the *Daily Echo Bournemouth* for the endless inspiration, witticism and criticism, and being responsible for some of the most hilarious moments of my life. You all know who you are, but special thanks to Lorraine Gibson, writer of superb non-fiction, for the tireless support and her helpful comments about this book; Andy Martin for the decades of relentless fun and kindness, Mr Ed Perkins (my deputy editor and non-fiction best-seller) and every sub-editor I've ever worked with – I hope I've done our trade justice in this novel. I'd also like to acknowledge my deeply missed late colleagues: super-sub and fab writer, Andrew Chappell (borrowed one of your best lines about amateur dramatics for the next novel – hope you'd approve), Chris Parnell – for disagreeing with me about almost everything but always making my work look beautiful and being a fine writer himself; Gareth Weekes, for letting me become a feature-writer – you turbo-charged my career; and the joy that was Neal Butterworth, one of the finest newspaper writers and editors in the business.

I'd also like to thank all my virtual colleagues on the A Few Good Hacks group for their kindness, support, and the endless banter, and to acknowledge the cogent explanation about second mentions from writer John Sturgis in his Spectator piece: 'The tabloid art of the knobbly monster'.

Closer to home, I'd like to thank my lovely friends for their kindness, generosity and encouragement and for putting up with me over the decades: Sarah Towlson, Claire O'Malley, Bernadette John, Frances Brewer, Julie Magee, Hilary Porter, Sue Lowe, Viv Wharf, Lisa Gallo, Heather Short, Jake Sugden, and Simon Clarke, take a bow. Thanks, too, to Mum and Dad and my best bro', Matthew.

Finally, I'd like to thank the amazing Zac and Louis, who may sometimes not have understood why Mum's always writing, but always believed in my dream.

A Note from the Author

In order to avoid falling victim to the pedants' revolt, I'd like to point out that for me, the newsroom described in this book reflects how newsrooms often were, how they occasionally are and how I wish they would always be.

About the Author

Faith Eckersall spent thirty years in the best job ever – as a reporter and feature-writer for a regional newspaper in Dorset. After gaining her MA in Creative Writing from Brunel University in 2015, where she was supervised by Professor Bernardine Evaristo OBE, she accidentally left journalism for PR and, missing her old newsroom, decided to invent one of her own. She was awarded the Grazia and Women's Prize For Fiction First Chapter Award in 2018 and now freelances for national newspapers and magazines. When she's not writing she can be found stalking museums and libraries, running the highways and byways of Hampshire where she lives, and ensuring that she is never, ever without a book to read.

About Embla Books

Embla Books is a digital-first publisher of standout commercial adult fiction. Passionate about storytelling, the team at Embla believe our lives are built on stories – and publish books that will make you 'laugh, love, look over your shoulder and lose sleep'. Launched by Bonnier Books UK in 2021, the imprint is named after the first woman from the creation myth in Norse mythology. Embla was carved by the gods from a tree trunk found on the seashore; an image of the kind of creative work and crafting that writers do, and a symbol of how stories shape our lives.

Find out about some of our other books and stay in touch:

X, Facebook, Instagram: @emblabooks
Newsletter: https://bit.ly/emblanewsletter